ER UNDER THE BRIDGE

Verna Simms

*To Dan
Best wishes
Verna Simms*

Cover design by Shannon Yarbrough, St. Louis, Missouri
Photo by Christopher Oleksiw
Copyright © 2014 by Verna Simms
All rights reserved.

The characters and events in this book are fictitious.

Rocking Horse Publishing
St. Louis, Missouri

Visit our website at www.RockingHorsePublishing.com

ISBN 10: 0-9910695-3-6
ISBN 13: 978-0-9910695-3-8

DEDICATION

I dedicate this book to the Jefferson County Writers' Society. Many thanks to Pat DeClue, who founded the group in November 2001, and asked me to join. I also wish to thank all the members—past and present—who critiqued the work and encouraged me to keep writing, and especially long-time members Elaine Becherer, Anna Wells, and Dennis Bentley.

ACKNOWLEDGMENTS

A special thanks to Faye Adams and Dorri Pease for their tireless editing and to Annette Rey and Kim Lehnhoff for sharing their computer know-how. I am also greatly indebted to Robin Theiss for the many months she worked hand in hand with me, planning scenes, giving me ideas to make Papa more likeable, bringing Dan and the mother cat into the story sooner rather than later, and encouraging me to mention holidays to show time passing. Most of all, I appreciate her believing in my made-up characters and my ability to bring them alive. Thank you so much. I love you all!

PROLOGUE

Late in the fall of 1918, two neatly dressed young men knocked on a farmhouse kitchen door. Chester Hall invited them in. These missionaries stayed two weeks with the family in rural Missouri, during which time they explained the mysteries of Joseph Smith—telling of the tablets of gold on which the Book of Mormon had been written, and of a new Church that thrived in the western states. They explained how Joseph Smith and his followers had struggled against disbelievers, and finally moved West in the hope of finding religious freedom to practice their beliefs, which included a theory that men could have multiple wives.

The young men's message fell on fertile ground in the mind of Mr. Hall, and he yearned to join the other new converts. He wished to participate in the building of a magnificent temple planned in the town of Mesa, Arizona, an infant state in the Union. Having been born to a poor family and struggled hard his entire life, he dreamed of finally tasting glory in this world, and even greater glory in the one to come.

Despite his wife's misgivings and reluctance to leave Missouri and her parents behind, Chester spent the next months selling the family farm and everything they owned. With that money, he purchased a new Model T Ford, and then he packed up his family of five and set out on the long trip over the dangerous mountain roads—to do God's will. Six months later, on April 27, 1921, in the outskirts of Mesa, Arizona, a baby girl was born to the Halls, their fourth child. They named her Amelia.

Time passed and time passed . . .

Verna Simms

CHAPTER ONE—THE FIRST DAY

My new life started on an autumn day in the first week of September 1927. It turned out to be a pivotal day, though not for the reason I'd expected. As I slept in the early morning hours of my sixth year, I had not yet learned, as everyone does sooner or later, that things never remain the same, that life is a process of people and events in constant motion, like ants. They alter plans and eliminate our options.

In my six years of life, I had only just begun to take into account how changes occurred, through my observations of events in our home, like Papa complaining that my sister's and my hemlines exposed too much of our black stockings, or the unexpected realization one day that Mama had grown rounder and softer, and that smile lines were permanently etched around her blue eyes.

Over the years I've often thought how fitting it was that Papa himself called me out of my sleeping innocence that September morning, forcing me to meet the new day—the one where, he correctly asserted, there would be new expectations of me as "a young lady." I'd been eager to cross that bridge, to join my siblings as a student and the rest of my family as among the schooled. I still remember the childish fantasies I toyed with as I tossed and turned beside my sister in our bed. I imagined myself in my beautiful new school dress walking alongside my sister and brother; me, carrying my new blue satchel and my very own silver lunch pail, and finally having something important to say at the dinner table when our family customarily shared all that had gone on during each day.

When Papa called me to wake up that morning, I felt the heaviness of my lack of sleep, but paid it no mind. I couldn't wait to begin my first day of school, never realizing it would also be the day that would mark a change in our entire family—the day the trouble began.

On that day, I first beheld Papa as a man, not as my father or as a god. And I realized it would be best to hold him at a distance, not unlike the way one appraises a powerful and charging river from a safe position on its bank. Even now, when my thoughts occasionally betray me and come to rest on his tall, lean frame, thick dark hair, and steely blue eyes, mixed-up feelings stir in my chest. Shame, sadness, anger—and a measure of love. Yes, still fond memories linger, also. Because, unlike Mama and the others, I can never fully let him go. Papa, the man I can always trust—or so I thought.

*****

"Rise and shine, Amelia," Papa called, "time to get up and dress for school!"

"I'm awake already." I sat up. "Mama made me a new dress."

"That's nice. Just remember what I've told you, a young girl who expects to be a lady one day does not go out in public with any part of her limbs uncovered." Despite Papa's tone, his eyes twinkled. "Well, look what I've found here," he said, examining a small object he pulled from his pocket. As he left my room, he laid it on top of my dresser.

Eagerly, I jumped out of bed and found a small, smooth stone, dark gray in color, with a tiny hole on one end through which a piece of twine had been threaded. Papa had given me a gift, evidently for my first day of school.

It was something he often did to mark a special occasion. At the smallest excuse for a celebration, like the time Aileen recited a poem in the school assembly, Papa came home with a little token. On that particular day, it was a hair ribbon. When Daniel had participated in his first baptism for the dead, he gave him a small penknife. Another time, Joseph was presented with a replica of our Model T for earning an A in Spelling. I'd been given occasional trinkets, too, but they'd always been given for no reason at all. The little stone necklace would be the first time I'd received a gift for something special I'd done—or was about to do.

Struggling out of my nightgown, I hurried to the nightstand and washed my face and sponged the night sweat from my body. Nearby, on a peg beside the door, hung the new cotton dress Mama had made just for me, white with pretty miniature daisies and yellow bias-tape trim on the neckline and across the top of one pocket. It fell straight from my shoulders all the way to the hemline, with long, narrow sleeves.

I pulled the dress over my head and tied two lengths of yellow bias tape in a careful bow beneath the simulated collar. I twirled in this lovely dress, noticing that unlike the many hand-me-downs from Aileen, this one fit perfectly.

Standing before the full-length mirror that stood in a frame in the corner, I slipped the stone necklace over my head. I brushed my short copper-colored hair and admired the grown-up-girl who stared back at me from the gilded mirror—a girl big enough to be on her way to school for the first time. I felt I could skip all the way to school, but I knew my sister, Aileen, would never permit it. She was five years older than me, and could be bossy.

Reluctantly, I turned away from the mirror to grab the black stockings and bloomers that covered my knees—hateful garments I'd be required to wear "for modesty's sake." I plopped down upon my bed to pull them on and by the time I stood again, perspiration trickled down my neck, a consequence of my exertion and the already stifling Arizona heat.

High top, button-up shoes stood next to my bed and I sat on a low stool to tackle them. Carefully I maneuvered the hooks, trying to insert each of the ten tiny buttons into their respective holes. You couldn't do it by hand; the holes were too tiny and the leather too stiff. You slipped the sharp point of a buttonhook through each buttonhole, slid its bent end over to catch the corresponding button, and struggled to pull that button through the hole. If successful, you then released the buttonhook with a twist. A complicated effort requiring considerable skill and, at six years of age, I wasn't good at it at all.

Finally fully dressed, I stood before the long mirror again and surveyed the now somber, flushed, and yet proper lady-like girl staring back at me—a girl of whom Papa would surely approve.

"Ugh," I snarled. "I hate you!" I stuck out my tongue and pushed my bangs back off my sweaty forehead, so that they stood askew.

Not finding Mama in the kitchen, I headed out the back door for the outhouse. Papa had built a deluxe toilet with two adult-sized openings and one smaller hole for children. A hinged lid covered each hole. I emerged from the small building hot and sticky in the bright sunshine, and ran across the yard and up the steps to the porch that led to our kitchen. Just as I stepped through the door, I brushed my short, stubby fingers across the wind chime that hung from the roof. I loved its tinkling, musical sound.

"Mama?" I called at the top of my voice. "Aileen? Joe?"

"My goodness, Amelia!" Mama answered, stepping into the kitchen through the short hallway that connected it to her and Papa's bedroom. "Must you holler inside the house?"

"I didn't see you," I said. "Where're Ailie and Joe?"

"Aileen left early," Mama answered. "She wants to catch up on the news and visit friends before the bell rings. And Joseph, well, he's across the street. He's going to walk to school with Billy."

"Aw shucks, I thought they'd walk with me," I whined, plopping down dejectedly on the bench beside the wooden kitchen table.

"No, I'm accompanying you," Mama said, turning her attention to the wood-fueled cook stove. Then she added brightly, untying her bib apron, "After all, it is your first day."

The stove chimney proceeded into a small warming oven. Mama reached inside and took out the bowl of mush she'd kept warm for me. I scowled at the food. Mush wasn't my favorite breakfast and this morning the mixture looked especially lumpy. I poured milk over it, but instead of eating, I fixed my eyes out the open window and on the mountain, where I caught sight of what appeared to be a golden halo surrounding one of the flat boulders. The sight was truly breathtaking, like a mist of brilliant green-blue sage.

"Well, I've changed my mind, Mama," I said, "I'm not going to school today. I prefer to climb the mountain."

"What?" Mama laughed, throwing her head back. She turned and followed my gaze. "Silly girl. Of course you'll go. That mountain was here long before we moved to Claypool, and will be here when you come home from school today. Now hurry and eat or you'll be going without breakfast. It's a long time till lunch."

Her face became serious with a deep scowl. She jerked the apron over her head, taking pains to avoid mussing her silky light-brown hair, which she wore piled into a neat bun. She hung the apron on its peg on the wall beside the stove, and sat facing me.

"Gee whiz, Mama!" I exclaimed, "you're wearing your voting dress!" The tan pongee was Mama's best dress. It flattered her with its low waistline and delicate sash, which she looped through two walnut-colored wooden rings sewn at her left hip. "I didn't realize my going to school was so important."

"Most momentous thing you'll likely ever do. I'm looking forward to walking you to school this morning, Amelia," she said. "I'll help you find your classroom, and make sure you're settled in. Now finish your mush while I change shoes, and if there's time, I'll tell you the story of how this dress got its name."

"Yes, Mama, do tell. Please."

"Okay, Amelia. As best as I can relate the tale. You must know why I never, ever want to hear you say you're not attending school. Never! Understand me, young lady?" Mama furrowed her forehead.

I nodded. I'd never seen Mama so determined. She sat on the edge of her wicker rocker, kept in a corner of the kitchen, and kicked the brown felt house slippers from her feet. I watched her deftly button her high-top shoes. They were similar to mine, although newer in appearance—black leather, with pointed toes.

Ugly, ugly, ugly. I sat quietly, waiting for Mama to continue.

Mama glanced at the clock, then leaned forward and let her hands drop to her lap. "Women have not always been allowed the privilege of voting. That first day—when I should have voted—we were traveling west, stuck somewhere between Missouri and Arizona. You should have seen me! My toes were encased in mud. My clothing hung wet, ragged, and muddy. My hair was tangled and hanging down like a wet dog's tail. Not fit to vote even if a polling booth had been handy." Mama let out a half laugh, half groan, again checking the clock.

"It's getting late; I'd better postpone the story until after school. If you've finished breakfast, let's see how you look."

"You're pretty today, Mama," I said, and wasn't surprised when the corners of her mouth turned up slightly, nor when she quickly turned away.

Obediently, I stepped around the table to stand before Mama, and she bent over to pin a white handkerchief to the front of my dress.

"Papa gave me a present, Mama," I said, lifting up the necklace for Mama to see.

"I see that," she stopped to examine the stone in her fingers. "I recall seeing it years ago. It was his lucky stone," she added. "One he found in a creek bed in Missouri when but a boy about your age. It already had a hole, see? Like formed by God to be a necklace."

Mama paused to look into my brown eyes. "It's a very special gift, and you must take good care of it, Amelia."

"I will," I promised. "I'll keep it forever."

She placed both hands on my shoulders and looked me up and down. Suddenly she pulled back, and then she licked her fingers and smoothed my bangs into place. "This morning you remind me of Aileen in that dress."

I smiled at the possibility that I might resemble Aileen. My sister, with her long, wavy blonde hair and clear blue eyes was often complimented for her beauty.

"Our hair and eyes are different," I said, mentioning our dissimilarities. I hoped Mama would confirm it was minor.

"Yes, they are," she agreed. "Like Papa says, Aileen's eyes are azure-blue, but yours are pecan-brown, with little specks of chocolate kisses in them."

I smiled then. I wasn't fond of brown eyes. I preferred blue or green, like the other members of my family. I wondered why God had chosen brown—like dirt—for me. Mama told me often that Daniel and I resembled her sister, Mildred, and my Uncle Willie, both who had brown eyes, but having never met them, I found it little consolation.

She reached over and took hold of my skirt in both hands and gave it a gentle yank. Then she attempted to smooth the fabric. "How on earth did you get your dress wrinkled already?"

"Which kind are better, Mama?" I asked.

"Which kind of what?" She sounded confused.

"My color eyes or Aileen's?"

Mama furrowed her brow and pursed her lips, pretending to think hard. "Hmm, I can't say." She shook her head and tapped her chin. "They're both charming. Why, I guess I'd choose whichever eyes I happen to be looking into at the time!"

I giggled. "Well, you're looking into mine right now."

That brought a laugh from Mama and a light spank on my bottom, too. "Well, they're beautiful enough."

I started toward the door, but she grabbed my arm. "Wait a minute; I see something not so lovely. You've a stocking sagging like the neck of an old turkey gobbler. Reach inside your bloomers and yank it up."

I struggled to gather up the dress, but the fabric kept getting in the way.

"Here," Mama said. "I'll hold the dress for you and pull out the elastic in the legs of your bloomers. You jerk up the stockings."

"See?" she said, patting my leg. "The elastic on your bloomer legs makes good garters. There, that's nice."

I didn't see anything nice about long stockings or drooping bloomers. "Mama, do girls have ugly legs?"

"Land sakes, whatever made you ask such a question," she exclaimed.

"Why else do we cover them with stockings and bloomers below our knees?"

Mama chuckled and pulled a hairpin from the side of her light-brown bun, something she always did when she wanted time to form an answer. After a second, she shoved it back, closer to her scalp. "Mormon girls are always modest," she said. "You'll understand these things when you grow older."

I pondered that answer to myself, but aloud I asked, "Did Papa and Dan leave already?"

"Yes, they're gone," she said. "They're working on a house for Mr. Brown on the west side of the mountain. Papa wanted an early start to beat this stifling Arizona heat."

She glanced at the kitchen clock and took a shiny new lard bucket from the cabinet shelf above the sink. I watched her fill it with an orange, two sugar cookies, and a sandwich, and fit on the lid. Then she leaned forward and pressed down hard on the lid with both hands.

"Time to go, Amelia. Here, you carry the lunch pail." She held it out. "You're a big schoolgirl now."

"Yes," I said proudly, taking it from her. Suddenly, I was glad the others had left. To have time alone with Mama was a rare treat.

We went out the door, crossed the yard, and opened the gate that met the dirt road. Something written on the outside of the wooden gate caught my eye. I could read some but was unable to make out the middle word. "*No polygamy allowed*" in bold red print.

"Wow. Who wrote that, Mama? What does it say? Isn't 'poly' a girl's name?" I looked at her inquiringly.

Her face turned scarlet, and then a deep, dark, angry color crept over it and down to her neck. "Land sakes, I don't know who would mark up our gate. What it says is unimportant. It'll wash off." She slammed the gates securely shut, with such force I feared it would pop off its hinges.

CHAPTER TWO—SCHOOL

I reached for Mama's hand as we started down the road that led toward Claypool. Her fingers were moving in a nervous twitch. Somehow, it made me feel uneasy.

At a sharp turn at the bottom of our block, I noticed the neighborhood busybody, Mrs. Jones. She stood close to the fence furiously shaking a rug, and a large German shepherd stood at her side. I ran up to the dog, Brownie, and slipped my fingers through the wire fence to stroke his head.

"Good dog," I whispered.

"What's between you two, Amelia?" Mrs. Jones asked. "Heaven help me, if any other person in town sticks their hands on this side of the fence Brownie'd bite it off."

I shrugged and continued petting the dog. Certainly it wouldn't be wise to admit the truth. Whenever my mama placed chicken gizzards on my plate, I'd hide them in my pocket. Later I'd run down the half-block to toss the food to the dog.

"You braid beautiful rugs, Sarah," Mama said, as she watched the neighbor vigorously shake the throw rug, "but they'll soon wear out if you don't stop beating them against the fence so hard. By the way, I'll have extra time now that Amelia is in school. How about coming to my house and showing me how they're made? I sew mine together after they're braided but yours are much nicer."

Mrs. Jones' face brightened as she nodded. "I would be pleased to. Let me know when." The hard lines disappeared from her face and she folded the rug as she leaned farther over the fence.

The copper mining settlement where we lived consisted of dusty dirt roads. This one meandered past the school and boasted a sign announcing its name as Elm Street. It continued on past the town, and eventually stopped at the entrance to the Inspiration Mine, the employer of most of the men of Gila County.

I knew that a few months before I was born, my family had moved to Arizona from a farm outside Crystal City, Missouri. Mama told us the elders in the Mormon Church had promised to let Papa help build a new temple in Mesa. It didn't work out. My parents, brothers, and sister had driven over the dangerous mountains from Missouri to Arizona expecting him to have a job, but he had had to look elsewhere for employment. Fortunately, being a skilled carpenter, he found he could make a living building houses and garages, mostly for other Mormons who were settling in this new state.

With rare exception, two churches sorted the residents of Claypool and the surrounding area for many miles into Methodists or Mormons. As Mama and I proceeded on our way to school, I could see the tall white spire of the Methodist Church beyond the rooftops of the few buildings in town. We attended the Church of Jesus Christ of Latter-day Saints in the neighboring city of Miami. Most people ignored the long name and called us Mormons—after the book. I didn't actually know any Methodists, but I wanted to. Aileen told me there would be plenty at school.

Very little traffic met us along our route that morning. The miners had left their homes hours before, hurrying off and into the dark shafts, where they spent their days underground like moles.

Suddenly, I caught sight of my brother and his friend Billy, up ahead. "Hey, Mama, there's Joe," I said, breaking into a run. "Hurry! We can catch them!"

"My stars and garters, no! We'll do no such thing," Mama said, shocked. "Imagine me running down Main Street. Why, whatever would people think?" But she quickened her steps. After a moment, she added, "Amelia, I do wish you'd not use nicknames for Joseph and Daniel. Papa chose good Bible names for them. He doesn't like them shortened."

"But he didn't hear me," I pointed out. I waited for her to scold, but she seemed to be studying the toes of her shoes.

"How come Aileen and I didn't get Bible names?"

"Oh, Chester let me name you and Aileen. Your name means industrious. You are too, but more importantly, you are smart. You've got gumption. I'm counting on you to see females never backslide, and lose their new rights. You like the name don't you?"

I nodded.

"We've plenty of time," she said. "You mustn't run and make me walk so fast. Do you want your mama to trip and roll all the way down to your school behind you?"

I laughed at the thought of Mama rolling down the dirt road. I knew she had partly been referring to her shape.

She'd been slender as a girl. One morning, while I helped her make her bed, Papa came in and picked up their wedding picture from the white lace doily atop the chest of drawers in their bedroom. It showed Mama in a long white dress turned just enough to show the large bustle in the back, boasting a big white bow. He looked it over a moment and then came over to the bed and showed it to Mama, patting her on her bottom. "You sure don't need a bustle anymore, Ida," he'd said, winking.

Mama had laughed and said, "Oh, you!" She grabbed the picture from him quickly and laid it face down on the dresser. I caught a look of sadness as she turned, and when her eyes raised and met mine across the room, she said, "Amelia, straighten this corner. A job worth doing is worth doing well."

Mama and I continued down the road to the schoolyard. I sneaked a glance at her and noticed the early morning sunshine lit up the gold strands of her light-brown hair. Her deep blue eyes seemed a window, through which I could see the clear sky above her head. *She's beautiful.*

"Mama" I asked, squinting. "Why didn't girls attend school years and years ago?"

"I don't know, hon, that's just the way of it. Sometime in history, men decided they knew better how to run the country than females, so girls needn't be taught."

"Tarnations," I grumbled, stomping my foot, "I've as much sense as Joe or any old boy." I made up my mind at that precise moment to study and learn all that I could cram into my noggin. Then, just as in the bedroom that morning, mama suddenly caught my gaze.

"Sixteen years," she said, with a sad smile.

"Huh?"

"That's how long it's been since I stayed home alone of the day," she said. "I had Daniel on the very day I turned twenty. I've almost an empty nest now, with my last little bird flying off to school." She patted my head, her eyes moist.

The schoolyard up ahead resembled an anthill, with children and adults streaming toward the front and moving up the steps. I quickened my pace.

"Is Papa going to pay Daniel for helping build Mr. Brown's house?" I asked, skipping ahead of Mama again, hoping to hurry her along. Joseph and Billy had already entered the building.

The whole structure had originally been white, but like every building in Claypool, the Inspiration Mine's copper fumes stained all the areas that were not exposed to the rain. From a distance, the two tones gave the school an odd, outlined appearance, with the siding immediately beneath the roof and the windows seeming almost to glow in the morning sunshine.

"Mercy, Amelia, I wouldn't know anything about that," Mama answered. "Business and money matters are for men to fuss over. We ladies needn't bother our heads over them."

"But Daniel said he's saving to build a house for himself," I said.

"Well, I don't think he plans to do that right away," she answered. "He's still a boy. He's got a lot to learn from Papa about the carpentry trade, and besides, he's got the lean-to built by the side of the tool shed now. He likes to sleep there."

She stopped at the entrance to the schoolyard and smoothed her hair with both her gloved hands. I watched her fingers account for her hairpins one at a time. I caught her hand and heard her mutter under her breath, "He'll surely not stay long if Chester doesn't treat him fair."

A long procession of steps began on the left side of Claypool Elementary School, which gave the impression that it jutted out of the mountainside. Steps continued across the front of the building, rising up at intervals with the terrain. There were three landings before the steps made an abrupt turn to the left and marched up to a porch-like landing before the school's front door.

I had long awaited my first ascent of those steps, but suddenly something else grabbed my attention. A large playground stretched all the way across the school's property in front and continued around the side toward the mountain. It held one tall slide with a ladder flanked by bright red railings. There were two rows of blue swing sets; four of them held swings that resembled small blue airplanes. It was the airplanes that held my eyes that morning. They were designed so that passengers sat facing each other, two on a side.

I let go of Mama's hand and started running up the steps. Before entering the front door, I waited for her. Children and parents maneuvered past me to go inside. From that height, I could make out the roof of the post office, and to the north beyond the Methodist Church, the dim gray irregular buildings of the town of Miami, five miles away.

Mama stood panting, her face red, when she finally reached the top of the stairs. I let her pass in front of me and waited inside the door for ages, while she caught her breath. Despite the burning lights that hung at intervals above us, the interior of the building seemed dark after our walk in the bright sun. Finally, Mama offered me her hand and I was happy to pull her down the long corridor, having no idea where it would take us. We passed several wall displays that held pictures of brightly colored books and pencils and some signs, welcoming students back to school. Groups of children milled around in the hallway and inside each open classroom. Their faces were all unfamiliar.

I gripped Mama's hand tightly. She squeezed mine back reassuringly. Halfway down the hall, Mama took a sudden right turn into a second hallway and stopped.

"Amelia, see the red balloons in the doorway? Bet that's your room. Let's go see." My heart pounded with excitement and worry. I strengthened my grip on Mama's hand.

"Yes, indeed, this is it," Mama said cheerily, at the classroom door. She took a few steps inside. Several heads turned and pairs of childish eyes looked our way. Then they went back to their various activities throughout the room.

Mama released my hand and bent over to smooth my bangs. "I don't see your teacher, Amelia, but I'm sure she'll be along soon."

She must have noticed the worry on my face because she added, "Now you'll be fine. Aileen will walk home with you after school. I'd best hurry home." Her face showed a sense of urgency. Then she turned and left me standing alone, looking after her. I watched as she headed back the way we'd come, until she turned left at the first hallway and disappeared out of sight.

Despite my galloping heart, I surveyed the bright room. Instead of the desks I'd expected, four low narrow tables were placed neatly into two rows. An aisle between them led to the teacher's desk. Sparkling white tables flanked by a set of four small chairs faced the front of the room. Each chair painted a different color—red, yellow, green, or blue. They are just the right height for my short legs to reach the floor and not dangle. Behind the teacher's desk, a large blackboard spanned the entire wall, beckoning me to come draw a picture or write my name.

The girls and boys in the room fluttered like butterflies. Some squirmed quietly in chairs or scooted in and out, scraping the floor. Others bobbed around in small groups, their heads close together, chatting excitedly. I wanted to join the girls, but lacked the nerve to approach them.

Suddenly, I heard a woman's voice behind me. "Hello, there," she said, finding me standing in front of the door. "What's your name?" There stood a pretty young lady with medium brown hair and brown eyes and deep dimples in her cheeks. She wore a stiffly starched black cotton dress that seemed contradictory to her youthfulness and sweet smile. The dress had a bright, white lace collar.

"Ameliahall." I said quickly, running the two names together as if they were one.

"Well, good morning to you, Ameliahall!" She laughed, mimicking me, but with a kind tone in her voice. "I'm Miss Barnes, your teacher."

Her voice was warm and welcoming, and her smile revealed a set of white, even teeth that matched the snowy collar around her neck. Her chestnut-colored eyes twinkled and lit her face.

"Come with me, dear," she said, slipping her hand in mine. "You'll be cooler over by the window. Why don't you sit in this yellow chair? Why look, it matches the daisies on your pretty dress!"

I wondered if I looked exceptionally warm. I gazed around and noticed that the girls who stood together in the back of the room wore short-sleeved dresses, and their legs were bare between the hems of their skirts and the tops of their white knee socks.

I stepped past three chairs to pull out the yellow one near the window and smiled at a girl I knew sitting behind me, Mary Brown. Her long sleeves and her high top shoes matched mine. Apparently, she'd sought a cooler place for herself.

"Hi there, Amelia," she said, wiggling the fingers of her right hand at me. Mary attended the same Mormon Church in Miami where my family worshipped. It was her house that Papa and Daniel were building.

"Hi Mary," I answered, glad for a familiar face. Just as I was about to lower myself into the chair, Miss Barnes said, "Wait, Amelia, let me re-do your bow, dear. It's come loose."

She stooped down until her face was level with mine. I looked deeply into her fawn-colored eyes and caught a whiff of an aroma not unlike the lilac bushes that grew in our backyard. Instantly and completely, I fell deeply in love with Miss Barnes.

She tied a perfect bow on my dress and stood. Then she pulled out the yellow chair for me. Nodding toward a dark-skinned girl with black hair who was now seated on my right, she said, "This is Blanca Romac. Blanca, meet Amelia Hall."

Water Under the Bridge

Blanca smiled, widely revealing an empty space between her two front teeth. Her blue-black hair hung in two neat pigtails with a fiery-red bow fastened on the end of each one. They perfectly matched her red dress. I longed to have hair like hers. Mine was auburn and cut so short it was useless to try and gather it in a ribbon. Mama once told me, "I'll let your hair grow longer when you learn to sit still for me to curl it." But Blanca's hair was long and straight.

"Did the tooth fairy come for your teeth?" I asked.

"No," Blanca said, shaking her head solemnly.

A small breeze wafted through the window, caressing my face and ruffling my short hair. Outside, I could see a trail leading from the back of the school up the mountain to my left, and in the distance, the sunlit boulders, green bushes, small cacti, and scrappy trees lifted my spirits, as glimpses of the mountain have always done.

I was grateful to Miss Barnes for my seat beside the window and although I hated my long sleeves, bloomers, and heavy stockings, I felt they were responsible for the privilege.

Suddenly, a bell tinkled. Miss Barnes walked to the front of the room and stood before the blackboard. A noisy scraping of chairs quickly replaced chatter as children took their seats.

Miss Barnes waited until every child sat quietly. Then she said, "Good morning, class. I am happy to see all your sweet faces this morning. We're going to have a wonderful time learning to read and write and cipher. You'll make new friends and probably even get to know old ones better. Then, before you know it, first grade will be over and you'll be ready for second!"

She smiled brightly and turned to write on the blackboard. I caught the words of a familiar song emerging from her hand—one Aileen sang at home.

Miss Barnes turned to face us, "We're going to learn a new song."

Tentatively, I raised my hand.

"Yes, Amelia?" she asked, smiling. "Do you have a question?"

I stood. In a loud voice that surprised me, I said, "I know that song already."

"You do?" Miss Barnes said, clearly surprised. "Can you read, Amelia?"

"Yes ma'am," I said, confused. I thought everyone my age could read. The incredulous looks on my classmates' faces told me otherwise.

"Well, good for you, Amelia! Why don't you read the words aloud," Miss Barnes said.

Suddenly sorry I'd spoken, I took a deep breath and obediently read,

Good morning to you! Good morning to you!
We're all in our places, with bright sunny faces,
For this is the way to start a new day.

"Nice job, Amelia." The teacher turned to the rest of the class, "Soon all of you will be able to read."

I glanced around the room to see what the others thought and caught a boy rolling his eyes, which made me ashamed. Aileen often scolded me for showing off, and her words came back to me. "You needn't call attention to yourself," she'd said. My big sister was right—always right.

Miss Barnes took a long stick from the ledge of the blackboard and used it to point at each word on the board as she led us in singing. Next, she asked us to stand and face the American flag in the corner behind her desk. She walked over and stood before the flag to set an example for us. We placed our right hands over the left side of our chests. This way she led us in the Pledge of the Allegiance.

Next, Miss Barnes asked us to take turns standing and telling our names. When it was my turn, I took special care not to run my two names together. "Amelia—Hall," I said, making my last name sound like a sigh.

Our first lesson introduced us to scissors and paste. Miss Barnes passed out sheets of colored construction paper—each of us received one light beige paper that bore the faint outline of a little Dutch girl wearing a large bonnet, an apron, and a pair of wooden shoes. She showed us how to lay the beige drawing on top of a sheet of colored paper, and using a pencil, press down hard to trace the image of the Dutch girl's dress, which created an imprint of it on construction paper beneath it. I chose sky blue paper and, following the indentation with my scissors, carefully cut out the dress. After that, I cut out the doll, so that she seemed to be released from her beige background. I pasted the dress onto her figure. Finally, with a pencil I drew a pocket on the skirt.

"That's lovely," Miss Barnes said, inspecting my work. When we were finished, she announced, "Recess time, children. Leave your papers on the table to dry and line up by the door—girls first—two by two."

I found myself standing beside Blanca admiring her pretty red pinafore. She also wore a pair of white socks and shiny black shoes. All the girls, except Mary and me, wore cool summer dresses. As my class marched down the hallway outside our room, I felt lonely and scared. I liked it better at home where I didn't think about what I wore.

Children in other classrooms talked or recited as we passed open doors. I strained to hear Aileen or Joseph, but the voices sounded to me like a gaggle of geese. Blanca clasped my hand instantly flooding me with a sense of calm and gratitude. I turned to her shyly and smiled. Together, we followed the children in front of us. Two by two, they turned left and walked toward the bright sunshine outside. I could hardly wait to leave the stifling building. As I stepped out on the landing, the breeze tickled some of the short hair on the top of my head. I shoved my sweaty bangs off my forehead.

"I like your hair, Amelia," Blanca said. "It's the color of a new penny."

I was astonished. My red hair disappointed me daily and I could not fathom how someone with Blanca's beautiful black pigtails could admire mine.

"I wish it was long like yours," I said. "Then I could wear ribbons."

"What are those pretty flowers?" she asked, releasing my hand to point at one of the yellow and white blossoms on my dress and, at the same time, effectively changing the subject.

"Daisies," I said, grabbing her hand back and pulling it gently down the stairs toward the play yard. "It's my favorite flower. My mama made this dress."

I forgot all my trepidations when the playground neared. "Hurry," I squealed. "Let's share an airplane swing."

Blanca nodded agreeably, and together we raced down the steps and into the play yard, but by the time we reached the airplane swings, they were nearly full.

"There's only one available seat and it's not facing the propeller." I moaned

"You go first, Amelia," Blanca offered.

"We'll take turns," I suggested, too eager to pass up the ride.

"No, that's okay," she said. "You go ahead. There'll be other recesses. I don't mind waiting."

My ride ended too soon, and the long line of children that formed in front of the swings confirmed that there would be no second ride that day. Blanca and I headed for the slide, joining the end of the line behind two boys and Mary Brown.

The slide stood in the middle of the yard away from any shade and the hot sun beat down. I lifted the skirt of my dress a little, trying to let some air on my legs, but they were so heavily covered it was futile.

"You must be awfully warm," Blanca said, sympathetically.

"It's these bloomers and stockings," I said. "I wish I needn't wear them."

Mary turned around. "After we're baptized, we'll wear holy underwear also," she said, shaking her head miserably. Then she turned to Blanca, "It's our religion."

"Oh," Blanca said. "I have no religion."

"You don't?" Mary asked. "What do you believe?"

"My family sings our native songs and we have prayers at night," Blanca said. "We're free spirits; that's what my mama says."

I had no idea what Blanca meant by "native songs" or "free spirits." I knew Papa wouldn't approve of someone having no religion, but I decided God must appreciate everyone who says prayers.

"You know each other?" Blanca asked, looking back and forth at Mary and me.

"Yes, we attend the Mormon Church," Mary said. "Amelia's papa is building our family a new house. I can't wait. We've been renting the apartment above the store since we moved here last year. It's much too small for eight of us." Then she turned to me and added, "I sure hope your papa's a fast carpenter."

"He is," I promised. "My brother, Dan, is helping, too. They'll be done in no time. Dan's my biggest brother. Daniel is his real name. I call him Dan. I have another brother named Joseph. He's eight."

Blanca seemed not to hear me. She reached past me to touch Mary's shoulder. "You'll have a lovely new room," she said.

Mary nodded enthusiastically. "Mama's making me curtains the same color yellow as Amelia's dress," she said. "We ordered material last week. It'll be a wonderful room and I get it all to myself, cause I'm the only girl."

"What color is your room?" she asked Blanca.

"Pink," Blanca said, "with lots and lots of ruffles. My mother made curtains, a bedspread, and a canopy—and they all match."

"A can of what?" I asked, shocked.

"A canopy, can—oh—pee!" Blanca enunciated the word for me. "It's a covering like a tent."

"Tarnations, you sleep in a tent?" I asked, impressed.

"No," Blanca said, doubling over with laughter. "Come see it and you'll understand. It's a bed with a pretty ruffled roof over it."

I did want to see that bed. I couldn't imagine how it would look, but I knew I'd love it. I pictured Blanca, with her dark hair, standing in a room surrounded by pink ruffles. My own room with Aileen now seemed drab. Our curtains and bedspread matched, but they were a pale, dusty blue color with tiny rosebuds sprinkled on them. Until a few moments before, I'd thought our room lovely.

Blanca clasped my hand again. "I'm sorry you've lost your room, Amelia, but I'm really glad to know you," Blanca said. "We can be best friends, want to?"

I nodded, thinking Blanca had an aura of mystery around her, but didn't mention I hadn't lost my room. It didn't feel important at the time. Pure joy welled up in my chest, filling my throat and making me speechless. I'd wanted to go to school for as long as I could remember, and the first day brought mixed feelings—mostly good, but with a few unsettling moments. Now I sensed pleasure. I'd expected to find a friend at school—never a best friend!

Recess ended and we went inside. The afternoon flew by. We practiced tracing the alphabet from a book onto paper and learned all the different sounds that *A* makes.

When we were dismissed, I didn't wait for Aileen. Instead, I ran the short distance toward home as fast as I could, partly to prove I was big enough, and also to tell Mama about Blanca and to show her my paper doll. As I rounded the corner near our house, I spotted a strange car parked in front of our porch. The sight I saw made me throw my hand over my mouth and stop in my tracks.

Verna Simms

CHAPTER THREE—STRANGERS

"Wow!" I gasped.

A car was parked in front, close to the fence. I stopped running and watched. Papa stood talking to a stranger. His foot rested on the running board of a black Model T touring car. Even in this position, he was half a head taller than the other man, slimmer and more muscular. I had never thought of Papa as handsome, but I had heard others describe him that way. He had wavy jet-black hair, high cheekbones, a cleft in his chin. His face changed with his mood, though. Today he appeared to be very happy.

I eased forward, keeping my eyes locked on the strange vehicle. What a sight to behold—bundles wrapped in canvas and tied to the fenders, on the roof, even on the back bumper. Everything seemed to be in turmoil. More strange people were scurrying about, carrying bags and boxes between the car and our home—like squirrels in the fall.

Who were these people?

"Papa!" I shouted.

He ignored me. I watched in horror as they continued to carry bundle after bundle into the house. I noticed the writing had been washed from the swinging gate that pushed inward into our front yard. I moseyed through and hurried over to stand under the lone cottonwood tree growing nearby. My gaze slid over to the tool shed and the lean-to Daniel built last month. Mama's prize rooster strutted in the chicken pen, watching over his flock of a dozen hens. Two pairs of overalls hung on the clothesline, drying. None of my family worked in the yard, as was often the case. Much of our chores were done outdoors, either heating water in the old iron kettle or washing clothing, chopping wood or hoeing in the garden—located in back, just west of the outhouse.

A freckled-faced boy with an armload of clothing approached me. He said, "Hey." I rushed passed him, up the back stairs across the porch and into the house.

"Mama?" I called.

She hurried into the hall from the bedroom that Aileen and I shared. In her arms, she carried bedding and two large feather pillows. She scarcely glanced my way—but pressed on through our small dining room, and into the parlor. I followed her. I loved our parlor; it was reserved for guests. A burgundy-colored nine by twelve rug, with a floral design decorating all four corners, graced the floor. It didn't completely cover the room, leaving twelve to fourteen inches of dark, highly polished tongue-and-groove flooring around the perimeter. A maroon davenport with beautifully carved mahogany legs and trim and a matching chair were placed a foot away from the large double windows. These were covered with ochre colored lace curtains, almost the exact shade as the hand-crocheted scarf draped over a library table. Tasseled fringe hung down six inches on each end.

Wallpaper with vines of light-green ivy ran up and down the walls. The only wall ornament to be seen was a large hand-painted mural of a waterfall. I always felt I had entered a different world inside this pleasant parlor. One door led outside to a covered wrap-around porch that circled the front and side of the house. Inside the room, Mama dropped her load on the davenport and threw her arms up in a gesture of despair. Joseph and Aileen followed.

Mama said, "Aileen, come help me shove this davenport farther away from the wall. We can make a nook to sleep behind it." Her eyes swept the room, as she adjusted hairpins and wiped sweat from her forehead with the tail of her apron. "Mercy me, but it'll be privacy of a sort," she said. "I need you too, Joseph."

I was still being ignored and plopped down on the davenport, holding my paper doll to my chest. Billows of dust flew from the seldom-used sofa.

"Shucks, Mama. Amelia is sitting on it," Joseph complained. He was tall for a boy of eight, and had inherited Papa's dark hair and blue eyes. In contrast to Papa, he had a quick, bright smile, but he wasn't smiling now. Aileen and I resembled Mama with her heart-shaped face and pointed chin. Only Mama's light brown hair had a tint of copper, mine more the shade of a persimmon

"Land sakes, Amelia, get off that davenport," Mama ordered, brushing wisps of hair from her forehead. "If you can't find anything to do to help, at least go somewhere and get out of the way of those who are working."

I bounced up and scurried from the room, and grabbed two cold biscuits off the stove as I passed through the kitchen. Out the back door I flew, letting the screen door bang shut behind me. I took the steps, two at a time, and made my escape.

No one noticed me dash around to the back of the porch. Only then did I pause to catch my breath, as I parted the morning glory vines. Mama had tied them up with strings attached to the roof of the porch. With my slender body sideways, I was able to slip inside my secret hideaway.

Sitting in the cool dirt, brushing a spider aside, I slowly removed my clean handkerchief. I wrapped the two biscuits in the hanky and re-pinned it to my dress. Then I removed my shoes and stockings. Leaving them behind, I stooped over and made my way into the cool, semi-darkness under the house: a five-room structure with two bedrooms, a large kitchen, a small dining room, and an average parlor. The bedrooms both faced the east, twin closets between them. A small closet opened into the hall adjacent to the dining area. We never ate in this room except when guests came for meals or on holidays. At night, Joseph slept in the dining room on a folding cot, but he kept his clothes in the hall closet. The entire family spent most of our waking hours in the kitchen or, if the weather permitted, outdoors.

Six concrete pillars supported the house. Joseph and I, being only two years apart, often separated from the rest of the family and found our own form of amusement in this crawl space under the house. Months ago, we carried in gunnysacks to make a seat and also a few flat rocks, with which we built a low privacy wall that doubled as a shelf. It was into this semi-dark hidden area that I crawled that day, duck-like, on my haunches. I plopped down. I reached for a shoebox on the shelf, opened the lid, and placed my little Dutch girl inside.

"You'll be nice and dry here, sweetie," I promised. "They don't have room for us upstairs."

I gazed up at the floor-joists above me, feeling sorry for myself. I thought how sad they'd be when they discover I'm missing. Then, continuing my conversation with the paper doll, I whispered, "I'll come here every day after school and visit with you. What happens at school will be our secret. We won't tell anyone else. It'll be fun, you'll see. We don't need them." I stammered as I pointed above me at the two-by-sixes supporting the floor. A tear rolled down my cheek and I reached for the bulging hanky. Slipping one of the biscuits out of its hammock, I began to chew. After what seemed like a long time, but probably wasn't, thirst drove me into the daylight again. I tried to brush the dust from my clothing.

I cranked the handle on the cistern and watched the tiny buckets follow the chain up until they tipped over from the weight of the water inside them and filled my pail. The buckets reminded me of seats on a Ferris wheel. A long drink of the water cooled me, and I did my best to wash my hands and face. Over on the far side of the lot I saw Daniel busy stacking lumber. I strolled over.

"Hey, Dan," I said. "What're you doing?"

"Wondered where you were, Amy. Wanna help? Joseph is inside." All the time he was speaking, he kept busy carrying armloads of short scraps of lumber from the back of a large truck to the lumber pile.

"This your truck?" I asked, as I climbed on.

"No, sis. Hand me an armload, so I needn't hop in and out. That way we'll be done in no time."

Daniel stood five feet-eight with broad shoulders and a compact frame. I liked watching his muscles ripple as he strained over a heavy load. Mama said he reminded her of her brother, my Uncle Willie. Square jaw and bushy eyebrows. Not at all like Papa or Joseph. I'd never been to Missouri to see any of Mama's relations, but I sometimes wondered about them. Both of Mama's parents were dead but she had two sisters living, in addition to Uncle Willie. Daniel's hair almost lit up like fire when the sun splashed down on it—burnt orange. His gray-green eyes looked sad.

"Truck belongs to Mr. Wallace. It's on loan so I could haul these lumber scraps away."

Mr. Wallace, the local banker, lived up the hill from us and had a big house with a veranda—all painted a snowy white. They didn't have any children, so we never visited them. I was glad to be able to help my older brother with his work. "Thanks," Dan said, as we unloaded and he stacked the last bit of lumber. I jumped down landing on the hard packed dirt, stinging the soles of my bare feet.

Entering our large, roomy kitchen, I eased the door closed behind me quietly. A wood-burning cook stove stood close to the back door, with only enough room for the wood box beside it. The fire had burned low, but I could still feel the heat. Our usually uncluttered kitchen was now strewn with bags and boxes. We had no running water in the house, but Papa had installed a sink with a drain that led to the back yard. The drain board was piled high. Mama's pride and joy, the Old Mother Hubbard cabinet, had doors hanging open and empty. I could only guess all of the dishes were dirty and waiting to be washed. A path to the icebox and an army folding cot was clear. I was tired so I headed toward my room, but Mama stopped me short. Shaking her head, she said, "Mr. and Mrs. Overberg and their infant are using your room."

"Where will I sleep?" I whined, rolling my eyes around the room.

"Why honey, in the parlor behind the davenport," she said, trying to sound cheerful. "We made nice pallets for you and Aileen. Joseph is on the other side, behind the chair." Mama wiped her hands on the apron she usually wore.

With a sigh, she glanced toward the closed door. "Be nice to them, Amelia. Pretend you are camping. It could be fun."

When I entered the parlor, Aileen put her arm around my shoulder and pulled me down to sit on the pallet beside her. She said, "Amy, remember the story I told you about when our family came West?" I nodded. "Papa thought we should come here and live close to the brethren," she continued. "He thinks we can be better Mormons near our own kind.

"Mama was raised in the Church of Christ back in the state of Missouri. Her sisters derided her because this new religion substituted white bread for unleavened bread, and water for grape juice at communion. Papa and her brother Willie, he's our uncle, had a heated argument about whether the revelation on the tablets of gold was real or a fake."

"I remember a little, but I don't understand why they can't just look at what was found. Surely no one would throw gold away." I said.

"An angel took the tablets of gold, so there's no proof. We have to go on faith." Aileen stared at the ceiling, then rubbed her tired eyes. "Probably the Overbergs were harassed also. So they came here. A lot of Mormons come out West, just as our parents did—the year before you were born.

"Well, if others hadn't helped us, we'd have starved," she said. "Now it's our turn to do for another family. These people are old friends of Mama and Papa from Missouri. They've talked about them a lot. You do understand, don't you?"

I didn't, but I nodded anyway. I had always thought God was everywhere, so I wondered why a family had to move to a different place in order to worship Him. I didn't bother to ask about this though. I knew I'd get the standard answer: "You'll understand when you are older."

"Why is Joe in here with us?" I asked. "I saw his cot in the kitchen."

"Oh, their daughter, Thelma, is sleeping there," Aileen said. "She's fifteen. Mama said we're to give the best to company."

"How long will they stay here?"

"Not long, I don't think," she said. "By the way, how was your first day of school?"

"Okay."

"Is that all? Didn't you like Miss Barnes?"

Suddenly I couldn't contain myself. "Do you know her?" I asked Aileen.

"Sure," she said. "I had her in first grade, too. Isn't she pretty? I love the way she pulls her hair back into twin buns and places those exquisite hairpins in it. Every day I couldn't wait to get to school and see what she would wear in her hair. Those hairpins looked like jewels."

"She wasn't wearing any other jewelry," I said. "Not even a wedding ring."

"Married ladies can't teach," said Aileen.

"How come?"

"They just can't," she said. "Come on, let's say our prayers and go to sleep. You first."

I knelt next to the davenport and folded my hands.

"Will you walk me to school tomorrow?" I asked Aileen.

"Uh-huh," she answered, her eyes closed and her hands folded.

"Promise?"

"Yes, yes, yes, little sister! I promise. Now, come on, you first."

"Our Father in Heaven. Bless Mama and Papa," I began. "And bless Daniel, and Aileen, and Joseph, and me. Help me be good. Oh yes, and bless my new friend, Blanca, too. In Jesus' name . . . Amen."

I lay down on the pallet while Aileen said her longer prayer. Before she was finished, I was sound asleep.

CHAPTER FOUR—THE OVERBERGS

"Get off'n me!" a child screamed. "Get off, or I'll tell Daddy. I will, I will, I will!"

An infant's sobs and an unfamiliar female voice followed this outburst, "Stop it, you two! Mama's in bed with a sick headache, and you'll make her worse. Here, Timothy, come sit at the table, and I'll tell you a story."

"Don't want no story," the child whined. "Wanna doughnut."

"They don't got doughnuts here," said an older, gruffer, yet childish voice. I suspected it was the red-haired boy I'd seen outside in the yard.

I got up and dressed as quickly as possible, slipping into Aileen's old blue chambray dress with the long puffy sleeves. I pushed my feet into a fresh pair of black stockings that lay on the davenport—where I'd left my soiled ones the night before. Then I pulled on fresh bloomers.

Aileen had awakened before me. Her pallet and blanket lay straightened, with her nightgown neatly folded on top of her pillow. It took so long to button my shoes, I decided to only half-straighten my bed. I stuffed my nightgown beneath my pillow and then rolled my entire pallet up, blanket and all. I hoped Mama would be too busy to worry about how it looked, or at least not notice until I'd left for school.

On my way to the kitchen, I found Joseph in the dining room standing before the large mirror combing his hair. I walked passed him and nearly tripped over a pillow lying on the floor.

Looking around, I gasped. "Gosh almighty, look at this place!" Everything lay topsy-turvy.

"Gee willicans, where were you last night?" he demanded, without looking at me. "Mama made me turn all the chairs upside down on the table, crawl under, and make pallets for the two boys all by myself. I could've used your help, Amelia Hall. You're big enough. Only two years younger than me and you act like a spoiled baby."

I caught his tone and the use of my full name. I knew no explanation would be sufficient, so I just stuck out my tongue, and proceeded on into the kitchen.

A blonde-haired boy of about three sat on the bench at the kitchen table swinging his feet. Directly across from him, a teen-aged girl struggled with a screaming infant, trying to wash its face. The red-haired, freckle-faced boy I'd met the day before stood, and planted himself in my path directly in front of the back door.

"Your name is Amelia," he said, accusingly. Then he grinned, revealing a mouthful of yellowed, crooked teeth.

"Hey there, Amelia," the teen-age girl hollered, "I'm Thelma and that there's James." Then she pointed to the two toddlers with her at the table, "This is Timothy, and this crying baby is Paul. So happy to meet you." She smiled warmly.

Just then a woman's voice drifted in from my and Aileen's bedroom, "Thelma, fix the baby a sugar tit. I've gone dry."

Thelma stood obediently, revealing a full figure barely contained in her snug green pinafore. "Where you keep your sugar, hon?" she asked.

I took down the sugar jar from the shelf over the sink, and handed it to her.

"Thank you," she said, smiling again. "You wouldn't happen to have a clean rag I could use, too?" She raised her eyebrows apologetically.

I pulled a clean dishrag out of the basket of linens Mama kept on the shelf. When I handed it to Thelma, she patted my arm. I studied this fresh, pretty, and very friendly-looking girl, and thought her face a might too broad and flat. At first glance, she appeared to be rather plain, but her smile changed that—it transformed her face. Dimples appeared in both cheeks and her blue eyes brightened, as if a light had been turned on inside her head. I stood gazing at this large-boned girl with strong, sturdy features, and straight, flaxen hair catching the light. *Will this person change my life?* Her hair had been gathered at the back of her neck in a green ribbon and tied in a careful bow. Except for her large bosom, I'd have thought her an oversize child, very girlish.

I stepped around James and out the screen door into the backyard. Our hens were making a commotion and, through the open door, I saw Mama inside the coop, carrying an egg basket. Mama's hair hung almost to her waist, still in braids.

She looked at me and called, "Oh, good, Amelia, I need help." I hurried over and her puffy eyes and flushed face told me she'd not slept well. Her gaze darted to the chicken house window and through it up the road. "Aileen's gone to the Wallaces' to borrow milk. Do you see her coming?"

I looked up the road and shook my head.

Mama sighed, "Well, take these eggs into the kitchen then, and while you're there, put a sign in the window for ice. Better make it twenty pounds. Land sakes, we're almost out of everything." She turned her back and attended to her hens.

"If my garden hadn't burned up in this hot sun, we'd at least have vegetables," she complained.

I stood waiting for Mama to hand me the egg basket. She straightened, finally, and counted the eggs. "Heaven help me, not even one egg apiece," she mumbled to herself.

"Mama, what's a sugar tit?" I asked, taking the basket. I lay my hand on the brown eggs. They felt warm and comforting.

"Oh," she said, her face registered surprise, then understanding. "It's for a baby to suck when the mama is low on milk—a spoonful or two of sugar wrapped up in a cloth. You go on now, Amelia, and put these eggs away. You'll have to fix your own lunch today. I haven't time."

I inhaled a deep breath of the familiar odor of chickens, relishing the sameness of it. Mama followed me as far as the gate to the chicken yard, but there she stopped, rubbed her neck, and studied the sky. "I don't know why we never have rain in this hateful dry climate. Sometimes it teases us by clouding up, but no moisture," she said, a hint of desperation in her voice.

I looked high into the deep blue sky. Not a cloud in sight. As I shut the gate behind me, I heard Mama muttering to herself, "I don't believe it rained once all summer long. Not one single drop."

Overnight, things became difficult in our home: cramped quarters, irritable children, and too little food for the household of four adults, two teenagers, and six children. I felt grateful for school, to be able to leave the crowded chaos for the day, but I pitied Mama trying to make the best of it.

The weeks that followed became increasingly hectic. Everyone expected Mr. Overberg to find work quickly and move his family into their own home, but they remained, day after day. Food had to be stretched to provide for all those mouths and laundry seemed impossible to manage. To make matters worse, Mrs. Overberg took to her bed most of the time, complaining of a headache.

Mama looked pale and tired. Dark circles surrounded her eyes and she took less care with her appearance than before, often wearing her cleaning dress and not bothering arranging her hair.

One evening I lay awake on my pallet after prayers. A slight breeze played with the parlor curtains. I could hear Aileen's even breathing beside me. As always, she'd fallen asleep quickly, while I lay struggling—for what seemed like hours—to shut down my mind. For some reason, I felt compelled to revisit all the day's events, turning them over, and considering what they meant. I'd done this for as long as I could remember, and indeed, Mama told me I'd never been a good sleeper. She said that as an infant I'd been difficult to put down, and always awakened at the drop of a pin.

I scolded myself, saying, *Amelia, go to sleep! Stop thinking!* I tried counting sheep, a suggestion from Joseph, and I played imagination games, like trying to picture every item in our silverware drawer, or fantasizing about myself as the queen of some foreign land, and imagining gorgeous details of my dress and crown and throne. Still, my mind would return to whatever events had occurred at school or in our home that day, or to something someone had said, either to me, or to someone else in my hearing. At an early age, I had observed that the adults rarely bothered to bring children into their reasoning, and not being one to appreciate surprises, I felt compelled to study them or listen to them closely. I'd often been reprimanded for asking questions about conversations I'd overheard. Lately, I'd been wondering how Papa could imagine we had enough room, enough food, and enough time to accommodate another family.

Suddenly, I heard a creak on the porch outside the window and Mama's voice, just above a whisper. "Land sakes, Chester, why do you suppose he can't find work?"

"I expect he's too choosy," Papa said, "and probably wanting an easy job like the one he had in Missouri. Remember he sold insurance there. He's not cut out for manual labor."

I pictured my parents seated together on the bench outside the parlor window.

"I'm working on him, Ida," Papa continued. "I told him I'd teach him the carpentry trade. He may not be good for packing lumber, but he could measure and cut."

"I suppose so," Mama said, absently. "I don't know how much longer we can make things stretch, Chester. This awful heat—it's making the hens not to lay, and I've used up most of our sugar and flour."

"Don't worry," Papa said. "We're doing our Christian duty. God will provide, and we'll be rewarded in heaven."

Suddenly, I thought of some words to a song we often sang in church, "Will there be any stars in my crown?" it asked.

I don't care about any old crown, God, I prayed, I just want our old life back.

Verna Simms

CHAPTER FIVE—JAMES

James became especially trying. He sassed his mother and refused to help with chores, but worst of all, he seemed determined to pester me. Yesterday, I pulled out a chair to sit at the dinner table and James raced over and plopped down in it so suddenly, I landed on his lap.

He hollered, "Get off'n me! Get your own chair, Amelia. I got here first." He pushed me to the floor and roared in loud, raucous laughter.

When I went outside, James followed. It was futile to try to find a place inside the house where I could be away from him and the other Overbergs. More and more I found refuge in the crawl space under the kitchen.

"No, Chester," Mr. Overberg said, "Mining doesn't appeal to me. I'll wait for something better and keep learning the carpentry trade in the meantime. I'm in no hurry. Better to wait."

Not in a hurry! I could hardly believe my ears. I looked at Mama, but her face remained stony. Mrs. Overberg appeared disinterested. She sat at the table holding Paul. She took a biscuit and began feeding the baby little pieces. James and Timothy squirmed, pushing at each other on the bench. One by one, I stared at the faces in that room, wondering if anyone felt as I did—that Mr. Overberg had to be the most selfish man on the earth, not to grab a job for himself and move his family out of our crowded house. Only my sister's face registered any reaction. A little vertical worry line creased the space between her eyes, but otherwise, her expression remained placid.

Finally, we sat down at the table and I reached for a biscuit. No sooner had my fingers wrapped around one than James shot his hand out and snatched it right out of my grip.

"Give it back!" I threatened.

Papa scowled at me and said. "Haven't I taught you to sit quietly at the table?"

"He took my biscuit," I said, knowing full well Papa had seen the incident. "He already had three. There's not enough left."

"Amelia!" Mama said, "mind your manners! There's plenty here for everyone." Then she placed her own biscuit on my plate.

Papa turned his attention back to Mr. Overberg.

"Will Payton told me something interesting, Ivan," he said, "You remember Fred and Hobart, those young missionaries who converted us both back in Missouri?"

Mr. Overberg nodded and helped himself to a large portion of Mama's potatoes, nearly a third, despite the fact no one had taken any yet.

Papa continued. "Well, Fred, he's married now and lives in a house in Mesa. I've been planning to go see him Sunday," Papa said. "It's not far, just over the high mountains to the west." Papa paused, with his fork pointing at Mesa in the air. He waited for an answer, but Mr. Overberg just continued shoveling food into his mouth.

"Those are good boys," Papa continued. "Two years teaching strangers the truth. I don't know what's become of Hobart, but I'd like to go see Fred. It was to those boys' credit that I became a Mormon—you, too. What do you say? Want to go?"

Without looking up, Mr. Overberg grunted, "Uh huh, sure," and continued eating.

Papa gazed out the kitchen door and up at the sky. "Those boys didn't get paid a dime—everything at their own expense. Think of the stars in their crowns when they get their reward." He looked again at Mr. Overberg, to no avail. Then he waved his fork over the table, indicating everyone there. "Here's a whole houseful of jewels for their crowns," he said.

Why could I be counted one of Fred and Hobart's jewels? I wasn't even born when Papa met them. I never saw them in my life. And besides, what choice did I have? Men made all the decisions.

I carried my plate to the sink and hurried out on the porch. I noticed that the door didn't slam shut behind me and felt a wave of dread wash over me.

"Race you to the lean-to, Amelia!" James said, shoving me out of the way and dashing off in front of me. "I'm faster than any old girl."

I stood on the step, my hand resting on the porch post.

"Red, red, red, there's a fire on your head!" James taunted me from in the yard. He seemed not to know the color of his own hair. After he realized I ignored him, he headed across the yard and disappeared behind the chicken coup.

Papa and Mr. Overberg climbed into the Model T and I watched as they drove toward town. Chimes tinkled softly from the breeze their departure had created and Martha, our yellow striped cat, looked up thoughtfully. I leaned over and scratched her head and patted her bulging sides wondering when the kittens would be born.

Then Mama came out the door with the empty dishpan. She stopped and rested an arm across my shoulders. "Just turn the other cheek, Amelia," she whispered, having evidently overheard James's commotion. "God gives a Christian the strength to ignore these kinds of things. Besides, James won't be here long and you must keep your manners, even if others don't."

Silently, I said to myself, let Mama be right. Let the Overbergs leave soon—real soon.

Aileen, Joseph, and Thelma remained indoors. I heard chatter and the clattering of plates as they cleared the table. The baby babbled happily. Thelma washed the dishes every night with Mama. I'd hoped for a walk with Ailie and Joe. Even though I knew I was selfish not to go inside and work clearing the mess, I couldn't bear the thought of all those people constantly bumping into each other—like marbles in a fish bowl.

"Mrs. Overberg sure is sick a lot," I said. "I wonder how she felt before we knew her, if she'd always left the chores for others. Do you suppose the noise and tension in our house is truly giving her headaches?"

Mama looked in the distance before answering. "Yes dear, all of us are feeling pressure—everyone, that is, except Papa, Daniel, and Mr. Overberg who leave every morning and come home to supper on the table. And for some reason, the situation appears not to bother Thelma. I do sometimes wonder why."

"Thelma does all the work," I said. "She takes care of Timothy and Paul more than their mother."

I waited for another scolding, but this time Mama just smiled.

"Yes, she's a jolly soul," she said.

It was true. Thelma had an open, lovable, cheerful nature, and a quiet, peaceful way of pitching in, or saying a kind word that soothed. Every afternoon after school, she met me at the kitchen door with a smile and a cookie, and evenings after supper, she jumped up and started clearing the table

"I'll do the dishes, Mrs. Hall," she'd offer, night after night, while Aileen and I, glad to let her, just helped to carry the dirty plates to the sink and then slipped off—Aileen into the parlor and me out the back door. Mama never took advantage of Thelma's offer though, never completely. She would let Thelma dry, but Mama washed. She was very particular about dishes.

"You have your hands full enough with those two babies," Mama replied one evening to Thelma's nightly offer. "A young girl like you should be out in the fresh air and sunshine." She made a point of saying this loud enough for Mrs. Overberg to hear. But Mrs. Overberg didn't seem to notice. She never grasped how much work needed to be done. If she didn't retire to her room, she might follow her husband outdoors and the two would go for an after-dinner stroll. I couldn't admire the thin, pale woman with a hair color that defied classification, like sagebrush when it has dried and withered on the mountain. The close-cropped blur of brown, gray and blonde always needed grooming.

Suddenly, Mama broke my daydreaming. "Go inside Amelia, and take this dishpan of water with you. Then knock on the bedroom door and ask Mrs. Overberg if she'd like to sit a spell with us. She's so pale—I think a bit of fresh air would do her good."

I obeyed and was surprised when the woman actually opened the door and followed me outside. I sat down on the porch floor with my feet on the first step. Mrs. Overberg sat down beside me.

"Why don't you work on your paper dolls," Mama suggested to me. I'd been cutting pictures of girls and boys from the old Sears & Roebuck catalogue.

I gathered the catalog and my scissors from the drawer in the Old Mother Hubbard cabinet. Aileen stood washing dishes while Joseph dried. Thelma had taken the baby in the bedroom for a nap, and Timothy sat on the floor eating chicken scraps out of the cat's bowl.

I decided to let him be.

Back outside on the porch, I sat down on the step with the catalog and found the page where I'd left off the evening before. While I labored to maneuver my scissors into the tiny corners of each picture, Mrs. Overberg watched.

"Often, after coming here, I find it hard to get enough air," she complained.

"Oh, dear me. It's the mine," Mama said. "The copper fumes make it hard to breathe sometimes. If we could remove shoes and stockings, it would at least be cooler," I glanced at her covered legs and feet. I was allowed to remove mine when at home.

"Oh, no, I don't think that would be a good idea," she said. "Ivan wouldn't like it if I went out and about uncovered. It's not proper."

"You don't go out anywhere," I pointed out, "and besides, it's too hot to be wrapped up all the time. I strip down the minute I enter the yard." I held my bare legs up and wiggled my toes to show her. "Mama doesn't cover her legs when she's working around the house. When I grow up, I'm going barelegged all the time. Yesiree."

"Oh, yes, you will," Mrs. Overberg said. "You'll understand better . . ."

"I know, I know," I interrupted her, "when I'm older!"

Mama sat fanning her face with a clean metal pie pan. "Sit beside me, Sadie," she said, "I'll share the breeze with you."

Mrs. Overberg smoothed her dress and joined Mama on the bench. "It was Ivan who insisted we come West," she said diverting her eyes from the glaring afternoon sun. "I think he'd follow Chester to the moon."

I paused and dropped my scissors hand in my lap at this information. *So, Papa had invited the family*, I marveled. *Why?*

"I wasn't sure at all about this new religion," Mrs. Overberg continued, taking the pie pan from Mama, "but Ivan felt sure it was God's will that we go. I was just hoping . . ." Her voice trailed off.

Martha, the cat, walked over to stand before Mama and Mrs. Overberg, as if to take pity on the pale woman. Then, suddenly, she jumped into her lap.

"My heavens above!" Mama exclaimed. "I'm sorry, Sadie. I've never seen her do such a thing. Just push her down. Amelia, take the cat somewhere."

"Oh no, please, it's okay," Mrs. Overberg said quickly. Her eyes lit up. "I've always loved cats."

"Martha's going to have kittens," I offered. "You may have one if you want."

"I wish I could," Mrs. Overberg said. "But Ivan won't have another cat. We had one once." Her eyes became distant and Mama and I fell silent, waiting for her to explain.

"I never told you, Ida," she began, "but Ivan and me, we had another son, Aaron, a beautiful boy, but he passed on—four months old."

"I'm so sorry," Mama said, reaching out to pat Mrs. Overberg's knee.

"Well, he was never really well," Mrs. Overberg said, as if that was a satisfactory reason. I felt very sorry now for the thin woman who now sat hugging our cat absently.

"Those missionaries were staying at our house," she said. "Chester had sent them over and Ivan invited them to stay overnight. I'd found a kitten shortly before Aaron was born and the kids and me became attached to it. A cute little black stray, too small to be away from its mother."

She leaned forward and began rocking slowly back and forth on the bench.

"Aaron had the croup. He'd had it before a couple of times and scared us to death, but that night he took a bad turn for the worse. One of those young men—Freddie—sat up with me. While I was fixing Aaron a poultice for his chest, Freddie sat rocking him in the chair. The baby was crying and coughing and wheezing. Then all of a sudden . . .he was quiet!"

A long silence caused my heart to pound.

Finally, Mrs. Overberg said, "The baby died in Freddie's arms. Freddie rose quietly and laid him in his bed. I said, "Surely he's not asleep." Another long silence. Mrs. Overberg stroked Martha's back.

Freddie whispered, "Your baby's gone, Mrs. Overberg. He'll never be sick again."

"For a bizarre reason, Ivan blamed the kitten and we had to get rid of it. Some old wives' tale he'd heard. He said he never wanted to see a cat in our house again."

Tears welled up in my eyes and a hard lump formed in my throat. Mama turned and pulled Mrs. Overberg toward her. The cat, disturbed, jumped down and ran past me into the yard.

I remained on the steps, listening, "The young men stayed for two whole weeks," Mrs. Overberg said. "They did the things we couldn't bring ourselves to do—wash Aaron's little body and dress him in his best clothing. A bad time," she shook her head. "Only our new faith sustained us.

"Ivan hadn't wanted anything to do with religion at all before Chester talked to him and those two boys arrived. I'd tried to encourage him to attend church with me, but he always said he had work to do. I took the children alone. We walked up to Main Street in Crystal City to the Baptist Church. I wasn't raised Baptist, but it was the closest.

"One evening one of the boys told us of Joseph Smith's vision. That was enough to make Ivan listen, and when he heard about the golden tablets, something changed in him. I wasn't so sure myself. But Ivan, he was so interested in the vision. Something came over him and he started reading the Book of Mormon and searching the Scriptures."

Mama nodded, "The same thing happened to us," she said. "I'd gone to the Church of Christ all my life and I wasn't at all sure about this new religion, but I have to say, it brought about a change for the better in Chester. Sakes alive, before this he had an anger in him that has all but disappeared, and he no longer compares what he owns to what others have, property-wise, that sort of thing."

Mama caught my eyes and lowered her voice, but not enough to prevent my hearing. "Chester's dad had been a preacher, you know. It left a bad taste in his mouth—religion did. He used to tell me how his dad left his family in want while he wandered all over the country preaching God's word, and then the man would stumble home drunk and, mercy me, he'd get upset over the littlest things and slap his wife in the face, or beat Chester and his brother. Chester called him a hypocrite and he personally didn't want anything to do with him, or with religion.

"I don't fully understand all the reasons behind the Mormons," Mama continued, "but as I see it, if it makes a better man of a husband and father, it's a better family life for all of us. Chester's always been a bit of a dreamer and the chance to come here and help build a beautiful white marble temple fascinated him." She looked down at her hands. "It nearly broke his heart when they wouldn't let him help work on the temple in Mesa." She took a deep breath, squinting against the setting sun.

Mrs. Overberg nodded "I know it did, and it wasn't right. Things would have been better for all of us and the elders, too, if they had. Chester's a good worker. Ivan talked of coming sooner, but Paul was born before he'd saved for gas money."

She reached down and picked up Mama's hand. "You've been most kind to me and my family," she said. "I don't know how you do it, Ida. You work from sun to sun and always have such a kind and generous way about you."

Mama's face turned red with embarrassment and her hands reached for her hairpins. I noticed how they moved over the hairpins like a bird flittering from one branch to another. "Come inside, Sadie," she said, standing quickly, "I have a cake tucked away for dessert. We'll have us a slice before the others return and gobble it all."

The two women rose and walked through the door, leaving me to wonder at how little I really knew about the Overbergs—how little I understood about anything at all. I'd been angry with Mrs. Overberg for not carrying her fair share of the work, never realizing that she carried a burden in her heart heavier than Mama had ever had to bear. I felt so sorry for little Aaron, the baby who never got to grow up, and I was sad for the little cat, too. I tried to find a good reason for it all. *Why would God take a little baby like that? And how could Mr. Overberg blame a little kitten?*

I wondered, but I wouldn't ask. Papa always said that God's ways were not always our ways. And Mama or Aileen had never been good at explaining His reasons for doing the things He did. Repeatedly, I was reminded that I'd understand better when I was older, and sometimes, to my greater frustration, I was told I'd understand it all in heaven.

CHAPTER SIX—THE FAIR

One Saturday morning early in October, the slamming of the kitchen door woke me. I heard Papa's touring car choke to life and chug down the hill. I rolled over on my pallet and tried to go back to sleep. No luck. Nature called. I rose to my knees and peeked out the window. No one in sight. *Papa and Mr. Overberg have driven to town to buy a donut and hear the latest gossip. They'll be away for hours.* I didn't bother to dress, but slipped quietly past Aileen and eased out the parlor's front door, and made my way to the back of the lot. As I came out the privy door, I heard what sounded like Papa's Tin Lizzy Ford roaring up the incline to our house, dust flying, and someone leaning on the horn. I panicked. Looking down I glimpsed my clothing—or lack of it. Only a skimpy nightdress, no shoes—and bare legs. If Papa catches me outside like this, I'm in big trouble. The kind of trouble spelled with a capital B.T. I forgot about being quiet. I sprinted toward the kitchen door for safety in the house. I leaped up the steps two at a time and collapsed inside the kitchen door, gasping for air.

Thelma rose from her cot and leaned on her elbow, her eyes wide. "What's wrong, Amelia?"

"Dunno."

Thelma sat upright and patted the spot where her pillow had fallen to the floor. "Sit here by me and tell me what's going on. Who's making all that racket?"

Before anymore could be said, Papa barged into the house and called in a loud voice. "Listen up, everyone! Throw clothes on, grab your shoes, and meet me in the car. I heard they're having a fair, and one of the newfangled flying machines will be landing at the fairground——at eight this morning."

The next second Papa vanished out the door, but before he left the porch, he stuck he head back in. "Anyone not in the car in three minutes will be left behind." With that, he was out of sight.

No one spoke. I hustled to throw on a dress, grab my shoes and flew out the door and fell into the back seat. Daniel sat next to the window. James jumped in beside me, with Joseph crowding into the vacant spot beside him. Mama had already been up and dressed, but had been caught brushing her waist length hair, and still carried a brush in one hand. "Oh dear me," she exclaimed as she closed the car door behind her. "Hope I can manage my hair. My stars and garters, what will the neighbors think if they see me with my hair down?"

Papa didn't wait for the Overbergs to be properly loaded, but geared the car and barreled down the road. Mama's long hair was flying out the window and whipping around her face. I fully expected Papa to complain but when I looked, he and Mama were glancing at each other laughing—much like teenagers.

Papa took the corners on two wheels, and each time James poked me in the ribs. I'm sure he did it on purpose. Daniel noticed, "Here, Amelia," he said, lifting me onto his lap. "You sit here and we won't be so crowded." I turned to James and stuck out my tongue. He made a nasty face back at me.

The fairground was located about a mile out of town. I believe it was the only available level spot in the area. Other vehicles had already taken up most of the parking spaces, but Papa squeezed into the first empty spot he noticed. We all piled out. I stood on the running board to try and see if I could locate anyone I knew. No one. I jumped into the air. Not a soul. I found myself left alone with Mama. Other members of my family had wandered off. Mama had somehow managed to arrange her hair in a topknot fastened by her large hairpins. I looked to see her face glowing with excitement.

"Oh, Amelia. This reminds me of the Fall Festivals we had every year back in Missouri. We planned for months ahead of time. My two sisters and I always made new dresses to wear, sometimes with matching bonnets. Gracious sakes alive, what I wouldn't have given to have had a few days' notice. Seems to me they would have advertised weeks in advance something like a new invention coming to town." She tried to smooth back her unruly hair and tugged at her dress. "Imagine all these people and me in my housedress." She chuckled softly before adding. "You look like your clothing came out of the ragbag. Whatever will people think?"

Water Under the Bridge

I looked around and saw with relief that Aileen had made it and stood with a couple of girls from school. I was feeling a bit blue when suddenly I saw someone waving a hanky. "Oh Mama," I squealed. "There's Blanca. May I go to her?"

Mama nodded her permission and I was off—like a rabbit let out of a cage.

"Blanca, Blanca" I exhaled. "I'm so happy you're here. Jiminy Cricket, however did you find me in this crowd? I looked everywhere but couldn't locate anyone I knew. I even jumped up so I could search over the heads of the crowd."

"You are so funny, Amelia." Blanca clasped my hand and pulled me away from the others. 'That's exactly how I spotted you. I glimpsed your lovely copper-colored hair flash in the sunshine when you jumped. Come over to the refreshment stand. Daddy was in a hurry to get home and to sleep so I didn't have time to eat. I brought a couple of tortillas, but we'll need something to drink. You like orange pop?"

"Sure do, but Papa didn't give me any money. You go ahead though. I don't mind."

Blanca laughed, "It's okay. I've an extra nickel."

We moved a bit away from the crowd and sat on a small boulder under a cottonwood tree and started munching on the treat. The orange pop fizzed and tasted so good sliding down my throat. We seldom had soda at home and this was a real treat. I turned and smiled my thanks.

And then I heard it—like a mosquito buzzing high above our heads. All eyes craned upward. In the far distance, I glimpsed a bright orange object—no bigger than a bird—too far away for a good look. I stopped chewing to better concentrate on this strange object headed our way. The buzzing became louder and louder and, except for the sound coming from the sky, all was eerily silent. The large crowd stood as if turned into many statues.

I gasped as I could see the aeroplane. It landed in a whirl of dust, taxied around in the roped in area, and then I could make out two men sitting in an open cockpit. You couldn't tell what they looked like. Each wore a helmet, and large goggles completely covered the top half of their faces, but they sported huge smiles and were waving to the crowd. I leaped in the air and waved back. I had noticed while the plane was still airborne it was pulling a large white banner with lettering, *"Be the first to ride high above the ground—we will circle the town for 10 minutes for 10 cents a pound."*

The strange vehicle had four wings, two on each side, one above the other. It reminded me of a box kite. In front, the large blades, similar to pictures I'd seen of windmills, rotated slowly. I learned later that they were called propellers and once stopped, one of the men had to manually turn the blades by hand to get the motor started again. Sort of like cranking our car.

I jammed the remainder of the tortilla in my pocket and gulped down the pop. Hooking my arm through Blanca's, I elbowed our way toward the roped-in area. "Hurry, Blanca. Gee whiz, we must push closer to the front. I can't see a thing back here."

A large man turned and allowed us to squeeze in front of him. My mouth hung open, my eyes wide. Such a wondrous sight. Oh, how I would love to climb into the seat and view the world from high above the birds and the clouds. I searched the crowd with my eyes and located Papa. He knew what I wanted and shook his head no.

I turned to my friend. "Blanca, I only weigh 40 pounds. You have $4.00 you could loan me? I'll pay you back." No better luck with Blanca.

"My parents said it was too dangerous, Amelia. We can watch. Oh look, your brother is standing in line."

Daniel waited second in line. I tried to get his attention. He wouldn't take his eyes off the plane. I glanced behind me for Mama's reaction. She noticed Dan and her face paled. Mama kept shaking her head but Dan didn't turn her way. I knew he had his own money and didn't have to ask Papa. Oh, how I wished I were a boy and seventeen!

After everyone with money had had a turn riding, the younger man hopped out of the cockpit and hurried over to the crowd.. "I'm going to walk on the wing while the plane is high overhead. I ask that no one make a sudden noise that might startle the pilot. He needs to concentrate to be sure and keep the aeroplane steady."

I gasped and looked around. You could have heard an ant crawling in the grass it was so quiet. I watched in amazement as high above the crowd the daring young man slowly hoisted himself out of his seat and onto the wing, and stood and stretched his arms for balance. He slowly walked the length of wing, and stopped and waved to the people below before he turned and inched his way back. I noticed that all around me people were holding their breath until once more he dropped down into his seat. The crowd erupted in loud cheers and hurrahs when the young man and the pilot circled the field and dipped the wings in farewell to the crowd, before roaring off into the distance.

Water Under the Bridge

It was over. Well, almost. Daniel didn't talk about anything but flying for the next few weeks. "One day I will be a pilot and fly. Someday!" He said.

Me too, me too!

Once more on the ride home, James bumped into me. I knew it was on purpose.

Just wait, I thought, just you wait and see, James Overberg, I'll get you, and get you good!

Verna Simms

CHAPTER SEVEN—PAPA AND THELMA

After dinner, Thelma and Mama stood and cleared the table. Papa also rose to his feet, "I'll help Thelma with the dishes, Cora. You go outside and get some fresh air."

We three Hall children were stunned to hear Papa offer to do women's work, and even more amazed to see him grab a dishcloth. But Mama's face lit up. "Why, I know better than to turn down an offer like that," she said, beaming.

She followed Joseph and Aileen and me outdoors and the four of us sat together on the porch steps. Mama must have been feeling guilty about not cleaning up the kitchen, because she started telling Aileen all the chores she'd done that day and the ones she planned for the next day, which included cleaning out the chicken house and polishing furniture.

After a while, Joseph leaned over to me and said, "Hey, little sis, come help feed the chickens."

"Naw, that's your job," I said, without making a move. Martha lay beside me and I rubbed my hand over her soft fur trying to feel the kittens inside.

"Great guns. Come with me, Amelia," Joseph said. "I've something to tell you—now." The tone of his voice convinced me. Once out of earshot, he put his arm around my shoulders and whispered in my ear, "James is afraid of spiders."

I stopped and looked into his face.

"How do you know?" I asked, a grin spreading across my face.

"Fiddledeedee, let's say these big ears aren't for decoration," he put his hands behind his ears and folded them forward. I laughed.

"Last night when we were on the front porch, he started screaming something fierce," he said. "Turns out a daddy longlegs had crawled on his arm. Mama sent Daniel to scoop the spider off."

He paused. "Get it?"

"Get what?" I asked, not entirely sure what Joseph had in mind.

"I'll show you, slow poke. Follow me," he said.

When we reached the back of the house, he pointed at the entry to our secret hideaway under the morning glory vines. That all he needed to do; I understood completely.

In the cool semi-darkness, we enjoyed a quiet respite for children—and a heaven for spiders! A wave of appreciation for my brother washed over me so intensely that I reached out and gave him a big hug.

"C'mon, let's fix him now," I said.

"Naw, you do it yourself," he said, "and not today, not till the right time. Wait till you can be alone with him." He looked up at the mountain and said, "Hey, how 'bout we go up yonder?"

I followed him out the backyard gate, and together we started up the gradual slope that began at the northeast corner of our yard and ascended upwards for miles. After a twenty-minute or so walk, a deep crevice cut into the mountainside. Joseph and I enjoyed slipping into this valley where we could play unobserved by the family below.

A large old acacia tree grew just at the point where the slope started up again on the far side of the crevice. Its ancient branches spread majestically, at least fifteen feet high, thickly covered with thorns. Joseph and I spent most of our Saturday afternoons under this tree, high above the house and surrounded by soft, light green mosses and other shade-loving wild flora.

"Joe," I said sitting down in my customary spot beneath the old tree, "did you ever notice the air smells better up here?"

"Yesiree," he said, "it's purer. Dan told me that on the southeast side of the mountain the air is even better. There are more nut and pine trees growing on that slope. Trees are good for the air."

He laid his back against the trunk, leaning his head on folded arms behind his head. "I hate that copper mine with its fumes," he said. "I don't blame Mr. Brown for building a house up high. His wife has asthma. She'll breathe much better on stifling hot days."

"Mr. Overberg said it's a bad place to live, they'd have to haul water and that's too much trouble for a family of six."

Water Under the Bridge

Joseph ignored that problem. "It would be nice to have a dwelling up here, wouldn't it?" he said, scanning the area dreamily. "Too bad Daniel can't afford the land Mr. Wallace has for sale. He's saved lumber already."

Suddenly I had an idea, "Hey, if Dan'll give us his scrap lumber, could you build us a tree house?" I asked hopefully.

Joseph bolted upright, "Sure I could," he said. Then he looked around. "Where?" He had a faraway expression in his eyes.

"I dunno. Anywhere up here," I said. "I wouldn't care where, but I would truly love a tree house, wouldn't you, Joe? Do you think Mama would allow us to sleep all night outdoors?"

"You're darn tootin', maybe she would," Joseph said.

And thus began our autumn of dreams. Joseph and I planned every detail of our fantasy tree house from the removable ladder we'd build to keep others out, to the roof and windows we'd include for protection from bad weather. All of our plans were scheduled to begin as soon as the Overbergs finally left. Then we hoped to convince Papa and Dan to hike with us to the summit of the mountain and maybe back down on the other side. We felt sure they'd see for themselves that there were several good places for a tree house.

Over the next few weeks, Joseph and I made frequent trips climbing the mountain to discuss plans, and as we did, problems at home receded into the background and our cramped quarters and strained tempers could be forgotten, until the sun dipped behind the tree-lined mountain ridge, painting the sky pink and changing the pitch of the shadows. A signal—time to head home.

As we emerged from the shelter of our hidden valley into the last warm rays of sunlight, Joseph and I often walked with our hands clasped together, swinging them between us, and singing loudly. Definitely something he wouldn't do in public. I knew he thought he was protecting me, trying to prevent me from tripping over a loose stone and tumbling down the hill. I also knew that I was big enough to safely negotiate my way down the mountain alone, but I always held onto his hand tightly.

Playing checkers, later that evening . . .

"Amelia!" Aileen said, "what's the matter with you? That's the second time you moved your king in harm's way."

"Gee whiz, I don't feel like checkers tonight, I guess." I muttered and turned to look outside. *I must slip into my sleeping quarters before everyone else, and before dark.*

"Hey, you spent all afternoon under the house," Joseph said. "What are you up to? Brooding?"

"Are you sick, hon?" Thelma asked, genuine concern on her face.

"I'm okay," I said, pushing my chair back with a scraping sound. "I've been doing some serious thinking and I'm tired. See you in the morning."

You better believe I'd been thinking—plotting something Mama wouldn't approve of—no need to involve Joseph.

In my dress pocket, I'd hidden a bottle with holes punched in the lid. Inside lived five live daddy long-leg spiders. Without thinking, I reached inside and turned the small bottle in my fingers.

"What's in your pocket?" Joseph asked.

"Why, an old medicine bottle Mrs. Overberg threw away," I said. "I'm going to use it for a pencil holder."

Tarnation—Joe'll guess later. He might try to stop me if he realizes now, but I know he won't tattle.

Slowly, feigning nonchalance, I strolled from the room and parted the curtain that separated the dining area where the younger Overbergs slept, and entered my sleeping quarters.

Inside the room, I walked to the window. Good, I thought, no one hovered close by. Mama had gone to visit Mrs. Wallace and she'd taken Mrs. Overberg along. When Mama and Mrs. Wallace got together, they usually talked for hours, so I banked on the probability that they'd be a while yet, what with a third woman involved.

James had accompanied Mr. Overberg and Papa on an errand. While I gazed out the window, Papa's car pulled up and stopped in front of the house. I could smell fumes from the exhaust.

My attention stayed on Mr. Overberg as he opened the door on the passenger side and slid out. Then I saw James jump out.

Papa slammed his door shut with a loud bang that made me jump. He opened the hood on the driver's side and stuck his head inside. James and Mr. Overberg joined him.

Dear me, I'd better hurry, if he has car trouble, he'll be in a bad humor for sure.

I waited quietly in the darkening parlor for my chance.

"I'm going to the outhouse," I overheard James say. He headed slowly across the yard in its direction.

"Darn it all, not much I can do tonight," Papa said to Mr. Overberg. "It's getting too dark. I'll examine the dang thing in the morning."

Water Under the Bridge

I heard the scooting sounds of chairs being pushed on the porch and a heavy creak as their cane seats strained under the heavy weight of the two men.

"Wow, Brother Chester. Let's settle out here a bit. It's cooler." I recognized Mr. Overberg's distinct whine. "I don't relish going in to the little woman tonight. I've had about all I can take of her sick headaches. Joseph Smith had the right idea when he decided a man needs more than one wife. It's just a shame the state passed a law against it."

"There are ways to get around the law," Papa said. "Out here, the sheriff looks the other way." The window rattled and I heard a bump. I imagined Papa's chair tipped back against the wall with his feet propped up on the porch railing, a position he assumed whenever he rested on the porch.

The kitchen screen door squeaked open.

"James, you wash up. Mama wants you in bed before dark. Hurry yourself now. She's at the Wallace's with Mrs. Hall and due back any minute."

Another screech of the kitchen door told me James had stepped out on the porch to wash. As fast as I could, I sneaked into the dining room and over to his pallet. I slipped the bottle from my pocket and unscrewed the lid. I tapped gently on its bottom to dislodge the spiders. Then I scurried into the safety of the parlor and resumed my position near the window.

My heart beat wildly. I wished for company in my mischief so I could enjoy it more.

Outside, Papa led the conversation, "You going to Phoenix to check on that carpentry job tomorrow?"

"Uh-huh. But I can't make up my mind about it. A man spends many years at one job. It's important it's the right choice. What do you think? You like building houses, don't you?"

"Yeah, but it's not for everyone. A carpenter needs to climb and carry heavy boards."

I visualized Mr. Overberg's chubby figure standing on the ridge-row of a roof, with the wind whipping up and bowling him over, and then the man rolling head over heels down the roof, landing with a crash far below. No, I wouldn't recommend that trade for him.

Papa might have had the same thoughts because suddenly he started a low down chuckle—that rose up into a full-blown laugh. "Ivan, my friend. Tell you what you should do. I know a man in Phoenix, a good Christian man who tells fortunes. Not a charlatan like these Gypsies around here. They'll tell a man good news and when he catches her stealing his watch, they change it to a curse. Did I ever tell you what happened to me?"

What's keeping James?

No answer from Mr. Overberg, so Papa continued, "It was last summer, while working over in Mesa—building this two-story house. Had a tall ladder and had just climbed down, all tuckered out and sweaty. This Gypsy woman, really no more than a girl, sidled up beside me and grabbed my left hand in hers and smiled. 'Let me tell your fortune, good-looking,' she practically cooed. 'Only costs a dollar.'

"I told her no and jerked my hand away and then I saw it—in her free hand—the chain to my own watch. She'd hidden it in her full skirt pocket, but the chain had dangled on the outside.

"I don't have a grip like a vice for nothing. I snatched hold of her skinny arm and squeezed. I refused to release her until she returned the watch. So anyway, she spat on me and cursed. She said, 'So, big strong man, I will tell your future for free! In arrogance, you will climb the tall, tall ladder and when you reach the top rung, it will break. Down, down, down you will tumble. And break your neck!" Papa paused briefly, "She threw my watch on the ground and I turned her loose to retrieve it. Then she spat at me again and traipsed off, swishing her hips like the Queen of Sheba."

A shiver ran up and down my spine as I thought about the woman's curse, but I quickly forgot as I heard the screen door open and slam shut and James make his way to the dining room.

I held my breath.

Mr. Overberg laughed at Papa's story. Then Papa added, "I wish someone would drive all the Gypsies and Mexicans out of the state of Arizona."

I tried to imagine James sitting in the dining room on his pallet, probably pulling on his nightclothes.

A bumping sound on the front porch told me that Papa had risen from his chair. I could hear his footsteps pacing back and forth. "Now, this man I'm telling you about over in Phoenix. Well, he's all right. He revealed to me I would have seven wives in the new millennium."

"Seven!" Mr. Overberg gasped.

"Yes, one for each day of the week."

I didn't know what to make of this. I hadn't any reason to believe the Phoenix man's prediction would come true—and I wasn't sure when the new millennium would come anyway. I'd heard Papa mention it before; he made it sound like it would be here any minute, but it always seemed to me like it was far off in the future. I just knew I didn't like the idea of Papa having seven wives.

Mr. Overberg's voice lowered, maybe he'd turned his head away, "You be sure you take proper care of . . ."

Aaargh! The scream I'd been expecting came from the dining room, drowning out the rest of Mr. Overberg's sentence. More screams, piercing the air. "Help! Help! He-ellp! Spiders! My bed's full of giant spiders! Somebody help me."

The people in the house ran into the dining room from all directions. Thelma arrived first, and James grabbed onto her like his life depended on it.

I lounged in the parlor, afraid my beaming face would betray me. I found it hard not to laugh out loud. I wanted to yell, "Gotcha, James Overberg!" in his face.

Another door opened and Mama and Mrs. Overberg rushed in, encountering Thelma and Papa who were preparing to carry James's pallet out the door. "My stars and garters, what's all this?" Mama asked.

"Spiders," Thelma said. "James had spiders in his bedroll."

I summoned up enough self-control to enter the kitchen chaos. James sat sobbing like a baby, his face now buried in Mrs. Overberg's bosom.

"Of all things, get hold of yourself!" Mr. Overberg shouted at him. "That's no way for a man to act. Afraid of little spiders? What's wrong with you boy, anyway?"

He grabbed James by the neck and pushed him out the kitchen door. "Ivan . . ." Mrs. Overberg said. He turned over his shoulder and said, "You mind your own business, woman or I'll be back to take care of you later!"

"Mama, Mama!" James screamed.

In the midst of the confusion, Mama stood pulling at her hairpins, her face flushed.

"Mercy me, where've you been, Amelia," she asked. "Don't just stand there like a lump on a log. Help me gather up all the bedding and take it outside and shake everything."

I glanced up at Papa who stood in front of the stove. I expected him to tell me to hurry up, but instead, I was startled to catch him wink at me.

My face instantly grew hot and I left the room, but not before I heard Mama say, "Imagine that, I can't even leave for a couple of hours without coming home to a ruckus. Spiders—and in my house!"

I felt sure I wouldn't sleep, but I did and I dreamed of women, seven women—all lying on the floor in a row and for each, a large hairy spider replaced her head. Every one of them had green, flashing eyes that darted pitchforks at me.

My scream was the second heard that night. It woke the entire family and started the two Overberg youngsters howling. Both of the senior Overbergs arose to attend to them. Thelma followed on Mama's heels to the parlor. Mama had not bothered to put on her housecoat and her braids hung loose.

Aileen and Joseph got to me first. Aileen held me in her arms and said, "It's okay, Sis. Only a bad dream."

I looked to see Joseph shake his head. He said, "Little sister, you went a might too far."

"What do you mean, Joe?" Aileen asked, rocking me.

Thelma looked at Joseph expectantly.

"Yes, what do you mean by that?" Mama said, kneeling down and taking me from Aileen's arms into her own. "Land sakes. What did Amelia do?"

Just then, Papa made his way into the parlor. He held a finger to his lips and said, "Everyone back to bed. Amelia had a bad dream and it's over now."

Mama didn't budge. "You okay, Amelia?" she asked.

"I'll handle this. She's fine, Ida—get back to your bed. You're out here in your flimsy nightclothes, bare legs and all."

"I'm okay, Mama," I said. "The bad dream's over now."

"Well, if you're sure," she said. She walked quickly back toward her bedroom, her arms crossed over her chest to cover herself as best she could.

"All of you back to bed," Papa said firmly to Thelma and Aileen and Joseph.

He waited until Thelma and Joseph left the room and Aileen settled herself in her pallet. Then he said, "I mean it, Amelia. This business between you and James—it's over."

"Yes, I know, Papa," I said.

The next morning when I prepared for school, my mind returned to the tumult of the previous evening and I played it over again in my mind, beginning with the afternoon's gathering of spiders from beneath the house and ending with Papa's words to me, which clearly meant an order. I remembered Joseph telling me I'd gone too far. I wondered what he meant. After all, he was the one who told me James was afraid of spiders and gave me the idea.

Then I realized my brother had misunderstood. He thought spiders caused my nightmare. Surely he knows I'm not afraid of spiders. I recalled the horrible seven women and Papa's words, "One for each day of the week."

Water Under the Bridge

CHAPTER EIGHT—DIRTY WINDOWS

Papa continued to dry the dishes every night, a gesture that met with our approval, but instead of taking it easy, Mama used the extra time to do more chores. Tasks that had been put off, like sweeping the porch and cleaning the henhouse, she now did in the evenings while Papa worked in the kitchen with Thelma, and the Overbergs—if Mrs. Overberg felt up to it—took an evening stroll up the road to the Wallace house and back.

One November evening when Mrs. Overberg took to her bed after supper, Mr. Overberg came out on the porch where Mama stood filling her cleaning pail with water.

"Ida, I do believe you're the busiest woman I've met," he said.

I sat on the top porch step with Timothy and Martha. The soon-to-be mother cat had been lying on the porch, enjoying one of the cooler evenings of late. She lay there tolerantly while I gently rubbed her sides, even though the toddler persisted in grabbing at her tail.

"No-no," I said, removing Timothy's hands from Martha's tail and stroking her fur. "See? Be gentle like this. She's a nice little kitty. Don't hurt her."

I spoke loudly, hoping his dad would take note and turn his attention to his young son, but he appeared to be more interested in Mama's work.

Inside, I could hear Papa and Thelma chatting over the clank and clatter of the supper dishes. Most everyone else had scattered, going off on various missions. Papa had sent Daniel on another errand, something he frequently did of late, and which Daniel clearly resented; however, Papa said it was important to take care of business in the evenings when people could be found in their homes, and he used Daniel as his business emissary.

That particular evening, Aileen and Joseph offered to go along with Daniel in the Model T, and Mr. Overberg had given them money for ice cream, making me regret that I'd not volunteered for the trip. He'd also told his wife to take their boys on a nice walk.

"Oh dear, Ivan. I'm not feeling all that well," Mrs. Overberg said, hesitantly.

"The cool air will do you a world of good," he told her. "You're too cooped up in this house all the time. That's what's ailing you."

She had gotten up from the kitchen table and gone into the bedroom. When next I saw her, she came out on the back porch wearing her brown felt hat with Paul straddling her hip, and wearing a different dress. She called to James and Timothy, who were leaning over the chicken fence out in the yard, to go with her, but Timothy spotted me petting the cat and refused to go.

"That's okay, I'll watch him," I said, not anticipating what trouble he could be.

Mrs. Overberg placed her baby on his feet and she and James each took hold of one of his chubby hands. I watched them walk slowly toward the Wallace house with little Paul between them. Occasionally he lifted up his legs so that he could swing between his mother and James in the air. After a few minutes, they disappeared from sight around the bend.

"You are a hard worker," Mr. Overberg repeated to Mama, obviously intent on a conversation.

"You don't say. Idleness is the devil's playground," Mama said, without looking up, "and there's always plenty to be done around here." She dipped her scrub brush into the pail of soapy water at her feet and scoured the wood frame surrounding the kitchen window.

"You're right about that," he nodded, "but why don't you let me do the job for you tonight, Ida? You made a fine supper and must be tired. Go for a walk and enjoy this nice, cool evening."

"I'm enjoying myself just fine, Ivan," Mama said, intent on her window. "I like a clean house."

"I know you do," the man said. "No question about it. I feel badly though. You do so much for us, and Sadie can't help, what with the baby and her sick headaches. You leave now and let me finish this job."

Timothy smiled up at me, his blue eyes twinkling beneath the shock of straight, white-blonde hair that covered his forehead. He resembles Thelma, I thought, they both have the same fair complexions and sturdy builds. I smiled back, seduced by his dimples.

Water Under the Bridge

Then, as if he'd planned a diversion, he took the opportunity to snatch quickly at Martha's side, pressing down hard on her bulging belly. The cat shrieked in pain and took off down the steps and around the house.

"No, no!" I said loudly, but still Mr. Overberg didn't pay any attention.

Instead, he persisted, "Ida, I mean to finish this job for you." He bent over and took the rag Mama had hung over the side of her pail and started wiping the glass on the window.

"Come and sit with us, Mama," I suggested. I agreed with Mr. Overberg. I was glad he finally showed interest in helping around the house like Papa, and I was anxious for an adult to help with the struggling toddler in my charge.

"No, the both of you go for a walk," Mr. Overberg ordered. His tone was oddly sharp. "I'll keep an eye on Timothy myself. You go now. I'll have this window sparkling when you return."

I stood, but then I caught a strange, determined expression cross my mama's face. Suddenly, she flung her scrub brush into the pail of water, letting it splash on Mr. Overberg's pants. Then she stalked over and sat down on the top step beside me. She leaned over and picked up Timothy and plopped him firmly on her lap.

"Mercy me, if you insist on doing my work," she said, "go ahead, but Amelia and I are going to sit right here with Timothy. I'm going on no walk."

I sat back down obediently. Even Timothy caught the angry tone of her voice. He turned his head to look into her face and she rubbed his leg as if to say, "It's okay." He accepted that little reassurance with a grin.

I wondered why she was so upset. Why wouldn't she take Mr. Overberg up on his nice offer? We all wanted Mama to take it easy, and I wanted our company to do more work around the house. Mama never used to do everything herself. The Hall children were accustomed to chores. We had done more work before the Overbergs came.

I also missed her. We never had long talks alone and we hadn't taken a stroll together since the first day of school.

"We're learning our fives at school now," I said, taking advantage of the space of time Mr. Overberg's idea now afforded me. "You know, five plus one is six, five plus two is seven . . ."

"That's nice, Amelia," Mama said, dismissively.

Mr. Overberg wiped the kitchen windowpanes until they squeaked, then stepped back to admire them. He looked over at Mama for approval, but she averted her eyes to Timothy who, sensing the tension, now sat quietly in her lap.

"I bet you'd like to go for a walk with your papa," she said.

Timothy looked up questioningly at his father, but Mr. Overberg didn't respond. Instead, he took the scrub brush out of the pail and went over the windows again, frames and all. Then he wrung out the rag and wiped them some more. Finally, he said, "Well, I do believe the sun will shine brightly into your kitchen tomorrow morning, Ida." Proudly, he picked up the pail and headed toward us on the steps.

Soon Papa and Thelma joined us on the porch. We sat talking and Mama went in the house and returned with glasses of sweetened iced tea for everyone, but Mr. Overberg refused a glass and continued washing windows. Finally, dark overtook us and we filed into the house.

I sat at the kitchen table doing my homework when Mr. Overberg finally walked through the kitchen door. Mama stood washing the iced tea glasses at the sink.

"I hope the windows meet with your approval," Mr. Overberg said. "I know you have very high standards for a clean house, Ida."

"Maybe they will," Mama said. "Perhaps, thanks to you, Ivan, tomorrow after supper I'll be able to look inside my own house and see what's going on in my very own kitchen."

CHAPTER NINE—A TREE HOUSE

Joseph and I came down the mountain early. Despite the shorter days of early December, it was still light outside and we separated as soon as we closed the gate to our back yard. Joseph headed across the road to Billy's house, hoping to get in a quick game of kick-the-can before dark. I planned to go indoors and pester Aileen for a game of jacks, but just as I came around the house, I saw Daniel sitting outside the door of his lean-to on a short bench he'd built, shining his church shoes. I squeezed onto the seat beside him and started swinging my feet.

"Hey Amelia," he said.

"Hey Dan," I answered, "What're you doing?"

"Nothing much," he said, "just shining these old shoes." He held them for me to see. "I mean to pay a visit on Mr. Wallace tomorrow and I want to look my best."

"Why?" I asked.

"Gee, I'm going to see him about a job," he said. "Papa doesn't have enough work for both me and Mr. Overberg. I plan to ask Mr. Wallace if he has anything that needs doing. What's on your mind, Amy? Did Joseph run off, and leave you alone?"

"He's at Billy's," I said, shrugging. "Gee whiz, Dan, I've been meaning to ask you . . .Joe and I . . .we . . .well, we've been wondering if you'd give us some lumber."

"My word. What for?" he asked. He stopped shining on his shoes to look at me.

"Well, Joe's going to build a tree house on the mountain," I said, smiling widely. I hoped he'd appreciate the idea.

"Wow. A tree house? Did Joe say he could build a tree house?" Daniel looked skeptical.

"No, not really, not all by himself. But I want one, and we've been planning it. He didn't say he couldn't build it."

Daniel slapped his leg and laughed. "Jiminy Cricket, if you don't beat all, Amelia—my girl! Why do you two want to be up on that mountain all the time anyway?"

"Oh, it's real peaceful up high," I said, hoping he'd connect that comment with the chaotic situation in our house of late.

"Well, I don't know about Joe building a tree house," he said. "I don't know about that at all." He held the shoe up again and turned it slowly, inspecting his work.

"You could do it," I suggested hopefully. "You could measure and saw and we'd help nail. We'd let you use it, too."

"Nah, I'm busy enough, Amy. I don't have time for tree houses anymore. I need to work. Besides, I already made Joe and you stilts last summer. Why don't you go find them and march around the yard?" He laughed and stood as if to go inside, but then he looked down and saw my face and stopped. Suddenly, he grabbed me up off the bench, lifted me high in the air, and sat me on the roof of the tool shed.

"How's that for being up high?" he asked. "Is it peaceful enough up there? See, you don't need a tree house, little sister. Up there the sky is your ceiling and the shed roof is your floor."

I smiled weakly, disappointed that Daniel wasn't taking my idea seriously.

"C'mon, jump" he said, holding his hands to catch me. "Let's wash up. I'm hungry, aren't you?"

"We already ate," I reminded him, leaning forward so I could drop into my brother's arms.

"Well, that may be, but I'm a growing boy," Daniel said, patting his belly. "Besides, I think I saw Thelma whipping up a batch of cookies."

He swung me to the ground, and leaving his newly shined shoes on the bench, took off for the kitchen. I followed slowly, frustrated that my petition for a tree house hadn't been successful, but I hadn't given up. I resolved to approach him again later. I'd wait for a good opportunity.

The days continued to shorten. Still, the Overbergs did not leave. Joseph and I grabbed every opportunity to escape up our mountain or sneak under the house. Weekdays were better than weekends. I loved school. Besides having a teacher I adored, school became a safe haven from our cramped house, and where James didn't bother me.

At recesses and lunch, Blanca and I sat together, our backs against the cool stone wall of the school building. Occasionally we managed a ride on the airplane swings or challenged each other in a game of hopscotch, but most days we sat and talked. Sometimes Mary Brown would join us. Her new house consumed most of her thoughts and she never tired of describing it.

"It's so much bigger than the house we had in Missouri," she said. "There's a second story for bedrooms and a dining room in this one. Our old house had only four rooms."

"How nice for you," Blanca said, enthusiastically. "You should have lots of room now for your big family to spread out. How many bedrooms are there?"

"Three," Mary said. "One for Papa and Mama, one big one for the five boys, and a smaller one just for me."

"All five boys in one room?" I asked. Then Blanca reached over and touched my arm. "What?" I asked.

She shook her head at me and turned her attention back to Mary, "I'm sure it's a big room," she said.

"It is! It's a very big room," Mary said, apparently missing Blanca's admonishment. "It's the whole side of the house nearest Claypool! My room is above the kitchen and the boys are other side of the hall."

"Gee whiz. Are your parents downstairs then?" I asked.

"Yes, their room is on the other side of the first floor."

"When will you move in?" Blanca asked.

"Before Christmas," Mary said brightly. "Mama said we're going to have a ten-foot pine tree in our new house and set it up beside the stairway so its top branches reach way up past the ceiling of the first floor."

"Gosh almighty. A Christmas tree?" I exclaimed. "Papa won't let us have a tree. Says they're pagan. You're a Mormon, too. How is it you have one?"

"Oh, my mother isn't Mormon," Mary said. "Besides, it's not against the religion that you can't have a tree. I heard one of the elders say it was okay. Your papa has his own notions," She looked at me sideways before adding, "I overheard the grownups talking. I'm sorry Amelia. I truly am. We've always had a Christmas tree and presents and always will."

I wish my own mama were so determined. She'd told us wonderful stories about Christmases in her childhood that included stockings and Santa Claus, but she always made it clear that she'd left that life behind. "Water under the bridge," she'd say. "A wife's duty is to follow her husband's ways and your papa's a good man. He knows what's right and he does not want us to follow pagan traditions." Still, she had always given us children one small gift every Christmas for as long as I could remember and Papa seemed to allow her this one indulgence.

CHAPTER TEN—BLANCA'S CAPE

A few days later, as James and I sat at the table finishing breakfast, Mama hurried into the kitchen carrying a pile of clothing in her arms. "Here, Amelia," she said, "there's a nip in the air this morning. I want you to wear a coat to school." She handed me Aileen's old black coat and then began sorting garments on the kitchen table.

"Perhaps this one will fit you, James," she said, holding up an old brown jacket of Daniel's with frayed cuffs.

"I ain't wearing that rag," James said. "I don't need no coat."

"Aw, me neither," I said. "I'll wear my sweater."

"No, Amelia," Mama said, "It's too cold today for a sweater. You need a warmer wrap and your old one was too small last year. This coat should be just right this year."

I pursed my lips and stared up at the ceiling in exasperation. "But I don't like it, Mama," I whined. "Can't I ever have a coat of my own? I always wear Aileen's old things! That coat smells like mothballs and it's, well—it's old and ugly!"

"It is ugly," James agreed, getting up to shovel a second helping of oatmeal into his bowl, even though Joseph and Aileen hadn't eaten yet.

I returned to finishing my own cereal. Silence filled the room, except for a soft meow on the front porch from Martha who wanted in. She had given birth to five kittens two days before and we had them corralled in a box near the stove.

Mama opened the door for the cat before turning back to me. "Amelia, be reasonable. We don't have enough cold weather for you to need a coat often or long. Money doesn't grow on trees, you know. This coat will air out quickly and be fine for you."

James looked up and grinned. "Yes, Ah-mee-lee-ah, that ugly coat'll be fine for you." He stood, leaving his bowl on the table and ran out the back door nearly tripping over the cat.

Mama looked after James and muttered, "That boy'll catch his death of cold, but I don't know what I can do about it."

I carried James's and my bowls to the sink. Then I snatched the old black coat. It felt heavy and rough to the touch. The large rounded collar, which was edged in black piping, showed signs of wear. The material had faded on the cuffs to a mottled gray. I put it on and found that, unfortunately, it fit me perfectly.

"Okay, I'll try it," I moaned.

"That's a good girl," Mama smiled.

I stepped out on the porch in my "new" coat and looked up at the mountain. Golden splashes of aspen were interspersed with green smudges of cacti. The bright sun illuminated the coral-colored granite boulders, giving the morning the appearance of a warm summer day, but in fact, the cool air made me acutely aware that Christmas would be here soon.

I took my satchel off its peg on the front porch and pulled the detestable coat closer to my body. I broke into a run across the backyard and through the gate.

A pinon tree, devoid of leaves, stood starkly against the blue sky and in the far distance above and at least a mile beyond it, a buzzard soared slowly in circles. As I watched, it suddenly swooped down toward earth and I lost sight of it. A queasy feeling washed over me as I realized some poor animal had become its breakfast.

Blanca greeted me in the playground, wearing a new pink cape with large pearl buttons down the front. Her forearms came out embroidered slits on either side of the buttons, but her hands were buried inside a fluffy, white fur muff.

"Oh, Blanca," I squealed, "How pretty you are! Where'd you get the outfit?"

"Mama made the cape." She said, twirling, so I could appreciate the total effect of its fullness. She held out the muff for me to feel. "And my grandmother sent my muff to me for Christmas," she said. "She lives far away in old Mexico and she thinks it's cold here in the United States." She giggled. "She always sends my presents early, too, because she's afraid they'll be late."

"Good for her!" I said. "I would love a cape. Mama made me wear this ugly old coat of Aileen's. I hate it."

"Does she sew?" Blanca asked. "I'm sure my mother would loan her the cape pattern. She said it was easy to make—no sleeves or collar to fuss with."

A brief stir of hope rose up in me as I pictured my mother at her sewing machine making a cape for me from Blanca's mother's pattern, but it was quickly dashed by another vision—the houseful of people at home needing meals, the large pile of mending she'd been meaning to get to, laundry, chickens to feed, and all the other chores around our house that Mama managed alone.

"Nah, she has too much work already," I said. "Maybe next year after the Overbergs leave." Then I added, "If they ever do."

"They won't be there much longer," Blanca smiled kindly, but then I thought I detected a brief worried expression in her deep brown eyes.

When class dismissed for recess, Blanca squeezed my hand and pulled me into the cloakroom at such a pace I had to run to keep up with her.

"Slow down!" I said. "What's your hurry?"

"Here," she said, taking her lovely cape off her coat hook and handing it to me. "Let's trade for recess!"

"Really?" I asked. I pictured myself in the beautiful cape, my hands thrust in soft, white fur.

"Yes," Blanca said. "It'll be fun."

Eagerly, I took the cape from her and wrapped it around my shoulders. Its silky lining felt luxurious and smooth to my skin. The garment hung from my shoulders in soft folds. I twirled around a couple of times in the cloakroom so that Blanca could see how the cape flared. Then I saw her beaming face above my stinking, old black coat, and felt ashamed.

"Gee, it's lovely, but here," I said, slipping the pink cape off my shoulders and handing it to Blanca. "Thanks for sharing, but we don't have to trade. It looks too pretty on you with your dark hair and skin color, and besides, my coat's warmer."

"Are you sure?" Blanca asked. She slowly removed my coat and handed it back. As soon as I put it on, she reached out and smoothed the front of it with her hand. "I was very warm in it," she said.

That evening, I helped Thelma fold clothes at the kitchen table while the others were involved in various indoor activities throughout the house.

Mr. and Mrs. Overberg and the baby were not among them. They had taken a drive after dinner. I matched socks while Thelma folded the clothing and placed the garments in stacks for every member of her family and mine. I told her about Blanca's pink cape and rabbit fur muff.

"I bet they're beautiful," she said.

"They are! The cape is soft like a baby's blanket. She let me try it on."

"How nice of her," Thelma said, "Where'd she get it?"

"Her mother made it," I said. "She makes all of Blanca's clothes and they're all lovely. She offered to loan us the pattern, but Mama's too busy to sew."

"I can sew," Thelma said. "I made this dress myself." She indicated the pale blue one she wore.

"Did your mother teach you?"

"Oh no," Thelma said. "I learned from my grandmother in Missouri. She came to stay with us a long while after my baby brother died. We spent the whole time together sewing clothes. You should sew, Amelia. It's not difficult and you could make yourself a cape. I'll help you."

So, I imagined myself sitting at Mama's sewing machine, but the image quickly faded. Sewing didn't appeal to me. Aileen liked it, but not me. The thought of painstakingly cutting out an entire dress and piecing it together with pins seemed torturous and I seriously doubted that I would want to wear anything I'd made.

"I'm not good at things like that," I sighed. "I'll have to wear hand-me-downs forever."

"Or you could marry a rich man and buy all store-bought," Thelma suggested. "There are lovely clothes in the Sears and Roebuck."

A week before Christmas, Miss Barnes announced, "Today we're going to draw names for the Christmas gift exchange." She started passing out little slips of white paper.

"Write your names on one of these papers and then, one table at a time, we'll come drop them in the box on my desk."

Busy hands grabbed at the little scraps of paper and labored to print their first and last names in big block letters. Table by table, and one by one, we slipped our names inside the festive red box on our teacher's desk.

"Now, tell your parents you're not to spend over twenty-five cents for store-bought and homemade presents are just as nice," Miss Barnes said. "We'll have a holiday party on the last day of school before the Christmas break and exchange our gifts then. Today you'll draw one name from a box, so you'll know who to buy a gift for. Now, one table at a time again," she

Water Under the Bridge

nodded at the table where Blanca and I sat in the front of the room. "Don't tell anyone whose name you draw because it's supposed to be a surprise."

As luck would have it, I drew James's name. It crossed my mind to ask Miss Barnes if I could trade my paper for one of the other children's, but I knew she wouldn't approve. I just hoped James didn't have my name, too.

James' behavior had improved tremendously at school. Miss Barnes was patient, but made it clear that he obey. Although he didn't seem to care when his own mother corrected him, he tried to please Miss Barnes. He also hadn't bothered me since the incident with the spiders.

That evening after dinner, I told Mama about the gift exchange at school while she swept the front porch. Aileen sat reading a story to Timothy and trying to keep Paul from crawling off the porch at the same time. Thelma and Papa stayed inside washing dishes.

"Come with me," Mama said. I followed her into her bedroom. She opened her top dresser drawer and took out a small package, which she handed to me. Inside I found two bright yellow pencils and a small round ball, mostly blue and gold. It resembled a miniature of the world. A seam broke the tiny globe into halves and revealed a pencil sharpener on one side.

"Mrs. Wallace picked them up for me in town this morning," she explained. "Hurry now and wrap these gifts for James."

I carried the package into the parlor and encountered Aileen curled up on the davenport, reading.

"Look what Mama bought," I said, thrusting the small globe under her nose. "What is it?" She said, sitting up straight and taking the small orb from me.

"It's a pencil sharpener," I said. I showed her how to separate the two halves of the globe and insert a pencil into the small round hole inside.

"For James?" Aileen asked.

"Yes," I said, "but there are two brand new pencils here, too, so I'm going to keep the sharpener for myself."

"You mustn't do that, Amy. It would be unfair to James and Mama wouldn't like it."

"But it's my gift to give," I said. "It should be up to me what to give him and I don't think it's fair that he end up with better things than us."

"You mean you don't want him to have better things than you," Aileen said. "You give that sharpener to James just like Mama told you. You know it's the right thing."

Dejected, I wrapped the two pencils and the little world sharpener inside a wooden box. Some of the children at my school had been talking about what Santa Claus would be bringing them. I wished that Papa wouldn't be so strict. Next morning, I got an idea.

"May I have a new cape for Christmas?" I asked Mama.

Her face immediately registered disappointment in me.

"Amelia, I thought I made myself clear. Aileen's coat fits you fine and it's plenty warm. We cannot afford to buy things we don't need and I have too much to do with all the mending. Besides, you might as well know now, you're a big girl, Papa declared we'll not be having presents for ourselves this year."

"Ahhh! Tarnations!" I said, stamping my foot, "Why not? The Overbergs are exchanging gifts."

"You know why," Mama said. "He's agreed that I can cook us all a nice meal and that will have to do."

That night, I lay awake for some time after the house was still. After a while, I became aware of a low hum. I sat up and leaned on my elbow to listen. The noise came from the back of the house, a familiar sound I couldn't place.

Sleep overtook me as I heard Aileen's even breathing and the night sounds outside my window. In the far distance, a dog barked. Just as I nodded off, I recognized the hum—Mama's treadle sewing machine.

On Christmas morning, I sat up and found something green draped over the back of the davenport. I pulled on it until it fell into my lap. Immediately I saw it was a cape—just like Blanca's! It had a note pinned on the front. It said, *"Dear Amelia, This is for church tomorrow. Love, Mama."*

I hopped up and threw the cape over my shoulders and slipped my two hands into the cross-stitched slits on either side. I twirled around the room, and it wasn't until I came back near my pallet that I saw the navy blue cape waiting there for Aileen.

"Get up, Aileen!" I nearly screamed. "Get up and see what Mama made us for Christmas!"

Aileen sat up and took the soft navy bundle I handed her. She read the note pinned to her cape and said, "You mustn't call it a Christmas present, Amy."

"I know," I said. "It's for church. It's not a present." But I thought to myself, dear, dear Mama, staying up late to surprise us. I ran into the kitchen to thank her, but saw only Joseph in the room. He told me Mama was outside feeding the chickens.

"See my cape," I said, twirling for him.

"Yeah," he said. "She gave me a pocket watch."

"Nice," I said. "Mama must've been up all night making our gifts."

"For a few nights," Joseph said. "I heard her in her bedroom sewing several nights this past week."

Verna Simms

CHAPTER ELEVEN—WINTER 1928

I was eager to return to school after our holiday break; the winter passed slowly. The increasing tension in our over-crowded home made me dread Fridays, knowing another weekend with the Overbergs awaited me.

One windy day in early March, Blanca and I stood in the middle of the play yard with the wind whipping our hair and my bangs, which needed a trim, and stung my eyes. "Have you ever flown a kite?" I asked Blanca.

I didn't wait for an answer, but continued, "We've got an orange crate at home. I've been thinking I could ask Joe to saw kite sticks from the wood. Then, you and I could attach string around the sticks and paste newspapers over everything and make a kite. I'd be fun. Want to?"

Blanca nodded excitedly.

"But where's a place without trees or houses where we can fly a kite?" she asked.

I realized it would be a real problem. Joseph and I had lost several kites to trees or rooftops. Once tangled in branches, it became useless to try and save a kite.

"I know. Up on the mountain behind our house there's few trees and no houses. Joseph and I play there all the time."

I beat Joseph home that afternoon and lingered in the yard, waiting for him. As soon as he reached the gate, I ran to meet him. "Joe," I said, walking with him toward the house, "Blanca and I want a kite. Would you help make one?"

I saw he wasn't interested, so I added, "We're going to fly it up on the mountain so it won't crash in the trees."

He frowned. "Hey, that's our hideaway, Amelia—yours and mine alone."

I wondered at this new side of Joseph I hadn't noticed before and hurried to put him at ease, "Oh, Joe," I said, "of course it's yours and mine. Blanca and I won't be going that far up—just far enough to get away from trees. We could play right above the path that leads to school."

He thought for a moment.

"Well, I guess that'd be okay," he said, nodding as he looked in the direction of our secret place, "just don't take her any farther."

"I won't," I promised. "So, will you help us?"

He agreed, and together we headed toward the tool shed to look for the orange crate I'd seen in the pile of scrap lumber. The next morning I waited in the schoolyard, barely able to contain my excitement. Joseph had sawed six sticks, enough for three kites. He'd even promised to help lash them together.

Finally, Blanca's father's car pulled up and braked to a stop in front of the school. When she emerged, I noticed she carried a brown paper sack. By the time I reached her side, several girls from our class gathered around to see what she carried.

One by one, she pulled out folded sheets of colored paper and began handing them to the girls. As she presented each one, she said, "And this one's for you, Mary . . . and this one's for you, Bess," in Blanca's sweet way of making everyone feel special.

I hurriedly opened mine, seeing straight away that it was an invitation. My eyes lit up at the picture of a lovely white birthday cake with six pink candles on top. Each candle stood in the center of a pink rose and a yellow fire blazed on top. Big scallops of pink icing looped around the side of the cake.

"It's lovely!" I squealed.

"Mama and I made the invitations," Blanca said, nodding. "She's baking a cake to look exactly like this picture." She pointed at the cake on the invitation. "My birthday's really on Friday, but we're celebrating on Saturday."

The writing on the invitations said:

>*You are invited to a birthday party.*
>*Where? At Blanca Romac's home*
>*When? On Saturday, March 17, 1928*
>*Time? Two o'clock*
>*R.S.V.P.*

Water Under the Bridge

From that point on, the prospect of attending Blanca's birthday party consumed my thoughts, making me forget how urgently I'd wanted to introduce her to the mountain and kite flying.

I beat my own time racing home after school. When I burst through the kitchen door, I noticed Mama sitting at the table peeling potatoes. With no breath left for talking, I thrust the paper into her hands.

"Amelia, my heavens!" Mama said, taking the paper and unfolding it.

She read the invitation and then said, "Oh, dear." She handed it invitation back and paused a moment to look out the kitchen window. Her hands flew up to her hair. I watched her remove a hairpin and slowly jam it back into place.

"What?" I asked, alarmed.

Aileen, Joseph, and James could be heard approaching the house. They were singing *I've been Working on the Railroad*.

"What's wrong?" I asked. "I can go, can't I?"

"Gracious me, honey, I'm afraid not," Mama said, pulling me close to her. She smoothed my hair and patted my back. "I know it's a big disappointment, but your papa'll be out of town with the car all day Saturday.

"Tell you what we'll do," she tried to sound cheerful. "I'll bake a cake, you may decorate it, and we'll have a nice party right here at home—a party to welcome in the springtime."

Instantly a large lump welled up in my throat, preventing me from answering her. I stared past her out the window and saw Joseph and James leaning over the fence in the chicken yard. I swallowed hard, trying not to blink to keep tears from falling.

"Gosh almighty, Mama, I have to go. I just gotta. Maybe Joseph could walk me." Then, without waiting for a response, I started for the kitchen door. "I'll ask him," I said, over my shoulder.

"No, Amelia," Mama said, grabbing my sleeve and stopping me. "It's much too far for you and Joseph to walk. Out of the question."

I knew the pain in my own face mirrored her own, but her expression quickly changed to one of steely resolve.

"There'll be lots of other parties, Amelia," she said firmly. "You have to make the best of this. Life is full of disappointments."

She turned her attention back to the potatoes she'd been peeling over a metal bowl when I'd burst into the room. I slumped down in a chair, letting the tears fall.

Aileen came in and, seeing me, said, "What's wrong, Amelia?"

"Nothing," I said between sobs, turning my head away. I didn't feel like explaining.

"Can I go play on the mountain?" I turned to Mama. I longed for its rugged beauty, my refuge.

She looked out the window and scanned the mountainside. Suddenly her eyes fixed on something.

"No hon, you'd better not," she said. "Not right now, anyway. I see Daniel and Thelma on the trail."

Then, under her breath she added, "They're holding hands." A smile pulled at the corners of her mouth, but she shook her head and went back to her potatoes.

"Gee sis, I'll take a walk with you," Aileen offered. I shook my head, realizing she'd be curious about my latest calamity and in no mood to share my sorrow. I also knew Mama would fill her in the moment they were alone.

Later, in my hideaway under the house, I opened the old shoebox and removed the little paper doll. I smoothed the apron the doll wore but it gave me no comfort. Somehow, nothing mattered now that I wouldn't be attending Blanca's party.

At dinner, Aileen tried her best to cheer me, "Put on your thinking cap, Amy. You and I'll do something really nice this Saturday. Maybe a picnic."

"Oh, that'd be fun," Thelma chimed in eagerly. She and Aileen had become nearly inseparable. I suspected Mama had told them both about the party.

"Naw, I don't want to," I mumbled.

All evening long I nursed my pain until finally, with a long face, I prepared for bed. Aileen knelt for prayers and waited.

"Go ahead without me," I muttered.

"I'll do no such thing," she said, shocked. "Don't take this out on our heavenly Father, Amy."

"Well, He could do something if He wanted to," I said. "He's God, isn't He? He could give Mama her own car, or change Papa's plans."

"God's ways are mysterious," Aileen said. "They're not for us to understand. But if you're smart, you'll say your prayers. When you have a problem, that's not the time to turn your back on God."

I knelt down next to her facing the davenport's seat and folded my hands, but I let Aileen say the prayer alone.

The next morning, I sat dejected on the steps of the schoolyard and watched Mr. Romac's car roll to a stop. Blanca jumped out and waved happily to me. She ran to me and immediately started telling me more plans for the party before I had a chance to speak. "My mother said we're going to play games outdoors," she said. "Pin the Tail on the Donkey. And we'll break open a piñata, too."

I held my gaze on Mr. Romac's car as it rolled out of sight. Then I turned and placed my hand on Blanca's arm. Without warning tears filled my eyes. I couldn't help myself.

"Oh Amelia," Blanca said, falling silent. "You can't come."

"No," I blurted out, unable to hold back the sobs anymore. I lowered my head and bit my lip. "Papa'll be out of town Saturday with the car. Mama doesn't drive. She claims it's too far for me to walk."

A pair of girls headed toward us, but when they saw me crying, they quickly turned and moved toward the slide, heads together, whispering. Chatter and squeals permeated the air as children tried to squeeze in a few more rides on the slide and swings before the bell rang. The brightness of the morning sun and their happiness seemed to sharpen my despair.

I rose and walked slowly up the steps toward the front door of the school building.

"Don't worry, Amelia," Blanca said, following me. She locked arms with me and stopped at the last step. Tugging at one of her pigtails, she said thoughtfully. "I'll tell my mother. She'll think of something. She always does. You'll see."

The next morning Blanca again bounced from the front seat of her father's car. She dashed toward me, calling my name and thrust a sheet of white paper at me.

"I told you! I told you!" she chanted, all smiles.

Mr. Romac sat a moment in his car, evidently waiting for his goodbye wave, but finally he gave up and drove away.

"Gee whiz, what?" I asked.

"Read it! Read it! It's a note for your mother," Blanca said. Then, unable to wait for me, she said, "We're inviting you to come home with me on Friday and—Guess what?—if it's okay with your mother, you get to stay over the whole night! Daddy'll drive you home after the party. Isn't it super, Amelia?" Her face beamed.

During noon recess, together we raced the short distance from the school to my house and squirmed anxiously while Mama read the note from Mrs. Romac. Finally, she folded it and slipped it into her apron pocket. "Well, sounds like a good plan," she said, smiling. Then she turned to Blanca, "Thank your mother and father for me, dear."

On Friday, my satchel contained my best Sunday dress, a pair of clean white stockings, two petticoats, a nightgown, and a pair of starched white bloomers. The dress was my favorite of all Aileen's hand-me-downs, pale blue organdy with long puffed sleeves and a row of tiny buttons up the bodice. I always wore two petticoats under its full skirt and glided across the room, listening to the swish the petticoats made against my bloomers. That dress made me feel like a princess.

Before I left home that morning, Mama warned me twice not to sit in the dirt. Then, as I ran across the yard toward the path that led to school, she hollered after me, "Remember, Amelia, I'll not be wanting to boil those bloomers!"

"Sure, I know," I yelled back. "I'll be careful, I promise!" I opened the gate and as I reached the dirt path, I heard her call, "Have a wonderful time!"

I squirmed, finding it difficult to concentrate on lessons and could scarcely take my eyes off the clock; its minute hand crawled slowly around its face. Finally, the bell rang

CHAPTER TWELVE—BLANCA'S PARTY

"Oh!" I gasped at the spectacle of Blanca's bedroom—a full-sized bed covered with a pink, ruffled canopy. More pink ruffles draped the bedcover and the matching curtains on her window. I'd never imagined such splendor, and stood transfixed in the doorway, unable to move.

That is, until I saw the dollhouse.

Blanca's eyes followed my gaze. "Want to play dolls?" she asked.

I nodded and knelt on the floor beside the miniature two-story house. On one side, it had a shingled roof, white clapboard siding, and black shutters flanking the windows. The other side opened to reveal the partitions for rooms and a staircase that led to the second floor. It stood nearly as tall as Blanca and me.

"Gosh almighty, where'd you get this?" I asked Blanca, incredulous.

"Daddy built it. He made all the furniture, too. Mama sewed the bedspread and curtains. Did you notice they match my room?"

The tiny bedroom was a replica of Blanca's own magnificent room.

"This one'll be me," I selected a golden-haired doll. "Does she have any party dresses?"

"Oh, yes, over here—in this wee trunk. It's full of all kinds of doll clothes. Choose anything you like."

I crawled over to the trunk and rubbed its glossy brown finish with the tips of my fingers. I inhaled the scent of cedar. "Blanca, you're so lucky to have parents who give you all these lovely presents."

Her dark eyes sparkled in agreement. "They make almost everything." Then she added, "I do love my parents very much, but sometimes I think you're the lucky one, Amelia. I have pangs of jealousy sometimes of the girls who have brothers and sisters. It's no fun to play alone all the time."

I couldn't imagine being alone. Even the days when only the Halls filled our home had become distant in my memory.

On a lighter note, Blanca said, "Hey, wanna have a wedding? You play the bride with your doll and my doll will be a bridesmaid. But later we switch, okay? So I can dress as the bride, too."

The next couple of hours we engaged in intense play as Blanca and I pretended that the pretty girl dolls met handsome boy dolls and enjoyed romances that were followed by glorious weddings. Dressing the dolls in wedding garb took up much of our time. We took turns pretending until we had each been a blonde and a brunette bride and had met and married a blonde and a brunette groom.

"You girls hungry?" Mrs. Romac called, peeking into Blanca's room. Her accent heavily emphasized her R's.

She looked to be no more than a girl herself, petite, her long black hair cascading over her shoulders, with Blanca's lovely brown skin and dark eyes.

At her waist, six tiny bells dangled on a gold colored sash, and they jingled as she walked. Her bare feet revealed toenails painted a deep red. I stared at her in fascination.

Seated at the dinner table, Mr. Romac looked our way. "Let us give thanks." Then he dropped his head and Blanca and Mrs. Romac did the same. I dipped my head also, but kept my eyes on Mr. Romac, expecting him to speak. The silence lasted a full minute as I studied this man. His dark wavy hair dripped water—wet from a shower—and ran down his forehead and face and handed in his lap. He looked up suddenly, catching my eye, and winked.

My face felt hot; I was embarrassed to be caught watching him instead of silently praying.

Mrs. Romac turned to her husband, "Did you have a good day at work, Fredo?"

"A fine day." He helped himself to the skillet mixture of potatoes, onions, peppers and sausage meat. "The men discussed conditions in Mexico." He pronounced it May-hee-ko.

"Some worry for their families' welfare—those still in the old country." Mr. Romac spoke with the same accent I'd heard in his wife's speech. He also had a rhythm to his words and every sentence ended on a high note, almost like a question.

"Ronaldo suggested we take up a collection. I told him to count me in."

"An excellent idea." Mrs. Romac stood and walked to the cupboard and returned with a bowl of tapioca pudding.

I ate two helpings but, remembering my manners, declined a third.

After dinner, Blanca's mother sang as she washed the dishes. Although I couldn't understand a word, her soft voice made her endearing to me.

Preparing for sleep, I asked, "Where does your papa work?"

"In the mine," she said. "We moved here with several other families from Mexico four years ago. The men wanted work and the mine hired everyone."

"That's good," I said, wishing Mr. Overberg would find a job, too. I suspected he hadn't tried.

Darkness and bedtime came too soon for me. I dreaded going home to my crowded home the next day. I sank down in Blanca's soft, thick featherbed. "When I grow up, I'll have featherbeds," I said, dreamily. I closed my eyes and imagined myself floating high above the earth on a fluffy white cloud.

Blanca gently shook me. I ignored her. The bed was warm and soft. I rolled over.

"Amy, wake up, sleepy-head."

I opened my eyes surprised to see a light-filled room.

"You smiled in your sleep while dreaming," Blanca said. "I hated to wake you. Mama is urging us to hurry and eat breakfast, so we can dress for the party."

I leaped from bed and dressed in my party finery. Blanca's dress was a deep shade of pink, almost rose. It hung straight from her shoulders without a defined waist, in the style popular in those days. A large rounded white collar framed her face, its edges trimmed in delicate white tatting. With her dark braids tied with matching ribbons, she reminded me of the doll Aileen had once admired in the Sears & Roebuck catalog.

The early morning hours helping prepare for the party flew by. We arranged colorful paper plates on the table and Mrs. Romac placed the cake—an exact replica of the cake on the invitations—in a place of prominence in the center of the table. As soon as the other girls arrived, Blanca suggested, "Let's play in the backyard. Do you all know *Pin the Tail on the Donkey*?"

"Me, I do!" I said quickly, running ahead so I could go first. Mrs. Romac laughed and held me by the shoulders. "I'll blindfold you, turn you around three times, and then you must try and pin the tail on the picture of the donkey." She indicated the large hand-drawn drawing hanging on a tree. "Whoever comes closest to pinning the black dot wins."

I didn't exactly cheat. I couldn't actually see the donkey, but peeking beneath the blindfold, I could see the ground. I noticed Mrs. Romac's moccasin footprints in the sandy soil and followed their direction. As it turned out, they led straight to the donkey's bottom.

"You won!" Blanca shouted. Then she presented me with a beautiful pair of white socks with lace trim, exactly the same as all the other girls were wearing with their shiny black, low-topped shoes. I clutched them to my heart.

Later, as I prepared to leave for home, Mrs. Romac came into Blanca's bedroom with a small brown paper bag. "I noticed today that your feet are smaller than Blanca's," she said. "I think these shoes might fit you and I would love for you to have them. I hate good shoes to go to waste."

Inside the bag, I thrilled at the sight of a pair of black, shiny shoes.

"Oh thank you!" I said, hugging her impulsively. I tried the shoes on immediately and found that they fit well, but I knew better than to show them to my parents. Papa would certainly not approve and Mama would take his side. So as soon as I arrived home, I ran around the house and slipped between the morning glory vines to hide my special shoes in my secret place.

Over the weeks and months that followed, I often stole beneath the house to try on the white lace-trimmed bobby socks and pretty new shoes. I longed to wear them to school, but knew that would be impossible. I also fantasized twirling around in them on my toes like a ballerina, but there was no room to stand in the crawl space. "I am a princess," I told myself as I conjured up a whole roomful of shiny low-topped shoes in my imagination—in every color of the rainbow.

CHAPTER THIRTEEN—LINDBERGH

One afternoon I sat under the house in my secret place wearing my socks and shoes, when upstairs I heard the kitchen door open and shut. Daniel called, "Where's everybody? Come quick!"

I scrambled to remove my socks and shoes, and barefooted I duck-walked out as fast as I could into the bright sunshine.

I found Daniel and Mama in the parlor. Mama wore her cleaning dress and Daniel stood cranking Mama's phonograph. Gently he lowered the arm on a black phonograph record that was spinning on top. First I heard a sound like an airplane propeller and then a man singing a song about a young man who had braved unknown dangers to fly over the ocean alone in an "aeroplane." He was the "Eagle of the U.S.A."

> *"Over the ocean, he flew all alone, gambling with fate and dangers unknown. Others will make that trip across the sea, upon some future day, but take your hats off to Lucky, lucky Lindbergh—Eagle of the USA."*

"Oh son, that's nice, but I haven't time for foolishness right now," Mama mumbled as she headed toward the kitchen.

Of course, I knew all about the Lindbergh flight. I recalled the day last May when Daniel had rushed into the room waving a newspaper, "He made it! He made it!" Daniel had hollered. "All the way across the Atlantic Ocean by himself!" I'd never seen Daniel so excited.

"Goodness gracious, Daniel, whatever are you talking about?" Mama had asked.

"Charles Lindbergh," Daniel said, waving a newspaper. "Haven't you heard?"

Mama shook her head. "Can't see any reason for the young man to worry his mother so. Bad enough we had the terrible war only a few years ago. My stars and garters, just when things are going peaceful, sons create hazards for themselves—tsk, tsk." Mama took a swipe at a speck of dust on the Victrola.

But I was interested. "Tell me about it, Dan," I asked.

"Okay," he said, happy to explain. "He's a pilot, you know, like I plan to be. He flew his plane all away across the ocean—from New York to Paris—all by himself. He's the very first person to do that. He's famous now and got a $25,000 prize."

Daniel had a faraway look in his eyes that day and he looked that way now. It had been all anyone would talk about the year before. Daniel wanted to be like Lindbergh and dreamed of flying someday.

"Where'd you get the record?" I asked.

"The general merchandise store in town ordered it for me. It came today." He lifted the needle arm, moved it across the record, and carefully lowered the needle at the beginning again and gazed out the window, seeing a future I could not.

"Play the song again," The music had ended a second time and I savored the time with my big brother. I'd seen little of him the past few weeks. "Nah, that's enough for now, Amy," he said. "Don't wanna wear out the record." He carefully removed it from the Victrola and slid it into its case. Then he went in search of Mama with me following him. Thelma and Mrs. Overberg were feeding the two youngest children in the kitchen.

"Your mama's in the bedroom," Mrs. Overberg said. We found her on her hands and knees scrubbing the floor.

"Lindbergh named his plane *The Spirit of St. Louis*," Daniel said. "He's put St. Louis on the map."

"St. Louis was on the map long before Charles Lindbergh came along," Mama said without looking up.

"Aren't you pleased, Mama?" I asked.

"Oh, I'm fine," she said. "But I'm tired and a little cranky today, I guess. I could hear the song from in here."

Mama stopped scrubbing and sat with her back against the wall.

"You must be careful with your money, son," she said. Then her face changed and she added, "But once in a while a boy deserves something special, I suppose."

Water Under the Bridge

She went on. "Crystal City is only thirty miles or so from St. Louis. Every year before school started, my mother took us shopping for school shoes in the city. It was something we looked forward to all year, taking the train in to Union Station and stopping for a soda downtown on our way to buy new shoes."

"Maybe someday you can go back, Mama," I said.

"I was born there," Daniel told me proudly, even though I already knew. "I'm going back. I'll learn to fly. Then I'll fly all over the country and come West in an aeroplane and soar over this house like an eagle." He held his arms and soared around Mama and Papa's bedroom. Then he picked me up and swung me around.

Verna Simms

Water Under the Bridge

CHAPTER FOURTEEN—CAMOFLAUGE DRESS

April, my birthday month, started out rainy. Several times Aileen, Joseph, James, and I were pelted on our way home from school. Then, for two Saturdays in a row, I was forced to play on the front porch with Joseph and the Overberg children while Aileen and Thelma had the parlor all to themselves.

I stood in the kitchen and appealed to Mama. "It's not fair!"

"You leave the big girls alone," she said. "Take your jacks and your paper dolls outdoors and amuse yourself on the porch."

I soon tired of these pastimes, and walked back through the house and stuck my head in the kitchen door. "Please Mama," I said. "I'm bored. When will it stop raining?"

"How do I know?" Mama answered, cross again. She'd been impatient with me a lot lately. "If you're so bored, come in then. I have something for you to do that will pass the time."

I followed her into her bedroom and to the closet. Inside were boxes. Lots and lots of cardboard boxes stacked up to the ceiling in some places.

"Quit gaping, Amelia. Help me get this box down." Mama pointed to a large box stacked higher than her own head. It was labeled "AILEEN—7/8."

"You've outgrown all your dresses," she said. "Let's see what we can find. I've no time for sewing now."

She pulled on the carton and it tumbled over into her hands. I helped her lower it to the floor. The heavy box landed with a thud.

Mama opened the box and held up garment after garment, every one faded and worn. Some patched. But all had been stored clean, ironed and neatly folded.

"Quit dawdling, Amelia. Go through this box and choose any you can use," she said.

I hated them all, old and ugly. I especially disliked a dull green dress with yellowish green speckles. I made sure to ignore it in the box, but Mama snatched it and shook out the creases and handed the dress to me. One day about a week or so later, I sat on a low branch of our tree, wearing the hated dress.

Joseph walked right past me.

"Joe," I called, swinging my feet to gain his attention.

"Why, Amy," he said, startled. "I didn't see you up there. With that green dress and your brown arms and legs, you blend into the tree."

I laughed and dropped down beside him.

A camouflage dress, I thought, instantly changing my opinion. The ugly green dress became my favorite.

A few days later, a balmy spring Thursday, I wore the dress to school on my birthday. I remarked to Miss Barnes and one of my friends, "Guess what? This dress makes me invisible when I'm climbing a tree."

Miss Barnes threw back her head and laughed, "How special, Amelia!"

After racing home that afternoon, I stopped at the cottonwood to try hiding again. I wish Miss Barnes could see me now. As I was hugging a lower limb among the leaves, suddenly a pretty canary flew past and lit on the end of the same limb on which I sat. I wondered if it might be our pet canary, the one who had escaped the previous summer, when Aileen had forgotten to latch its cage door.

Maybe if I climb quietly and inch towards the tree limb I can see it better. Perhaps catch the bird for Aileen. I edged my way slowly toward the bird, but it noticed me and flew away.

Men's angry voices coming from the tool shed nearby startled me. They rose and filled my heart with anxiety. I couldn't distinguish the words but I recognized Papa's and Daniel's tones.

Their voices came closer. I sat perfectly still, desperately hoping the dress would again make me invisible. I knew Papa wouldn't tolerate me overhearing his conversation with my brother. He had told me many times not to snoop, not to listen to conversation not meant for my ears. I squeezed my eyes shut, pressed against the tree's trunk, ignoring the roughness of the bark on my cheeks, and tried not to breathe.

"You'll mind what I say, boy!" Papa said. "You're not to talk to her again, you hear, boy?" He emphasized the word 'boy.' Daniel walked quickly away from his lean-to and across the yard toward the house.

"Tarnations! You turn around and face me, boy!" Papa demanded.

Daniel turned and kicked the dirt with his feet. They were only a few yards from the tree now.

I felt my heart pounding so hard that I feared they would hear it.

Sweat glistened off both men's foreheads.

"Aw, Thelma and I were just talking," Daniel said. "I told you. She came by to suggest we take a walk on the mountain. I didn't have time for walking—not today. She mentioned you bought the lot next to where the temple will be built in Mesa. All excited about it." Then he added, "Did Mama know about it? The lot, I mean."

"That's none of your concern," Papa said. I could almost smell his anger. "You're not to say a word either, if you know what's good for you. Meddling in my affairs."

Daniel's reply was at once low and calm. "I don't care what property you buy. That's your privilege. But you promised to pay me for the work I did. We had a deal and you went back on your word."

Then Papa said, "This is my house and the Lord saw fit to make me the head of it. You're almost seventeen, a grown man now and you can make your own way. High time you left. Do you understand me?"

Daniel's doubled his fists as if to strike Papa, and I shut my eyes again, but they wouldn't stay shut. Next, I saw my brother drop his arms limply and walk past Papa to the tool shed. He didn't look back but called over his shoulder. "Fine, then," he said. "I'll get my clothes. Farewell, Papa dear."

Papa watched as Daniel entered the lean-to and then he stomped toward the house. He sat on the front porch gazing into the sky.

Afraid he'd notice me if I jumped down, I hugged the tree's trunk trembling until an hour later when Mama called, "Dinnertime!" I waited until Papa rose and closed the kitchen door and then I dropped to the hard dirt below.

When I entered the kitchen, Mama said, "Amelia, run and tell Daniel to come eat."

"He's running an errand," Papa answered quickly. "He won't be home tonight. We had a talk. In fact, now that the Brown's place is finished, he plans to take his pay and be on his own."

"What?" Mama said. The color drained from her face. Papa's eyes fell to his plate and the room became silent. Not a sound came from the Overberg children, or from any of us.

"There're a lot of mouths to feed here and he's a big boy," Papa continued. "He can make his own way."

"When was this decided?" Mama asked. "Why didn't he tell me?"

"He asked me to tell you," Papa said. "He didn't want you upset."

I'd kept my head down. When my eyes met Mama's, I saw her expression change from shock to anguished understanding.

After the dinner dishes were cleared, Mama brought a cake out of the Old Mother Hubbard cabinet. "We have a birthday today," she said brightly, even though her face contradicted her tone. "Amelia is seven years old."

I sat weakly through the "Happy Birthday" song and tried to look pleased when I was presented with a ball and jacks by Papa and some cards with animal pictures on them from Mama. Aileen and Thelma gave me two embroidered handkerchiefs they'd made, and Joseph gave me another I.O.U. for making my bed. Finally, Mr. Overberg reached in his pocket and handed me a shiny nickel. "Don't spend it all in one place," he said, which made everyone laugh.

Later that evening, Joseph and I met in our secret place beneath the house.

"I can't believe Daniel'd just go off like that—and on your birthday," Joseph said. "He didn't even say goodbye to Mama." Then he reasoned aloud, "Well, he's not too far. I'm sure we'll probably see him as much as before."

"No, I don't think we'll see him hardly at all," I said. "He and Papa had an argument and Papa ordered him off the place." We looked at each other and shook our heads.

CHAPTER FIFTEEN—WATERMELON

On Saturday, the spring-summer sun was burning brightly for a change. Aileen, Thelma, and Mrs. Overberg sat across the table from me. Timothy and Paul romped around on the floor. Mama stood at the window studying the sky through the kitchen window

"Let's hurry up and finish breakfast," she said. "The men won't be home until late tonight and no telling how long this nice weather'll hold. I want to air the bedding."

There goes my Saturday. I hated Mama's spring housecleaning.

"We'll leave everything out to soak in the sun," Mama said. "I do enjoy the fresh smell of sunshine when I slip between the covers at night, don't you?"

"Well, I can't take the Arizona sun," Mrs. Overberg sighed. "It dries my skin dreadfully. I'll stay indoors with the two young-uns."

Thelma, Aileen and I struggled to carry our thin mattresses and heavy blankets outdoors and drape them over the clothesline. Mama adjusted the clothesline poles every ten feet to keep the bedding from dragging the ground. Then we thoroughly shook the feather pillows making the dust fly before pinning each one to the clothesline. Finally, we all stood back to admire our work.

Just then I saw Daniel approaching from the gate. "Hey," he called out to us. "Anybody want company?"

I ran to him and gave him a big bear hug, then grabbed one of his arms and pulled him toward the house. "Come on," I said. "I missed you. Where're you staying now? Do you like it up there? When can I come visit?"

"Slow down, little sis," Daniel said laughing. "A guy can't answer so many questions with one breath." He kissed Mama and Aileen and nodded at Thelma.

"Are you getting enough to eat?" Mama asked. "You need anything?"

"I'm fine, Mama," Daniel said. "I do miss everyone and figured Saturday morning'd be a good time to drop by." We all knew what that meant. On Saturdays, Papa always headed out after breakfast.

Mama made a big noon meal and we spent the afternoon sitting at the table talking. Finally, dusk settled in and Mama said, "Well, we'd better take down the bedding or we'll not have any covers tonight." We followed her outside.

I expected Daniel to take off then, but he lingered and helped carry the aired bedding into the house. It was warm inside, so we returned to sit on the porch. We'd only been there a few minutes when Papa's car drove up. Mr. Overberg got out of the front seat, followed by Joseph and James who stepped out from the back of the car.

Daniel and Papa stood still a moment looking at each other. Then Daniel walked over and stood next to Mama. If he reasoned Papa wouldn't argue in front of Mama, he was right.

"I hope you saved room for dessert!" Papa said, smiling. He reached into the car and produced a large striped watermelon.

"Let's cut it and eat it right now!" I said, nearly colliding with Aileen to run down the steps to Papa.

"Amelia, watch what you're doing!" she said.

Papa placed the melon on the porch. "Run get the butcher knife. The melon is already cold. I stored it all day in the water that runs from Mr. Charter's icehouse. Feel how cold it is, Amelia."

I placed my hand against the smooth green skin and instantly my mouth watered. Aileen dashed in the house to fetch the knife and Mama called after her, "Bring the oilcloth from the kitchen table, too—and the turkey platter."

Mama and Mrs. Overberg spread the red-checkered oilcloth on the ground under the cottonwood tree and Papa sliced the big green melon in two. Rich, red juice ran out on the platter and I inhaled the sweet freshness of it. Then he sliced each half into wedges and again into smaller wedges. The melon was so ripe it cracked with the slightest pressure of the knife.

"Here you go," Papa said, handing me a slice. "There's enough for all of us."

Water Under the Bridge

He handed the wedges around to everyone, including Daniel. Thelma took hers and sat down next to my brother. "Isn't this nice?" she asked.

Daniel had a troubled look on his face, but he said, "Sure is!" I looked up and caught a frown crossing Papa's face, but he bit into his own slice of the melon.

"Mr. Pirtle gave it to me," Papa said. "He has acres of watermelon. I've been thinking we ought to move closer to Phoenix. You can grow anything there—two crops a year. They irrigate. Canals are being built to divert the water from the Colorado River."

No one looked up from eating the fruit. We'd become accustomed to Papa's elaborate plans, most of which never came to be. We also knew that he made all the decisions in the family, so he would do whatever pleased him anyway. But, while he was speaking, I noticed Mr. And Mrs. Overberg exchanging glances and I wondered what that could mean.

Maybe they'll move to Phoenix, I thought hopefully.

Joseph, Daniel, and I saved our watermelon seeds, spitting them into our hands and laying them on the turkey platter to dry. Then we spent the next couple of hours shooting them with our thumbs and forefingers at each other. We chased around the yard until it was too dark to see and then Daniel said, "Time for me to go, little sis."

"When're you coming back?" I asked, walking him to the gate.

"Oh, I'll be around again soon," he said. He leaned over and gave me a hug, and then he headed down the road that led to town—alone.

CHAPTER SIXTEEN—A NIGHT STROLL

Around midnight or so, I awoke suddenly with an urgent need to use the outhouse. I lay still and put off the trip as long as I could, but finally resigned myself to getting out of my comfortable pallet to go out. I started to tiptoe through the dining room door, but changed my mind, remembering that sleeping boys would obstruct the path.

Silently, I unhooked the screen door and slipped out onto the front porch and into the dark night. Millions of stars shone brightly and I imagined that the Big Dipper winked at me. On the front stoop, I paused before heading out towards the backyard.

There's nothing to be afraid of, I reasoned. Night was the same as day out in the country. But just to be on the safe side, I held close to the side of the house as long as possible. When I reached the corner and stood a mere twenty feet or so from the outhouse, I started across the yard, but suddenly realized how dark the outhouse would be and also that no one could see me where I stood. I looked around and then hitched up my nightgown and squatted, relieving myself in the sandy soil.

Guiltily, I stood and took another look back at the house. It remained completely dark. All the kerosene lamps had been extinguished hours before. Both relieved and anxious, I again hugged the shadows as I made my way toward the front door.

Then, just as I passed the kitchen window, I heard a man's voice, low—almost a whisper. I froze in my tracks and my mouth went dry, but then I heard him again and realized that it was only Papa.

I paused, expecting to hear Mama's voice, too. I wondered why they were up whispering in the kitchen in the dark. Instead, I heard a giggle, a girlish giggle, and then the man's voice again—low and murmuring. It was Thelma and Papa.

Confused, I stood still in my place beneath the window. I could hear breathing and something that sounded like a soft moan. It seemed very secretive and, in a flash, brought back to my mind a memory of something I thought I'd forgotten.

One night when I was very small, maybe three or four, I'd been awakened by strange noises from Mama's and Papa's room. I got up out of my bed and found the door open enough for me to peek inside. At first I thought they were wrestling, but as I watched, I slowly began to understand that was something else, something private.

The next morning, I asked Mama what they'd been doing and her face instantly turned red with embarrassment. That very day, she moved their bed to the other side of the room. Their bedroom door had always been shut tightly since then, so that not a flicker of light could escape.

I didn't quite understand the connection between this situation and that long ago event, but I had the same sense of forbidden discovery. With my heart pounding, I inched past the window and made my way quietly to my pallet. As I slid between the sheets, I thought how fortunate I was on two counts: not to have been caught relieving myself in the yard or caught eavesdropping on Papa.

I lay quietly until the sky began to lighten, trying not to imagine what had been going on in our kitchen, and knowing with certainty that Mama would not approve. I wanted to understand, but knew better than to reveal to Mama that I'd been listening through the window. I finally decided it should be a matter best left for the adults.

Fortunately, school and chores kept my mind and body occupied every waking moment for the next several days. The weather had improved and I longed to spend my days outdoors instead of in Miss Barnes' classroom. I always enjoyed the days of early May and the fresh, clean air that lasted such a short while before the heat stayed the copper fumes on Claypool.

CHAPTER SEVENTEEN—BETRAYED

On the last day of the school year, I walked home with Aileen and Joseph. Something had been puzzling to me all during the day. It was strange that James would miss on the last day of school. I turned to them.

"James didn't come to school today. I wonder why. He's usually late but today he didn't show up at all."

They didn't appear interested. James and I had kept a respectable distance between us since the event with the spiders, which suited me fine. As we rounded the corner before our gate, I stopped in my tracks. Unusual activity surrounded the Overberg's car, parked haphazardly, as close as possible to our front fence.

Mr. Overberg and James each loaded a bundle of something into the back seat

'Look, look. They're leaving!" I screamed, "Yippee!" I let out a whoop of joy, recalling the account of David from the Bible dancing in the street when he came home from battle. I grabbed Aileen's arm and tried to pull her into a dance.

"What on earth is the matter with you, Amelia?" Aileen asked, removing my hand.

"Don't you see?" I practically squealed with delight. "They're packing up. We're going to have our room back!"

We'd barely had time to enjoy our new bedroom before the Overberg family invaded our home. A few weeks earlier, Mama had decorated it with blue print curtains and matching bedspread

The day our family had made the long trip over the tall mountains from Lehi to Claypool, Aileen and I had expressed sadness. We hated to leave our friends. Mama had consoled us by displaying the fabric she'd set aside for our bedding and describing how she would decorate our new bedroom. I had thought it lovely fabric, but after seeing Blanca's room, I'd secretly planned to ask Mama to make a change.

Aileen's brow furrowed and she quickened her step. I struggled to catch up.

"Shucks, Aileen. Aren't you glad?" I asked, puffing. "They've been here forever!"

"Oh, no. We should hurry, Amelia," she said softly. "I want to tell Thelma goodbye." Then she broke into a run.

"Well, go ahead," I called after her. I looked over at Joseph who ambled along unusually quiet. He nodded.

The two of us dawdled as we watched our sister race up the path toward the house. In our line of vision, we saw Mama step out the kitchen door. She wore her faded blue gingham work dress. Suddenly she staggered to the porch railing and leaned over it, as if she might faint.

"Mama!" I screamed. Joseph and I both broke into a hard run.

Mama raised her left hand and placed it on her chest.

Aileen got to her first. She dashed past Mr. and Mrs. Overberg, jumped up the porch steps and draped her arms around Mama.

Joseph runs faster than I do. I watched as his wavy dark hair bounced and his long stride reminded me of Papa's. He reached Mama's side several seconds ahead of me and he and Aileen helped Mama into the house. I followed.

"Oh dear. Do you want a doctor?" Aileen asked, guiding her towards a chair beside the kitchen table.

"A doctor? No!" Mama shook her head firmly. "Just hand me a wet cloth for my head, please."

I ran to the sink to dampen a clean dishcloth. I wondered why the Overbergs didn't help. They couldn't help seeing Mama on the porch—they stood close by.

"I've had a bad shock, that's all, but I'll be all right," Mama said. "You needn't worry, child."

She avoided eye contact with me and when I handed her the cloth, her hands shook visibly. She rubbed the damp cloth over her face and held it in place on her forehead a moment.

"Let me help you lie down, Mama," Joseph offered. All color had drained from his normally tanned face.

Mama stood up shakily and Joseph took a couple of steps toward Aileen's and my room, but Mama didn't follow. He stopped and looked at her quizzically.

She dropped into the chair again. "You're going to find out soon enough anyway," she said. "I might as well tell you. The Overbergs are moving out, but Thelma isn't going with them." Her hands rose to her hair in her familiar way, but stopped before her fingers reached the hairpins and dropped limply into her lap.

She looked at each of us in turn for a moment. When her eyes fell on me, I couldn't wait.

"Land sakes. What's wrong? Why not?" I blurted.

Aileen sank into the chair beside Mama and buried her face in her hands.

"Did something happen to Papa?" Joseph asked.

"No, your father is fine," Mama said. Her voice had no emotion in it.

"Where's Thelma? Did you say she's staying?" Joseph asked, startling all of us with the angry tone of his question. Mama seemed to be struggling for words.

"Oh, I saw them as I ran up the hill," Aileen said. "The two of them drove off in Papa's car."

"Where'd they go?" I asked. "Tell me! Where's Papa taking Thelma?"

"It doesn't matter where," Mama said. "And I don't know or care if he returns." She bit her lip and stood. Then she turned her back to us and went to the sink where she started rearranging items on the windowsill. I knew she wished for dirty dishes, or busy work, but our kitchen was spotless. She walked to the cabinet and we watched as she cradled her big mixing bowl in her arms and opened the door to the flour sifter.

"But, Mama . . ." I said. I felt like everyone understood something I'd missed.

"Amelia," she said wearily. "Please don't ask any questions. I need to gather my thoughts. There's nothing you children should worry about. This is not about you. Please, just help me prepare supper."

In the icebox, I found a bowl of freshly churned butter and set it on the oilcloth in the center of the table. Aileen placed a pitcher of milk in front of Mama. Then she started assembling other ingredients: lard, baking powder, baking soda, and salt. No one spoke. We four had become machines, hoping routine could bring normalcy to our lives.

"Are we having biscuits?" I asked weakly, trying to make conversation.

Mama didn't answer. She poured the ingredients into the large blue mixing bowl.

Aileen opened the oven and peeked inside. For the first time I smelled the roast beef. Papa's favorite. Mama had planned a very nice meal for the Overbergs' departure, I thought.

Mrs. Overberg hastened past us in the kitchen with her head down, opened the bedroom door, and disappeared from our sight. Moments later she returned, with a bag in her arm. "Forgot this," she mumbled with a look of apology and slipped out the door into the yard.

My heart sank as Mama reached up with flour-dusted hands and adjusted her braids, leaving a trail of powder on her cheek and in her hair—the hair that Papa called "Mama's glory."

"Why don't you lie down, Mama?" Aileen said. "I can finish dinner."

"Everything's ready," Mama said. "We'll just wait for the biscuits to brown."

"Then come with me," Aileen suggested softly. "Let me brush your hair for you. Remember how you used to brush mine before you rolled the strands in rag curlers? It felt so good. Come with me, Mama."

I looked at Aileen, incredulous. At twelve years of age, here she was treating Mama like Mama was her child. But together, with Joseph's help, my sister got Mama into the bedroom and left me alone in the kitchen.

I felt pleased that the Overbergs would finally be gone, but then something Mama said came back to me, "Thelma is not going with them."

Suddenly my recent night trip toward the outhouse flashed into my mind—the girlish giggles I'd overheard—the strange manly sounds that came from Papa. My heart started pounding like it did on that night and my face felt like fire. Suddenly I grasped what was wrong with my mama. Thelma was staying—with Papa. And Mama knew!

At the same time, I realized something else—something awful. I could have prevented it.

I'd heard them together. I should've warned Mama. If I'd only told her, she might have been able to do something.

I took off, letting the screen door slam angrily behind me. The Overberg children, including James, were sitting in their car looking somber. "Goodbye, Amelia," James called out, for the first time using my given name without a slur.

I didn't answer. Instead, I ran randomly to the chicken coop and the hens started a ruckus. I leaned on the fence.

Water Under the Bridge

Papa—and Thelma? How could he? How could she? She wasn't much older than Aileen. Younger than Daniel.

Mr. Overberg's motor started, but I didn't turn around. I listened while the car backed away from the fence and pulled onto the road that led past the Wallaces' house.

"Don't come back," I snarled under my breath. Then I realized I meant Papa, too. Just drive off with Thelma and leave us forever! We don't want either of you.

Then to Thelma, I added, "Why did you have to come here and ruin everything? I hate you!"

But something deep inside seemed to whisper, *You don't really hate her.* And then the voice added, *besides, it's your fault.*

Verna Simms

CHAPTER EIGHTEEN—RUN, AMELIA, RUN

After a while, I walked back to the house, taking the long way around to the parlor door where I let myself in quietly. I tiptoed to my pallet and kneeled against the davenport and tried to pray, but no words came. I fell on my back staring at Mama's wall painting. Somehow the beautiful waterfall made me angrier with Papa. It seemed ruined. In my misery, I could see no beauty in anything.

One fine spring day, I told myself, as a light breeze ruffled the parlor curtains, Amelia Hall lost her family. It would never go back the way it was—the way we were before the Overbergs came. The way we were yesterday. The way we were this very morning! Never!

I counted all the losses that had, amazingly, occurred in one short day. Mama had lost Papa—and I had lost him, too. I never wanted to see him again and vowed I would just pretend him dead. In a way, I thought, I've lost Mama, too, at least the way she'd been before. Somehow I knew things could never be the same with Mama and Papa and us again.

In the deep place inside where I reviewed all the things that were closest to my heart, something else was missing. I felt an awful emptiness like a hole in my stomach, one that no amount of food would ever satisfy.

Suddenly I sat straight up. An urge to get away overcame me. I couldn't bear to face Papa when he returned, if he returned. I felt I could never carry my secret knowledge of his night in the kitchen with Thelma—not now.

It might kill Mama to know, I thought, remembering how she staggered on the porch and held her hand to her heart.

I pulled the cover off my pillow. I rolled up my bedding as small as I could make it. Then, gathering the bundle in my arms I tiptoed outside, closing the front screen door quietly behind me.

My feet flew across the dusty yard and made a sudden veer to the right, past the house, to the wooden back gate that led to the mountain. Quickly, I pulled the rope off the post and slipped through the opening.

I hate men, I avowed, starting up the incline. After only a dozen steps or so and despite the bundle in my arms, I broke into a run. I could hear stones rolling down behind me and the sound was strangely comforting.

"How could you? I screamed into the spring air on the mountain. How could you take Thelma over Mama? How could you do that to her? To us?"

I had barely covered half the ground to the acacia tree when a sharp stitch in my side forced me to sit down on my bundle and catch my breath. From where I crouched, our entire property was visible: the roof of our house and it's back side, the well, the chicken coop, the tool shed, the road that ran alongside our property and connected us to the Wallaces', the two gates, one that led to my school and the other that ushered me up the mountain. Suddenly it all seemed like a photograph—a picture from history. Amelia's old home, I thought.

Then I became aware of the wetness on my dress from the tears that had been rolling down my cheeks and pooling there.

My throat felt parched. I forced myself to my feet and dragged my bedding the rest of the way to Joseph's and my thorny, but welcoming, acacia tree. Leaning against the rugged old trunk, I jerked the hated high-top shoes and black stockings from my feet.

I rolled the despised black horrors into a ball and stuffed one inside each shoe. There I sat wiggling my toes in the air and feeling very unsure of my next move. I'd never thought to run away before and had no plan.

But every time my thoughts returned to Papa and Thelma and the prospect of facing Mama with my terrible secret, the hard rock in my throat ached and I knew I couldn't go back.

Papa did this, I thought, as anger welled in me once more. He chased Daniel away and now he's going to run Mama off. I wondered how he would explain this to God, the same God that heard his frequent long prayers. The God that he credited for all our good fortune in having a home and food on the table. The God that made Aileen and me wear black stockings!

Aileen and I had said our prayers every night as long as I could remember and where had they gotten us? Our papa had betrayed our mama.

Water Under the Bridge

I picked up my high-top shoes, one in each hand, and heaved them as hard as I could toward the house. I watched them tumble through the air and hit the ground, bouncing separately until they disappeared into the sagebrush below.

"I hate you! I hate you! I hate you!" I screamed, not sure who I meant; the shoes, Papa, Thelma, the Overbergs . . . or me?

Verna Simms

CHAPTER NINETEEN—RESCUED

Hours later, I huddled against the tree wrapped in my blanket. I wished I'd thought to bring food and more clothing. The stars gave off an astonishing amount of light in the inky blackness of the sky. Despite the chill and my wariness about being alone, sleep began to overtake me. I struggled to keep both eyes open, but no use.

A twig cracked. My heart pounded. Then I heard a scuffing, crunching, rhythmic sound that seemed to be coming closer. In terror, I held my breath and squeezed my eyes shut. Rolled up, as I was, in my blanket, I knew it wouldn't be wise to jump up and attempt to run. It could be a mountain lion. My only option was to play dead and hope to do so convincingly.

Suddenly something grabbed me. I felt myself lifted up in the air. Fear prevented me from opening my eyes and so engulfed me that I went limp. This thing was clearly a person holding me tightly.

I dared to open one eye a peek and looked straight into Papa's face and began to sob.

"Shh, child, Papa's here," he whispered. "I'm taking you home, Amelia. Everything will be okay."

In the starlight, his face looked kind and tender, and he drew me into his chest and cradled me like a baby as he lumbered down the mountain trail. No other words were spoken.

When we arrived at the kitchen door, Mama opened it and he carried me past her and through the dining room, all the way to my pallet in the parlor. He kissed me on the forehead as he laid me gently on the floor.

In utter confusion, I lay still, grappling with my feelings, unsure of the future. What should I do? Perhaps if I closed my eyes, I could imagine everything was normal. The Overbergs are gone. Mama and Papa are at home with me, Aileen and Joseph. If only Daniel had been here, my fantasy would have been complete. But there was someone extra to consider, too. Thelma.

I knew things were not normal, whatever normal was. Things hadn't been normal since the day I started school and the Overbergs arrived. I'd been hoping and praying for the day they would leave, never realizing that it would hasten a calamity, that Papa would keep Thelma for himself and betray Mama.

"Good night, Amelia," Mama said. She leaned over and patted my head. Then she turned down the wick and extinguished the light.

I rolled on my side to face the stars still gleaming like diamonds in the black sky. I didn't know what to do about Papa. I realized I didn't really hate him. I just hated what he'd done.

Just put it out of your mind, I told myself, lacking other options.

I awakened next morning to a glare in my face. I sat up and noticed the source. The sun reflected off Mama's prized possession, a large bronze mirror that once adorned Aileen's and my bedroom. The mirror now stood majestically in the corner of the parlor. I could tell that the morning was gone and without thinking, I jumped up, worried that I had wasted a precious Saturday morning sleeping. Then I remembered the events of the day before and a cold, sick feeling invaded me.

On the davenport next to my pallet I saw my high-topped shoes, freshly polished and with new buttons replacing the ones I'd ripped off the night before. My mind felt stunned and not ready to sort out my feelings about the new developments in our family.

The house remained strangely quiet—the quietest it had been in many, many months with no children crying and apparently no one in the house.

CHAPTER TWENTY—DANIEL

I called, "Mama, Joe, Ailie!" No answer. Then I stepped out the kitchen door and headed for the outhouse. On my way back, I spotted Daniel stacking lumber behind the tool shed.

"Hey Dan," I called, "Where's everyone?"

"Hey. yourself. There's Mama now," he said, pointing up the road toward the Wallaces'.

Mama walked alone toward the house. I suspected she had confided her troubles to her good neighbor friend, Mrs. Wallace. I watched as she slowly crossed the edge of our yard and made her way to the porch. When she saw Daniel and me watching her, she waved and smiled before going inside.

"Land sakes, I'm glad you finally surfaced," he said. "Aileen told me you had quite a night."

With no words to describe it, I sat down on the bench near the door of the lean-to and pulled my knees up. I rested my chin on them.

"Don't worry yourself, child. Everything will be okay, Amelia," he said. "What's done is done and I feel badly for Mama. I'm not ready to forgive Papa—or Thelma either, but somehow we'll get through this and things will work themselves out. I promise." He gave me a bear hug.

The two of us sat together with our own thoughts for a while. Then I asked, "Did you get a job?"

"Yesiree, you bet I did," Daniel said brightly. "Mr. Wallace hired me to work on his cabin. He's building high on the southeast side of the mountain. It's a long walk from there to here, but I mean to buy a car soon. The cabin is already under roof so he's letting me sleep in it, too. Isn't that neat?"

"I wish you could live here," I sighed. "Maybe Papa would let you come back now."

"What do you mean?" Daniel asked.

"I just mean, now that he has Thel—," I halted, remembering that Daniel didn't know I'd witnessed his fight with Papa.

"What do you know, Amelia?" Daniel asked, "And more important, how do you know it? Did Thelma say something to you?"

"Heck, no," I said, quickly. "I don't know anything. Really, I don't!"

"Well, you seem to know something," Daniel said. "Just make sure you keep it yourself. Don't let Papa think I tattled. He's only tolerating me coming around now because of Mama," he gave a slight chuckle. "Which is the same reason I'm tolerating him. If it weren't for you and Mama and the others, I'd leave and never be back. He'd be right happy about that, but I'll never give him the satisfaction."

Then, noticing my worried face, he patted my leg and said, "Hey, guess what? I have a secret."

That got my attention. I looked up at him, searching his blue eyes for a clue. "A secret? What?" I asked.

He leaned over and whispered in my ear, "Sure is a nice day, isn't it?"

"Tell me!" I said, hitting him on the thigh.

"Okay," he said, laughing. "But you must keep it to yourself. I want to be the one to tell Mama. Promise?"

"Sure. I promise," I said.

"I'm buying land." He pointed to the southeast.

"Oh, you already told me that," I said, disappointed.

"Oh no, this is different. That was dreaming for the future. I'm actually buying today. I already bought it, in a manner of speaking. I'll finish paying for it soon."

"Really?" I said. "Land of your very own? Where is it? Can I see it?"

"Right up there," he pointed again toward the southeast side of the mountain. "And yes, you can see it, but not today."

"Gee whiz. How'd you manage that?" I asked.

"The Overbergs decided against living in Claypool. They moved to Phoenix. Mr. Overberg has an office job of some sort. Papa told me to forget about the money he owed me as he'd spent it." He crossed his leg and rocked a little as he spoke. This was a habit he'd had since childhood, according to Mama. She'd always said Daniel couldn't sit still.

"I wouldn't have been upset if he'd told me earlier, but he kept working me—without a salary. I thought he might cut back what he'd agreed to pay, but I didn't get a penny."

"Shucks. So then how did you buy your lot?" I asked.

"Mr. Wallace agreed I could pay for it by working on his cabin and later doing some other jobs at his town house. Half of what I earn is going toward the price."

"But he's not Mormon," I reminded him.

"No, he's not Mormon," Daniel said. "That's a fact. I don't happen to agree that I should only work or buy on credit from Mormons. There's not enough work around for Mormons to hire everyone who wants a job."

Then he smiled a mischievous smile. "That's not the only secret I have," he said.

"Tell me!"

"Okay. Well, I've been thinking about something you said not long ago. Remember when we talked about a tree house?"

"Yes!"

"I've a plan to build me a tree house on my land—just until I have enough money and lumber stocked up to start a proper structure. What do you think of that idea?"

"A tree house? Oh, goody." I squealed, jumping up and down clapping my hands. "Can I use it, too?"

"Yes, ma'am," Daniel got up and grabbed my hand. "Climb up here," he said, helping me onto the bench. Then he pointed back at the mountain. "It's really not too far for you to walk on a good day if Joseph's with you. See that rock way up yonder behind the ridge? You have to pass it. Then it's half a mile beyond."

I imagined Joseph and me climbing the steep incline. We'll have to get up early in the morning, I thought.

"I'm going to live in it," Daniel said.

"In the tree house?"

"Yes! I'll be finished with Mr. Wallace's cabin before long and I'll need a place to stay while I'm working on his place. It occurred to me that I could make do in a tree house for a while."

"How many windows will you have?" I asked, picturing the elaborate structure Joseph and I had fantasized about building. "I like lots of windows."

An apologetic smile showed me his slightly crooked white teeth, "No windows or roof, I'm afraid," he said. "Just a platform—about ten feet up between two trees."

He shaded his eyes and studied the sky in the direction of his land. "I'm going to stretch a hammock between the trees and build a platform above it. It will give me a place to sit and double as a roof when I sleep. It'll help keep the rain off. Clever, huh?"

His face became dreamy as he stretched high and cut a wee twig from the cottonwood tree and whittled a toothpick. I heard a dog bark in the distance. It sounded like Mr. Jones' dog, Brownie. Somehow the fact that Papa was afraid of dogs suddenly entered my mind. Why?

"Remember the two months we lived camping in the desert?" Daniel said, trying to dislodge a seed from his teeth.

I nodded.

"I learned to enjoy sleeping under the stars that summer. You were only three or four. I'm surprised you remember."

"I've forgotten some, but I can still see Mama cutting the light brown curls from Ailie's head. I was surprised they stayed curly as they lay in the sand. I picked up all I could carry. Stuck them in my pocket."

"Oh, yes," Daniel replied. He patted my head. "We needed to haul every drop of water we used. Short hair is easier to take care of." Again he gazed into the sky. Hawks soared high above. "I'm going to learn to fly an aeroplane someday. Imagine zooming through the sky like a bird with the wind in your face." His square face shone with a faraway, dreamy look.

He stood up then and said, "I must return to the mountain now before Papa rolls in. I bet you're hungry, aren't you?"

"Yes," I admitted. "Come back and see me again soon, okay?"

"You can bet on it," he said. Then he got up and started toward the gate that led to the mountain. I felt sad as I watched him go high above us. I ran to catch up with him again.

"What about flying?" I asked. "Are you still going to learn to fly a plane?"

"Yes," he said. "You bet your bottom dollar. I'm going to be a pilot someday, but for now, I must build a home of my own. I need a place to live first."

"Well, I'm going to move to a big city and be a rich lawyer," I announced proudly. "I'm going to own two homes, just like Mr. Wallace, both with running water right in the kitchen and a bedroom for each one of my children."

Water Under the Bridge

"Amelia, you beat all!" Daniel said, laughing. "Girls aren't lawyers. How did you even know about lawyers?"

"Miss Barnes told me," I said. "She told us we'd be electing a president this year and we must all remind our mamas to vote. Did you know that Arizona allowed women to vote in 1912, but the state of Missouri where Mama lived didn't pass a law to let females vote until 1919? Mama didn't get to vote. That was before I was born. I'll vote all the time when I'm grown. That way we can have a say in how the country is run. Mama told me women worked to pass that law and some became lawyers. She said women go to college and become all kinds of things that only men used to be."

Daniel laughed and mussed my hair, a gesture that I usually loved, but today it made me angry. "I'm going to vote that boys can't be lawyers anymore," I said, stomping the ground and feeling my fury heat up and rise into my cheeks.

"So there!" I stomped off to the house where I snatched biscuits from the Mother Hubbard cabinet. I crammed them into my mouth so fast I almost choked until I could gulp a bit of water. I slumped down on the davenport in the parlor, hoping to find Aileen or Joseph.

Verna Simms

CHAPTER TWENTY-ONE—ARRANGING FURNITURE

Aileen's pallet had been put away, leaving her area behind the davenport neat as a pin. Mine, on the other hand, was a mess of rumpled blankets. I knelt down, folded my bedding, and stowed it beneath the davenport.

I ran my fingers around the davenport's carved wood trim and over its smooth curved legs. It had been a wedding gift from Mama's papa. That day he told Mama that it would be the first fine piece of furniture for her home with Papa. It was still the best piece of furniture we owned.

Mama came to the door and said, "Good! I want you to clean up your bedding." She carried an armload of clothing.

"Where're Ailie and Joe?" I asked.

"Joseph's playing with Billy and Aileen went with me up to Mrs. Wallace's house. They've been canning. Aileen stayed to help. She should be back any minute."

"When she gets home, may we move back into our room?"

A shadow crossed my mama's face. "No, I'm afraid not," she said. "Papa and Thelma will be using that room, Amelia. You and Aileen must think of this as your room—at least for the foreseeable future."

"But the Overbergs are gone . . ." I stopped, realization slowly coming to me. Papa would not be sleeping with Mama anymore. Thelma would be sharing his bed.

I became aware of the screen door slamming shut in the kitchen.

Seeing the pained expression on my mother's face, I quickly said, "May we rearrange this room better?" I wanted something to do, something that would take my mind off our family and give me more control over my life.

"Joseph's going to be sleeping in the dining room," Aileen announced, coming into the room. She'd obviously overheard part of our conversation.

Mama let out a pent-up breath and waved her hands as if to throw the matter at us—more a gesture of defeat. "Do whatever the two of you decide," she said wearily. She carried the clothing into the dining room and began sorting and folding them. I could hear her talking to herself. "Just as well. We've no need of a parlor. I should offer the davenport to Mrs. Wallace. She admires it." Then she added, "I'm too ashamed to have company now anyway."

Aileen looked at me and shook her head.

"Come on, Sis, let's rearrange our pallets," I suggested. "I don't like being jammed against the wall."

"Okay," Aileen agreed. She took a pad of paper and a pencil from the drawer of the library table. "I'll draw the room first. That way, we'll see how it'll look before we move the heavy furniture."

"Let me get scissors!" I jumped up and opened the drawer to find the scissors. "I can make cut-outs of all the furniture."

Aileen handed me her pad and pencil and I carefully drew the outline of each piece of furniture in the room, as if seeing it looking down from the ceiling. Then I cut them out.

"Okay," I said. "Bring your paper and we'll see where to place the furniture."

"Oh Amelia, you silly goose!" Aileen said, laughing. "You drew them too large. They cover the whole room!"

It was true. I'd been so focused on the shapes that I'd failed to notice the size of the paper. I started giggling at how ridiculous the gigantic davenport looked. "There's no room for us," I said, grinning at Aileen.

"No room at all!" she said back, doubling over to grab her sides. Suddenly we were both on the floor, rolling around, hysterical with laughter.

Joseph came in. He couldn't help but grin himself, seeing us. "What's so funny?"

"We're . . . we're . . ." Aileen tried, but she couldn't stop laughing. "We're rearranging the furniture."

"Yes," I giggled uncontrollably. "Mama said we could."

Joseph looked at us, puzzled.

"Here," said Aileen, picking up the paper and letting it bend slightly to hold the paper cutouts from falling. "Amelia made a plan." She turned toward me and doubled over again.

"It's not that funny," Joseph said, taking the paper to study it. Then his face took on a serious expression.

"If you use the davenport to divide the room in half," he said, "it will seem like two small rooms."

He took the scissors and trimmed each of my cutouts to about half their original size. Then he slid the miniature davenport, chair and table onto the paper to show us what he meant. "See? The sofa could be a dividing wall."

Aileen and I had sobered up by then. She said, "Gee, that's a good idea. Which side do you want, Amelia?"

Surveying the real room my eyes rested on the library table. On more than one occasion I had seen Aileen rub her hands reverently across its highly polished oak surface. A vase for cut flowers stood in the center and Aileen always filled it. It was a beautiful piece of furniture with rose-colored glass and a lower shelf held books between two bookends that, together, formed the shape of an elephant. Daniel had won the bookends at a carnival by throwing hoops over a stick.

Mama kept the table covered with an ecru hand-crocheted scarf that her mother had made for her. I walked over and fingered the soft fringe and its nice little tassels on the corners.

Although the side with the table tempted me, I knew Aileen loved it more. My eyes traveled over to the two living room windows, side-by-side. They took up most of the west wall of the room and through them you could see anything going on in the side yard and part of the road. Before I could claim them, Aileen, who had been following my gaze, pointed outside.

"There's Thelma," she said. "Hey, Thelma, come help us!"

Sure enough, Thelma could be seen getting out of the front seat of our car while Papa lumbered over toward the tool shed.

Turning back to the room and my sister, I said, "I don't care about furniture, and I don't care about her."

"Amelia!" Aileen said. "Watch your tongue. What has happened here with Thelma is just as much Papa's doing. We're going to have to make the best of things now. Besides, Thelma has always been nice to you. She's good to all of us."

"Not good to Mama," I said boldly, but I wasn't sure of myself. I wondered how Thelma could have resisted Papa. I wondered how she really felt about him. I also wondered how Aileen could juggle her loyalty to Mama with Thelma's friendship.

I shot a look over to Joseph, hoping he might be of help, but he'd turned toward the door of the parlor when Thelma entered the room.

"We're rearranging furniture," Aileen explained. "Joseph came up with a good idea. We're going to divide the room in half with the davenport, and Amelia and I each get one side to ourselves."

"That's wonderful!" Thelma said, enthusiastically, and I knew she was sincere. As much as I hated to admit it, Thelma didn't have the capacity to be mean or deceptive. Before all the trouble, Mama had admired her, saying, "That girl has a heart of gold and she wears it plainly on her sleeve."

As Aileen and Joseph showed Thelma the drawing for our new bedrooms, I struggled with my thoughts and feelings. If Thelma's not to blame, then Papa is, I decided. But I already knew that. Deep down inside, I'd seen the situation as a result of the sins of three people: Papa and Thelma for getting involved with each other—and me for not trying to stop it.

With Thelma's help, we pushed the heavy davenport to the center of the room. Then Joseph and Aileen carried the table to stand behind it. I brought its chair up to face the table.

"It's lovely," said Thelma, surveying the room, "and there's a lot more space here for both of you now." She turned to me and asked, "May I come and visit you here sometimes?"

Unprepared for her question, I looked down at my hands.

"I'll take this side," Aileen said, indicating the area nearest the windows.

"No," I said, finding my voice. "That table is yours. You like it best."

"Thank you, Amy," she said, beaming. She placed her hand on my shoulder in a gesture of affection. "We'll move the mirror to the back wall where we can share it. You may keep your school papers on my table any time."

"No need," I answered. "I'm going to ask Papa to bring home an orange crate. They give them away free at the grocery store. It'll serve as two shelves for me to set things on."

"I'll help you paint it," Thelma offered. "We could make it look pretty."

Again, I didn't answer, but decided that I didn't blame Thelma as much as I blamed Papa. I wasn't ready to forgive either one of them. Maybe never. I really didn't know.

I avoided her face and went out the front door.

CHAPTER TWENTY-TWO—A VISIT

In the yard, I ran around the side of the house and squeezed into the small vine-covered space that led beneath the house. I longed for Joseph to follow me. We hadn't spent time in our secret hideout for a long time. I wanted to discuss our tree house or maybe to get his thoughts on Papa and Thelma. But he didn't come. Alone in the dark, I took my shoebox from the shelf and examined its contents—my paper doll lay inside with the lucky necklace. I placed it in my hand and rubbed my fingers over the little hole in its stone. It seemed like the man who'd given it to me and the man who'd hurt my mama were two different people.

I missed Blanca so much it hurt. She comforted whenever the problems at home became too hard to bear. Aside from Joseph, who I thought didn't count, she'd become my only playmate.

Things settled into a routine at home. Papa and Mama barely spoke to one another, but separately they acted pleasant to my siblings and me. Mama didn't speak to Thelma anymore. She continued to cook meals for all of us and Thelma washed the dishes after dinner, but Papa stopped drying. He now ran errands, attended to chores around the house, or read his Bible at the dining room table in the evenings.

I believe he knew I harbored anger towards him because he tried to be especially nice to me. One Friday evening he said, "Amelia, you still have your birthday nickel?"

I nodded

"Well, I've errands to run in Miami tomorrow. Maybe you'd enjoy tagging along to spend it. I'll give you another and you'll have ten cents."

I thought the situation over and made an agreement with myself: If Papa will take me to visit Blanca, I'll forgive him.

"Papa," I said. "Would you mind dropping me at my friend's house instead? Blanca is my best friend at school—in the whole world—and I miss her. You could stop for me on your way back."

"I guess that'd be okay," Papa said. "Better ask your mother, though."

Mama gave her approval and I went to bed early that night, trying to hasten the coming of the next day.

Early the following morning, I brushed my impossible hair, and slipped on a school dress, the one with a detachable, wide, white collar and long sleeves that fastened with snaps. I chose it because I could unsnap the hooks and roll the sleeves above my elbows as soon as Papa left me at Blanca's. The blue and yellow print had faded, but I didn't let that bother me.

"Gee whiz, Papa, I'm ready to go." I announced immediately after breakfast.

"Oh yes, Amelia. I did promise to drive you to see your friend, didn't I?" He laid his napkin on the table, pushed his chair back and rose.

Thelma remained seated next to him. She spoke up. "Could I go along? I'd like to stop at the general store on the way back if there's time."

Papa shook his head. "No, not today, Thelma. It's been ages since I've spent time alone with my girl. Today is her day, just the two of us."

Thelma smiled, "Have a good time then."

"What did you learn in school lately?" Papa asked.

"I learned that Arizona is an Indian name that means 'Small Spring.' Do you know where any springs are?" Papa shook his head so I changed the subject and prattled nervously, "Did I tell you Blanca's name means white? I wish she knew I was coming. It'll be awful if no one is home or if they're too busy to let me stay."

"If it doesn't work out, you can ride with me to Miami. I have to see a man about a job there." Then he added, "Someday we'll be able to speak to each other by telephone. They're stringing wire now in Miami. People can talk to others miles away from their homes.

"When I lived in Missouri as a boy we hitched horses to a wagon to travel any distance. Now we drive our own automobile."

His whistling told me was in a jovial mood.

"Would you like to ride in an aeroplane, Papa?" I asked.

"Not really." Papa said. "I'm satisfied to stay close to the ground until the last day when the archangel Gabriel blows his horn and we'll rise up to meet Jesus in the sky. We won't need wings then—and I don't need them now.

Water Under the Bridge

"Maybe I'll invite Blanca and her family to attend Sunday services with us," he announced. "You'd like that, wouldn't you?"

"Oh yes!" I said, clapping my hands. "I could see her every Sunday, then."

When our car braked in front of the Romac's home, I noticed Blanca sitting on the porch. She ran over to greet me.

"Amy!" she squealed, "What a nice surprise!"

"Her name is Amelia," Papa said crossly. I was shaken by his tone and the dour expression on his face.

"Good morning, Mr. Hall," Blanca said. "Thank you for bringing Amelia for a visit."

Papa didn't answer. Instead, he said, "Say hello to your friend, Amelia, we'd best be going soon."

"Going? I thought I'd stay all day with Blanca—if it's okay with her mother."

Just then Mr. Romac stepped out to see who'd stopped a car in front of his house. Recognizing me, he waved. Then he called over, "I'll just be a minute here," and disappeared back inside his house.

"I have to go," Papa said. "Are you coming or going, Amelia, make up your mind."

There was no decision to make, I wanted to stay.

"I'll visit with Blanca," I said, confused.

"Then scoot out. I'll be back at three."

I opened the door and stepped into the yard just as Mr. Romac came down the steps toward us. Papa hit the gas and the car rolled away.

"I hope it's okay if I stay a while," I said. My mind raced. Why did Papa act so rude? Why didn't he want me to stay? Why did hurry away? What about inviting the Romacs to church on Sunday? What happened?

"Your father's in a hurry," Mr. Romac said, slowly shaking his head.

"Well, I guess so. He said something about looking for a job," I answered.

Blanca reached for my hand, "Let's go inside. Mama'll be thrilled to see you!"

Later, when I was alone with Blanca, she said, "Are you okay? How's your mother doing?"

I looked at her closely. She always guessed my troubles. I wondered about telling her what had happened at home, but I hesitated against it. Did I really want to confide in her the terrible things Papa had done?

"We're okay." I hedged and changed the subject to other family members.

"Dan no longer works with Papa constructing houses. He's lives on his own up on the mountain. He bought a lot and plans to build a house, but first he's going to build a tree house!"

"That's wonderful," Blanca said without enthusiasm.

"Ailie and Joe are fine. Joe spends all his time at Billy Farmer's house."

"Are the Overbergs still living with you?" Blanca asked.

"No, they moved out."

"So you and Aileen moved into your bedroom?" she persisted as I stood. Her questions disturbed me.

"Can we play with your doll house?" I asked, changing the subject.

"If you want to." Blanca paused a moment before asking, "Did Thelma move, too?"

I moseyed over to the dollhouse and chose the blonde-haired doll and examined her in my hands. I opened the small doll-sized trunk and sorted through all the lovely dresses. I needed to choose something bright and cheery. I loved Blanca dearly but wished she'd stop prying and play—or talk of something else. I could hear her mom singing softly in another room. I felt I had slipped into another world.

"She's not a bad person, Amelia," Blanca said. "You'll find that out. You must forgive her."

"Who told you?" Blanca's insight boggled my mind.

"No one told me anything," she said, moving away from the door as if she might be overheard. She lowered her voice to a whisper. "Sometimes I just know things."

We enjoyed the next hour playing with the dollhouse until Mrs. Romac called us to lunch.

Later, in the back yard Blanca offered, "Wanna swing?"

A tire swing hung from an old oak tree. I'd never seen anything like it before. As usual Blanca invited me to have first turn. I tried to see how high I could push before jumping to the ground and then relinquishing the swing. I studied to see how it had been made, hoping Joseph would help me make one in our yard.

At three o'clock sharp, Papa pulled up in front of the Romacs' house and honked the horn.

"Goodbye," I called. "I hope you can visit me, too."

"I doubt your papa would agree," Blanca said. "But you come here anytime, Amelia. You're my best friend."

Water Under the Bridge

On the way home, Papa kept his hands on the wheel in stony silence. I sat scrunched on my side of the car, unsure what had made him angry and decided not to ask. Finally we pulled onto the road that led past the Wallaces' home to our house. As we turned into our driveway, he stared into my eyes, "I hope you had a nice visit, Amelia, but you'll not be going again."

"Why?" I stammered, "Why not?"

"Because I said so, that's why," he answered with finality.

CHAPTER TWENTY-THREE—THELMA AND PAPA

Papa and Thelma shared the bedroom that had once belonged to Aileen and me, and Mama kept her original room to herself. Neither she, nor we children, ever spoke of it.

It became clear that Mama no longer loved Papa as she once had. Over dinner when he launched into one of his sermons, I often caught her giving him a look of disdain; when she left the kitchen and walked down the hall to bed at night, she made a noisy show of locking her bedroom door.

Papa appeared more conscientious of Mama than he'd ever been before. He wouldn't make any decisions concerning us children without her approval. He often ordered Thelma to do more chores. "Help Ida with the laundry," he'd say. But Mama would have none of that. "If I need help, I'll ask my children," she said.

One evening at supper, Papa said, "I'm tired. Thelma and I are going to turn in early." Then I saw him wink at Thelma.

Mama saw it, too. She stood up from the dinner table, "Well, I'm tired, too. I am so tired, you can't imagine." In an angry tone of voice she added, "I hope you children never get so tired as to share your bed with someone of the opposite sex—without the sanctity of marriage."

We didn't dare glance at Papa, so Aileen and Joseph and I all busied ourselves with our meal. Thelma got up from her place and quietly drifted out the kitchen door. Papa followed.

"I'll wash dishes tonight," Aileen offered standing with her plate in her hand.

"No," Mama said, "Thank you, but I'd rather clean the kitchen myself. You find something else to do."

Aileen hesitated before going out on the porch. I finished my dinner and gulped down the last of my milk. When I took my plate to the sink, I saw Thelma and Aileen walking up the road together. Papa was nowhere to be seen.

"Want to go up the mountain?" I asked Joseph.

"No, Billy invited me over after dinner for cake. It's his birthday," Joseph said.

So I headed down to my secret place beneath the house.

I had no sooner reached the wall and taken down my box of treasures when I heard angry voices inside the house above me. I couldn't make out all the words, but I heard Papa shout, "This is my house" and "my children." I only understood one word from Mama: "hypocrite," and then I heard a loud crash.

As fast as I could, I crawled out and came around the side of the house. Mama stood, legs apart, vigorously sweeping the porch as if she were chasing demons from the premises.

Papa stormed out the screen door and let it slam shut loudly behind him. As he passed Mama, I saw her raise the broom as if she was going to crack him over the head, but suddenly seeing me standing below, she swung around and stabbed its bristles at the corner of the porch roof, where the porch met the house.

"Spider webs!" She glared at me.

Papa didn't notice. He'd stepped next to the car and waited, watching Aileen and Thelma on their way back from their walk.

"Thelma, get over here," Papa ordered.

She obeyed, but stood uncertainly near the back of the car.

Papa frowned, his face flushed a dark red with fury. He stomped over and up the steps and to the water pail where he lifted out a dipper of water.

I meandered up the steps, too, then and saw him take a long drink, his Adam's apple bobbing up and down as he swallowed the deep gulps of water. He handed the dipper to me.

"We're heading to town," he said. "Get in the car, Thelma. Hurry up."

"Do you want me to buy groceries, Mrs. Hall?" Thelma asked. She hesitated, looking at Papa before adding, "You need anything else? I remember you broke a hairpin last week."

"I am perfectly capable of doing my own shopping," Mama said.

Papa grabbed Thelma by the elbow and almost dragged her to the side of the car. Then he opened the door and shoved her inside.

Water Under the Bridge

We watched the Model T turn around and disappear down the road.

Mama collapsed onto the bench and put her hands in her face. I could tell by the way her shoulders heaved that she was crying. Aileen sat down beside her and started patting her back.

About a week later, Mama and I sat on the front porch matching socks. Papa had taken Joseph to town with him, leaving Thelma alone. She closeted herself in their bedroom with the door shut most of the time, but occasionally she and Aileen would walk around the neighborhood together. Perhaps I should have felt sorry for the young girl, finding herself in the middle of adult quarreling, but I'm ashamed to say I didn't. Hadn't it been her own doing—choosing Papa over Daniel?

"My goodness, Sis, How can you be friends with her?" I asked Aileen one day.

"She's not any different than before," Aileen said. "She's my friend. Besides, she's going to be living with us and we must make the best of it."

"But what about Mama?" I asked.

"Mama understands," Aileen said, "we talked about it. She told me I should make my own decisions about Thelma and Papa."

Verna Simms

CHAPTER TWENTY-FOUR—MAIL

As I sat and petted the cat, I noticed the mailman walking up our street. He stopped at our front gate. Mama rose to meet him. "Good evening," he said, touching the bill of his cap as he handed her a white envelope. She took it and went into the house.

"Mama!" I called after her, leaving Martha behind.

She was seated at the kitchen table reading a letter several pages long. When I approached, she got up and went into the dining room. I followed.

"Amelia, go find something to do," she said.

"But who's it from?" I asked.

"Uncle Willie," she said. "Now leave me be so I can read."

I sensed that Mama was being secretive. She usually shared the letters that came from Missouri. I went back into the kitchen and took a couple of cookies from the jar in the Old Mother Hubbard cabinet. I sat down at the table to eat them. After a few minutes, I heard Mama go into the parlor where I could make out a drawer opening and shutting.

Thelma came out of the bedroom then and said, "Oh, I'm sorry. I thought Chester had come back." She turned and went back into the bedroom and shut the door.

"I'll finish matching the socks, Amelia," Mama said. "Then I'm going to turn in. I trust you can put yourself to bed on time?"

"Yes, Mama," I said. I could hear the chickens cackling outside, but otherwise the house was eerily quiet. I admit I almost wished for James and his family back. At least then Mama seemed happy. I decided to join the chickens outdoors. I wondered if one of the hens was setting. I'd be nice to have a few wee chicks running around, scratching in the sand. I loved nature.

I busied myself outdoors until Joseph returned at dusk. Then we both came in to the parlor where Aileen already lay in her pallet reading.

"Oh, you startled me," she said when we came around the side of the davenport. From her new sleeping area, she couldn't see the door. That was one of the reasons I had wanted to be on the other side.

"What are you two doing?" she asked.

"Mama got a letter," I said.

"I know. I saw the mailman."

"Do you know who it's from?" Joseph asked.

"Uncle Willie," I said. "She put it away."

"Well, I'm going to bed," Joseph said, disinterested.

"I think she put it away in here," I said, pointing to the drawer of the table.

"Maybe she did, Amelia," Aileen said, "but if she stored it there, don't you think that makes it clear that she doesn't want us to read the letter?"

"Okay," I said, "I just wonder what it says."

I prepared for bed and joined Aileen on her side of the room for prayers together when we heard Papa quietly close the kitchen door. He walked into the parlor and said, "How's everyone? Ready for bed?"

"I guess so," I said, unsure who he meant by "everyone."

"Well, good night then." He headed toward the kitchen.

Aileen and I finished our talk with God. Then I scooted to my side of the room and lay down. Somehow, I couldn't get the letter out of my mind. Mama had definitely acted strangely. I wondered why Aileen and Joseph weren't curious.

Finally, Aileen's even breathing told me she'd fallen asleep, and I tiptoed over to the table. Quietly I slid the drawer open and removed the envelope. I carried it over near the window and removed the folded sheets of paper. Out fell four ten-dollar bills. I held the letter up to the light of a full moon shining through the window. Disappointment flooded over me. The words were in long hand and I couldn't read them.

Turning over the envelope I was glad to find writing I could read, in even block letters, the return address said WILL ABERNATHY. I could also make out the words CRYSTAL CITY, MISSOURI.

I wondered how I could decipher the handwriting and an idea came to me. Quietly I stepped back over to Aileen's side of the room and took the pen and two sheets of paper out of the drawer. I held the letter, covered by a blank sheet of paper, to the windowpane so that the moonlight shown through and I traced the lettering as best as I could.

Water Under the Bridge

It took a long time to trace all of the unfamiliar words, but when finished, I hid the sheets of paper that held the tracing in my pillow case and folded the dollar bills back into the letter and tucked everything into the envelope. I replaced the letter in its hiding place and crawled in bed. Later, I'd try to find help deciphering the scribbles.

I felt guilty about snooping on Mama, but I felt a pressing need to know all that happened in our household. Why had she chosen to keep the letter to herself? It must have something to do with money. Then I realized that if Uncle Willie had written to her and sent money, it must have been a response to a letter of hers. Had Mama asked for money? I wondered. And if she had, why?

Verna Simms

CHAPTER TWENTY-FIVE—A TRIP OVER THE MOUNTAIN

One lazy day in late August, it was way too hot to do anything but hang around the kitchen out of the sun. Papa strolled in to where Aileen, Joseph, and I sat crunching sugar cookies and turned to Mama, who stood scrubbing the shelves of the Mother Hubbard cabinet. Papa cleared his throat before speaking.

"Ida, Thelma and I are driving to Phoenix on Saturday morning," he said. "I've put new tires and spark plugs in the Model T and I plan to take the young'uns along; that is, if it's okay with you. They haven't been on a trip in a long while and I think they'd enjoy it." It sounded like he had rehearsed the speech.

Papa had been careful lately not to plan any activities that included us children without consulting Mama. He never ordered Mama to do anything anymore, but instead made it appear she'd made the decision.

"I'll think on it," Mama hedged. Wiping her hands on her apron, she nonchalantly opened the kitchen door and stepped out onto the pack porch. Aileen and I rose from the table and followed her, me swishing my hands through the water in the wash pan we kept on the back porch. I dried them on my dress tail. I felt my jacks in my pocket, so I crouched on the packed dirt under the shade of our lone tree and called, "Come on, Aileen, join me in a game."

I liked playing with my sister; she let me use both hands to catch the ball, which helped me win once in a while. I counted up to three before missing catching the ball. "Shucks," I groaned, and handed the ball to Aileen.

A bird was singing on one of the lower branches. "Gee whiz, Aileen. That looks like your lost canary. What do ya think?"

"I dunno, but it seems happy. I sometimes think it is wrong for humans to put birds in a cage. If it is, I'm glad it's free."

I shuddered to think of being in a cage, especially if you were able to fly.

A tree stump that had been left when the land had been cleared for our house made a good seat, and Mama strolled over and sat near us. Joseph traced words in the dirt next to her. They watched our game for a short time.

"You heard your Papa invite you to drive with him to Phoenix tomorrow. Would you like that?"

Before we could answer, Papa interrupted. He'd crept up on us, evidently worried what Mama would say.

"We'll stop at Superior for ice cream," he said. "You children can play on the playground there. They have a circular slide, remember?"

We all turned eagerly to Mama, and seeing our faces, she nodded. "Go ahead. It'll give me a day of rest. Maybe I can read a little or page through the Sears and Roebuck catalog."

Papa quickly reached in his hip pocket and produced his wallet. Extracting a five-dollar bill, he set it down in the dirt between Mama and him. "Here's a five, Ida. Order something for yourself." He turned and walked toward the house.

Mama didn't answer. She waited until Papa walked out of sight and then reached over and snatched the money and folded the bill safely in her apron pocket.

Aileen and I returned to our game. After a few minutes, Mama strolled over to pick the dead blooms from her lilac bush. Her sister had sent a small lilac root to her three years before, and Mama had taken very special care of the bush she'd planted, often telling us that it became "her little bit of Missouri."

I watched her bury her face in the purple blooms and wondered if she longed for her family. She still had Uncle Willie and her two sisters living, Uncle Willie being her favorite and closest to her age, just two years older—like Joseph and me. They'd played together as children.

Uncle Willie and his wife, Aunt Cordelia, had no children. They lived in the big old rambling house where Mama had grown up outside of Crystal City. I loved hearing stories from Mama's childhood, although she rarely told them anymore. My favorite was when she and Uncle Willie used to stay up half the night making up stories. One would begin the story and tell it for a while. Then the other added to it. She said some of their stories went on for months if not years and were never really finished. When they tired of one, they started a new one. I thought it sounded like fun and begged Aileen and Joseph to fantasize with me, but they never agreed.

"What do you suppose Mama'll buy?" I asked Aileen.

She paused with the little red ball in her hand and thought. "Probably material for a new dress," she said. "She's been complaining that all her dresses are too tight."

"Mama always says it's a sin to throw good food away," Joseph said, "but it's also a sin to eat more food after you're full. Gluttony, it's called. Papa doesn't like a fat woman. I heard him say so to the iceman."

"Mama is not sinful," Aileen said.

"And Papa should keep his mouth shut," I said.

Aileen and Joseph both looked at me in shock. "Amy!" they both said at the same time, but I was spared a lecture because Papa came out of the kitchen door then and called to us. "Wear your good clothes Saturday," he said. "I mean to stop and say hello to the bishop."

We all watched him turn and stride back to the house.

"That's kind of strange, don't you think?" I asked. But Aileen and Joseph had begun a new game of jacks.

The next evening, after clearing the table and wiping the oilcloth, Aileen said, "Anyone want to play a game?"

"Oh yes," said Thelma, looking anxiously at the rest of us.

Joseph got up and walked to the high shelf on the far wall of the kitchen. "Checkers, dominoes, or Fox and Geese? Tic, Tac, Toe? What'll it be?"

"Dominoes," Aileen answered. "We can all play at the same time."

Joseph took the box down and opened it.

"You and Joe always win at dominoes," I complained.

"You'd win if you'd tried harder," said Joseph. "You're too lazy to add up the dots ahead of time." He turned the black tiles over so that we couldn't see the white dots. Then he shuffled them around on the tabletop to mix the pieces up in case we remembered which was which.

"Be careful, Joseph!" Aileen said sharply, "You'll wear out the tablecloth. Nobody can remember where anything is anyway."

"I'll just watch," Thelma said, "and I'll find books to hide the pieces behind."

She knows her place, I thought. I wasn't clear on exactly what it was, though.

Later, after Aileen had won again and the dominoes were put away, Joseph went to his cot and I carried the glasses to the sink. Thelma stood, wiping the oilcloth again.

"Want me to brush your hair for you, Amelia?" Thelma asked. "It's getting longer."

I hesitated. I enjoyed having my hair brushed and it had been a long time since Mama or Aileen had taken the time. But I wasn't convinced about Thelma yet.

"I'd really love to do it," she said. Her sparkling eyes and dimples attested to her good intentions.

"I guess so." I retrieved my hairbrush from my orange crate shelf in the parlor and brought it into the kitchen. Thelma motioned me to sit on the floor with my back toward her. She stayed in a chair behind me.

"You have lovely hair," Thelma said. "Sometimes when the sunshine hits it, it looks similar to copper."

I didn't respond, not being sure that I liked copper—with its smelly fumes—and I also didn't want Thelma to believe I liked her again, so I kept quiet.

Thelma began brushing, very gentle smoothing out the tangles and caressing it with her hand after every stroke.

A twinge of guilt made me try a little conversation with her. "Do you miss your family?" I asked.

"Oh yes," she answered quickly. "I believed I wanted to be away from the noise of my brothers more than anything else in the world, but I miss them terribly."

A long silence filled the air as Thelma continued to tenderly brush and smooth my hair. I guessed her thoughts had wandered far away.

"Missouri is different from Arizona," she spoke suddenly. "Grass and trees grow everywhere. We had a lovely creek that meandered through our farm. In the summertime, we fished and swam in the crystal clear water."

She paused with the brush in the air above my head.

"I had a good friend in Missouri. Her name is Lorena. She lived on the farm closest to ours. She had a rope swing—just a long rope with a thick-round stick tied on the end, bigger than this brush handle. It hung over the branch of a big tree. We could grab onto it and swing way out over the deepest part of the creek. Then we'd let go and drop in the water."

"My best friend, Blanca, has a swing made from a tire," I said, "but it doesn't go over water. It's in her back yard."

Thelma stood and walked to the window. "The creek felt so good on a hot day, with the cool, clear water caressing my skin." She stood at the window, staring into the darkness. Then abruptly she said, "I miss Lorena, too. I miss Missouri." Then very quietly she added, "I'm only sixteen." But somehow I knew her words weren't directed to me.

***

"Ida," Papa said. "Do you have time to pack us a lunch? I'd sure enjoy some of your biscuits and fried chicken."

"Heavens no," Mama shook her head. "Remember? This is my day of rest. Buy the children hot tamales from a street vendor. They like them. Get 'em pop to drink, too." She removed her apron and hung it on the peg beside the stove.

Then she said something odd, "It might be a good idea to do something fun with them today—something nice they'll remember."

Papa looked at her closely, but said nothing.

She kissed us goodbye and we crowded into the backseat of the black Model T Ford behind Papa and Thelma. It had been a new car when our parents made the trip out West in 1920. I remembered being told Papa paid for it with money from selling their farm in Missouri.

When they arrived though, the elders of the church told Papa that he couldn't help because he didn't have a Recommend, a card that judged him, in the opinion of the elders, worthy of entering the temple. Papa was too new in the faith and didn't have any elders to recommend him. He almost cried with disappointment. Mormons in Lehi sheltered our family and we lived with them while Papa searched for work, taking odd jobs as a carpenter.

He eventually moved the family to Claypool, a new development that needed housing. When we first arrived, Mama said we couldn't afford to rent or buy so we lived in a tent in the desert for a couple of months. Eventually, Papa saved enough money to buy a lot and build us a home.

Papa's voice interrupted my wandering thoughts. "Aileen," Papa said. "Sit in the middle so Joseph and Amelia can't pick on each other. I want this to be a pleasant trip."

Mama handed me two pairs of black bloomers through the window. "You and Aileen put these on over your white bloomers and tuck your dress tails inside. I'll not be wanting to boil your bloomers once you're home. And Amelia, you go down the slide after Joseph, you hear? If it's dirty, his pants will wipe it clean. They're getting too short anyway."

I had to lean over and stick my head out the back window to hear the last of her instructions. Papa let the handbrake off and he pushed the clutch halfway down to neutral. We started coasting down the hill. When he released the clutch, the car jerked hard and the motor came to life.

I enjoyed the scenery of the mountains that ran from Claypool to Phoenix. Joseph sat on the side with a view of the valley.

"Look down," he yelled suddenly, "there's a wreck below! It isn't rusty so it must be a fairly new wreck. Do you see it?"

I didn't. I shoved Aileen out of the way, but we'd already passed.

"I'm missing everything," I grumbled.

"Stay on the same side of the car for the trip back and you'll trade views then," Papa said. "We're coming up to the hairpin curves in the road soon. You remember the area where you can look ahead and see where you've already been? You can admire that from either window.

"You should find the scenery interesting too, Thelma," he said. "Nothing like it in Missouri." He smiled widely and winked. I'd never seen Papa in such good humor. His sky-blue eyes danced with pleasure. Thelma scooted a few inches closer to him and smiled back, showing her deep dimples. She'd dressed especially fine for a road trip in a new white dress that I thought would surely be filthy if she spent any time at all on the slide in Superior.

Papa called back to us, "Those small caves on the side of the mountain are bootlegger's hideouts. Shortly up ahead we'll be entering the tunnel—now, get ready!"

Suddenly it became dark as night. We whooped and hollered, "Hello, hello!" and covered and uncovered our mouths to make an eerie echo sound. Back in the sunlight, I noticed Thelma's red face and Papa glancing her way, laughing. We reached Superior at 11 o'clock. I hopped out first, jerked black bloomers on over my whites, and raced for the slide.

"Me first!" Joseph galloped after me. "Mama said so."

"Look, Aileen's still in the car," I pointed, ignoring his protests. "She doesn't want anyone to see her pulling on bloomers."

"Wouldn't hurt you to be a bit modest yourself," said Joseph, climbing the ladder a few rungs behind me. "You're eight years old now."

The circular slide was enclosed for safety and gave us a great thrill. We had to be careful not to scrape our elbows on the metal sides as we zoomed around and around, before spilling out onto the gravel below, laughing.

Joseph and I made ten trips up and down. Aileen and Thelma both watched.

Water Under the Bridge

Then Papa called, "Ice cream, anyone?"

"Me!" I shouted and rushed to him. At a small convenience store adjacent to the school playground, Papa ordered vanilla cones. I pushed my mouth into the hollow cone, smearing the delicious vanilla ice cream over my face.

"You're so messy, Amelia," Aileen said, shaking her head. She daintily licked her cone, careful to follow its contour.

Verna Simms

CHAPTER TWENTY-SIX—A SURPRISE

Papa pulled a watch from his pocket, "Time to go. We need to see the bishop. Mustn't be late for an appointment."

When we arrived at the bishop's home, he surprised me. "You're early. I didn't expect you for another half hour."

"We made good time," Papa said.

"Well, follow me," the bishop said, climbing into his shiny black touring car. I stared at the short, stout white-haired man with a pink face and wondered what Papa had in mind.

No one spoke as we drove the narrow streets, keeping the bishop's car in sight. Papa kept his eyes straight ahead and his hands firmly gripped the steering wheel. Thelma seemed giddy. She brushed her hair and smoothed her dress and examined her face in a compact mirror. I noticed a gray Chrysler parked in the church parking lot close to the door.

"Looks like the Overbergs' car," Joseph whispered, leaning over and poking Aileen with his elbow. I threw him a questioning glance but he ignored me. We piled out.

Aileen turned to Thelma, "I think your new dress is very pretty, Thelma."

"Thank you," she said, beaming.

Thelma really is a pretty girl, I thought. Her light hair, the color of sunshine reflecting on fresh straw, shone with a white bow neatly tied at the nape of her neck. Her face glowed with youth and happiness.

Inside the church, we found Joseph was right. Mr. Overberg and James sat in the first row on the left side of the room, both dressed in suits. James waved his hand in a 'hello.'

Joseph acknowledged him with a nod and I raised my hand and gave him a slight wiggling of my fingers. James and I had unofficially declared a truce after the spider episode.

"Where did Papa go?" I asked Thelma, noticing that he'd disappeared.

"He's changing clothes," she said.

I turned and asked Aileen, "What's going on? Why'd we come here?"

She didn't answer, but raised her finger to her lips for silence. The side door of the sanctuary opened with a slight squeak and a pretty, dark-haired young woman stood at the doorway, hesitating for a moment.

"Oh, here's my wife," the bishop announced. "Come on in, Alice. We're ready."

His wife? I thought she couldn't have been much older than Aileen. She seemed to glide into the room and her silver-gray taffeta dress rustled as she moved; its wide cummerbund hugged her hips. Long slim sleeves, finished with three-inch flounces, covered her hands to the knuckles.

She sat at the organ and playfully twirled around on the revolving stool. Then she leaned toward the organ, plucked a single blue cornflower from a floral arrangement on top and shook the water from its stem. She wrapped the blossom in a white handkerchief trimmed with delicate white tatting.

Alice walked over and handed the flower to Thelma. "Here, take this. It'll give you something to do with your hands and it's a borrowed hanky—with something blue." She flashed Thelma a smile and glided back to her place at the pump organ and softly started to play.

As the rich organ music filled the room, Papa entered, wearing his best suit. The bishop walked to the front. "Chester, you and Thelma stand here facing me." Then he nodded at Joseph and said, "Young man, you stand at your father's right side—and you girls, beside Thelma will be fine. There, that should do it."

He opened a book and, clearing his throat, began to read in a deep, solemn voice.

Only at that instant did I grasp what was happening. I'd never been to a wedding, but all became clear. I'd been tricked into witnessing the marriage of our papa to a girl who was not our mama.

I wanted to turn and run, but I knew it was futile. Tears welled in my eyes and my legs shook. I bit my lower lip and did my best to compose myself. Did Aileen and Joseph know about this? Poor Mama! To be betrayed in this way. What will become of her? What will become of us? A fury rose up inside me—an anger like I had felt that day on the mountainside. I felt my cheeks burning and I dared not move or speak.

I told God that I might have to stand there, but I would not be a witness! Defiantly, I turned my face toward the stained glass windows and fixed my eyes on the colorful panes reflected by the sun. In my mind, the words to a song emerged:

> *If an angel will loan me her wings,*
> *I'll fly up, up ever so high,*
> *Up over these walls that hold me below,*
> *And vanish forever in the sky.*

I noticed the intricate design of the stained glass, how at first there had been no noticeable pattern, but then a white dove took shape. Its pearly white wings were spread in flight. Noah had used a dove to know when to escape from the ark. I concentrated on seeing myself sitting astride the lovely little dove soaring out the door and over the tall building, all the way to freedom.

"Let us all join hands while we pray," the bishop's voice boomed, bringing me abruptly back into the church. But I'd been successful. I did not hear and do not recall a single word of the ceremony. I had willed my mind elsewhere. I do remember the last statement I heard the bishop make that day. He said: "Go forth and bring children into the world for the glory of all."

Papa pulled Thelma toward him and planted a kiss on her lips. She looked adoringly at Papa. After congratulations by the bishop and his wife and hugs for Thelma from Mr. Overberg and James, Papa finally turned to us and said, "Hungry? How about hot tamales? We'll buy from a street vendor in town and perhaps we'll have time to stop in Superior again on the way home."

My enthusiasm had long gone and, in its place, a stew of boiling anger churned in my heart—with extreme sadness, worry, and pity.

Apathetically, I accepted orange soda pop and a piping-hot tamale. A man cooked them on the sidewalk while we watched. Wrapped in cornhusks, they smelled delicious. Until that day, they had been my favorite. I tasted only a couple of bites and wrapped the remainder of my tamale in a hanky.

"Will Mama be there when we get home?" I asked nervously.

"Of course she will," Papa said.

During the ride home, he and Thelma chatted gaily and sang spiritual songs. Usually I enjoyed Papa's deep bass, and joined in with the family, singing loudly. That day though, the three of us sat mute in the backseat of the Model T Ford.

I felt like a bitter persimmon had lodged in my throat, giving me difficulty swallowing.

I longed to talk to Aileen and Joseph in private, to try and sort out with them and understand this latest development in our family. Did they have any idea of Papa's plans? Did Mama know? She wouldn't have told me, I was certain, but she may have warned Aileen. With a heavy heart, I sat staring at the deep ravines below. I could no longer appreciate its beauty.

Suddenly, I felt an overwhelming pain and lurching feeling in the pit of my stomach. I pressed my hand over my mouth and closed my eyes, trying to force calm thoughts about happier times.

"Papa!" Amelia yelled. "Stop the car. Amelia's turning green!"

At almost the same time, Joseph shouted, "Truck, truck!" and Thelma let out a loud scream. Papa made a sharp right turn of the steering wheel and forgot his religion, spewing out a string of words I'd never heard before. I lurched forward and held the car door with both hands. I hung my head over and opened my eyes in time to see my lunch sliding down the side of Papa's clean Model T. I could feel my weight on the door and realized the car wasn't upright; but leaning. Below, I could see nothing—wide-open space. We were suspended over the side of the mountain!

I don't know if it was shock, or if I had bumped my head in all the commotion, but the next thing I knew, my shoulders were being shook and Aileen crouched over me crying, "Amy, wake up! Please, sister, wake up!"

"Good gracious, turn loose of my legs," I snapped groggily, trying to sit up. A worried Joseph stood holding both of my knees. "What happened?"

I found myself lying in the road with my family over me. Behind us, Papa's car rested diagonally in the road, three wheels on the gravel and the right rear tire hanging precariously over the edge. A flatbed truck parked in front of Papa's car, idling.

Aileen tugged on my arm to help me to my feet. "Oh, Amelia, the car almost tumbled down the ravine! It still might fall. Hurry, we must get out of the way. Joseph, help me!"

"Hell's bells. I'm okay," I said. "I can walk." My legs felt wobbly. "I'm thirsty though. Feel like I swallowed a cocklebur."

"Come over here," Joseph said, pulling me toward a shady area created by the cropping of overhanging rocks.

"You got chewing gum?" I asked Aileen. They both shook their heads.

"Try this," Papa said, producing a piece of hard orange candy from his pocket.

He crossed the road to a short stocky man wearing overalls and carrying a large rock—the driver of the truck.

He and Papa placed stones behind three wheels of the Model T to prevent them from rolling. Joseph ran to locate more rocks. The sun beat down as Papa removed his hat and wiped the sweat from his forehead. Finally, he opened the door of the car and slid behind the wheel.

"I'm not getting back in," I said, looking at Thelma and Aileen.

"Wait, mister," the strange man shouted. "I'll back my truck and hook a cable to your car. You mightn't have good traction with only one back wheel on the road. It'll be safer if I pull too." His voice was deep and loud.

We heard the truck's gears grind as we watched anxiously from the side of the road, praying that the car would not tumble down the side of the mountain. Papa turned the wheels to the left. Slowly the car inched forward.

"What a day!" Thelma said, running over to join Papa. He and the truck driver disconnected the cable linking their two vehicles, before shaking hands.

"You're telling me!" I said. "And now we go home and find out what Mama thinks about Papa marrying Thelma."

"We're not telling her," said Joseph, the tone of his voice oddly defiant.

So, he hadn't known either, I thought, and he's angry.

"Why should we do his dirty work?" Joseph said. "Let him tell Mama himself."

He reached down and picked up a rock, and ran across the road where he threw it as hard as he could throw. We heard it bouncing down into the deep canyon below.

Aileen remained silent, but her forehead revealed the small vertical worry line that always gave away her feelings.

The last few miles of our journey passed quietly, all of us immersed in our own private thoughts. Thelma laid her head on Papa's shoulder, and he draped his arm across the back of the seat. I rested my head in my sister's lap, pretending to sleep. I tried to imagine where the car was at the various points between Superior and Claypool.

As the car rounded the corner near our house, I recognized the familiar crunch of the earth and the incline of the road and I opened my eyes. The sun had dropped behind the mountain, leaving the path dark from the car to our door. We five weary travelers made our way to the back porch and toward the always welcoming and cozy kitchen that seemed so much a part of our mama.

Mama opened the kitchen door, holding the oil lamp high to help us see the way. "Did you children enjoy your holiday?" she asked.

Then she caught a glimpse of me. "Good heavens! What happened to you, Amelia?"

"Leave her be, Ida," said Papa. "She's had a rough day." He let Thelma walk in and then he abruptly turned around and went back out into the night. Over his shoulder he called back to us, "Someone tell her. I'm going for a walk."

We all glanced at each other, unsure of what to say. Thelma had stopped in the middle of the kitchen, but panic spread across her face and she nearly ran into the hallway to reach the bedroom she shared with Papa. We heard the door shut.

Aileen said, "We went to Superior, Mama, and we rode on the circular slide and had tamales."

"And we bought ice cream, too," said Joseph. "And then Amelia got carsick."

"Well, I imagine the heat, the circular slide, and too much food caused it," Mama said. "Sounds like a recipe for sickness to me." She smiled sadly and patted my head. "We must get you cleaned up. You'll feel better then."

Aileen and Joseph looked at each other.

"I was sitting behind Papa," Joseph continued, more from a sense of wanting to keep Mama busy listening than of giving her any important information. "Aileen sat in the middle and Amelia was behind Thelma. We'd unsnapped the Isinglass windows to get fresh air. Amelia had her head stuck partly out the window. I think that's what made her sick."

He stopped and intensely stared into my eyes, willing me not to contradict him, but I couldn't resist. "Nah, the pop and hot tamale and the winding road did the damage."

Then I remembered that the rest of my tamale I'd brought Mama. I pulled it from my pocket. The tamale had deeply stained my once white hanky with the food smashed beyond recognition. *Just like me..*

"You forgot to tell her Papa wrecked the car," I said.

"Oh my goodness!" Mama said. "Thank heavens no one is hurt. Are you all okay? Amelia? Aileen? Joseph?" Mama turned to each of us.

"She was knocked out," Joseph said.

"What?" Mama said; her face drained of color and her eyes opened wide. She grabbed my chin in her hand and took a good look at me.

"I think I'm okay," I said, but then I added, "I just have a little pain right here." I pointed to my heart.

"Well, I never," she said. She stood up and soaked a rag in the pan of water in the sink. She washed my face and smoothed my hair. "I sure hope you had some fun today, Amelia."

Before I could say anything, Aileen answered. "She did. She had fun riding the slide in Superior."

"I wanna go to bed," I announced.

"I'm tired, too," Joseph said quickly. "Let's all call it a day and go to bed."

Verna Simms

CHAPTER TWENTY-SEVEN—A PACKAGE

Mild weather and short days followed. Joseph and I enjoyed our time outdoors in the yard or on the mountain. One afternoon we pulled out the pair of stilts Daniel had made the year before and took turns walking from the porch to the chicken coop. I was on the stilts when my brother suddenly yelled, "Mailman!"

I hopped off and let the stilts drop to the ground. We both ran to the gate as fast as we could, but Joseph beat me, as always, and took the package—a large bundle wrapped in brown paper and reinforced with tape and string.

"Who's it from?" I squealed. "Maybe presents from Missouri!"

Joseph examined the label and said, "Sears and Roebuck."

I remembered the five dollars Papa gave Mama on that fateful day he and Thelma married—a day I'd tried to forget.

"Let me feel. If it's soft, it's dress material."

Joseph lifted the package high and away from me as we walked to the house.

In the kitchen, Mama stood with her hands on the large sifter hanging from the Mother Hubbard cupboard. The sifter held ten pounds of flour and I loved the job of turning the crank and watching the snowy white flour drop into a mixing bowl. Mama never measured the ingredients—she had made biscuits so often she knew it was enough when the pile of flour reached a certain height in the mixing bowl. I took a quick look inside the bowl and it reminded me of small peaked mountains covered with snow.

Joseph set the package on the table. "What did you order, Mama?" I asked. "Can we see? Aileen hoped you'd order material for a dress. Is that it?"

"My goodness, Amelia. You don't have the patience of a tadpole. Let me get this apron off and I'll let you open the package. Sure wouldn't want flour all over the place, would we?" Mama's eyes crinkled when she laughed. "Carry it into the dining room please, Joseph."

Mama pulled her apron over her head, opened the screen door, and shook the apron over the porch railing. I waited impatiently, watching her wash her hands and smooth back her hair.

"Okay, Amelia, open away, but be careful you don't cut anything but the string," she said, handing me the scissors. I clipped the binding close to the knot as she had taught me. We saved all string and wound it into a ball. String is handy for kites and fastening straps on bean shooters, and so many other fun things. I handed the twine to Joseph.

The brown paper crinkled as I tore it open and slowly, carefully unfolded each layer. Inside, lovely soft material lay before my eyes in two shades of blue and fire engine red—also a small folded stack of white fabric. "Oh!" I exclaimed. "Red! I've never seen you wear red, Mama. Hold it up to your face and let's see how it looks."

Mama lifted the red fabric to her face, smiled and batted her eyes like a schoolgirl. "No, Amelia, the red is for you for a dress. I remember you admired Blanca's red dress. About time you have one of your own, don't you think?" She gave me a light squeeze and continued to finger the material.

"Feel how fine and soft cotton percale feels to your fingers. The colors look to be true to the samples in the catalogue. You never know when you order if it's good grade or not." Then she added, "This light blue will make a pretty dress for Aileen. See, it has a slight tint of green. It'll bring out the color of her blue eyes."

Aileen had left early that morning to meet friends in town. I could hardly wait for her to return and see what Mama had bought.

"Who is the white for?" Joseph asked hopefully.

"Collars," Mama said. "I'm planning to make removable collars for the dresses, square with ruffles all around. We can tack them onto any dress to make them appear to be new."

She noticed his disappointment. "I'm afraid I didn't order anything for you and Daniel this time," she teased, "but there should be enough white left to make a nice soft handkerchief."

Seeing the look on Joseph's face, she laughed and stood. She opened the door to the hall closet and removed a small package. "You really didn't think I'd forget you, did you, son? This came earlier."

Joseph eagerly untied the string from his package while I held my red fabric to my chest and twirled around the room. "Will you make a full skirt, Mama? I'd like that. Can you have it sewed it in time for Christmas?"

"Have it sewn," Mama corrected me. "Page through the catalog and choose a dress you like. I'll copy it. Just be sure it has no collar. I once worked at a factory in Crystal City and stitched collars for men's shirts. I got the idea then to make detachable collars, but they wouldn't do for little girls that'd take them off and lose them. You and Aileen are both old enough now. I'll try to finish it by the holiday," she said. "But it must be a secret between us. You know how your papa feels about Christmas."

"But they have a Christmas program at church," I pointed out.

Joseph had already removed the paper from his package and his hands shook slightly as he cut the string tied around a small, brown rectangular box.

"Yes, they do, but your papa has his own notions about religion. Mostly he keeps them to himself because they are different from that of the elders—on many things."

"Can I wear my dress to school on Valentine's Day, too? Red is for valentines."

"Yes, honey, it will be your special occasion dress. Now be quiet and see what I ordered for Joseph. By the way, the proper grammar is 'may I wear it to school.'"

Joseph lifted the lid and his face lit up instantly, his blue eyes sparkling. I leaned over to see a shiny two-bladed pocketknife on a bed of white cotton. He removed the knife and held it in his hand for me to admire. Then he opened one of two blades and ran his finger over its edge to test the sharpness.

"Land sakes. You be careful, son," Mama said. "A new knife is very sharp. You're going on eleven now and should be old enough to handle it safely. The way you like to whittle little toys, you need a sharp knife. Daniel will show you how to keep the blades sharp."

"I already know how," Joseph said proudly.

"Everyone got a present but you," I pointed out.

"My present is the smiles on your faces," Mama said. "I wouldn't trade them for the world."

"Papa didn't get anything either," Joseph said.

"No, that's true; he didn't," Mama said lightly. She reached up to adjust her hair and a hairpin snapped as she tried to push it into her bun.

"Oh dear, that's the second one I've ruined this week. However will I manage to keep my hair in place with only six pins?"

She headed for the parlor with her hands holding her hair. I knew she'd use the bronze mirror to redo her hair.

"Mama didn't buy anything for herself," I said to Joseph.

"Papa's money," he answered. "I doubt she'll ever use his money for herself."

The holiday month passed uneventfully. Mama finished our dresses in time for Christmas, and I wore the fancy full-skirted dress to school on the last day before winter break. I showed Blanca the detachable collar and she agreed it would be useful.

Christmas came and went, a big disappointment. Without the Overbergs in our house, Papa saw no reason to tolerate any celebration. Mama placed small gifts beneath our pillows on Christmas Eve, some candy and a new toothbrush, which I thought went together well. Aileen and I traded hairbrushes. She liked pink and I preferred blue. We said we'd consider the brushes our gifts to each other. Joseph presented me with an I.O.U. for another kite. He promised to build two to make up for not giving me the one he'd planned the year before.

There had never been any mention made of Papa's marriage to Thelma, not by him or Thelma, and certainly not by Aileen or Joseph or me. As if we had all made a pact, Joseph had said to let him do his own dirty work and we'd been relieved to do so. None of us wanted to be the bearer of distressing news to Mama.

CHAPTER TWENTY-EIGHT—THE BIG NEWS, 1929

One evening, we crowded around the kitchen table after dinner. Mama sat quietly darning socks, Thelma writing a letter to her parents, and Aileen reading *Little Women*. I lay on the floor on my back with one ankle crossed over my knee. Mama had told me to wash the soup pot and I lounged, waiting for dishwater to heat on the stove. Suddenly, she said, "Amelia and Aileen, you girls go outdoors. I'll wash the pot myself. I want to speak with Thelma in private."

I jumped to my feet happily and headed for the door. Aileen hesitated a moment, but then she found her bookmark and marked her place. "Coming?" I asked.

"Sure," she followed me outside.

She sauntered out and settled down beneath the cottonwood tree, leaning against the trunk, the book on her knees. She resumed her reading.

I perched on the bench inches away from the open kitchen window, avidly listening. My heart pounded. I'd become an eavesdropper. I knew better. I just couldn't shake a powerful desire to know everything.

"Thelma," I heard Mama say. "Will you stack the plates while I clean the pot?"

I heard the sounds of water splashing and metal clanking against metal.

"How've you been feeling?" Mama's voice filtered through the window.

"Not so well."

"I noticed that you barely touch your meals these days."

"I've been tired," Thelma said, "and the heat gets to me sometimes."

"I've been wondering about something, I'll come right out and ask. Could it be that you are with child?"

I clasped my hand over my mouth to hold down a gasp. No response came from Thelma.

"I won't be angry if you are," Mama continued quietly. "I just . . ." She seemed to struggle for the right words. A shocked silence followed.

I felt sorry for them both. Here they were, two women, both basically good people. They both loved the same man. And because of that, they hardly spoke to each other.

Suddenly, a sharp crash, the sound of a shattered glass broke the silence. I jumped to my feet.

"Oh, no!" Thelma shrieked. "I'm so sorry!"

"No, no, I'm the sorry one," Mama said, calmly. "It's not your fault. I shouldn't have upset you. Step outside and get a breath of air."

If more conversation followed, I didn't hear it because the threat of Thelma coming out and finding me lurking under the window had me frightened. I ran around the house into the yard. Looking around to see if Mama had seen me from the window, I quickly began jumping rope and reciting a rhyme:

> *Ted, Ted went straight to bed,*
> *Pulled the covers up over his head.*
> *How many blankets did he use?*
> *One, two, three, four, five…*

After a few minutes of this, I became exhausted and thirsty. I crept back up the stairs as Thelma disappeared into the kitchen. I drank deeply from the pail of water we kept near the door. Then I held the dipper high and poured water over my head. The cool liquid ran down my back and refreshed me. I peered through the screen door and was stunned to see Thelma in Mama's arms.

Before I could turn away, I heard her say, "Don't worry. I will help you."

Soon enough, I noticed that Thelma had been gaining weight. Despite the conversation I'd overheard, she seemed very happy and eager to help around the house.

One evening, Mama took Joseph, Aileen, and me aside. "I must tell you that Thelma is 'that way,'" she said. "We must be kind to her. And you three do more housework. Understood?"

None of us answered with a word. What could we say?

As we prepared for bed later, Aileen said, "Mama has changed toward Thelma, hasn't she? She's fond of her again—like she felt at first. I've noticed that she looks for any opportunity to comfort her."

"Mama's never been unkind to anyone," I said.

"Yes, but this is different," said Aileen. "Did you ever tell her that Papa and Thelma had a marriage ceremony?"

"No, I didn't tell her. I'm sure Joe didn't either. He promised he wouldn't."

I pulled my nightgown over my head, my mind racing. "Well. do you think she'd feel differently about her if she knew?"

Aileen stopped brushing her hair. Its golden brown highlights shone under the lamplight.

"Gee, I'm not sure," she said thoughtfully. "Marriage is supposed to be permanent." She tapped her white teeth with the brush handle. "The other way," she added carefully, trying to put it to me delicately, "is a sin. I've heard that an affair often doesn't last. In that case Mama could get Papa back."

"Heck no, I wouldn't want him back," I blurted, startled at the thought. "Besides, what would happen then? Thelma would go back to her parents. Mama and Papa wouldn't be the same together. I know I wouldn't take him back if I were Mama."

"You don't know what you'd do if you were grown and had four children," Aileen said. Then she added, "I hope to have a good husband that loves me. I want a nice home, and lots of children. Do you ever study the pictures of men in the Sears and Roebuck catalogue and imagine being married to one of them? Someone tall and handsome?"

"No," I said emphatically, and meaning it. I didn't understand this side of Aileen and thought the idea farfetched.

"Besides, I'm going to be a busy lawyer," I announced, "I'm going to fight for women's rights. Maybe I won't marry at all. Men are trouble. Always want to be boss."

We both lay down in our pallets then and fell silent, each immersed in our own, very different ideas of a happy future for ourselves.

By January of 1929, Thelma had grown very round. Her feet swelled and she could no longer stand for long periods at the kitchen sink. Aileen and I took over the chore of doing our nightly dishes. Ordinarily I would have complained, but I felt sorry for Thelma and anxious for the baby's arrival.

Aileen and I often tried to guess whether she would have a boy or girl, and we suggested names for both.

"Your papa says if it's a boy, he'll give him a good Bible name," Thelma said. "But if it's a girl, I hope to name her myself."

"What will you call her?" I asked.

"Lorena," she said. "My friend from Missouri's name."

CHAPTER TWENTY-NINE—BENJAMIN

February 25th was Aileen's thirteenth birthday. Thelma and I had stayed up late the night before to decorate a birthday cake for her.

I awoke Tuesday morning to excited voices in the kitchen. I noticed Aileen's pallet was uncommonly messy and wondered if I was missing a very early surprise party.

I scrambled to dress and button up my wretched high-top shoes. Then I ran to the kitchen. "Happy Birthday, Aileen!" I called.

No one was in the kitchen.

"In here, Amelia," Mama answered from the room I used to share with Aileen. I wondered why. She hadn't been in that room in months. Not since Thelma moved in with Papa.

Before I got to the door, Mama emerged and met me in the hall. "Take your lunch pail and go on to school. Your breakfast is inside." Her face looked worried.

"Hey, what's going on?" I asked. "Where are Joe and Ailie? Is everyone okay?"

"Everyone is fine. Joseph is drawing water for me. He'll walk to school with you. Wait for him under the cottonwood tree"

She lowered her head and whispered in my ear, "Thelma is having pains. Her baby is on the way. I need you to be a very good girl and go to school. Aileen is staying home to help. I don't need you and Joseph underfoot."

"Where's Papa?" I ventured to ask.

"He's gone for the doctor," she said. "'Now get, before I sweep you out with a broom!"

Moaning sounds came from my former bedroom then. Part of me wanted to stay, but the other part urged me to escape.

"Out!" Mama said, pushing me through the door and settling the matter.

I set my pail down and washed my hands and face in the gray metal wash pan. I noticed dirt at the bottom and, feeling useless, added water and carried the pan out to the sandy ditch that stretched between our house and the road. I scooped a handful of sand into my hand and scoured the pan, rubbing round and round until it shone.

"What're you doing?" Joseph called as he stood on the path that led to the gate. He clutched his school satchel in one hand. I ran to take the wash pan back to the porch, grabbed my satchel, and took off running to catch my brother. We heard Papa drive in from the road then and watched as the doctor climbed out of the passenger side of the car. Both men hurried into the house.

"When I get married," Joseph said on the way to school, "I'm not asking my wife to have any babies."

We walked the rest of the trip to school in silence, me weighing this information in my mind.

Throughout the day I struggled to concentrate on my work. "What's wrong, Amelia?" Miss Barnes asked. "Your mind seems elsewhere today."

I'd never shared any of the events in my home with my teacher. I wanted her to like my family and me. I wasn't sure what she'd think about us if she knew Papa had married two women, and they were living together in our house.

"I'm just tired," I said.

When I forgot my place in our reader for the second time, Blanca leaned over and whispered, "Everything is okay. You have a new baby brother."

I looked at her, flabbergasted.

As Joseph and I raced the distance between school and home, I told him what Blanca had said. "It's a guess," he said. "Like true or false questions, you have a fifty percent chance to be right. We'll see when we get home."

But the prediction turned out to be true. We did have a sweet baby brother. Thelma and Papa had a new son. Papa now had five children. Only Mama remained the same. She still had four children and a husband who loved someone else.

"What did you name him, Papa?" I asked when he came out of the bedroom to join us in the kitchen.

Water Under the Bridge

"Well, I've always liked the name Benjamin," he said. "And Benjamin is a good Bible name."

"I like it, too," I said. "Benjie." For once, Papa didn't object to a nickname.

We all adored the baby, especially Mama. She shared her rocking chair with Thelma. She offered to rock Benjie so that Thelma could take a walk or a nap, or have a little free time for a bath.

Aileen and Joseph and I also vied for turns holding the baby, and Papa remained in the best humor he'd been in for as long as I could remember. He even suggested that Mama ask Daniel to come for dinner one Sunday. It appeared as if our love for Benjie had changed us from two separate families to one big happy family of eight. Laughter came easily over the next couple of weeks and past offenses, if not forgotten, were pushed far back into the recesses of our minds where they were never considered.

Those were happy days.

Verna Simms

CHAPTER THIRTY—BIRTHDAY GIRL

On April 7, a very special day, I awoke, hopped up, and looked out the window. The sun shone brightly. I could see its rays moving through the branches of our lone tree, like the feet of tiny fairies doing ballet. My eighth birthday and I had big plans.

It must not rain, I thought, surveying the blue sky where large, cottony clouds seemed to hold out the possibility of rain.

The week before, I'd asked to have a birthday party but Mama said, "We really can't afford it, honey. We barely make ends meet now." Then she looked at my turned down mouth and added. "You may invite Blanca, if you wish. We'll churn homemade ice cream.

"We don't have room for a nice party inside," Mama twisted wisps of hair between her finger and thumb. "Let's plan to eat outside. Homemade ice cream is messy anyway."

"Sure, but what'll we use for a table?" I'd asked.

"The rock will do just fine." Mama answered. "I'll hem the white sheet that ripped last week. After we boil it to kill germs and hang the cloth in the sun to bleach and iron the wrinkles smooth, it'll do for an adequate tablecloth."

Joseph had been standing nearby listening. "I'll go with you, Amy," he offered, "if you want to roll out of bed early that morning and gather wildflowers. They'll look festive on the table."

"I'll plan games," Aileen volunteered. "What contests would you like?" She looked to Mama. "May we have candy for prizes?"

"If you cut and paste little baskets for candy, we could fill them with one sack of gumdrops. We can surely spare that." Mama nodded.

And so the planning began and I could scarcely contain myself waiting for the day to arrive. Now here it was!

I waited at the front gate for Blanca. She arrived at two o'clock sharp. Mr. and Mrs. Romac both gave me a big smile and called "Happy birthday, Amelia." And then they turned to their daughter, jumping out of the back seat. "Have a nice time, dear. We'll come for you tomorrow." The car started to roll down the hill when Mrs. Romac stuck her head out and called, "And don't forget to brush your teeth." The wind whipped her hair around her face, making me think of the day Blanca and I had planned to fly kites on the mountain, but never had.

Blanca handed me a package wrapped in white paper decorated with little stars of different colors and tied with a pink ribbon. "It's a gift for my very special friend. Happy birthday, Amy!" I placed it with the other gifts on the rock.

Everyone gathered around the table. We didn't have chairs, but standing suited me fine. Even Papa stayed in a good humor and smiled, with his arm around Thelma. He lit eight candles and sang his version of *Happy Birthday, Amelia* in his deep baritone voice.

"Open your presents, Amy," Thelma said. "Open mine first. It's the one wrapped in red paper."

I snatched the red package, shaped like a baseball bat. "Wonder what it is," I said, first feeling the wrapping to try and guess. "Too soft for a bat. Maybe clothing rolled tight and disguised to fool me." I laughed, throwing my head back.

"Hurry. Open it!" Thelma squealed. Suddenly I realized she was really a young girl not much older than Aileen.

I undid the paper, and inside a small fire-engine-red child's umbrella lay before my eyes.

"Oh, Thelma, I love it, I love it!" I pushed the gadget to open it wide and twirled around and around. "How did you know I adore umbrellas?" Thelma's and Papa's eyes met.

I unwrapped Blanca's gift next, careful to save the ribbon. I smoothed the ribbon flat and felt the softness of it as I slipped the delicate pink length safely into my pocket. I saw a lovely pink pocketbook with a chain handle. "Oh gee, Blanca, thank you," I gripped her hand. "I'll carry it to church every Sunday and always think of you."

Water Under the Bridge

The other gifts were nice, but those two were my favorites.

Aileen gave me a small blue drawstring pouch she'd made of scraps of material. Inside, I saw a small red ball, nestled among her set of jacks.

Joseph, not to be outdone, offered me a brand new bean-shooter. My old one had broken some time ago. I'd seen him up in the tree, sawing a fork from a small limb, just the week before. Mama presented me with her long black, hand-beaded necklace, which I'd often admired, and Papa had wrapped up a picture frame he'd made himself, covered with a paper that held a drawing of a peacock.

Not all of my presents were new, but Mama said, "No one has money these days for foolishness, but a gift that a previous owner has treasured is a gift of love."

We heard a howl from the house and Thelma jumped up and ran. She soon returned with Benjie—in time for the delicious homemade ice cream.

The day went wonderfully well. Now I wished for rain. We seldom had a normal, steady rain in Claypool, Arizona. Instead, a loud clap of thunder ripped open the skies and dumped torrents of rain. Then, just as suddenly as it began, the deluge stopped. But that didn't dampen my enthusiasm for the new umbrella. I opened it and proudly marched around the yard while Joseph teased me, singing.

> *No rain for Amelia, no more rain,*
> *It ain't gonna rain, it ain't, it ain't.*
> *How can Amy use her umbrella?*
> *It ain't gonna rain, it ain't, it ain't!*

I don't remember the ingredients Mama used for her homemade ice cream, but I do recall she added evaporated milk in place of real cream. I thought it tasted fantastic, savoring every cold and sweet bite of the vanilla flavor.

As soon as we finished eating, Papa stood up and turned to me.

"You had a nice birthday, Amelia. I see you're almost grown and it hardly seems possible. Not that long ago, I held you on my lap like I do Benjamin. Now, you're a young lady and I hope I've taught you well." He turned to Mama then. "Thelma and I are driving to Mesa tonight. I have plans I need to discuss with the elders there. Goodbye." He kissed me on the cheek, waved goodbye to the others, and the three of them were gone.

Aileen and Joseph had agreed to let Blanca and me have a sleeping 'room' all to ourselves. Aileen bedded down on the cot in the kitchen and Joseph spent the night in the shed in our yard—the room that Daniel had used before leaving home.

Not having males in our house made it seem oddly quiet. Blanca and I retired early, preparing for bed, but not for sleep. We talked late into the night. For the first time, Blanca told me of her parents' hardships in the past.

"My grandparents traveled with my mother all over the world." I couldn't see her face in the dark, but I caught a wistful tone in her voice. I'd often noticed that it is easier to tell confidences in the dark. You cannot read facial expressions. I would have liked to study my best friend's face as she continued her tale.

"They were living in Old Mexico when Mama and Daddy met and fell in love. When Mama became pregnant with me, they traveled to the border between Mexico and the United States. They camped close to the border, and when Mama's labor began they sneaked over the river to the Arizona side. Right before entering the area where the guards stayed, Mama insisted that my daddy let her go alone." Blanca hesitated and for a while I thought it was too painful for her to continue.

"She waited all alone until the contractions were only minutes apart. Then she approached the guard, well on the American side. I made my entrance to this world fifteen minutes later." She gave a little half laugh, her voice trilling up and down the scale. "Mama always said the best present she ever gave me didn't cost her a penny but was worth a fortune: American citizenship."

"Did that make your parents citizens also?" I asked.

"No, they had to go back. Did you notice my parents have a slight accent?"

"Yes, I did, but I like it. I love everything about your parents. They're so nice."

Silence hung heavy and we neither one asked any more questions. The subject changed to silly girl talk and we laughed until Mama called, "Lower the volume, girls. Some of us prefer sleep."

I reached over to Blanca's side of the bed and squeezed her hand and fell asleep thinking what a happy day I'd experienced—one that I will remember always.

Each day when I arose from my bed, I went outside to check the weather. "Why won't it rain?" I complained. "How can I try out my new umbrella if it doesn't rain?"

"Oh, Amelia. You tire me out with your nagging," Mama said. "Use it as a parasol and keep the sun from your face. When I was a young girl living in Missouri, we always wore sunbonnets to keep the sun from drying our complexion. The sun wasn't nearly as hot and dry as it is here in this horrid desert, yet modern girls don't protect their skin at all. You're going to be as brown as black walnuts by the time you're grown."

I still longed for rain. One morning as I gazed at the sky, I saw a few clouds. "Think it might rain today, Mama?" I asked.

"Well, honey, it just might." Mama turned her face to the tree. "See how the leaves turn up? That's a sign of rain. The leaves try to soak up all the water they can. In Missouri, if the grass didn't have dew in the morning, we took that as a good sign of a coming rain, but out here, we've no grass."

"You like Missouri better, Mama?" I asked

"Land sakes. Of course I do." Mama wore a wistful expression on her face.

Rain came; in fact it poured—a long, warm rain. I walked to the henhouse and gathered the eggs, carrying my new red umbrella proudly. I skipped outdoors to the mailbox. I strolled around the yard and even trudged a short distance up the mountain to gather flowers, enjoying every minute. High up, I sniffed the air. I'd heard horses could detect rain. Why can't humans? The umbrella didn't leak and when I entered the kitchen, my hair felt dry. Of course, my feet were wet. No matter. At home, I wore no shoes and my bare feet were used to all kinds of weather.

The rain stopped and I left the wet umbrella on the porch and listened to the birds chirp. Little sparrows flew by, dipping and splashing their wings in puddles of water. It had been a full day and I felt very happy. Rain left a fresh smell in the air and the trees glistened with wet leaves like pretty little diamonds in the sky. I slowly prepared for bed, hating for this special day to end.

Tucked under a light sheet, I heard the wind howl and worried for the safety of my red umbrella. I rose from my pallet, rescued it from the porch and brought it into the kitchen. It still felt damp to my touch, so I opened the umbrella and placed it in front of the still smoldering fire of the cook stove to dry and then slipped back into bed—and a peaceful sleep.

Verna Simms

CHAPTER THIRTY-ONE—WHY?

The next morning, I awoke last. Upon entering the kitchen, I gasped, "Oh, my gosh!" My hand flew over my mouth. "What happened to my umbrella?" There it lay—broken and slashed—thrown onto the wood box in the far corner of the room. I dashed over and snatched it in my arms.

"It's ruined!" I cried. "Who could have broken it? Why?" My treasure had indeed been damaged beyond repair. The handle broken, the red silk material slashed with a knife or other sharp instrument. I turned my startled face to Mama.

"Chester lost his temper when he saw you'd left it open in the house. You do remember we told you it brought bad luck to open an umbrella inside the house, don't you? I'm sorry, but it's your own fault. Someday you'll learn to think and be more considerate of others' feelings." Mama saw the stricken expression on my face and added more kindly. "I know it's a hard lesson, dear, but we must accept the trials in this world. It'll be better in the next life, I'm sure."

"Who decided an open umbrella was bad luck, Mama?" I asked.

"I don't know, but you had bad luck, didn't you?"

She turned and left the room but not before I retorted, "What Papa did wasn't luck. He did it on purpose!"

I didn't accept the defeat graciously. Cradling the broken gift, much as I would a small red bird with a broken wing, I carried it into my sleeping area and hid the remains under my pillow. I will think what to do with it later, I promised myself.

The next day, I sat cross-legged on the porch, needle and red embroidery thread in hand, and labored to repair the rips in the material. I used a feather-stitch. One after another, I sewed until all were somewhat held together.

"You can't make it waterproof, sis." Joseph said, shaking his head.

"Hell's bells, I know, Joe," I answered. "But I'll not leave it to be burned like driftwood. It's mine and I'll do the best I can." Then hide it where no one can get their mitts on it, I mused stubbornly.

"I'll help repair the handle," Joseph volunteered. He leaned over and examined the damage. "I'd need Papa's brace and bit to drill a hole though both parts and then run a short length of baling wire, to hold it firmly together. He keeps his tool shed locked and I don't know when he'll be back."

I saw my chance to get even with Papa. "I know where he hides the key," I bragged.

"You do?" Surprise showed on Joseph's face.

Gathering my finished work with me, I walked to the far side of the yard. "See," I said, pointing to a loose board about half way up on the back side of the shed. "You twist that a little to the left and you can reach your hand inside and get the key. It's to the right, hanging on a nail under the shelf."

"How'd you know that?" Joseph asked, his face incredulous.

"Papa never notices if I'm in the yard or not. I could be a stump as far as he's concerned. One day I saw him remove the key and then watched as he put it back. Had to feel around a bit to find exactly where it hung. You try."

Joseph found the key and together we drilled holes and secured the umbrella's handle. I couldn't be proud of my umbrella anymore but I intended to carry out my plans. After Joseph left the yard, I slung the umbrella over my shoulder and climbed the tree in our front yard—the cottonwood close to the road. I scooted out on a high limb as far as I could without the branch dipping down enough to break, and there, using a length of baling wire, I fastened it to the branch above, leaving the umbrella open like a bright fire burning in the tree.

I shimmied back down, being careful not to rip my blue gingham dress. I trotted over to the steps and hopped up on the back porch. I whooped in delight, seeing the results. It would be impossible for a long, long time to leave the house by way of the back porch without seeing a fire-engine-red umbrella hanging high in a tree. Even Joseph would be too heavy to climb on that tender limb to pull it down, and I knew Papa had no ladder so tall. To me the message said, "Don't mess with Amelia Hall."

CHAPTER THIRTY-TWO—BAPTISM

I had to do what Papa said, even though I stayed mad at him. I bit my tongue to keep quiet, as he walked to where I relaxed in a comfortable chair. "Amelia, do you remember a letter coming last week?" I nodded, but didn't understand what it had to do with me.

"Well," Papa continued, "The bishop wrote. You're a very lucky girl." He paused for effect and looked around the room to be sure he had everyone's attention. "The letter commented that you are eight, the age of accountability. Time to be baptized, and he's invited you to come to Mesa and be baptized in the temple's baptistery." He studied me for my reaction. "Aren't you pleased? Not everyone has that honor. The temple hasn't been finished very long, you know. What do you say?"

"Yes, Papa. Will Mama come with me?" Suddenly I felt young and almost afraid, not of the water—I'd pretended to be baptized by my brother or sister in the Salt River, but this was different—serious, very serious.

"Of course, we'll all go," Mama spoke up. "I wouldn't miss an important day in your life for anything."

Sunday, I dressed in my best. For once, Thelma and Benjie stayed at home and Mama rode in the front seat beside Papa. We three siblings huddled close together in the back. I tried hard not to think of the day I'd last made the trip and gotten sick. I managed to prevent dizziness by staying in the middle and not looking down. Chewing gum helped, also.

Inside the temple room, I gasped. Twelve life-size golden oxen stood in a circle, each facing the baptistery. Mama had me undress in a small room to one side and I slipped on something resembling long underwear. Next we entered the main room and I walked down three concrete steps into warm tepid water. It felt good. I expected cold water.

A man I'd never seen before took my hand. "Amelia Hall, do you believe that Jesus is the Son of God?"

"Yes, I do," I answered, nodding.

He placed a white handkerchief loosely over my nose. In a loud voice as if the angels needed to hear, he spoke: "I baptize you in the name of the Father," a slight pause, "the Son," a longer pause, "and the Holy Ghost." With that, he tightened the handkerchief over my nose and lowered me into the water and quickly raised me again. Somewhere in the background, an organ began playing *When the Role is Called up Yonder*.

I walked up the three steps, water dripping on the concrete floor. Mama reached over, clasped my hand and led me back into the room where my clothing lay on a chair.

"Here, Amelia," she said, handing me a new white garment. "From now on, you are to wear a holy garment under your regular clothes. It represents holiness and obedience to God."

I dressed in this unfamiliar undershirt and then my regular clothes, and we left the temple. Somehow I didn't feel any different than before, which surprised me. Well, maybe a smidgen warmer. I'll ask Aileen about it when we are alone, I thought.

That night I asked Aileen, "Have all my sins been washed away?"

"Why, Amy, you haven't sinned; but if you had, I understand they have all been forgiven."

I rolled over and went to sleep, and all at once I felt a great relief as if a great burden had been lifted from my shoulders. I'll try and do better in the future, I promised silently under the covers.

CHAPTER THIRTY-THREE—SECOND GRADE

Imagine my surprise when I entered the second grade in the fall to find that Miss Barnes would again be my teacher. A new first grade teacher had been hired. Blanca and I sat next to each other, too. I loved the routine of school and was pleased to be back. Second grade seemed easy. I became the best reader in my class, and my other subjects weren't difficult. I especially loved art, and felt lucky that Miss Barnes had moved up to be our second grade teacher.

One day, Miss Barnes showed our class how to make stand-up valentines. I was ecstatic. Carefully, I cut stiff red paper into the shape of a heart. Next, I folded a white paper in quarters and cut small shapes from it. When I opened the paper, it resembled a lacy handkerchief or a doily. I pasted together two strips of paper and folded them like accordions. Then I attached one end to the heart and one to the white lacy paper. I'd created the most beautiful valentine I'd ever seen and marveled that I'd made it myself.

At the end of the day, Miss Barnes said, "You may take any valentines home tonight to show your parents, but be sure and bring them back in the morning if you plan to give them away here. Also, ask your mother for a paper bag to hold all your new valentines. We'll exchange tomorrow."

"I made a valentine for everyone in our class," Blanca told me during recess. "How about you?"

"Naw," I said. "I haven't had time. I'm going to make mine tonight and I'm only giving them to girls, but I've made a special one for you because you're my very best friend."

That evening I worked until way past my bedtime to cut out and paste a valentine for every girl in my class. Then I pulled out the beautiful pop-up heart I'd made in class and carefully wrote Blanca's name on the back.

"It's lovely," Thelma said. She'd been sitting at the kitchen table nursing Benjie. "You must show me how sometime."

The next day I wore my special red dress with the removable white collar. I felt a little hurt that no one complimented me on my dress, but they'd seen it before at our Christmas party.

After lunch, our class stopped all schoolwork and Miss Barnes surprised us by handing out iced pink and white cookies.

"Place your valentine bags on your desks, boys and girls," she said. "We're going out in the hallway and when I call your name, you will step in, one at a time, and drop your valentines in your classmates' bags."

Later, when the bell rang, I ran down the steps of our school carrying my full bag of valentines. Miss Barnes hadn't allowed us to look at them in class. "You may enjoy them later," she said.

When I arrived home, Thelma stood peeling potatoes at the sink and Mama rocked Benjie.

Thelma said, "So how did Valentine's Day go, Amelia? Did Blanca enjoy the pretty valentine you gave her?"

"She hasn't seen it yet," I said. "Our teacher wouldn't let us open our bag at school."

Aileen came in behind me, "That's because she doesn't want anyone's feelings hurt. Some children receive more valentines."

I hadn't considered that. Now I wanted to count my valentines.

"Well, dump them on the table and we'll admire how pretty they are," Mama said.

I threw my satchel on the table and suddenly felt a wave of panic.

"They're gone!" I said. "All of my valentines are gone!"

"How can they be?" Mama asked. "Do you remember carrying them out of your classroom?"

"Yes! I had them in my bag. I remember carrying it down the hall. I held it in my right hand with my satchel slung over my shoulder."

"I'll walk back to school with you," Aileen volunteered. "You must have dropped the bag along the way."

We retraced my steps and looked everywhere, but not a brown paper bag was to be seen. Back at home, no one could cheer me up. In my mind, I imagined all my valentines blowing away in the wind.

The next morning, Blanca waited for me in the playground. "What's wrong?" she asked when she saw my face. Then she said, "Oh my, you lost your valentines!"

I could only nod. I no longer marveled at Blanca's ability to figure things out. She pulled on a braid in deep thought. Then she said, "I know. Go look on top of the slide."

In a flash, it came back to me. After school the afternoon before, I'd taken a trip down the slide before running home. Blanca hadn't been with me. Her father always waited in the car as she waved goodbye to me at the bottom of the school steps.

Today, I raced over to the slide, worrying that my bag might have blown away or spilled, but there it lay—sitting on the platform near the top steps where I'd left it the day before. In my haste to cram in a ride, I'd forgotten my bag.

"Land sakes. How do you do it?" I asked Blanca, hugging her.

Blanca tossed her head and laughed. "I don't know. Mama is good at figuring out things, too. I guess I inherited the talent from her."

"I wish I had that talent," I said, "but I have the next best thing."

"What's that?" Blanca asked.

"You. I feel a sense of peace when you talk to me."

.

Verna Simms

CHAPTER THIRTY-FOUR—A CRASH HEARD AROUND THE WORLD

When Benjie turned seven months old, he learned to sit alone. One afternoon, a month later, Joseph and I watched him while Thelma occupied her hands mending socks. We sat on the floor of the parlor playing with him while Mama rested on the davenport thumbing through the Sears & Roebuck catalog and Aileen slumped next to her reading a book. The child vied for our attention and was an immense comfort to the whole family

"Look Mama," I said. "Benjie is trying to stand. Isn't he cute?" I held both of the infant's chubby hands and he pushed up on his feet.

"Yes, he's a sweetie," Mama said. "Aren't you?" she asked Benjie. The baby smiled at her.

"Peek-a-boo," Joseph teased, hiding his face behind his fingers. Benjie giggled and placed his own chubby fingers on Joseph's hands to pull them away.

Supper simmered in the oven that lovely Tuesday in late October. Papa had not returned from work. The family had never felt so carefree. We waited as we enjoyed a cool breeze that blew through the open window. Mama started humming a little ditty and because I was wearing a yellow dress with a flared skirt, I saw an opportunity.

"Look, Mama," I said, "I'm a ballerina!" I tried to stand on the very tips of my toes.

Aileen joined me, laughing. "I'm a willow tree," she said, holding her arms out, swaying back and forth in her green dress.

Benjie clapped his hands, delighted with the show.

"Put him on my back," Joseph said, dropping to the floor on all fours. Aileen and I lifted Benjie onto Joseph's back and held him in place as our brother crawled to the kitchen. Mama followed us. "Hold onto him," she said. "If anything happened to Benjie, I'm sure I don't think I could stand it."

I couldn't visualize anything so terrible. Our love for the little fella is the only thing holding this family together. For no reason I felt a chill slide up my back, like a cold wind had blown up my dress. I stopped dancing and started to leave the room.

Suddenly, the screen door burst open and slammed against the wall. Papa appeared, waving a newspaper in his hand. His face shone pale as a ghost and his mouth was set firm. I could not imagine what horrible thing had happened.

"Chester, what's wrong?" Mama rose from the davenport, alarmed.

He looked past her, shock on his face. "Wall Street crashed!" Papa slumped in a chair. "No one saw it coming. The market's been shaky for weeks, but . . ." He lowered his face to his hands, breathing heavily. "The paper said that last Thursday over twelve million stocks traded. Today it was pandemonium!"

He wiped sweat from his brow with his sleeve before adding, "Do you know what this means, Ida? People have lost their life savings. Thousands of people. The newspaper reports that people have committed suicide over it. Jumping out of tall windows! Glad we don't live in New York. Anyone who had their savings in stocks is bankrupt."

"Oh, my goodness!" Mama lifted her eyes to mine before collapsing in the nearest chair

Joseph gathered Benjie in his arms and walked outside. Mama continued staring at Papa. Aileen and I stayed near the dining room door where we could hear. I wondered if Papa would tell us to leave, but he didn't notice us. I felt as if the world was beginning to tilt and I left the room, but their voices followed me out.

"Whatever could have caused such a terrible thing to happen?"

"I'm no expert," Papa answered, "but the paper says it's the most disastrous and far-reaching event in the history of the stock exchange. Too many people buying on margin, I say. I've always said that if you can't afford to pay for it now, don't buy it.

"Ted Wallace has lost a fortune," Papa continued.

"Oh no!" Mama said. "Will they be okay? What can we do?"

"Everyone owes him money," Papa continued. "Everyone except me. He can only hope they come through."

Water Under the Bridge

Then he said, "And we can only pray the bank doesn't close. The meager amount we've managed to save is stored there. I mean to go first thing in the morning—me and everyone else in town, I expect." He dropped his head on folded arms to the tabletop, gasping. "Oh Ida, I suspect it's all gone."

No one had noticed Thelma coming to the door of the kitchen until she asked, "Will we lose the house?"

"No," Mama answered. Then she said, "The house is paid for, right?"

"Yes, thank the Lord," he answered.

"Thank the Lord," Mama repeated, barely audible.

Later Thelma asked Aileen, "What will happen to us?"

"Papa and Mama will manage somehow," Aileen answered.

The next morning, Papa's fear became reality when he arrived at the bank in Miami to find a sign on the door. CLOSED.

"We're going to have to tighten up around here," he said to Mama. "Don't buy anything but necessities—and don't buy them unless you ask me first."

And so the Great Depression began. In the following months, thousands of men across the country lost their jobs and banks began foreclosing on homes. Although the citizens of Claypool were not wealthy enough to have lost substantial sums in investments, it suddenly seemed that everyone was scraping by, including us.

"Won't President Hoover do something to help?" I overheard Mama ask Papa.

"No, Ida. He believes government shouldn't interfere with individuals. They mostly tax our property to fund schools and roads. Lucky if we can make the assessment so they don't steal our house. Dang the politicians. We're on our own—you and me."

I often heard Papa and Mama in the kitchen, late into the night, discussing the effects of the crash on the neighbors or planning how to make ends meet at home. Mama and Papa had always been frugal. They raised chickens and tried to grow vegetables when it rained. There were not many places for them to cut back.

One evening at dinner, Papa said, "I can no longer make a living in Claypool. The mines aren't being worked much. No one has money to build anything, not even a lean-to. The banks aren't loaning. What a mess!"

"I know," Mama answered, "And I've been thinking, Chester. Most of our neighbors don't have cars. Those that once owned one don't have them anymore."

Papa stared off into space. He seemed not to be listening. Mama continued anyway. "It's so far to walk to Miami. I'm just wondering, what if we convert our parlor into a little neighborhood store? I have a bit of money tucked away and there's a need for a store close by."

Suddenly Papa looked at her. She obviously had his attention.

"We wouldn't have to carry much," she added, "just flour, bread, coffee, sugar—the staples. Maybe some candy. Just merchandise that isn't perishable."

"Would you like to take a walk?" Aileen asked Thelma.

Thelma looked at Mama, but she was engrossed in conversation with Papa.

"I'll listen for Benjie and go to him if he wakes," I said, eager to hear more of Mama's plans for a store.

"Thank you, Amelia," Thelma said, smiling. She, Aileen, and Joseph crept outside. I'd noticed everyone refrained from making loud noises—as if silence would help solve the tragedy.

CHAPTER THIRTY-FIVE—A STORE

Papa leaned back in his chair, his long legs out in front of him crossed at the ankles, with his head cradled in his hands, which were clasped behind his head. He seemed to be imagining the store Mama was describing.

Mama's words poured out, "Thelma and the other kids can manage the housework and I could run the store while you look for work."

I think I was the only one that caught "other kids." Papa didn't change his expression or his posture. "Well, I'm guessing that if I sold the car and bought a one and a half ton truck with what money we have, I could haul things," he said. "I suppose, in addition, I could use it to carry goods from Phoenix for a store. Maybe peddle some vegetables and fruit around town and between, too. I've often longed for a truck."

Benjie began to cry in Papa and Thelma's bedroom. I moved to fetch him, but Mama said, "You run along outside, Amelia. I'll see to the baby."

I obeyed and lounged on the porch. After a while, Aileen, Thelma and Joseph returned. They sat on the steps with me. We could hear Mama and Papa talking inside with some intensity.

Suddenly, we heard the screen door slam and looked up to see Papa dash out of the house. Without a word he crossed the yard and walked quickly up the road toward the Wallaces' house.

"What do you think he's doing?" Joseph asked. "Great guns, he's moving fast. Didn't know he had it in him."

We all sat immobile, speculating. Joseph stopped working on the toy car he'd been whittling for Benjie.

After almost an hour, Papa came hurrying back down the road with Mr. Wallace, a portly man, puffing at his side. They went in the front door together, which surprised us on two counts since Mr. Wallace had never been to our house and we seldom used the front door. After a few minutes, Aileen looked in the parlor window and exclaimed, "Oh no! Come look. They're taking the davenport!"

It was true. Papa and Mr. Wallace carried the sofa out to the road and headed up toward the Wallace house, lugging it between them.

"We need the money," Mama explained simply. "Mr. Wallace is going to sell it for us. He knows a man who might buy it."

"His wife loves it," Aileen said. Then we all remembered that the Wallaces had lost money in the crash. I felt sad. It was as if both Mama and Mrs. Wallace were losing the davenport.

Reading my mind, Mama said, "My stars and garters, it's only a davenport. Besides, we need the space for the store." And before we had any time to adjust to that idea, Mama announced, "Hop to, we're going to give the front room a thorough cleaning." And when Mama said "clean," she meant clean!

"Joseph, fetch water and start a fire under the kettle."

Turning to Aileen and me, she said, "You two start with the woodwork. Leave the floor until the windows are washed. I'll do them myself." Mama was picky about glass.

"It was bad enough to sell the davenport, but did Papa have to sell our lovely maroon chair, too?" Aileen asked. He had hauled it out with him that morning in the truck he'd bought in trade for our Model T.

"We need the money and the space, dear," Mama said. "Mr. Wallace's friend bought them both." Then, under her breath she added, "Never grieve that which cannot be helped."

Aileen and I hustled to gather our cleaning supplies. Mama had placed the laundry washtub on the porch and it was full of bedding. So much work to do. I looked up to see Joseph beckoning to us from the window.

"I'm slipping over to see what Joe wants," I said. Joseph pointed toward the parlor.

I walked across to the parlor windows and peered inside. I gasped and placed my hand over my mouth in horror.

"Gosh, almighty. Hold onto your hat, Aileen," I yelled. "Papa's sawing the dining room table in half! Think he's lost his mind?"

I forgot the chores. I stood mesmerized, watching—Papa knelt on the dining room table in his stocking feet. He'd placed sawhorses beneath the table and marked the exact center with a chalk line that ran lengthwise. Now he held the saw on the edge of the table, at the top of the line, and sawed through the beautiful cherry wood.

Seeing it for herself caused Aileen to push me to hurry. "Before we start scrubbing the woodwork, let's hang the bedding on the line to dry," Aileen said. "Mama is sure to be in a bad humor now."

I helped her wring the excess water from the blankets and hang them on the two clotheslines.

When next we saw the parlor, two long skinny tables stood against the two main walls. By adding four two-by-fours as extra legs, the tables now formed a countertop in the shape of an L.

We surveyed the room that had once been Mama's pride and joy. I felt a lump in my throat, but Mama didn't appear sad at all. "So be it," she said, placing her hands on her hips. And, without another word, she started working on her business of setting up a new store.

"Gee whiz, Mama. Will you have to stay in this room all day?" I asked.

"No, honey, we'll hang a bell that tinkles when the front door opens."

Aileen and I had been instructed to move our pallets into the dining room. We laid them end to end on the window side of the room and Joseph's pallet stayed on the far side.

We still owned six dining room chairs. Mama distributed them—three for the store, one for her, and two for customers. "People might enjoy sitting and visiting a while," she explained. "Land sakes, but it reminds me of the old country store we had in Missouri when I was a child. Customers would even play checkers. Nice, friendly place to meet." Mama dropped wearily on a chair and propped her feet on another. "I'd like that."

The other three chairs were kept in the dining room where they were positioned side-by-side and covered with a blanket at night to make a privacy wall between Joseph's area and the space shared by Aileen and me.

Word got out quickly about our new store and the townspeople came to purchase small items between their trips to Miami. Before long, Mama and Papa increased the supplies they carried and I noticed that we again had plenty of food on our table. We also had little treats of candy and over-ripe fruit.

Mama appeared happier than we'd seen her in a long, long time. She thrived on running a business. During the day, she scrubbed and straightened and served the customers that stopped by. At nights she took out pencil and paper and tallied her sales or made lists of items for Papa to bring from Miami. She wouldn't let anyone help with her books. She had "a system," she said.

Things went well and the family made do. We lived and worked together in harmony. Although Papa and Thelma still shared a bedroom, there seemed to be no tension in our home. Thelma now kept the house clean and Mama never turned down an opportunity to cuddle Benjie. Papa happily took the money Mama handed him every Saturday. Life became good and I felt content once again.

CHAPTER THIRTY-SIX—MOVING WINTER 1930

One afternoon in February, I came home from school and found Thelma in the kitchen with Benjie on her hip. I'd been recalling the fun of his first birthday and was anxious to plan something else. Maybe a nice picnic for the family to share.

"Where's Mama?" I asked. "I'm making plans to teach Benjie to walk. When he doesn't need to be carried, think of all the good times we can have. We can go to the school playground and ride the merry-go-around."

"Your mama's here," said Thelma. "She's resting. Her head hurts her some."

"Gee whiz, is she all right?" I asked.

"Sure, she is," said Thelma. "Don't worry. I'm afraid I've upset her."

She placed Benjie in the highchair Papa had made for him. Then she straightened, rubbing her hand over the back of her neck and started wiping the already clean highchair tray.

"Where's Aileen?" she asked. "Your mother wants her to mind the store."

"She stayed after, to talk to her friends." I said. "She won't be long. What did you say to upset Mama?"

She reached over and touched my hair. I noticed then that she had tears in her eyes. "I'm really going to miss you, Amy," she said. "Your papa and I are moving away. He thinks Benjie and I should be with him in Phoenix. Perhaps he can find steady work there."

"Shucks! When was this decided?" I stormed. "Tarnations. No one told me."

"Oh hon, I just found out today," said Thelma, with skepticism in her face. "Only your mama and me know so far—and now you."

"But why?" I asked. "We're doing great here. Mama's store is making lots of money." A thought intruded in my mind, *We're finally happy as a family and now Papa has to ruin it all.* I turned to leave so she couldn't see my tears.

"We'll come and visit a lot," Thelma called with finality, as I escaped out the screen door to hide under the house. As usual, I welcomed the solitude I found there.

It had been a shock to all of us, but I was surprised at how upset it made me. First I hadn't wanted Thelma to stay but now I didn't want her to leave. We'd grown fond of her, despite the circumstances that had made her part of our lives, and we all dearly loved Benjie.

I awoke early the next morning—for a Saturday. I heard someone stirring in the back bedroom. I dressed hastily and entered the kitchen at the same time as Thelma opened the bedroom door, carrying Benjie.

"Good morning, Amy." she said sleepily. "Your papa wants an early start before the sun beams down. I can't get over the winters here. Cold at night but hot around noon."

She appeared nervous, and I suddenly realized that from now on Thelma would have the responsibility of caring for her child without Mama.

Mama appeared in her doorway wearing her old faded housedress and she hadn't bothered to unbraid her hair. She turned to Thelma, "May I carry Benjie to the car?"

"Of course," Thelma said and handed Benjie to her. "Chester said we'd breakfast along the way, but I'll pack a snack for Benjie—if it's okay?"

Mama nodded and opened the cupboard door with her free hand.

"All ready?" Papa boomed. He laughed, in a jovial mood in contrast to the rest of our sad faces.

"One minute," Thelma cried. "I forgot Benjie's blanket. She rushed to the bedroom door and grabbed the doorknob, then turned back, surprise on her face. "It—it's locked."

Papa rummaged in his pocket for keys and stepped over and unlocked the door, stood there for a moment, and locked the door once more as soon as Thelma returned, carrying Benjie's favorite blanket. No one in the room said a word. Shock registered on all our faces. Locked door—in our house!

Out in the yard, I stood to one side and watched, still stunned. Thelma and Papa opened the car doors and scooted in. Mama gave Benjie a quick kiss on the cheek and handed the child to his mother through the open window.

Aileen had been silent until now. "Papa, may we ride with you for a ways and then walk back?"

I jumped at the idea and not waiting for an answer, jerked the back door open and hopped in.

Papa roared in laughter. "Might as well. Amelia has already taken up homesteading. Not too far, though."

I waved at Mrs. Jones and called to Brownie as we turned the corner and then a terrible thought hit me. Mama had looked forlorn as we drove off, leaving her all alone. What if Papa was playing another one of his tricks and wouldn't let us out of the car but would keep us forever? I'd never see my mama again. Fear gripped my heart.

Then the school loomed close. The day Mama and I had walked to school that first day came to me in a flash as the scene unfolded in front of my eyes. "Let me out at the schoolyard!" I cried.

Papa braked. "You sick?"

I shook my head but it was a lie. I felt deathly ill.

As usual, Aileen took charge. "We'll take the shortcut over the mountain home. I have no desire to answer Mrs. Jones' questions—perhaps a nice lady—but unbearably nosey."

Joseph and I both agreed. We loved to race over the mountain. I only wished I could find flowers blooming so I could carry a bouquet home to Mama.

The house seemed lonely now with just Mama, Aileen, and Joseph. Daniel had not visited for a couple of weeks, not since Papa and Thelma moved. I missed him.

One afternoon I came home from school with an idea. "Mama, can Joseph and I go visit Dan up on the mountain?"

"Heavens no," she said. "It's much too far for you to walk and I'm not even sure how to get there."

"Gee whiz, I know the way," I said, remembering our conversation at the tool shed on the day after I'd run away. "He told me how to recognize the path. Joseph will walk with me."

"No, it's out of the question," she said. "I'm not about to have you two roaming around the mountainside. Why don't you write him a letter?"

"How would I mail it to him?" I asked. "He lives in a tree house."

"A tree house?" Mama said, shocked. "Who told you that? Your papa said he stayed at the Brown's."

I realized I'd probably said something Daniel didn't want Mama to know. "I told him to build us a tree house," I said. "I told him he could live in it and we'd come and visit."

Mama laughed. "I think you better write a letter," she suggested. "You're big enough. I'll let you have a sheet of my special paper with the birds on it."

"Should I mail it to the Brown's?" I asked, trying to cover my tracks regarding the tree house. Then suddenly I had a thought. "I know! I could give it to Mary tomorrow at school."

"Good idea," Mama said.

So I spent the next hour laboriously writing out a letter to my brother and wondering how I would get it delivered. I wrote:

> *Dear Dan,*
>
> *Please come home. We're missing you terrible. If you come, you can share Joseph's spot in the dining room. Aileen and I will move over. Papa won't mind. He's not here. He left with Thelma.*
>
> *Love, Amelia*

Fortunately, I didn't have to wonder long how to send the letter. The next day was Wednesday. When we sat down to supper, the kitchen door opened and Daniel walked right in. "Sure hope you made enough biscuits for me," he said.

"Daniel!" Joseph and I shouted in the same breath.

Mama ran over and gave him a long hug. Then she quickly started filling another plate with her chicken and dumplings.

Daniel lowered his sturdy frame into Papa's chair, a half smile on his face. "Sure feels good to be here," he said, patting the armrests.

"How've you been, son?" Mama asked. "Gracious sakes, but we've been missing you."

"I found work in Miami," he said. "A man, Mr. Farrell, needed carpenters to finish a lean-to he'd started before the crash. He told Mr. Wallace and he recommended me. Mr. Farrell put me up while I worked—me and a few other guys. We got board and pretty good wages."

"I wanted to go visit you," I said.

"Me too," Aileen said. She and I both rose from the table to give Daniel a hug. He squeezed our shoulders, with Joseph getting a friendly shove.

"I've good news," he said. "Tomorrow I'm walking to Miami to pick up a truck I bought. With it, I'll be able to visit more often, especially since . . ." his voice trailed, but we all knew he referred to Papa's absence.

"Great guns. What kind of truck?" Joseph asked eagerly.

"Oh, it's just a 1914 Model T pick-up," Daniel said proudly. "It runs good though, and it's as clean as the day they built it. It was supposed to be ready for me when we completed our job, but we finished a day early. Maybe I'll ask Mr. Wallace if I can ride with him tomorrow morning to pick it up."

He turned to Mama. "Okay if I stay the night?"

"Of course it is," she said. "This is always your home."

I suspected we all thought Papa would see things differently. Daniel kissed Mama on the cheek and asked, "Should I sleep in the lean-to or is there an extra bed available now?"

We searched each other's faces to see who should tell him about Papa's locked room. Finally Joseph spoke. "Papa locked his bedroom. He said we're to keep it for his own use when he comes on weekends."

Daniel bounced out of his seat and bolted over to check for himself.

"Well, I'll be . . ." he growled, stooping to examine the keyhole. He turned back to where we'd remained in the kitchen and said to Mama, "So, where're you sleeping?"

"I've kept my old bedroom. Heaven help the person that tries to take it from me!" Mama exclaimed. "The girls sleep in the dining room with Joseph now—on the opposite side near the window."

"While a perfectly good bed remains unused?" Daniel snarled.

"It's not worth the trouble," Mama said. "We each have a place to lie down. Best to let sleeping dogs lie."

But Daniel wasn't listening. He stared out the open screen door and appeared to be studying the sky. "Tell you what I'll do," he said. "Tomorrow I'll buy a skeleton key at Woolworth's in Miami. They're only a nickel."

I expected Mama to protest, but instead she got her purse and handed Daniel a coin. "You'll be needing to save your money for gasoline now, son," she said, dragging out the word "son" like a caress.

Joseph interrupted. "Gee, Dan, can I go with you tomorrow?" He rose and walked to his brother's side.

"You have school," Aileen reminded him.

"Ah shucks, can't I miss just this once?" Joseph begged. "Please? It isn't every day that Daniel buys a truck."

"I guess it'll be all right," Mama said.

Later the next day I heard voices. "Joe! Dan!" I yelled, coming into the kitchen.

"They're not home yet, Amelia," Mama called from the parlor. I joined her as Mrs. Wallace reached the front door to leave. She'd either been shopping in the store or visiting with Mama.

"You must come by for a visit soon," Mrs. Wallace said to Mama. "You work too hard. How about after dinner tomorrow and we'll chat?"

"I'd love to," Mama said. "It's just so hard to leave the store."

"I'll watch the store," Aileen announced, coming in behind me.

"I'll help, too," I offered.

Mama looked uncertain, but then she appeared to gather her resolve. "Yes," she said, "I'll plan on tomorrow. It's high time the girls learned to handle things in my absence, and I would enjoy time away."

After Mrs. Wallace left, Aileen asked, "When will Daniel and Joseph be home? They left before we went to school this morning."

"I know," Mama said. "I've been expecting them to pull in all day. I hope that truck's reliable."

"Mama, I've been thinking," I started, "with Papa gone, do you think Daniel could move back?"

A glimmer of hope crossed Mama's blue eyes, but it soon faded.

With both my brothers gone, I had time on my hands, so I decided to clean my shelves—the ones made from orange crates.

I scooped everything onto the floor in a pile and then sorted through all the papers to decide what to keep and what to pitch.

"Oh my," I muttered to myself. "I'd forgotten this letter from July 1928, the one I'd copied by tracing the writing using the windowpane!"

We'd learned cursive this year, so I forgot the mess on the floor and spread the papers on the library table and began to read.

Dear Ida,

Hope you and your family are well. We feel fine except for Cordelia's back. She hurt it last spring digging in the dirt planting peonies.

The writing was smeared and I couldn't make out the next paragraph so I turned to the last page.

Water Under the Bridge

I worry about your girls' safety with you all alone in that wild-west country Chester dragged you to. It appears to me that his new religion dwells on the opposite sex far more than is healthy.

Come back to Missouri if you feel you or your family need help. Your old room is always available. Promise me you'll keep a keen eye out for trouble concerning Aileen and Amelia. I often think of you at that age and how I tried to protect you.

A last, but hopefully unnecessary, warning. Men have been known to use the Bible as an excuse to take advantage of women, especially young girls. I even heard of one dad who tried to convince his daughter it was permissible for fathers to sleep with their daughters (in the knowing them way as told in the Old Testament) because of the example of Lot and his daughters. Shameful!

I didn't understand the meaning but thought it best to burn the letter at the first opportunity. A car braked and I jammed the letter in my pocket and ran to greet Daniel and Joseph.

The next day, Mama explained to Aileen and me how to make change and record sales in the store. "Be sure and write down anything you sell that's getting low," she said. "Your papa will need to know what to buy on his next trip."

It found it fun sitting on a chair beside Aileen as she served a customer. Occasionally she'd hop up and dust a spot on the candy counter or rearrange the candy. I knew better than to ask for a treat. We had few customers, so I soon became bored and went outside. Around suppertime, Mama rushed home and took over.

"Mrs. Wallace says things are bad with them. Wish I'd taken her a dozen eggs. We could spare them."

"I'll go, Mama," I volunteered. Mama looked relieved and packaged a dozen eggs and handed them to me. I watched as she counted the money and her face glowed with pleasure and I thought, when Mama is happy, she is as pretty as she was that morning she walked me to school; too bad she can't be happy all the time.

Before prayers that night I said to Aileen, "Mama needs to be with grownups more and have freedom from the store. Let's you and I help."

Aileen nodded.

CHAPTER THIRTY-SEVEN—SAD NEWS

Papa returned once a week to bring laundry for Mama to wash and to leave goods for the store. Thelma and Benjie rode in the front seat with him and we enjoyed their short visits. Over the months since they'd left, I didn't seem to miss little Benjie any less with time. I hadn't realized how the child's gleeful laughter and playful ways brightened the whole house.

One Saturday in June, shortly after school closed for summer vacation, Papa arrived alone.

"Where's Thelma and Benjamin?" Mama asked, running the tip of her tongue over her lower lip.

"They're at home," Papa said. "The baby has the croup. Thelma stayed up with him all night. I'm not sure she knows what to do." A frown creased his forehead.

"Oh dear," Mama's voice choked. "Maybe she better move back to Claypool so I could help."

"No," Papa said. "It does no good to take him out when he's ailing. Better for you to come home with me. You could show Thelma the steam treatment."

Mama didn't answer right away. "What about our children?" she asked, shaking her head. "And the store?"

"Oh, don't you remember, Mama, Aileen and I know how to run the store," I said.

"Yes, but I mustn't leave you alone overnight," Mama clenched her fists in her lap.

"Daniel could stay with us," I suggested.

"No," Papa said sharply. "That won't be necessary." He turned to Mama, "Just write instructions. I'll make sure Thelma follows them."

"I'd feel a lot better if they were with us." Mama fussed with her hair, removing the pins and then jamming them back in place one at a time. "I'd like to observe Benjamin with my own eyes. It's hard to tell how sick a baby is without looking into his eyes and feeling his forehead."

"Just jot it down," Papa ordered impatiently. "I'll make sure she follows instructions. If he doesn't get better soon, I'll call the doctor."

Mama wrote several pages of instructions for Thelma and handed them to Papa. Then he thrust the papers deep into his pocket, walked briskly to the driver's side, slid behind the wheel, and left. I stood in the yard, gazing at the dust billowing up from the road, until the truck turned the corner and was out of sight. I could see two hawks floating low, gliding on motionless wings. A heavy load crowded my heart and a chill ran up my spine. My darling little Benje lay sick and helpless.

On the following Friday, Joseph and I sat in the yard building roads for our toy cars. Our yard was mostly sand and it was easy to scoop the sand to one side. I looked up when I heard the front gate squeak open. "Here comes the mail carrier," Joseph said. "I'll get it!"

I jumped up and ran to meet the postman at the road, but when I reached for the envelope in his hand, he shook his head. "It's registered. Your mother must sign for it." His voice was laced with a hint of foreboding.

The postman stepped up on the front porch and before he could knock, Mama met him at the door. I stood close by, curious about the letter he held in his hand. I saw an average-sized envelope, very thin, but edged all around in black. I seemed to remember seeing an envelope like it before. But where?

Mama took one look at the envelope and caught her breath, shock on her face. Her hand flew to her heart. "Oh no," she said, snatching it. Then, forgetting her manners, she turned and let the door shut in the postman's face.

"I hope everything is okay." His eyes asked a question and he shook his head. He was an older man with gray hair, and he looked unsure of himself as he turned to go back down the porch steps toward the road.

Aileen and I hurried inside and found Mama slumped in a chair at the table studying the envelope.

"Want me to read it, Mama?" Aileen offered.

"No," Mama said, "oh dear, it's from Chester." We plainly heard the dread in her voice. Her hands trembled as she broke the seal and removed a single sheet of paper. Almost immediately she cried, "Oh no! Please God, no!"

The paper slid from her fingers onto the floor and she lowered her head onto the table.

Aileen rushed over and quickly embraced our mother. "What is it?" she asked.

In the meantime, Joseph reached down and retrieved the fallen mail. After reading it, he dropped his head and stared at his shoes, before he handed the paper to Aileen. I peered around her elbow to read the writing:

> *March 17, 1930*
> *Ida—*
> *The baby died last night. Pneumonia, the doctor said. I believe you might have saved him, had you been here.*
> *Chester*

"No!" I screamed, pounding the table. "No! No! No!"

Then great sobs racked my body. Mama pulled me onto her lap to comfort me, but it was no use. I fought her. It was all she could do to hold onto me.

"There, there, Amelia," she said. "It's all right. Benjie is in heaven now. He'll never be sick again."

I understood about death, but I had never thought it would happen to anyone I knew, especially a little baby. I felt as if my heart had been torn apart; an important piece of me gone forever. I couldn't imagine a world without Benjie's bright eyes and dimples. How could God let such a horrible thing happen?

Aileen had collapsed in the chair next to Mama. She was crying quietly, tears streaming down her face.

Joseph snatched something off the shelf behind the table and walked over to the kitchen stove. He grabbed the handle to lift the cover and out of his pocket drew his knife. With it, he scratched deep grooves into the wooden car he'd been whittling for Benjie. Then he dropped the little car into the fire and replaced the stove's lid. Without a word, he turned and ran out the kitchen door—and never looked back.

Mama retrieved the short letter and read it again. She turned it over and examined the back. It was blank.

"Land sakes, I do wish Chester had written more," she said. "He didn't say anything about Thelma, poor thing. She needs her mother."

"Mama," I asked. "What made the mail carrier suspect it was bad news? He seemed to know."

Mama jammed the note back into the envelope before answering. She slowly traced her fingertips along the black edging. "The black edging around the envelope, honey," she said. "Black is a sign of death."

"Why?"

"It's like a warning. It gives a person a chance to sit down before reading bad news." She fiddled with the topknot of her blonde-brown hair. "In earlier times, women used to faint on bad news. Especially if they were with child."

She reached out and placed her hands on both Aileen's and my cheeks. "The Lord knows best," she said. "We must be brave and trust Him."

The house seemed strangely empty after that. Even though Benjie had not lived there for months, every piece of furniture reminded me of him: the old wicker rocker that we used to help him fall asleep, and the table with its red-checkered oilcloth where we placed his small tub to bathe him. His cup, which Daniel had bought for him, still sat on the cupboard shelf. It had brightly colored animals painted on it.

We moped around the house for days. I dreaded the day when Papa would come. I didn't know how to talk to Thelma about Benjie. There seemed no right words to say. What I had on my mind could certainly be the wrong words to tell her: "Why would God allow such a thing to happen? Why would he take one so young and innocent as Benjie?"

"Tarnations, but I'm angry with God," I blared loudly, stomping my heavy shoes on the kitchen floor.

"No, child. You must not blame God for the unpleasant things that happen in this life," Mama said. "He made man and woman and He gave them everything they could ever want and need. He also gave them both free will and they chose to sin. That's what brought all kinds of trouble like this into the world. It's been that way from day one."

"But Thelma and Benjie weren't even alive then," I said, "and God could have saved Benjie if He'd wanted to. It's no use to pray if God can't or won't help!" I crossed my arms and puckered my lips into a pout.

"Amelia! Don't you ever talk like that! Of course, God can do anything He desires. His ways are not our ways. We can't understand now, but we must trust that He knows best. He doesn't do our bidding every time we ask Him. I know it hurts sometimes and it's hard to understand, but we must always trust God. We'll understand someday—*someday*."

She ran her fingers through her hair to give herself a few more seconds to gather her thoughts. "Let's go to the Bible," she said. "Call Joseph. Aileen, get my Bible."

Aileen dutifully went to Mama's bedroom to fetch the leather bound Bible while I went outdoors to find my brother. He was hidden under the house, sitting in the dark.

"Mama wants you," I said. "She thinks we should read the Bible."

"Aw, it won't do any good now," Joseph said. "Papa shouldn't have taken Thelma and Benjie away. Mama might have saved him."

"Mama said God took him away," I said.

"Naw, Papa took him," said Joseph, crawling out from under the house behind me.

Back in the kitchen, we sat at the table while Mama turned the pages of her large Bible. Finally she stopped at First Corinthians 13:12, ". . . for now we see through a glass darkly; but then face to face. Now I know in part; but then shall I know even as I am known."

"We will all understand someday," she said. Then she got up and turned her back to us at the table. I could see her shoulders heaving. Then, in a low voice I heard her say, "Oh God, I am so sorry I didn't go to them."

"Tarnations, it's not your fault!" I shouted. "God did it. He did it all by Himself! Why would He do this and make us wait to die and go to heaven to understand why. Why?" I stomped my foot.

Aileen grabbed my hand and pulled me into the dining room. "Stop it!" I said, "Turn loose of me!"

"Amelia, you must be strong for Mama," she whispered. "She's blaming herself. That's awful. She loved Benjie. You must stop questioning God. There is nothing that can be done about this and you make Mama feel worse."

I wasn't the only one blaming God, though. That Saturday, Papa entered the house alone carrying two large bags of laundry.

"It's over, Ida," he said, dropping them on the floor of the store where Mama sat busy working on her sales figures.

"Did you hear me?" he said, louder. "I said, it is over!"

"I heard you, Chester. I'm not deaf," Mama said, "but you still haven't told me what is over."

"Thelma's gone," he said. He held out a folded piece of paper, but Mama didn't reach for it, so he laid it on the table and stalked out the front door. A moment later, I heard the truck door slam shut, but after more than enough time had passed, the motor hadn't started.

"Amelia," Mama said, finally. "Please read the note to me aloud."

Surprised, I walked over to the table and scooped up the note. As I was unfolding it, Mama said, "I want to be able to honestly say that I did not read what was written."

Slowly, I read aloud the wide looping letters of Thelma's hand:

> *Wednesday, March 26, 1930*
> *Dear Chester,*
> *I have gone home to my parents. Please don't try to follow or contact me. We have sinned, you and I, and because of that God has seen fit to punish us just as he did David. Jesus tells us to 'Go and sin no more,' so that is what I mean to do. I believe you should return to your wife and ask her forgiveness. I only hope that someday she can forgive me, too.*
> *Thelma*

Shaken, I refolded the note neatly and laid it back on the counter where Papa had left it. I searched Mama's face for a reaction, but I couldn't see her thoughts there; she said not a word, but dismissed me with a wave of her hand.

"Guess I'll go outside," I said, and shuffled out the kitchen door into the yard. Papa sat stiffly in the front seat of his truck. I didn't go to him. I headed straight for the cottonwood tree and sat down beneath it. After a few minutes, Papa slid from behind the wheel of the truck and came over to the tree. He stood awkwardly with his arms folded across his chest.

"Amelia, what did Ida say about Thelma's letter?" he asked.

"She didn't read it," I said truthfully, kicking the sandy soil at my feet. "It was laying folded on the counter when I walked out the door."

Cautiously, I raised my eyes and saw that Papa's face held a blank expression; he never lifted his eyes to mine.

"I have to go to the toilet," I said apologetically. I walked toward the outhouse, but when I reached it and knew I was out of his sight, I veered suddenly off to the far end of our property and opened the rickety wooden back gate.

"Sis, wait for me!" I heard Joseph shout.

I turned to see him running toward me, taking long strides through the rocks and low-growing cactus. The glorious mountain view broke upon me and I sighed and waited for my brother.

"C'mon, Amy. let's go up to our tree," he said, when he caught up with me. "We must make a plan."

We walked in silence. I had hoped to be alone to ponder this new development, but I also welcomed my brother's insight. Up ahead, I could see some birds darting in and out of the trees. A mother bird was busy teaching her babies to fly. As we approached them, the birds swooped up to the trees on higher ground to gain more distance from Joseph and me.

"Amy, what do you think?" Joseph asked, sitting beneath the acacia tree. "Do you think Papa is coming back to us?"

"Gee, I don't know," I said, rubbing my hand over the light green moss at the foot of our tree. "I like the way this moss feels on my hand."

"It's nice," he said, "but I want to talk about Papa. Ailie is happy. She said maybe Mama will forgive Papa and things will go back to the way they were before."

He reached over and rubbed the moss thoughtfully himself. Then he added, "I suppose Mama can decide what's best."

"I don't think she should forgive him," I said. "She's gained a lot of weight since he married Thelma. I doubt Papa wants her anymore."

"Well, I'm going to go live with Dan if he stays," said Joseph. "I couldn't bear him treating Mama badly. Not again."

"Gee whiz, Joe. Don't go," I pleaded. "I couldn't bear it here with just Ailie and me. She spends all her time reading. Blanca would be all I have left and I don't see her in the summer." I hesitated before I added, "Promise me. Promise me you won't leave. Please Joe! Promise!"

"Oh sis, don't worry," he said, standing up. "I won't leave—or I'll take you with me." He rose to his feet and looked toward the top of the mountain. "Want to come see a cave I found?"

Joseph led the way and I scurried to keep up. The path became steeper as we climbed higher. Perspiration beaded on both our faces. I rubbed my cheeks with my dress tail and almost stumbled with the sweat pouring down into my eyes.

"Golly, it's a long, long way," I said, gasping for air.

"Want to turn back?" he asked with an anxious expression on his face.

I shook my head and dropped down on a flat rock. "I'll just rest awhile."

After a few moments, I looked over the landscape and said, "Oh Joe, isn't it lovely up here? Next time we come, let's bring a lunch and picnic on this rock."

Then I added, "I'm really thirsty."

"Me, too," he said. "We should probably start back." He gazed up to check the position of the sun. "We mustn't get caught up here in the dark."

"But we aren't there," I complained.

"We'll come again—soon. I promise. Have I ever broken a promise?" He turned toward the house. We hadn't gone far when he reached over and gripped my hand. Together we started the long trek back home to our uncertain future.

CHAPTER THIRTY-EIGHT—SUMMER 1930

Mama let Papa stay, but as before they slept in separate bedrooms—Papa in the room he'd shared with Thelma—while our mother remained in the front room she'd always used. Papa appeared nervous around Mama. When at home, he did more work around the house than before. He often asked Mama if she needed anything and when she'd say no, he'd say, "Are you sure?"

He continued to live and work in Phoenix during the week, so our daily lives didn't change noticeably. We still saw him only on weekends. He'd return home late Friday evenings and eat the dinner Mama left for him on the stove. On Saturday mornings, he took his pay to Miami and bought supplies for the store. Then he busied himself around the house, repairing things, cleaning out the chicken coop or tool shed, whatever needed doing, until Sunday afternoon. Then he'd gather a load of clean clothes and once again he'd drive over the mountain to Phoenix.

Usually on Mondays, Daniel would come by for dinner. Sometimes he slept over, but usually stayed only a little while after we ate and then headed back up the mountain, where I could only imagine the wonderful tree house that had become his home. I longed to see it and hoped that before summer ended, Mama would let Joseph and me walk the trail—or Daniel would invite us to ride with him in his truck. But neither happened.

With no school, I missed Blanca terribly. Joseph had Billy to play with and Aileen kept busy doing housework or helping serve customers in the store. A book occupied her spare time. I found myself spending many hours alone beneath the house or up in the cottonwood tree.

One Monday morning as Aileen and I cleared the breakfast dishes, we heard a car stop. Mama waited in the store and since it had become common for customers to stop by at all hours, we paid no attention.

Suddenly, I heard a knock at the kitchen door and looked up to see Blanca, a big smile on her face. "Surprise!" she said, jumping up and down.

She beamed. "Mother wrote your mama a letter to arrange this visit as a surprise for you."

I clutched her hand and pulled her inside. Mama came into the kitchen looking pleased. "You girls have the whole day before you," she said. "I have penny candy and we received a new Sears & Roebuck catalog yesterday. If you want, you can cut up the old one and make dolls. Whatever makes you happy." She left us alone and headed through the dining room to her private sanctuary—the store.

"Thank you, Mrs. Hall," Blanca called after her. Then she reached into one of the two ample pockets of her light blue pinafore and extracted a hand written invitation. She handed it to me.

"Amy, I'm so excited," she said. "Mama's cousins, the ones I told you that live in New Mexico—you remember—they have a boy Joseph's age. Joe is twelve, isn't he?"

I nodded.

"They have two older girls, too, but I don't recall their ages. Anyway, they've bought a car and are driving to Arizona to stay at our house over the Fourth of July holidays. Mama's throwing a big party and your whole family is invited! Isn't that super?"

She waited for an answer. I didn't know what to do. Papa had made it clear that he didn't like Blanca's family. Not knowing what to say, I said nothing, just gave her a quick hug and we went into the back yard to play.

"What's your pleasure, Blanca?" I looked around the yard. Everything seemed old to me, but I hoped Blanca could see something of interest.

"Could we walk on your stilts?" she asked, hopefully. "I've never had any to try."

"Oh, yes," I exclaimed, and ran and retrieved Joseph's and my old stilts from under the porch. They were a bit dusty, but I wiped them with my dress tail.

"You want the pair lowest to the ground, or the tall ones?" I asked. Without waiting for her to answer, I stepped up on the low pair and took a few steps. "These are the ones I learned on, but you're welcome to try the higher pair, if you want."

Blanca laughed and pushed her lovely black hair, which was hanging down loose, behind her ears. "I'd better start out safe. Not so far to fall."

I showed her how to hold her hands and slip her feet through the inner tube straps onto the wooden blocks that held her feet and helped her balance. She gleefully took a couple of steps and soon the two of us were circling the yard.

"Hey, sis," Joseph called from across the street, "wanna borrow my new stilts?"

"Sure," I hollered back. Daniel had presented Joseph with a highly polished pair of stilts for his eleventh birthday the week before. He'd been stingy about sharing, so I hadn't had a chance to try them. He ran and carried the set from inside the tool shed where he kept his things out of the weather.

"Company first," he said. He turned to Blanca, "I'll help you on and balance you until you feel steady." I'd never noticed Joseph being so helpful to another girl. I felt a sudden pang of jealousy. As the day went on, he continued to linger near Blanca even after Billy called him to come over.

During lunch, he asked Blanca, "How about a second helping?" She politely shook her head. "Would you like to walk up the mountain? Amy and I know a lovely nook to rest and watch a mama bird." Fortunately, Aileen said no to that idea. "She's not dressed to climb the mountain," she pointed out. "She'd ruin her pretty pinafore among the cactus."

When Blanca looked disappointed, she said, "Maybe you can wear an old dress of mine or Amelia's." But Blanca insisted on helping with the dishes and then she suggested we walk on stilts again. Joseph said, "C'mon, you can use my new ones again. You have the hang of them now."

I'm ashamed to say I was actually glad when Mr. Romac pulled up in front of our house to take Blanca home.

Joseph is my brother, I mumbled silently. But as the car disappeared around the bend toward the Jones' house, I felt my loneliness return and I wished her back.

I entered the house and discovered the invitation Blanca had brought laying on the table. In a fluid hand, it was addressed to "The Hall family." I read it through and then hid it behind the games on the kitchen shelf.

That evening, I waited for the family to gather at the supper table. Daniel was visiting. Impatiently, I watched Mama heap meat, potatoes, and beans on each plate and we sat through her prayer. Finally, the room fell silent as everyone began eating.

"May I read something aloud?" I asked nervously.

No one glanced up. I unfolded the paper and began reading. "The Romac family wishes to extend an invitation to the entire Hall family to come to an informal Fourth of July party on Friday at one o'clock. The parade passes by our home and you are all welcome to enjoy it with us. RSVP."

To my surprise, everyone stopped eating and looked at each other.

Aileen spoke first, holding a fork in midair. "That would be nice, don't you think, Mama?"

"Yes, it's high time we got out of this house and went somewhere as a family. And on our national holiday, too."

She touched her bun before adding. "Stars and garters. What on earth shall I wear?" We all laughed.

Daniel spoke first, "You look lovely in your light blue dress. It brings out the blue in your eyes. You have real pretty eyes, Mama. When I marry and have children, I hope the girls inherit your azure-blue eyes."

Mama's face turned pink. "Why, thank you," she said quietly. She began toying with her food. I could almost read her thoughts: *Don't eat! Lose five pounds before the Fourth!*

"I can drop you off, but I won't be coming with you," Daniel said, "I already have plans."

"What are you doing?" Aileen asked.

"Well, I'm not telling," he said. He smiled and raised his palm towards us "No more questions."

I hated secrets, but Daniel loved them. I fumed to know his plans, but I knew he wouldn't tell until good and ready. I suspected he might have a surprise concerning his tree house, or maybe he'd begun work on a real home. I hoped not. Although eager to visit him in the tree house, I still hadn't seen it.

The next day, a letter arrived in a pink envelope. It was addressed in large loopy letters that nearly covered the entire front side. It was addressed to Mrs. Hall, Aileen, Joseph, and Amelia Hall I noticed the return address as Phoenix, Arizona.

"Who do you reckon it could be from?" Mama said studying the unfamiliar handwriting.

"Open it!" I urged.

"Here," Mama said handing the unopened pink envelope to me. "Your name is on it, too. You read the letter aloud."

The letter was written in cursive, but I was able to read it with no problem.

Water Under the Bridge

Tuesday, July 1, 1930

Dear Mrs. Hall,

I hope you will keep this letter a secret from Chester and that you won't mind my writing to you. I miss you, Aileen, and Joseph and Amelia. I miss you so much I had to take a chance. My parents moved to Snowflake but I stayed in Phoenix with friends. I am working now in their restaurant washing dishes.

I've never thanked you all for what you did for me. I know I didn't deserve the kindness you showed me. Someday I hope to repay it. Until then, I will think of you often and hope to see you again soon.

You'll never guess what I saw. A friend and I went to a picture show and it actually talked. Not like the silent ones where the lips moved but you have to read the words. The title was "The Jazz Singer" and Al Jolson sang three songs—one he kneeled down with his face painted black and sang "Mammy." I wish you and Benjie could have been with me.

I get so lonesome at times. Even the movie reminded me of home in Missouri. We had minstrel shows there where they sold patent medicine.

I miss Benjie dreadfully. It is almost more than I can bear. He loved you all so much. Somehow I think he wants me to reach out to you. If you are not too angry with me, please write back.

Thelma

The room became quiet at the reminder of little Benjie. I pictured his blonde curls and blue eyes, his chubby dimpled smile. He had looked a lot like Thelma. I wondered why Thelma didn't mention missing Daniel. I knew he'd be hurt if we told.

Finally Mama said, "The poor dear." She took the letter from me and slipped it into her apron pocket. "You mustn't tell your papa about this."

"I won't," I promised.

We enjoyed the large gathering at the Romac's spacious home on Friday. In addition to their houseguests—relatives from New Mexico—two of their neighbor families came. They'd decorated their home with American flags, and Mrs. Romac had baked a large cake showing a picture of an eagle.

Mama took Daniel's advice and wore her blue dress. I wanted to wear my best red dress, but Mama said it wouldn't be appropriate for an outdoor holiday. Instead I wore an old blue gingham dress. Mama brought a basket of fried chicken and a peach pie.

Aileen noticed girls she knew from school and joined them in animated conversation. Joseph stuck close to Blanca and me, even though he'd been introduced to her cousin, Amos, near his own age.

At first I worried about my friend and my brother and didn't enjoy myself, but soon the festivities captured my attention. By the time the parade came along, I'd lost sight of Joseph and Blanca and stood at the side of the road waving my little American flag at the passing marchers.

Later, I joined a group that had gathered around the piano to sing patriotic songs. I loved singing, and Dolores Romac's beautiful voice should not be missed.

Too soon, it was time to go, and Mama said to the Romac family, "Thank you for a very lovely time."

Aileen, Joseph, and I climbed into the back seat of Mr. Romac's car and Mama sat in the front. On the way home, Mama turned to Mr. Romac. "We had a thrilling afternoon. I must tell you how happy I am that Blanca and Amelia have become fast friends."

"Si, friends are important for a successful childhood."

He braked in front of our house and we all echoed a polite "thank you" and gathered our belongings and carried them into the empty house.

"Blanca's parents are nice," Mama said. "Did you have a good time?" She looked at all of us.

"Oh, yes," we answered in unison.

"I hope Dan had a pleasant day too," Joseph commented.

"How you think he spent his day?" Aileen asked. "Don't you think it's strange he wouldn't tell?"

"Hey, I'll bet he met a girl," Joseph said, smiling. "What do you think?"

"I don't know when he'd have the chance," said Mama.

"Oh, Dan doesn't come here every night," Joseph said. "We don't know anything about what he does when he's away." He shrugged his shoulders.

"Well, I hope she is pretty and cheerful like Mrs. Romac," Aileen said. "Dan deserves a nice girlfriend."

Suddenly, I thought back to the day when I'd overheard Papa and Daniel quarreling. Papa had warned Daniel to stay away from Thelma—a girl close to his own age—a little younger, actually. Too bad he'd interfered, I thought to myself. How much better life could be for the two of them together than Thelma with my papa.

As if she read my mind, Aileen said, "Let's write to Thelma, Amy. We mustn't let her think we're mad at her."

Verna Simms

CHAPTER THIRTY-NINE—MORE TENSION

The Great Depression still gripped the country, but thanks to Mama's store, our family felt very few effects from it. We'd managed to recover much of our previous income and were eating well. Even enjoyed a few extras now and then. That is, until Papa came back. Before long, we noticed a severe reduction in the amount of food available to eat in our house. Daniel still dropped by during the week and Mama often packed biscuits and other meal items for him to take home, but we no longer had cookies in the jar, extra helpings on the table, or penny candy as a special treat.

"We're struggling to make ends meet," Mama explained. "The customers seem to be buying less and less."

They weren't coming any less frequently though. People walked in or cars pulled up throughout the day and Mama worked long hours to tend to the store. On Fridays, she continued to make a list for Papa, but it was smaller than before and the money she gave him to cover new supplies became less.

Again our cat Martha gave birth to three kittens. All gray, but one had the distinction of four white paws. Instantly, she became my favorite.

"How come they're blind?" I asked Aileen, worried. I'd been watching the little furry fluffs squirm their way to their mother to nurse. "Their eyes are tightly sealed."

Aileen said, "I don't know. I've read that squirrels are born with their eyes closed, too. Mama said we're not to name the babies. We can keep Martha but the little kittens must be given away as soon as they're weaned. Papa said no more cats."

From that day on, I tried to hide Martha and her brood from Papa. On Friday afternoons, I placed an old braided rag-rug under the back porch and carried mother and kittens there. It was shady and cool; maybe Papa wouldn't notice them.

Papa began to act strangely. When at home, he spent hours sitting under the cottonwood tree, his back against the trunk, and his bowed head resting in his arms. I couldn't tell if he was sleeping, praying, or daydreaming. Sometimes he sat inside his truck, worrying the steering wheel back and forth. He never started the vehicle, but sat alone, gazing out the window toward the mountains or sky.

"Mama," I asked one morning, "Why does Papa sit outside like that?" I pointed out the screen door toward the cottonwood. She didn't look, but said, "I'm sure I don't know. You can ask him yourself. I'll not be doing so."

I did ask him, but he didn't favor me with an answer.

Although our home remained quiet and peaceful during the week, when Papa showed up on Friday, a noticeable tension became apparent between Mama and him. In fact it seemed as if silent battle lines had been drawn. The only words they exchanged concerned practical matters, such as the need for store items or maintenance and repairs on the house or buildings on our property.

Papa asked Mama's opinion on every decision that involved her or we children. At first she answered his questions briefly and factually. Then, over time, they began to argue again, but it seemed different than before. Papa used to have the upper hand in all matters of family and religion and Mama never contradicted him. Now she made it clear she had her own very different opinions and she held her ground. Both used scriptures from the Bible or the Book of Mormon to support their positions. Although I hated to hear them disagree, I sat motionless, enthralled by the knowledge and delivery of the scriptures that both of my parents could muster.

Most of their arguments centered on how young people should live, especially young ladies. They usually began when Papa objected to how Aileen and I dressed or what he noticed Aileen reading. Papa often said he was fighting for our souls according to the Mormon belief, while Mama said God had given us all free will and a conscience to know right from wrong.

"It is our God-given job as parents to plan their futures for them," Papa announced. "We have the wisdom and experience to see ahead. Young people are too naïve to know what is best for them."

Mama said, "They have the right to choose for themselves whether to marry and whether they wish to bear children or not."

Papa had always claimed a woman couldn't enter heaven except through being married to a faithful Mormon man. "Without a husband, a woman is nothing in God's eyes," he said.

That didn't sound right to me. What if no man ever asked a girl to marry him? I wondered. Would she die and go to hell? Still, I wondered if Papa might be right. I had observed that an unmarried lady was considered an "old maid" when she reached age twenty-five and that most people pitied her. I wished never to marry, but didn't want anyone to feel sorry for me because of my decision.

As time passed, their arguments escalated. We never sat down for a weekend meal without hearing diverse opinions and scriptures flying across the table faster than our forks could pierce the potatoes that had become our mainstay diet. Joseph had taken to gobbling down his food and running out the door to Billy's house. Aileen often complained of "knots" in her stomach. I just wished that Papa would leave again for good and let us live in peace, but I was conflicted about this idea. Once in a while, he did something kind—like bring me home some candy or take Joseph and me to Miami with him where he bought us ice cream. Every weekend night before we went to sleep, he came into the dining room and said, "Good night children. Sleep well," and kissed us.

Despite the animosity between my parents that Aileen and I prayed nightly for God to take away, they worked well together to run the house and store and take care of their children. I made up my mind to choose my own future in my own time, but I kept that fact to myself. No hurry. I humored my parents by asking them questions. I soon discovered that they would each call a little truce long enough to search the scriptures for my answers.

One evening at dinner I asked, "What does the Bible say about marriage in heaven?"

Papa said, "There is no marriage in heaven. A person needs to marry here and be sealed in the temple." And then Mama asked him to back it up with scripture.

When Aileen and I were clearing the table, she said, "I don't know how you can make fun of them like that. You're tormenting Mama as badly as Papa is."

"I am not!" I countered. "If you knew anything, you'd see that Mama enjoys it. She gets to best Papa, and I'm just helping her by asking good questions. Without his Book of Mormon, or his revelations, he has nothing in his favor."

A couple of days later, Aileen said, "You're right, Amy, Mother does enjoy those debates with Papa. Tonight she told me she planned to ask him a question herself. Perhaps she figures a bad marriage is better than none at all."

"Not for me," I said. "I'll either have a good one, or no marriage at all."

"What are you saying?" Aileen asked.

"Shucks, I'm just saying—good marriage or no marriage."

CHAPTER FORTY—MOUNTAIN CALLING

On one of the last days of our summer break, I awoke one morning to the sound of Joseph hollering, "Amy, get up! Come and help me!" His voice came from outside, but when I looked out the window, I couldn't see him.

Hurriedly, I dressed and ran through the kitchen toward the back door.

"Your breakfast!" Mama called after me.

"I'll be back," I said. "Joseph's calling." I ran out in the yard and began looking for my brother. "Joe! Joe! Where are you?"

The lean-to door stood open.

"Dan?" I called.

Joseph came to the doorway then, a broom in his hand. "Hey, it's about time," he said. "I need your help. I'm cleaning the lean-to. It's full of cobwebs. Dan said I could have it." As he spoke, he took a swipe on the wall with the broom, stepping back and turning his head away from the dust.

"Gee whiz, you're gonna sleep out here?" I asked, impressed.

"Naw," he answered. He combed his dark wavy hair with spread out fingers. "I like being inside with the family. Billy and I are going to use this as a clubhouse."

He caught my look and answered my unspoken question. "It's boys only, sis."

I didn't think that was fair, but chose to let it pass. "Let's go back up the mountain all the way to the cave today, okay?"

He propped the broom upside down on the handle in the far corner of the little room, away from the door. "Sure, run and ask Mama if it's alright." He closed the homemade door, slipped the latch secure, and snapped the lock in place.

"I'd better fill the wood box first." Keeping a bucket of fresh water in the kitchen and a full wood box beside the kitchen stove were Joseph's chores. My responsibilities were feeding Martha and helping with clearing the table and dishes. "Want to give me a hand?" Joseph asked.

"Not today," I said. "I should eat breakfast and I'd like to pack a lunch for our trip."

Mama stood in the store talking to Mrs. Wallace. I noticed quite a few items between them on the counter, and Mama wrote down her tally on a pad and added up the purchase. I knew better than to interrupt so I busied myself arranging the candy while they talked.

"Are you sure it's not too much trouble, what with the store and all?" Mrs. Wallace asked Mama.

"Oh, it should be fine," Mama said. "Aileen knows how to tend the store now and I'll enjoy a day away, too." She placed some items in a bag and took a dollar and slipped it in the jar for change.

"Go carry this bag to the car for Mrs. Wallace." Mama motioned to me.

"Okay," I said, following our neighbor out the front door and to her car.

"Thank you, dear," Mrs. Wallace said. "I'll bet you're a wonderful helper for your mama. She works so hard!"

"I try," I said, not feeling very honest.

Back inside, I asked mama what she and Mrs. Wallace had been discussing.

"Oh Amelia, your ears are too big," she laughed. "I promised to help her give a dinner party to introduce her sister to some of the ladies in Claypool. She's visiting for a few weeks from Florida. She came in to invite me and buy some items for the party. It's on the 27th—that's a Wednesday. I'm going to be gone all day."

"What are we going to do then?" I asked.

"You'll do what you always do," Mama said, "your chores, and you'll play with Joseph and help Aileen cook dinner for you three. Aileen will be in charge, that's all."

I wasn't thrilled with that idea, to say the least, but I wanted to be on Mama's good side so she'd let Joseph and me climb the mountain again.

"You must stay together," she said, "and you be back home in time for dinner, so don't get busy playing and forget the time. You'll be lost in the dark and I'll not be wanting to search for you."

"No, we won't," I said, impatient to be off. "Joseph and I know the mountain too well to get lost."

Joseph and I scrambled to fix a lunch and head off on our adventure. Half way up the mountain, we stopped on the far side of a giant rock tower to rest. The sun beamed hot and made me thirsty. I plopped down on a flat rock.

"Let's eat here, Joe," I suggested. "Tarnations, but I'm dry." I took out a jar of water from my old school satchel and gulped it.

"Go easy," Joseph said. "You'll drink it all. Save some for me. Besides, you can't drink so fast in this heat. You'll be sick."

I stopped and looked around. The mountain was different at this level. "How do you think a rock becomes so many shades of red and brown?" I asked, inspecting the looming boulder beside me. "From down below you can't see the colors at all."

Joseph didn't answer. His eyes were fixed on a distant spot several yards ahead. A cloud had drifted across the sky, momentarily obstructing the sun. Some lizards had come alive in the brief shade.

"Do you think lizards are happy, Joe?" I asked.

"Oh, I guess so," he said, "as long as they feel safe." Then he gave me an impatient look and said, "You sure ask a lot of strange questions."

He stood and stretched. He'd grown over the summer and he looked thinner, too. From where I sat, he seemed as tall as a mountain.

"We'd better get climbing again, sis," he said. "We don't want to have to turn back the minute we get there, and it's a long way. It'll be easier if we zig-zag back and forth instead of climbing straight up."

We headed out and struggled for another hour or so. Then we stopped for lunch. After gobbling down sandwiches and consuming almost all the water, we started climbing again and managed to arrive at our destination. By the sun's position, I figured it to be around one o'clock.

Out of breath, but exuberant, we stood at almost the very top of the mountain. The air was cool and a breeze blew our hair.

"Come on, sis. The cave's over here," Joseph said, leading the way around some plants and rocks to a small opening large enough for me to stand up, but Joseph had to stoop. I stuck my head inside.

"Jiminy Cricket, I can't see very well," I complained, "Could wild animals be in there?"

"Oh, I doubt it," Joseph said, "but we won't go very far in today. We need to borrow Papa's lantern to explore all the way to the back. For today, we'll just crawl inside and take a look. Then we'd better head home, don't you think?"

I nodded and stood aside so my brother could enter the cave first. He hunched over to avoid hitting his head. He held a hand out for me behind his back and I took it and let him lead me.

The temperature was much cooler inside. It took a moment for my eyes to adjust to the dimness, but I made out a small, elongated room that led into a larger space with a higher ceiling. In that room of the cave, Joseph was able to stand upright.

Several large rocks jutted out toward the back and, behind them, a jagged path led into blackness.

I held Joseph's hand tightly.

"What do you think?" he asked, turning to inspect my face.

"Gee whiz, I like it," I said. "It's better than a tree house. Daniel should move in here instead. It's big enough for a whole family."

"You're darn tootn'—a family of snakes!" Joseph said, squeezing my hand suddenly to make me jump.

On Monday of the last week of our summer break, heavy rain forced Joseph and me to play inside or on the porch. Both restless and disappointed that we would soon be back in school and unable to spend our days doing what we pleased, I grumbled loudly.

But Tuesday morning the sun reappeared and by Wednesday, small green sprouts, cacti blooms in deep purple splotches, and a profusion of orange ground-hugging California poppies lured us up the mountain once more.

Inspired by the fresh scent of new growth that had obscured the persistent stink of the copper fumes, I asked Joseph, "Want to go back to the cave?" He and I were under the cottonwood tree surveying the spectacle on the mountain.

"Sure. Run ask Mama," he said. "School starts next Tuesday, day after Labor Day. We won't have another chance with Papa home on weekends."

Martha was supervising her kittens from a perch on the kitchen windowsill. She watched them closely as they played together on the porch. I stepped around them and into the kitchen. "Mama!" I yelled.

No answer.

Hurriedly, I made my way through our sleeping area and peeked through the partition curtain into the store. Aileen sat behind the counter immersed in a book.

"Where's Mama?" I asked, walking over to stand in front of the candy counter.

"She's helping Mrs. Wallace today, remember?" She answered without looking up. "She'll be back after supper tonight."

My mouth watered at the sight of the colorful suckers, bubble gum, peppermint sticks, and gumballs lying temptingly before me in glass bowls. I could smell chocolate.

"No candy," Aileen said firmly. "Feed Martha and then go play outdoors with Joseph." She turned a page in her book.

At thirteen, Aileen clearly believed she'd become a grown lady. But her order to go play outdoors sounded like the permission I'd been seeking anyway, so I headed back to the kitchen to grab an afternoon snack for Joseph and me to enjoy on the mountain.

Outside, I could hear Joseph splashing water in the washbasin on the back porch. I leaned out the door and watched him wet his dark hair. Beads of water streamed down his face. Nature wanted bangs and Joseph battled against them daily, convinced that only little boys or sissies let their hair grow over their foreheads.

"Hurry. We can go," I said. "Soon as I locate food."

I knew he was hungry. At eleven, he ate more than any of us and seemed always to be ready for more. I spied a tray of blueberry muffins in the warming oven of our wood cook stove, snatched four, and dropped them into a paper bag. Then I charged out the door.

"Great guns, slow down," Joseph chuckled. "The mountain isn't going anywhere."

As always, we ignored the steps and jumped down onto the hard-packed dirt path that led to the back of our lot, cramming muffins into our mouths as we ran. Joseph opened the swinging gate and let me slide through first. Then he fastened the rope that held it securely shut.

I was ten feet ahead of Joseph when he called, "Race you to that purple blossom!" He always gave me a head start, but I never won anyway, not unless he allowed it. That day we reached our mark in a tie though, and collapsed on the ground, exhausted.

"Oh Joe, I love it up here," I said, when I could catch my breath. I rolled over on my back and stared up at the blue sky.

"Me too," Joseph sprawled out on his stomach next to me with his chin propped up on one hand. He smiled at me and I thought how handsome my brother would be when he was grown.

He rolled over on his back to join me in looking at the sky.

"There's a polar bear," Joseph said, pointing at a large puffy cloud.

"Nah, it looks more like a ship," I said. "See? It has a billowy sail."

"We'd better not lie here too long," he said.

I nodded lazily. The warm sunshine and quiet mountain with its pure air made me drowsy. I sat up reluctantly and noticed a bird fly to a nearby boulder, tip his head, and take a drink of rainwater that had collected in a hollow stone. He raised his beak toward the sky as he swallowed. Next, he jumped into the puddle and splashed around a great deal, thoroughly enjoying the cool bath.

I looked at Joseph and we both laughed at the sight. Hearing us, the startled bird rose several feet above the rock and flapped his wings a few times as if to dry them before he turned and flew away.

"Amy, I wonder if a person could drill a well and find water this high up," Joseph said. He squatted down and pushed a large rock over. I knew he was looking for dampness beneath it. It was bone dry.

"I don't know," I answered, "but I'm sure thirsty. My mouth feels like it's full of sand."

Joseph pulled up his shirt and unbuckled a metal water canteen he had hanging around his waist. It was round like winter squash and encased in dark gray canvas. I watched as he unscrewed the cap, and offered me a drink.

"Gee whiz, where'd you get that?" I asked.

"Daniel gave it to me yesterday," he said, smiling.

I felt a pang of jealousy. Mama had let Joseph go home with Daniel the day before. I'd begged to go, too, but she refused. Why did all the nice things always go to boys? It wasn't fair. Girls should get useful presents too, not just frilly stuff.

Suddenly Joseph pointed down the mountain at our house, "Look, Papa's home! We'd better get back."

"But we haven't even gotten half way to the cave yet," I said.

"We'll go again another day," he said. "C'mon, Aileen's there by herself and he'll be mad that we took off if he doesn't find us at home."

"It's only Wednesday," I said. "What's he doing home?"

"Who knows?" Joseph said.

Too slowly we made our way back, using the same route we'd taken up the mountain, which took us all the way down into the crevice where we couldn't see or be seen by anyone at the house. When we arrived on the upper side nearest the house again, Papa's car was gone.

"He left," Joseph said.

"Good," I said. "Let's go to the cave."

Water Under the Bridge

"Nah," Joseph said, "it's too late now and too hot. I'm tired of climbing. I'm going to Billy's house."

Dejected, I headed alone to the house, pausing on the back porch to wash my hands and face. There, I noticed an acrid odor.

I entered the kitchen and found Aileen huddled in the corner. She sat sobbing, with her knees pulled up to her chest.

"Ailie! What's wrong?" I asked, alarmed. The stench inside the kitchen was so terrible I had to cover my mouth and nose with my hands.

There was no response from my sister, just sobs. I looked around for a clue. Nothing seemed out of order, except that the oven door was open.

"Did you burn dinner?" I asked, leaning over my hysterical sister. She shook her head.

"Tarnation! Did you burn yourself?" I took a gentle hold on her elbow, meaning to help her to her feet where I could get a good look at her, but she pushed me away and turned her face to the wall. Her sobs continued. Then I noticed large purple bruises on both of her forearms.

"Oh, Ailie!" I exclaimed, "who did this to you?" And the minute I asked the question, I knew the answer.

"It was Papa, wasn't it?" I said. She turned to face me and nodded miserably, her face red and wet with tears.

I stood up, stunned. Papa had never physically harmed any of us. I knelt on the floor next to my sister, wishing desperately for Mama or Joseph to come home.

"Why?" I asked, trying to connect the wretched smell in the kitchen with the bruises and my sister's despair.

Aileen just resumed her sobbing, but it became softer now. After several minutes, I said, "Come on, let's open the door and air this place out. You'll feel better if you do something.

"Please try," I urged. "I'll help you." Standing, the heavy odor was stronger.

"Come on, Aile. You need water," I said. "Come on, sis—let's go outside."

I tugged until she relented and followed me out the door and onto the porch. In the bright sunlight, my sister's always pretty blue eyes possessed a haunted expression that scared me.

"Oh my, Ailie, it can't be that bad! You've hurt yourself before. You've been hurt a lot worse than this, playing games."

"It's not me," Aileen said, beginning to sob again. "It's Martha."

I looked around for the cat and her kittens, but saw no sign of them on the porch.

"Where is she?" I asked, alarmed, opening the door and stepping back into the kitchen.

Aileen followed me, sobbing, viewing the empty room. I turned to look at my sister as she stared at the open oven door.

"Papa killed her?" I asked, incredulous.

Then the words that my sister had been holding back flooded out: "Oh, Amy, she screamed so! The most awful yowling and shrieking!"

I froze, wanting to cover my ears and run away, while holding my nose against the stench. Then I felt a slow-burning rage welling up inside me.

"I tried to save her," Aileen continued. Now I wished my sister would stop talking. "I ran to the stove, but he grabbed me and held me back. Heaven help me, I couldn't stop him!"

I reached for my sister and held her tight. "It's not your fault," I said. "Let's run and get Mama."

Aileen didn't hear me. It was as if the floodgates had been opened and she could no longer hold back the terrible details of her afternoon. "He came in and found Martha on the kitchen table eating from my plate. A customer came while I ate my lunch and I left it there. It's my fault."

Suddenly I remembered that I had not fed Martha before I left with Joseph for the mountain. The realization that I had been responsible was almost overwhelming. I started sobbing with Aileen. I looked around wildly, trying to think what could be done. I wanted to turn back the clock to that morning, but I knew that wasn't possible.

"It was horrid, Amy," Aileen continued. She was hugging me so hard I could barely breathe. "I'll never forget the screeching. I'll have nightmares forever and ever." She clamped her hands over her ears as if to shut out the memory.

"The kittens?" I asked weakly. My eyes frantically searched the porch—searched, but did not find them.

Suddenly we heard the engine of a car in front of the house. Aileen and I looked at each other. "Papa," I said. "Run!"

Aileen let go of me and hurried toward the front of the house. "Customers," she answered. "I must see what they need." She quickly wiped her eyes with the tail of her dress and headed toward the front room.

I stepped out to the back porch, picked up the newspaper and made a fan. I went inside and began waving the air around my face. I grabbed the box of baking soda from the shelf near the icebox and shook handfuls into the oven, but I dared not look inside. While Aileen waited on our customers, I made a plan. I knew where I'd go. I hoped to somehow persuade Joseph and Aileen to come with me.

Joseph came in shortly after I returned to the kitchen, just after six o'clock.

"Any food left?" he asked. Then he noticed the smell. "Whew, it stinks! Did Aileen burn supper?"

I told him what had happened and watched his face change to the same haunted expression I'd seen on my sister's face.

"Great guns. Where's Papa now?" he asked.

"I don't know. He left and he hasn't come back."

Aileen shuffled into the kitchen then. "I think there's biscuits," she said. "I need to tally up the sales for the day and then I want to go to bed." She had a tired, beaten face like an old person who had lived a hard life.

Joseph and I nodded. Supper was the last thing on our minds.

"Think I should lock the door?" she asked. "Or leave it unlocked for Mama?"

"Leave the door unlocked," Joseph said, reaching over and turning up the lamp wick. "I'll wait up for Mama."

I walked over and gave my brother a big bear hug—a hug meant to say goodbye and I love you.

"Good night, Amy," he said quietly.

"Good night," I said, and I dashed from the kitchen and into our sleeping room. There I fell across my pallet and buried my face in my pillow to muffle the sound of my sobs. I grieved for Martha and also for myself. Once more Papa was causing me to lose everything that I loved.

Verna Simms

CHAPTER FORTY-ONE—GONE

"Hey, Mama sent me to wake you, Amy," Joseph said, standing over me. Then he knelt and whispered, "She knows everything. I told her."

"Is Papa home?" I asked.

"No, Mama said he dropped off supplies and left. He might have taken the kittens with him. I didn't want to press Aileen for details, but only Martha—" He stopped talking. Neither of us wanted to be reminded of what Papa had done.

In the kitchen, I could hear the usual morning sounds of my mother walking about and clanking pans together. I wriggled into my dress and moved slowly toward them. A pleasant aroma of frying bacon permeated the air. Joseph sat at the table with a plate of two untouched biscuits.

Mama stood at the stove and, out of the corner of her eye, nodded to me as I entered the room. I could see the stove had been taken apart and every section thoroughly scrubbed.

"Hon, your papa didn't return last night," she said. "And I don't expect him until Friday." Her face had paled and her eyes were weary. She paused before taking a deep breath and continuing, "I'm warning you the same as I did Joseph. You're not to make a big issue over the cats. Aileen is upset enough already. I sent her up to the Wallaces. Best she not dwell on it anymore. It's a terrible tragedy, but what's done is done—water under the bridge."

Her analogy made my stomach sink. Thoughts of the rain barrel we kept near the tool shed flashed into my mind. Papa had threatened to drown the kittens. He had also told us once that he'd found a dead bat floating in the rain barrel. I pictured Martha's three little kittens floating in the dark, cold water. The image became unbearable, but it still seemed a better way to die than what had happened to their mother.

Mama grabbed hairpins from her topknot and put them in her mouth. I watched her take one at a time and jam it back into her hair—an angry motion of her hands.

"You don't understand," she said. "With the crash and all, life's difficult. It's all people can do to hold their families together. We've been very fortunate because of the store, but your papa has had a tough time finding work. He's worried that the store won't be able to sustain us forever. I'm sure he saw the cats as more mouths to feed."

"But they ate scraps," I said, "and the kittens ate so little!"

"Water under the bridge, Amelia," Mama repeated. "It's a heartbreak, but there's no changing it now. All is in God's hands."

"Maybe Daniel will help," Joseph said. "He has a job now. Maybe he'll move back home and . . ."

"With a wife to support?" Mama said. Then she gasped and covered her mouth with her hand. "Oh my, I slipped, didn't I?"

She turned around to face Joseph and me. "Whatever you do, don't mention this news to your papa."

Shock registered on my brother's face and I knew it mirrored my own expression. After a moment he recovered enough to say, "What?" Then his eyes narrowed in a queer way, "Who—who did Dan marry?"

Mama sat down at the table and placed her face in her hands. We waited. Finally, without looking up, she said, "It's going to come out sooner or later."

"So—say it," Joseph demanded.

"Daniel has married Thelma," Mama answered. "They aren't living on the mountain at the present. They're at Thelma's place in Phoenix. Now that you know, you don't breathe a word, understand?"

I plopped down into a chair beside her. It seemed like the room was spinning. "When did this happen?" I asked.

"They've been seeing each other for some time," Mama said. "Daniel went to her as soon as he heard she'd left your papa. He wanted only to console her, but they were in love before, you know. Thelma was just confused. She didn't know what to do. Her dad had instructed her that God wanted her to be Chester's wife."

"Gee whiz, so that's where Daniel went on the Fourth of July," I said.

"Yes," Mama said, "he visited Thelma that day."

"Golly gee, but when did they get married?" Joseph asked. "Does Aileen know?"

"Two weeks ago. Thelma told Aileen; she and Thelma are very close." Mama stood and took bread and jam from the counter. "Eat breakfast, Amelia," she said, "you look ill."

"Tarnations, I don't want anything to eat," I said, amazed at how much information had escaped me again. I worked constantly at trying to stay abreast of the developments in our family and couldn't believe how I had missed this one.

My feelings were jumbled. I feared Papa's reaction to the news about Daniel and Thelma, whenever it would come—and I knew it would come too soon. I also felt joy that Thelma was not lost to us and I felt betrayed that Mama and Aileen and Daniel had kept this secret from me.

"Land sakes, I felt disappointed not to be there to see my first born get married, but it became impossible for me to leave without your papa knowing," Mama said wistfully.

I heaved a sigh as I stretched my arms before going out the screen door, leaving Mama and Joseph to talk without me. I didn't want to know any more, not right now. Too dangerous.

The cool morning air made me feel a little less queasy. I glanced around, half expecting to see kittens on the porch, which instantly brought a sharp, new pang to the pit of my stomach. At the chicken pen, the hens stopped their scratching and clucked expectantly at me, cocking their heads from side to side, to see me with each beady eye.

"I've nothing for you," I said, showing my empty hands, "except good advice. Run away! Go live on the mountain and never, ever come back. Papa means to kill you all, you and your baby chicks, too."

I headed over to the cottonwood tree and wrapped my arms around its trunk. Somehow, the rough bark against my cheek felt reassuring, as if something hard and real still remained of my life. I plucked a tiny green leaf from a branch and unfurled it, running my fingers down its stem and over its feathery veins. Then I hoisted myself up and onto the big lower branch. From there, I started climbing, higher and higher, until I became well hidden in the foliage above the roof of our house. A tiny bird flew from its nest in my damaged red umbrella.

Joseph came out the back door and down the porch steps. He opened the gate and headed across the road toward Billy's house. He looked back several times and I feared he would spot me, but his gaze never took in the tree. I wiggled my fingers a slight wave goodbye.

Watching him as he disappeared into their house, an idea came to me. Mama visited with customers in the store—a good opportunity to slip into her bedroom and removed a suitcase from beneath her bed. I carried it into the dining room and quietly rolled my nightgown into a ball and stuffed it in the bottom. I packed all but one set of my clean undergarments and stockings and tried to fit two of my three school dresses in, but the case was too small. I settled for one dress.

I could hear Mama chatting with customers as if nothing was wrong in our lives. Fearing that Aileen would come in at any second, I carried the suitcase out the kitchen door and hid it beneath the house.

When Papa came on Friday, we acted as if nothing unusual had happened. He avoided our eyes, which made it easy. On Saturday, he drove to town with Mama's list and bought groceries. Pretending not to watch, I averted my eyes as he busied himself repairing our roof the rest of the day. After dinner, he claimed being tired and headed for bed.

Sunday morning he finally spoke to us directly. "Would you children like to join me for services today?" he asked. It was the first time he'd ever asked us to do anything. We'd always been told what we would be doing or ordered to do whatever he wanted.

Given a choice, I answered, "I'd rather stay home."

Mama said, "Will you be staying over this evening? Tomorrow's Labor Day."

"No," Papa said. He looked sad and tired. "I leave tonight."

When I entered the classroom on Tuesday, my third grade teacher, Miss Zimmerman, turned from the blackboard and glared at me. "You are late Amelia. What's your excuse for being late the first day of school?"

"Our kittens are missing," I said, having rehearsed this explanation all the way to school. "I went to search for them." I didn't dare look her in the eye. Instead, my gaze surveyed the classroom, stopping at a friendly face, Mary Brown.

I spotted Blanca and averted my eyes from her. She had that uncanny way of knowing what I was thinking and I felt ashamed of having told a fib.

"Well, bring a note from your mother tomorrow and I'll excuse you," Miss Zimmerman said, her tone softer. I guessed that she might be fond of kittens. She directed me to an empty seat in the back of the classroom.

"Now children, copy these words from the blackboard. I'll expect you to know their proper spellings tomorrow." She turned back to the board to complete the task I'd interrupted.

The morning passed quickly and finally the bell rang for noon recess. In the schoolyard, Mary rushed up to me just as Blanca and I joined her group of girls.

"Hey Amy, I want to thank you for the kitten," she squealed. "I named her Amy after you."

Stunned, I stood speechless, then overjoyed. One little kitten! I could hardly wait to tell Aileen and Joseph.

Only then I remembered—I planned not to go home.

Blanca grabbed my arm and took me aside. "Tell me, what's wrong?"

"Nothing," I lied. "Our kittens are missing. Papa gave them away." That part, at least, was true.

"There's something more," Blanca said. "You're different. Is someone sick?"

Recognizing the opportunity this idea presented to me, I said, "Yes, Uncle Willie's sick and Mama is going to Missouri to help care for him. Be okay if I stayed at your house while she's away?"

"I'm sorry about your uncle," Blanca said. "Will Aileen and Joseph need to come, too?"

"Uh—no," I answered, uncertainly. "They're old enough to stay home alone."

"I see," Blanca said. Her eyes seemed to bore into mine. "Did you bring clothes with you?"

"Yes," I said, pulling her hand and leading her over to the stone steps. Behind them, I brought out the concealed suitcase. Not wanting anyone to see it, I'd waited in the cottonwood tree until Joseph and Aileen left for school and I was sure the playground would be clear of children.

Blanca no longer wore braids, but had pulled her lovely dark locks back and tied a green ribbon at the nape of her neck. Small strands escaped and she twirled one in her fingers.

"What about a note from your mother?" she asked. I shrugged and turned my head. *What was I going to do? What a mess!*

Fortunately, a girl interrupted us to see about a game of jump rope and I followed her.

I worried the remainder of the school day, trying to figure a way to cover my tracks if I saw Aileen and Joseph at the school, dreading the lies I'd be telling Blanca's parents, and wondering how to get the note my teacher had requested from my mama.

I recalled Mama once saying, "Oh what a tangled web we weave, when first we practice to deceive." Now I understood.

When the school bell rang, I had a new story ready. "My mama isn't leaving until tonight," I told Blanca. "Would your papa be willing to drive me to our house so I can get the note from her?"

"I think so," Blanca said, "but let me speak to him privately first. I must explain things and ask permission for you to stay with me. I feel sure it's okay." Blanca's face showed doubt

That possibility had never occurred to me. I'd felt so welcome at the Romacs' home.

Blanca touched my arm, "Everything'll be fine, Amelia. Just wait here a minute while I talk to Papa."

I stood in front of the school steps holding my suitcase, waiting. Several children asked me where I was going and I said, "To spend the night with Blanca," hoping it didn't turn out to be another lie. Finally, Blanca beckoned me to the car and Mr. Romac drove toward my house. There, I noticed Mama bent over, wrestling with a hen in the chicken yard. She looked up when the car stopped.

"Wait here," I said, jumping out, giving no time for a response.

I dashed to the chicken pen and yelled, "Mama! Blanca's invited me to her house for the night, but my teacher wants a note from you that says our kittens are missing."

"What?" Mama asked. Then she said, "Here, help me! Shove these eggs under Red when I lift her up. No sense in her trying to set for weeks on only one egg."

Her golden-brown hair had fallen down in heavy layers as a result of her struggle with the hen. Thinking she'd given up the fight, the bird sat placidly on the nest. Feathers flew as Mama grabbed her and I forced eggs beneath her body.

"There!" Mama said, reaching up to re-pin her hair. "Now what do you need? Why is Mr. Romac waiting?"

She started toward his car. I ran along beside her. "Can I have permission to stay over at Blanca's tonight?" I asked. "Also, my teacher wants you to write her a note because searching for the kittens made me late today."

"Hello. What a surprise," Mama said to Mr. Romac.

"I'll run get a pen and pad," I said, fearing the reactions of both my mama and the Romacs when my story about Uncle Willie came out.

I galloped inside and grabbed Mama's tally pad and a pen off the counter in the store. When I returned she said, "Well, a night away from home might do you good. Give me the tablet and I'll write your teacher that note."

Stunned, I handed Mama the pad and pen. When she finished, she said, "Now Amelia, if you will come inside for a moment, I'd like to send cookies to Mrs. Romac as a thank you." I saw her exchange a look with Mr. Romac. He smiled and nodded.

Alone with Mama, she sat in a chair at the table and pulled me onto her lap. "I do hope you wouldn't ever run off and leave me," she said. "If you did, my heart would be broken. I couldn't imagine not having you here."

"I'm sorry, Mama," I said, tears welling up in my eyes.

"It's okay, dear," she said. "I know it hasn't been easy for you lately. I explained some things to Blanca's papa and he's happy for you to stay the night with them—but it's just overnight, agreed?"

"Okay," I said, relieved. I hadn't known what to do the next night, or the night after that. I also didn't want to leave Mama and Aileen and Joseph.

"Gee whiz, it wasn't a very good plan," I said.

"Oh, I think it's a good idea to spend a night away with your best friend. That's a very good idea," Mama said, rubbing my back. "Next time you must ask me first, though. Do I make myself clear?"

"Yes, Mama." I nodded.

She stood and held my shoulders, looking into my eyes. "God will not give us more than we can bear, Amelia," she said "You must trust me. Someday you will understand."

She turned and took a tin from the Old Mother Hubbard cabinet and filled it with peanut butter cookies. Then she kissed me. "Now run outside to your friend with these. Tell Blanca's mother I said thank you."

"I will, Mama," I said. "I love you."

"Have a wonderful time, Amelia," she said, "and I'll see you right here after school tomorrow."

When we arrived at the Romacs' home, Mr. Romac said, "You girls play outside awhile. I'll talk to my wife."

"Blanca, I'm so sorry," I said, sitting down beside her on the swing that hung from her front porch roof. "I should've told you . . ."

"No need," Blanca said, patting my hand. "Everything is okay. I told you it would be."

Mrs. Romac came out then. "Welcome, Amelia," she said with her delightful accent. "What a happy surprise! We're always glad to have you." She leaned over and gave me a hug.

"Thank you," I said. Then I held up the tin container that held the cookies. "My mama sent cookies and says thank you, too."

"Well then," Mrs. Romac said, "you girls get busy with cookies and milk!"

We followed her into the kitchen and I watched, fascinated, as she stopped at the counter and began rolling out dough.

"Tortillas," Blanca explained.

"I love tortillas," I said, watching as she placed a mixture that included black beans onto a piece of dough before rolling it into a neat roll.

"Blanca told me you might come home with her today, and I knew you liked tortillas," Mrs. Romac said.

Blanca knew? I hadn't seen her since the Fourth of July. No one had known my plan. In fact, I hadn't known my plans myself until last night.

Alone in her bedroom, Blanca said, "I know a game. Let's play grownups. Mama gave me her old blouses and skirts we can wear." She started to lead me out the door, but stopped short. "Wait," she said. "I'll curl your hair."

Happy to forget the events of the past day, I followed Blanca to her dresser.

"This is new," she said, pointing to a metal contraption. "It's a curling iron. You place it on top of the oil lamp chimney until it's hot, and then grab a lock of hair between the thongs, roll it around and around, and then hold the prongs in place until the iron is cool. Presto! Curls! It's easy and you'll look lovely with curls, Amelia. Want to try?"

I was a little apprehensive thinking about a hot iron so close to my scalp, but I trusted Blanca. Besides, my poker-straight hair now hung down past my shoulders.

That evening, I joined the family at the dinner table sporting copper-colored ringlets and Mr. Romac whistled a catcall when he saw me. "Will you look at this? Two prettier girls I've never seen before!"

The evening was pleasant and restful. After dinner, Mrs. Romac insisted on washing the dishes herself, while Mr. Romac drilled us on our spelling words. "Miss Zimmerman will be happy when we both get every word correct tomorrow," Blanca giggled. When I didn't respond, she asked, "Are you listening?"

"Yes, I heard you," I said absently. Then I added, "If I ever get married, I hope to have a husband just like your papa."

Blanca smiled. "He'd be pleased to know."

Later, in the darkness of her bedroom, as I felt myself drift off to sleep in the oh-so-soft featherbed, I felt a movement next to me and Blanca's fingers clasped my hand.

The following afternoon, Blanca and I dashed out of the school building and stopped short, surprised to find Mama standing beside Mr. Romac's car.

As I approached, she turned away from him and said, "Thank your wife for me, too. I can't tell you how much I appreciate your help with Amelia."

"Anytime," Mr. Romac said.

I looked at my friend and saw a strange and disturbing expression wash over her face. Was it fear or apprehension? After saying goodbye, Mama and I headed toward home.

"Why did you come to meet me?" I asked.

"To have time alone with you," Mama said. "Also, to thank Mr. Romac again."

We walked in silence. Then Mama said, "Your papa's home. He's leaving in the morning and will be gone until Saturday. Help me make this evening a pleasant one. Understood, Amelia?"

"Is he angry with me?" I asked, gazing into her eyes trying to read her feelings.

"Oh, no," Mama said. "He has no reason to be mad at you. He doesn't know anything about your plan. I just want you to be nice to him. Do it for me, will you?"

"Okay," I said, "for you. . ." I searched Mama's face uncertainly. It had been three years since that September day we'd walked together, on my first day of school. I could still see her vividly in my mind—how she'd looked then. The light tan pongee dress, with its low waistline and cute ornament over her left hip, had long ago been stored away.

Mama has gained a lot of weight and looks much, much older, I thought, sneaking a look at her as we continued up the road. I wondered if I had changed as much. I hoped I looked more mature.

Verna Simms

CHAPTER FORTY-TWO—COMPANY

Despite Papa's worries, Mama's store continued to thrive. She expanded it to sell used clothing, handcrafted crocheted doilies, and embroidered linens sewn by the ladies of Claypool. Word soon spread that Mama would barter for supplies when someone ran short on money. Mama always tried to help when groceries were needed. The store became popular with the town citizens as a place where handmade gifts could be purchased.

Every evening after closing the store, Mama counted the money and balanced her books. She wrote lists of items to buy and kept money in a cigar box for Papa's use in purchasing merchandise. We couldn't help but notice how radiant her face appeared on some days when sales had been especially good. When few customers came by, she spent her time thinking up new things to buy that would increase profits.

On the same day that Mama and I walked home together from school, she made a nice meal of ham and beans and cornbread for dinner. Papa ate three helpings and said, "Ida, you've outdone yourself." Then he announced to Aileen and Joseph and me that he was going to Snowflake. He appeared in a very good mood.

"I hope to do some good swapping there," he said. Then he turned to Mama. "I would appreciate it very much if you'd have a couple of chickens cleaned for the evening meal when I return on Saturday. I may bring company home with me. Be sure the girls are home, too."

The next morning he'd left before I awoke.

"What's he swapping for?" Joseph asked Mama over breakfast.

"Oh, he didn't say," Mama said, "but my guess is that he plans to trade the truck in on a new car. Ever since Daniel came home sporting that shiny Model A Ford, Chester's been dissatisfied."

"I wish I knew which hens weren't laying," she said. "They'd be the ones to kill." She headed for the door. "Maybe if I gather the eggs now I can catch them on their nests. I'd sure hate to lose a laying hen. We're selling dozens of eggs."

I followed her outside and Joseph tagged along behind. I perched on the porch step and immediately thought of Martha. Joseph ran out in the yard and grabbed his stilts, which were lying on the ground where he'd left them the day before. He hopped on them and clomped over to me.

"If only Dan and Thelma could visit," he said. "Wouldn't it be fun to go to their place?"

"I doubt that will happen anytime soon," I said.

"I wonder if he knows," Joseph said. He started stepping toward the front of the yard, his eyes searching across the street in the direction where his friend lived. "I'm going over and see if Billy will stay the night with me in the lean-to. What're you going to do?" He didn't wait for an answer, but marched on out the gate, the stilts making him more than six feet tall.

I wished Joseph had hung around long enough for me to ask his opinion on who Papa might be bringing home with him. I found myself alone again with my thoughts and lately, they'd not been very good company.

Suddenly I had an idea and I ran over to the chicken yard where Mama gathered eggs.

"Mama, I have a neat idea. Can I ask Blanca to come home with me tomorrow and stay the night?" I asked. "Joe wants to sleep in the clubhouse and Papa will be gone. May I?"

"I don't see why not," Mama answered, fingering the eggs in her basket.

So, Friday afternoon, Blanca went home with Mr. Romac, but he drove her back to our house before supper. Since Daniel had given us a key, we often took turns sleeping in Papa's room when he was away. Mama said Blanca and I should have the room to ourselves that evening.

Joseph and Billy left for the lean-to early, and soon after, Blanca and I decided to prepare for bed. We pulled our nightgowns on over our heads.

"It's weird," I mumbled, talking through the cloth. "Something is gnawing at my insides and I can't understand what the problem is. I feel uneasy for no good reason. Do you ever do that?"

"Yes, I think we all do at one time or another. I talk to my mother and it helps. Don't you? Talk to your mom, I mean."

"No way, Mama won't ever admit anything is wrong. Her philosophy is to ignore problems and they'll go away."

The sun had slipped below the treetops and we could barely see each other in the darkening room. Even near the window, Blanca looked like a dark shadow as she brushed her dark, silky hair.

"Start at the beginning," she said softly, "tell me every little detail. Perhaps talking aloud will help you decide what's best to do. I'll sit quietly and listen. Okay?"

So I began. "It sounds silly when I tell it, but Papa has been acting strange lately. Suddenly he's going to a town named Snowflake. I'd never heard of the town until the Christmas card came from the Overbergs. They live there now. Papa said Aileen and I must be home when he returns because he might bring company, but he didn't mention any names. Mama is to prepare a nice meal for them, whoever they are, but she refuses to ask questions. Papa's doing some kind of trading in Snowflake." I turned my face to the wall. "I'm being foolish, aren't I?"

Blanca didn't answer.

"Jiminy cricket, let's forget it," I said. "We'll talk about something different."

"You're not being foolish, my friend," she said. The serious tone of her voice alarmed me. "I can't answer your questions, but I feel danger in the air. You must be very, very careful. Don't trust strangers. Snowflake is a pretty name, but the image I get in my mind is dark and stormy. When you are not sure, you must say no to any question. I'm sorry, but that's all the advice I can give you. My intuition is failing me today. If I could only ask Mama. She's much better than I am."

"Gee whiz, I know what we can do to lighten our mood, let's sing songs," I suggested. We sat on Papa's bed and sang every song we knew. Then finally, Mama stuck her head in the door and said, "It's very late, girls, and I'm going to bed. You'd better stop singing now and go to sleep."

I drifted off into a troubled sleep, waking up several times and feeling my friend's hand in mine. With early morning, it seemed my worries were behind me. Blanca and I made Papa's bed to be sure no sign of our having slept there remained. Then we locked the door and gave Mama the key.

We used up the morning marching on stilts and chasing each other around the yard. We climbed the cottonwood tree and I showed Blanca the eggs in the henhouse. Then Mr. Romac drove up and honked his horn and it was time to say goodbye—until Monday, when we would see each other again at school.

"Remember my warning last night," Blanca whispered. "Caution!" Then she put her finger to her lips and skipped to her father's car. I had a sinking, lost feeling as they drove away.

Papa arrived in the early afternoon in a jovial mood. Three strange, middle-aged men entered the room with him. He introduced the strangers, but I didn't hear their names clearly. One sounded like Corn and it seemed to fit. The man's brown and weather-beaten face, with small lack-luster eyes hidden beneath bushy eyebrows, combined with tangled blonde hair and a matching beard reminded me of a scarecrow hiding behind dry corn shucks. He stood tall and lanky with dirty, bony ankles showing beneath too-short work pants. The man's eyes seemed to dart around the room like an animal trapped in a cage. I decided later that he must have been looking for a spittoon because he repeatedly made trips to the kitchen door and spit tobacco juice on Mama's blue morning glory vines. When he returned, spittle drooled down his unkempt beard. I remembered that Papa said Mormons weren't allowed to smoke. I wondered if chewing the tobacco weed was acceptable. My stomach lurched in disgust.

The second man, Mr. Popsky, or something close to that name, was short and fat. Rolls of flesh protruded over a belt slung too low. I scarcely dared to look his way, expecting his trousers to fall around his ankles any minute. His long ears and sharp, pointed chin protruded out from two double chins. He heaved a sigh as he lowered his heavy frame onto a straight ladder-back chair, and much of his body hung over the seat. Out of the corner of my eye, I noticed his pudgy face glow red with the heat of our kitchen. Although Mama hadn't mentioned dinner being ready, he snatched a cloth napkin and tucked it under his chin as a child might. I knew I shouldn't, but secretly I nicknamed him Fatso.

"Dandy" seemed an appropriate name for our third guest; he reminded me of a carnival barker, dressed in black pants, a white shirt, and a red vest. A gold chain hung from a small vest pocket. He made a big show of removing the watch, pushing a button to release the case, and sticking it under my nose. "See, girlie. Nice watch, yeah?" I didn't know what to say, so I muttered "Thank you, sir." All the men roared with laughter. Oily, coal black hair plastered down and parted in the middle matched a curled mustache beneath a large, prominent hooked nose. With dark beady eyes, it gave his rather thin face a hunted look. Pale skin testified that he stayed out of the sun. Thin lips appeared fixed in more of a leer than a smile, and he fidgeted around the room, inspecting everything his hands could touch. Papa introduced him as Mr. Lasch.

As soon as Mama placed the heaping plate of fried chicken on the table, Papa turned to her and said, "Ida, I've brought a sack of fresh oranges for Mrs. Wallace's sister. I thought she might enjoy them—a taste of home." He diverted his eyes from us, and explained to the three men, "She's our neighbor's sister and visiting from Florida."

"Ah." The men nodded.

"I'd like you to take them to her, now." He gave Mama a blatantly apparent order, meaning don't you dare disagree. "The girls can serve us. You gentlemen would like that, wouldn't you?"

I noticed that Papa didn't say please when he asked Mama to take the oranges to the Wallaces. It sounded strange.

Mama looked uncertain, but then she said, "Okay, I won't be but a few minutes."

As soon as she left, the men began filling their plates. Aileen and Joseph and I stood back, waiting for them to have their fill so that we could eat. I doubted that much, if anything, would be left.

I looked at Aileen, wondering about these strange men, but she didn't notice me. Instead she admired a long, double strand of beads that Dandy had pulled out of his pocket. They were a pretty shade of Robin's-egg blue. He said, "I have six sons and one daughter. She is about the same age as you, fourteen, that's right, isn't it?"

Aileen nodded. He turned to Joseph, "Son," he said. "Would you do s little favor for me? Take your bicycle and ride into town. Go to Mr. Gilmore's filling station and tell him we'll be there in an hour to gas up. Tell him if he's there, I'll pay my outstanding bill."

He pulled out his bill and handed Joseph a crisp dollar bill, making a big show of how much money he had.

He turned to Papa and grinned. "That's how to keep the station open." The men all laughed.

Joseph scooted his chair against the wall and looked questioningly at Papa.

"Times a wasting. Scat now, that's a good boy," Papa said.

Mr. Corn spoke up, "Now that's a real coincidence. My own daughter is a teenager, too. Then he turned to me. "How old might you be now, lass?"

"Nine," I said, averting my eyes away from his shadowy ones. Somehow they frightened me.

Fatso was mopping gravy from his plate with one of Mama's biscuits. My stomach was growling as I smelled the delicious aroma of her fried chicken and watched the platter emptying.

Mr. Lasch said, "You know, I've been thinking." He leaned toward Aileen. "How would you like to come home with me tonight and visit my two daughters? They're both near your age. One is twelve and the other thirteen. I'm sure you'd have a good time. We own a cabin on the hillside and we go fishing and boat riding."

Aileen looked like a trapped animal in a cage. I panicked, remembering Blanca's warning.

"What do you say?" the man asked.

"Gee, I don't kn-know," Aileen stammered. "I'd have to ask my moth—"

"It's a great idea!" Papa said, interrupting her. "Thanks for asking. You girls would enjoy that, wouldn't you?"

I hadn't been invited, but I shook my head vigorously. "Not me. I've plans with Blanca tomorrow. Mama already said I could go." It was a bold-faced lie.

Aileen's face brightened. "I'll run up the hill and ask Mama."

I felt funny inside—alarmed. I knew I needed to get my sister aside and talk to her alone. Mr. Lasch stood and reached into his pocket then. He pulled out a gold locket.

"My daughter loves lockets," he said. "I found a sale, two for the price of one. You can have this one. See? You place pictures inside. Does that sound like fun?"

Without waiting for an answer, he stepped over and slipped his hands around Aileen's neck and fastened the clasp. With his face inches from hers, he took his time opening the locket to show how the miniature pictures would fit inside.

It was exquisite. I wished for one myself, but not if it came with an old man to fasten it on me.

My sister blushed and turned to look in the small mirror hanging over the sink where Papa shaved. Her blue eyes shone in delight.

"That's settled, then," Papa said, winking at the men. "Go pack what you'll need, Aileen. Not much. Just for the night."

"If she needs more, I'll take her shopping," Mr. Lasch said. "You won't complain if I want to buy you new dresses, now, will you? Every girl I know enjoys dressing up."

"B-but I have to ask Mama," Aileen said, hesitating.

"No need for that," Papa said. "I'm head of this house." Then he pounded his fist on the table, making the dishes rattle.

While everyone stared at Papa, I took the opportunity to grab a cloth napkin and two chicken wings and slipped them into my pocket.

"I'll explain to your mother when she gets home," Papa said.

Aileen went to the dining room where we slept to gather her clothing. I started to follow her, but Papa stuck out one of his long legs and blocked my path.

"Leave your sister alone, Amelia. If you choose not to go, fine, but you wait outside. Don't delay Aileen."

Blanca's warning came back to me. I walked out in the front yard and scanned the road for Mama, but she wasn't coming. I tried to think what I could do. The feeling of foreboding was intense. Please God, I thought, don't let my sister go with these men.

On a whim I ran over to the cottonwood and leaped up to grab its lowest branch. Then I walked my feet up the trunk and hoisted myself up. It was twilight and I could barely be seen in the thick foliage.

After a few minutes I heard the door open. The men and Papa came out with Papa holding Aileen's hand.

Quickly I crawled out on the limb until I was no longer over my thinking rock. As the group started down the porch steps, I turned loose my hold on the limb and let myself crash to the dirt below. At the same time, I let out a bloodcurdling scream, "HEEEEELP!"

Aileen pulled loose from Papa's grip and rushed over to me. "Amelia! Are you injured?"

"Yes!" I groaned. "I'm hurt bad. Run and get Mama. I need her something awful!"

"Oh, dear me. I'll find her," Aileen cried, and without waiting for an answer or for Papa's comments, she flew out the gate and up the hillside like an eagle had loaned her its wings.

Papa knelt down. "Where does it hurt?" he asked.

"Everywhere," I said.

"Does one place hurt more than another?" he asked.

"It's an all-over pain," I said. I gave out a loud moan.

Suddenly Papa grabbed me by the hand and pulled me to my feet.

"Trickster!" he said. "I'll show you what hurts!" He raised his arm back as if to strike me.

I jerked free and ran. Where to go, I didn't know. With each step, my mind screamed, "Run, run, run!"

Aileen had left the gate ajar, barely enough for my small frame to slide through. I galloped down the hill with all the speed I could muster. Footsteps echoed behind me and I heard heavy, labored breathing. A hand grabbed at my sleeve and caught, but I made a quick turn like a rabbit and that took my pursuer unaware.

Instead of following the bend of the road that led into the schoolyard and town, I kept going straight and found myself at Mrs. Jones' fence. I grabbed hold of a wooden post and hurdled the gate. Both my feet landed on sandy soil and the Jones' German shepherd dog, Brownie, greeted me with a growl followed by one friendly bark.

I crawled behind an old oak tree and sat in its shadow where I couldn't be seen from the road. The dog joined me, licking my face. Finally, sure I was no longer being pursued, I walked around the Jones' house into the back yard. There I spied Brownie's doghouse. It might be large enough for two. Dropping to all fours, I squeezed in and the dog followed me happily.

"You sure are friendly tonight," I said. Then I realized that he could smell chicken wings in my pocket.

"Okay," I said. "You're sharing your house, so I'll share my dinner." I gave him a wing and ate the other one. In the cramped doghouse I stayed all night.

CHAPTER FORTY-THREE—EASTER

I awakening in the early morning when the sun rose. Brownie had left me at some point. I tried to crawl outside, but my legs were stiff. I began to wonder if the fall from the tree really had hurt me.

"What in tarnation are you doing in there, little girl?" Mr. Jones asked.

"It's just me—Amelia, Mr. Jones." I said. "I'd been playing hide-and-go-seek and I'm afraid I fell asleep."

Mr. Jones looked skeptical.

"Does your mother know where you are?" he asked. "It's five in the morning."

"I'm going home now," I said. "Thank you for letting me sleep in your doghouse." Once again, I tried to get up, but it was no use. I was unable to use my legs. "I think I'm stuck." I looked up at him sheepishly. "Can you help me out?"

Mr. Jones chuckled and his fat belly bounced up and down. He leaned over and lifted the doghouse up over my head and set it down away from me.

"I'm paralyzed," I whimpered, searching the friendly face hovering several feet above me. "I can't move either leg".

"Oh, dear!" Mr. Jones said. His face suddenly became serious and sympathetic. He leaned over and gathered me in his strong arms. He carried me into the warm and cozy front room where his wife was dusting. "Get a cushion, will you, Sarah?" he said.

"What's wrong, Harvey?" she asked.

"Amelia's hurt. She claims she fell out of a tree while playing hide-and-go-seek and thinks she's paralyzed. We better call a doctor."

He gently placed me on the sofa while his wife dropped the feather duster and hurried over, fussing over me. She rubbed my legs, and little by little, they began to tingle and life started to return to them.

"I'm feeling my legs again. It's a miracle. Or maybe they were only asleep. Anyway, I'm better. I'll walk home." I started feeling guilty and nervous and wanted out of their house.

"Oh, no!" Mrs. Jones said. "No one leaves my house on an empty stomach. You rest right where you are, dearie. I'll stir us up some pancakes and then after a nice breakfast you can tell me all about it. Harvey will walk you up the hill when you're ready. I've heard that dad of yours has a terrible temper and maybe you'll need a man around to protect you. I don't hold with some of the things that go on in these modern days. Why, when I was a girl, dads cherished and took care of their daughters.

"Who ever heard of girls playing hide-and-go-seek in the dark and falling out of a tree. Not that I am blaming you, Amelia. If your dad would stay home more often and not run after the young women, things would be better at home."

"Now, Sarah, don't go on like that. The child will think we aren't good Mormons the way you talk. It's just some of us believe differently than others. We mustn't judge. The Bible says to judge not, lest we be judged."

"Humph." Mrs. Jones snatched the feather duster from the floor and stomped off into the kitchen, but before closing the door she added, "On second thought, we'll all go. I need some sugar and I've wanted an excuse to speak with Ida. She should have taken my advice and left that no-good man when he took Thelma into the house. Afraid she'd lose custody of the children. Never heard of such a thing. Fiddlesticks."

"Don't you get all riled up now, Sarah. Ida knows what's best for her and the children. It's not easy for a woman alone. All of them don't have your strong constitution, Pet."

"Or good sense." They were in the kitchen now with the door closed and probably didn't know I could still hear.

"Ida doesn't see what's going on in front of her nose. I'd advise her to pack up, take her brood and head for her brother—you know, the one she keeps bragging that he has a large, beautiful home in Missouri. All Ida talks about is what a good husband that rascal of a man was years ago, when they first married."

"Can't live in the past forever. You told me Chester is yakking about moving to Snowflake. We all know they practice polygamy there. Sure no safe place for young girls, and their family has two. I'd never forgive myself if something happened and I hadn't warned Ida. So, don't you tell me to mind my own business! What happens in our neighborhood under my nose is my business.

"Men have been treating women as inferior beings long enough. Now that we have the vote, it's high time we showed them we are as good as they are. One woman for one man; none of this multiple marriages nonsense."

Mr. Jones spoke up quickly, "The main body of the church no longer teaches polygamy, just a few stray sects."

"Yes, I know. When Governor Hunt wanted to join the union in 1912, the Church stopped their teaching of multiple wives. Don't know if that was the reason or not. Maybe the other states didn't want us in unless we conformed to their notions, don't ask me."

I could hear pots and pans rattle and cupboard doors open and shut with a loud bang. "I do know one thing for certain, I'll not tolerate it in my own back yard. Makes a bad example, that's what it does!" his wife said, emphatically.

"My goodness, Sarah, how you do go on. You're going to burn the pancakes if you don't watch what you're doing."

I tried to make myself smaller and hoped to disappear entirely. I studied the walls, trying to get my mind off the conversation in the other room. They were completely covered with photos. One, I reasoned, could be a wedding picture of Mr. and Mrs. Jones. She looked young and pretty. Hard for me to visualize her as an old grouch. I walked over for a better look and decided to sneak out the front door, but Mr. Jones came in and I'd missed my chance to escape.

"Here, child. Come and eat, Amy. You'll feel better with food in your stomach."

I must admit the pancakes tasted delicious, smothered with butter and maple syrup. I ate four and drank two glasses of milk, trying to delay the trip home.

As we approached our house, Joseph stood at the cistern, drawing water. He gazed our way as we entered the front yard. I strolled over to him. "Joe, tell me what happened last night? Are they awfully mad at me?"

"Everyone is either worried sick or in a bad humor," Joseph almost growled. "Our guest didn't stop and get gas or pay his bill like he promised he would. We watched, horrified, as they raced passed in that long black Grand Pam sedan the braggart drives. Mr. Gilmore sure appeared angry. I know he blames me. Ailie is pouting because you kept her from having a good time with new friends over the Easter holidays, and Mama walked the floor half the night crying and worrying where you could be. We didn't know if you really were hurt or if you had run away again. Aileen says you had no business being jealous of her and ruining her fun. A lost weekend, I'd say. Does that answer your question?" He chuckled dryly.

I remained in the yard until the Jones' left. Then Mama opened the kitchen door and walked out and surveyed me. "Amelia, come over here. I need to talk to you, young lady. Just look at you! Will you just take a good look at yourself? Your new dress is ruined, your hair is a tangled mess. You even smell bad!" She curled up her nose in disgust.

"Wherever have you been? I worried myself sick! Do you have any idea how embarrassed you've made me?"

"Aw, Mama, I didn't think," I stammered.

"That's the trouble; you never think. You leave others to sort out your messes. Oh well, it's done now. Water under the bridge, you might say. Take a bath. It is Easter Sunday, after all."

I felt hurt. Mama seemed more concerned with keeping up appearances than my welfare, but I realized she'd forgiven me so I didn't say anymore. I felt bad about my dress. I shook it to try and remove the dirt, but no luck.

I walked over behind the tool shed and carried the galvanized washtub we used for bathing. I didn't expect any help pumping the water or building a fire to heat it. But to my surprise, Joseph strolled over to me and said, "You can use my shower if you like, little sis."

It pleased me. I knew Dan had built a shower outside the clubhouse, attaching an old washtub about seven feet above the ground, with a half-inch hole in the bottom and jammed a cork in the hole to plug it up. The tub caught any rainwater that ran off the roof of the lean-to, and by painting the tub a dull black, the hot Arizona sun heated the water. Pulling a string opened the cork and the water was released. Burlap bags, hung in a circle with baling wire, made a curtain.

"Thank you, thank you!" I called as I hurried into the house looking for a clean dress. I decided to punish myself by choosing the most ugly dress I owned. I snatched the hateful camouflage dress. The hem had been let out, and with the crease caused by the fold of the original hem the dress was even more distasteful than before. Maybe people will feel sorry for me dressed so poorly.

Showered and dressed with dripping wet hair and no shoes, I entered the house. "Mama," I asked. "I hear Dan and Thelma are working on their place up the hill. If Joe will walk with me, may I go visit them? I can help build a weekend retreat. Dan says I'm good at handing him lumber."

Mama scowled at the puddle on the clean linoleum floor and acted as if she hadn't noticed the dress I chose to wear. Her eyebrows drew together in a frown. Then her mouth crinkled in a smile that traveled to her sky-blue eyes, "Let's all go."

"It's four miles uphill, Mama," Joseph cautioned. He had followed me in. "Do you think you can walk that far?"

"You'll never know if I don't try," Mama laughed. She moseyed into her bedroom and returned wearing walking shoes.

Aileen danced out of our room wearing her new lavender dress. It had no collar but the gold locket hung elegantly down in front. Her face shone aglow with a rosy color.

"Where did you get that locket?" Mama asked with surprise in her voice. "I never saw it before."

"Papa's friend bought two for the price of one and didn't have any use for this one, so he gave it to me. Do you think it's pretty?"

"The strange old man who—" I started to say, but my sister flashed me a look that said 'keep your thoughts to yourself.'

"Yes dear, it's very pretty," Mama answered. "But it must be returned. Nice girls don't accept jewelry from men who're not related. I'm surprised Chester didn't tell you that.

"When you next see your papa give it to him to return for you."

Aileen's face showed disappointment. "I suppose there's no harm in wearing it until then."

We didn't make it up the hill. After only walking a short mile we heard a car—Daniel and Thelma headed to our house for Easter dinner. Will I ever see the land where Dan plans to build?

CHAPTER FORTY-FOUR—A LETTER

More than a week went by, and our family quickly settled into a peaceful contentment again. We realized it wouldn't go on indefinitely, but life became pleasant without Papa around. One day Mama received a letter from him.

Ida and family,
I made it to Old Mexico and found a job picking oranges. Instead of pay, they will give me a truckload of oranges that I hope to barter for merchandise for the store, and anything I can find to improve our lives. See you all when I return, but I can't tell when that will be.
Chester

A few days later while we sat together on the porch after dinner, Daniel drove his truck to a stop in front of the house.

"Daniel!" I said, jumping up and down, running to greet him.

He waved big before hopping out and rushing up on the porch to give each of us a hug. "I brought a couple of rabbits to eat," he handed a package to Mama. "How're things going without Papa around?" I wondered how he knew. I could also see a concerned frown on his face.

"We're doing fine," Joseph answered. "Papa hasn't been away long."

"Are you hungry?" Mama asked. "Where's Thelma? How long can you stay?"

Daniel laughed. "One question at a time," he said.

"Thelma didn't come with me because I can't stay long. I have the promise of a job in Miami and drove in to go see about it tomorrow morning. I couldn't pass up the opportunity to spend a night with you guys."

He walked over and hurriedly wiped the dust from the windshield.

"What kind of job is it?" I asked. "Flying?"

"Nah, there're no flying jobs in Miami," Daniel said. "It's a carpentry job. They're building a warehouse and mean to hire a bunch of men, but you have to get a jump on it. Lots of folks are looking for work. I'll be up at five, waiting in line."

"You might be the first in line at five," Aileen said.

"Well, that'd be a good thing, but I doubt it," Daniel said. "What've you got to eat around here, anyway?"

Mama stood, entered the house and walked to the icebox. "I have eggs," she said. "Would an egg sandwich fit the bill?"

"Sure would," Daniel said. "Scramble it and I'll share good news with you, too."

"No!" Mama said, smiling, hugging her checks with her palms.

I looked at Daniel and back at her. "What?" I asked.

"Is she?" She nodded like she was trying to encourage Daniel to say yes.

"Yes, she is," he said, beaming.

"What?" I asked. "Tell me! Quit talking in riddles and somebody tell me what you are talking about!"

"Okay," Mama said, "Thelma is 'that way.'"

"She's going to have a baby," Daniel explained in modern language. Why Mama's generation couldn't say the word pregnant was a mystery to me.

That evening, we stayed up late and listened to our brother talk excitedly of his new life with Thelma.

"Gracious sakes, I hope you get that job," Mama said. "It'll be nice to have you closer."

But I couldn't help thinking they'd be closer to Papa, too. That night, Daniel slept in Papa's bed. Before I woke the next morning, he'd left for Miami.

My mind was still on Daniel and Thelma, thinking how nice it would be to have a wee one in the family once more, when class was dismissed the next day.

"Let's sit in the swing until my dad gets here," Blanca ran to plop down on the closet swing. Perfect weather, not too hot or too cool. A slight breeze blew the copper fumes away from the schoolyard. It felt good to be out of the stuffy classroom with the western sun on my back. I took a deep breath.

"How does your papa manage to bring you to school and then come after you every day?" I asked, pumping my legs to start the swing. I wanted to make it go higher and higher—all the way into the sky to visit the birds!

"Oh, Amy, didn't I tell you?" Blanca said, sitting still. "He works nights now. He says as long as he's working below ground where it's dark anyway, it makes sense to work nights and be home in the daylight. He always waits up to take me to school in the mornings. Mama worries that sometimes he doesn't get enough sleep, though."

"Maybe that's why he's late," I said, as I stretched my legs on descent and let the swing carry me past Blanca. Then I bent my knees to ride backwards until I passed her again.

Blanca's eyes searched the road. All of the other students in the lower grades had left for home.

"I don't mind him being late," she said. "It gives us a chance to talk." She gave me a warm smile. "It's nice of you to wait with me."

I pumped my legs to make the swing go higher and higher. Feeling the breeze through my hair, I suddenly felt very free. Perhaps Daniel is right to want to fly.

"Remember how we used to see how high we could swing and then jump off to see how far from the swing we could land?" I giggled. "I could usually outrun you, but when it came to jumping, you'd beat me every time."

"Want to do it now?" Blanca said.

I heard a car honk and glanced behind me. "Aw, there's your papa," I said, disappointed. But I took the opportunity to jump anyway.

Blanca left the swing and headed toward her father's car. "See you Monday," she called, waving goodbye.

After she left, I remained in the swing a while, thinking. Aileen would be leaving her classroom soon. Her class dismissed fifteen minutes later than mine. If I wait, I can walk home with her. I hadn't talked to Aileen in private since the day Daniel visited.

I walked to a spot near the road to watch for Aileen. No sooner did I arrive there than I noticed a movement behind one of the large trees that stood across the road from the schoolyard. Something or someone hid behind the tree. The tree crowded a telegraph pole, leaving barely a crack between them. I froze and watched the space.

I wondered if Brownie might have jumped the fence and roamed down to the schoolyard.

Whatever hid there moved again. This time I saw a light flash, as if the sun had reflected off glass or gold. It's much too tall for a dog.

Suddenly a story I once heard of a young girl being kidnapped and killed back East came to my mind. I took off running toward the school and climbed the stone steps two at a time. Breathless, I burst into the hallway where I almost bumped into Aileen standing with arms locked with another girl. "Amy," she asked, startled. "Why're you still here?"

I didn't know the blonde-haired girl beside my sister. I hesitated, not wanting to sound silly or childish in front of Aileen's friend. "You know Amy, don't you, Mildred?"

"Sure, I've seen your little sister. But, we haven't met before. Hi, Amy!" Then she turned to Aileen, "I have to go. My mother scolded me last night for not coming straight home after school. See you!" She smiled and waved and hurried out the front door of our school.

"See you Monday!" Aileen called after her. Then she turned her attention back to me. "Now, what'd you want?"

"I thought I'd walk home with you," I said. "You are my big sister, aren't you?"

Aileen smiled and held out her hand. I was glad to take it and hand in hand we stepped out the door and down the steps.

"Of course I'm your sister," she said. "And we'll walk home together every day, if you like."

We started up the road and I craned my neck to scan the area around the tree and pole. I saw nothing. Then, as we rounded the corner by the Jones' home, I gasped. "Look, Ailie, look at that car! It's exactly like the one Papa and those men drove. You think it's the same one?"

"Not likely," she said. "Papa is in Mexico. Why would the men come here?"

"It's black like his," I said.

"All cars are black, silly! It's hard to tell them apart. You get excited too easily." But I noticed that she gripped my hand a little tighter and moved a bit faster the rest of the way home.

Joseph and Mama sat at the kitchen table. Mama looked up. "Where've you been, Amelia?" Mama said crossly. "Joseph has been home half an hour. You know I worry whenever you're late."

"I saw a man lurking between the tree and the telegraph pole in front of the school," I gasped, plopping down on the bench by the table. "I decided to walk home with Aileen."

"What?" Aileen said, shocked. "Gee whiz. You didn't say a word to me about that!"

"I didn't want to scare you," I said. Then I continued talking to Mama. "When Aileen and I opened the school door, I didn't see anything. Whoever lurked there had left. But tarnation, as we passed the Jones' house, I noticed a car exactly like the one those men drove. You know, the men Papa brought home with him from Snowflake." I looked over to Joseph for his support. "I memorized the number: 5-2-7."

"A lot of good that number'll do," Mama complained.

"Wait, that is the number," Joseph spoke sharply. "I remember thinking it's the same as Amelia's birthday—5 and 27."

Wide eyed, we glanced at each other, incredulously.

"What could they be doing in our neighborhood?" Aileen asked. "Wonder if Papa is with them?"

"My stars and garters. I can't imagine. You three stay here in the house and tend the store," Mama said. "I'm going to the corner. Land sakes, if Chester is in town, I want to know it."

She pulled her apron over her head and hung it on the peg behind the kitchen door. She started for the door and then stopped abruptly. "Oh dear, I almost walked out of the house in my slippers. Run get my shoes, will you Amelia? They're in the hall closet."

I obeyed and brought her the shoes. Then she smoothed her hair back with the palm of her hand and scurried out the kitchen door. We watched as she headed down the road. I could tell by the way she hurried that she was upset. I wondered if it was because of the strange men, or because Papa might be in town and hadn't told her.

Joseph fidgeted in his seat, rolling his eyes. "Dang it all, I'll bring in wood and start a fire in the cook stove," he said, jumping from his seat. "You two stir up supper and we'll surprise Mama by having the meal ready when she returns." He looked to see our reaction before continuing.

"Okay," Aileen said. "Mama seemed tired."

An hour later when Mama returned, we had supper on the table; leftover chicken and rice. Her eyes darted from one of us to the other, her face flustered.

"Chester isn't with them but you're right, Amelia, two of the men who came here that day are in town. Mr. Corren didn't leave the car, but I recognized him and the driver, Mr. Danbury—no mistaking him!"

"My goodness, what could they want?" I glanced at Aileen.

"I've no idea," Mama said. "But I'd like the opportunity to give that man back his gold locket." She stared at my sister, shaking her head. "You never should have accepted it."

Mama removed her shoes and stepped back into her felt slippers. Then she dropped to the table. "My, but it's sweet of you to have the evening meal ready for me. You're good children."

In our room that night, Aileen turned to me, "What do you think, Amy? Why did strange men come without Papa?"

"Tarnations, but I don't know," I said. "I don't like it." Suddenly I felt exposed. I stretched my arm high and pulled down the dining room shade so tightly that not even a sliver of light could escape.

"I wish Papa'd come home," Aileen said. "I'd plead with him to return the locket. Mama doesn't want me to have it and I'd rather not be near the man. Think he came for the locket?"

I bit my lower lip. "Actually, Mama said to return the jewelry, if you see him, Ailie. Here is what we'll do. I'll wait at your classroom every day after school. You stay in the hall, even if I'm a bit late. Then we'll leave by the back door of the building and cut across the mountain, and enter our yard by the back gate. That way you can keep away from the man, even if he's waiting across the street from the school. You may keep the locket and wear it every day." I didn't mention that no one hiding behind a tree could see us, either.

I became excited at my plan. "You won't be disobeying Mama and we won't ever have to gaze at his ugly face; he looks evil to me." I gasped for breath after my long sentence.

"Oh, Amy," Aileen smiled. "Sometimes you are clever." She turned out the light, reached over and raised the shade to let the cooler night air in, and soon fell asleep. I lay awake a long time, taking turns listening and staring out the window. I saw no movement and heard nothing except the normal night sounds of a hoot owl and an occasional dog barking.

Tuesday, after school, I stuck to my plan. As soon as Blanca left, I hurried to Aileen's school building and waited in the hall outside her classroom door. Imagine my surprise when Joseph and Billy came in right behind me.

"Hi," I said. "What're you two doing here?"

Joseph grinned his wide smile and said, "Same as you. Seeing my sisters home safely. Billy and I agreed four are better than two." He turned and looked at his friend. "Isn't that right, Billy?"

Water Under the Bridge

Billy's face turned as red as a beet, and for the first time I noticed how handsome he had become, with his blonde hair, cute little dimple in his chin, and amazingly gray-green eyes that twinkled when he looked my way.

As we hiked over the mountain path that led to our back gate, I couldn't help noticing that Billy looked sideways at me several times. Suddenly, I realized that he liked me and when Joseph had tried to keep me from following him to Billy's house, it was Joseph's idea, not Billy's. But I was only nine and Billy eleven. Much too young, as Mama would say. But if he wanted to help protect us—good. I enjoyed the hike home, stopping often to smell the cacti in full bloom.

Verna Simms

CHAPTER FORTY-FIVE—A CALL IN THE NIGHT

A few nights later, I had almost forgotten my scare of that Monday at school. Safely tucked in my bed, with the west window open—the one that faced our wrap-around-porch and the side yard, I felt secure. Our room remained dark, but the moon shone brightly and I lay quietly listening to my sister's and brother's soft breathing. I needed to rehearse my spelling words in my mind. The teacher expected us to know the proper spelling and, for me, the task was difficult. I'd often wondered why words weren't spelled like they sounded.

I jumped with a start when I heard my name called. "Amelia," a man's voice said in a low murmur. "Come outside, Amelia."

My blood froze. I gasped, holding my hand over my mouth, trying not to scream. I slithered over, like a snake, on the floor close to the wall to my sister's side and shook her gently and whispered, "Ailie! Wake up. Please wake up. A man's outside! He called my name!"

Amelia sat up, circled her arms around me. "You sure, hon? Maybe you've been dreaming."

"No, I was awake. I haven't been to sleep," I whispered, almost too scared to speak, and then I heard it again. "Amelia, it's me," the voice urged. "Come on out. You know you want to. I won't hurt you. Come to me."

I'd heard the voice before, but I couldn't recall the face.

I could feel Aileen's body tense as she pulled me down closer to the floor. Together we scooted over to where Joseph slept and shook him. This time Aileen spoke, "A man's calling for Amy to come out. Should we wake Mama?"

Joseph grunted and jumped to his feet. He didn't answer but strode over and opened Mama's bedroom door. We waited, much too terrified to move. There was just enough light for me to see him return, carrying Papa's shotgun. Mama trailed behind Joseph, wearing a tight-fitting flowered seersucker nightgown. Under normal circumstances I might have laughed at the sight of her, but to me, nothing appeared funny that night.

Mama walked from room to room closing and locking the windows.

"Who do you think could be in our yard?" Joseph asked.

I shook, afraid to answer. They'd laugh at me if I told them the men Papa had brought to the house had come for Aileen and me. The more I thought, I reasoned the voice belonged to Corn—the repulsive man with ugly-dead-corn silk hair and a scraggly beard.

All through the long night, Joseph watched, wide-awake, as he sat quietly with papa's gun on his lap. We heard no sound from outside. No ventilation in the hot stuffy room prevented sleep, even if we'd not been too scared to close our eyes.

At daylight, Mama said, "Amelia, I've been noticing how tired you look lately. You're losing weight. I'm afraid a gust of wind will blow you away." She tried to laugh, but failed. "You're becoming thin just at the age when a girl needs nourishment to mature into young womanhood. Do you think Mr. Romac would allow you to stay a week at Blanca's home?"

I glanced at Mama, grateful for the chance to escape the nightmare that seemed to be closing in around me. "I'll ask," I said, "but I'm sure I may. They've often told me I could stay as long as I wish. Thank you, Mama." I slipped over and gave her a kiss on the cheek. She pulled me into her arms and patted me on the back.

And so it was arranged. I slept in Blanca's soft bed with her for all of next week and there I felt safe and loved.

CHAPTER FORTY-SIX—A PRESENT FOR PAPA

Washday. Always a busy day. That Monday toward the last of July, our family of four stood in the side yard. A fire burned brightly under the iron kettle where Mama boiled white clothing, every so often poking the clothing down in the bubbly water with a forked stick.

"Here, Aileen" Mama said. "You scrub the overalls and I'll do a blanket."

"Okay, Mama," Aileen agreed, and leaned over the tub to scrub Joseph's overalls on a washboard.

"Amelia," Mama called shortly, her face red with the heat from the water, "come over here and help me wring water out of this double blanket. I've scrubbed it enough; it should be clean by now. Anymore rubbing and I'll wear it completely out. "

I dashed over and grabbed one side of the heavy wet cotton blanket—her twisting one way and me the opposite, squeezing out every possible drop of water. Then, the two of us draped it over the line. All the while, Joseph adjusted the clothesline props to keep the heavy wash from dragging the ground. As I helped fasten it securely against any wind, I could smell the acidy odor of the lye soap bubbling up in the pot, and my eyes stung from smoke drifting my way. I rubbed them, which only made it worse. We stayed busy with boring, routine household chores, nothing unusual—when we heard a vehicle.

A truck stopped and I looked up, shading my eyes as I squinted into the sun. "It's Papa," I called. "Gee whiz, someone's with him."

We couldn't see who. He slid from the driver's side of the truck, gave us a slight salute before walking around to the passenger's side, and opened the door. We each stopped our work and gazed.

Aileen commented, "Who could possibly make Papa go to that much trouble? I've never seen him be chivalrous before. He sure doesn't open doors for us."

A petite, dark-haired girl slid out. She didn't glance our way, but kept her eyes riveted on Papa's beaming face. My mouth dropped open. Mama snorted and went back to poking the wash that had bubbled up again.

"Hey. Who's with Papa?" Joseph asked. He stopped his work and shaded his eyes from the morning sun. Suddenly, his eyes widened and he stood, frozen in his tracks. "Whew!"

"Morning, everyone," Papa called, and escorted the girl into the house. We females followed, wiping our wet hands on our aprons. Joseph hung back—waiting—for what, I didn't know.

"Son," Papa stuck his head out the screen door. "Bring those boxes in the house. The ones that are in the very back of the truck bed."

Joseph hopped over to the truck and removed the tailgate. I rushed over to help, or at least watch, and see what Papa had brought—hopefully presents.

I wish I could recall all the truck held that day when he returned from Old Mexico. He brought us children each a matchbox containing jumping beans. I stood amazed. After seeing our bewilderment, Papa said, "Little bugs in the beans make them jump up and down." I could hardly wait to try and trick my friends into thinking I'd become magic!

He handed Mama a large oval ostrich egg. "What do you think of this, Ida?" he asked. "I'm told you can prick a hole in each end and blow the yolk and white out to cook, and then keep the egg shell intact, indefinitely."

The gifts were nice, but what I remember best of all is the present Papa brought back for himself! Juanita, a thirteen-year-old beauty with dark, wavy, shoulder-length hair and flashing cobalt-blue eyes, half hidden under thick dark, curly eyelashes. Her complexion shone with a healthy glow—smooth as ivory pearls. When Papa introduced her, she tossed her shiny hair and gave us a timid smile. Little laugh lines crinkled in the corner of her eyes. Her figure was slight, but definitely not girlish.

A tasty present for himself, indeed!

"We were married in Santa Ana," Papa announced with a sly smile and a wink at Joseph.

I glanced up to see Mama's reaction. Instead of the daggers I'd fully expected, her sky-blue eyes registered unconcern. Her face remained as calm and tranquil as the face of a sunflower turning to greet the afternoon sun. She appeared much more interested in the ostrich egg in her hands, turning it this way and that, peering at it as one might a crystal ball.

Our lives changed drastically today, I was thinking, as I watched Mama place the cream-colored ostrich egg in her lap and pull her printed-percale apron around it. She stiffly rose from her wicker chair, cradling the egg to her bosom, much as a kangaroo hides its young in a pouch. Not a word was spoken as she quietly drifted from the room.

Papa stood, "Anyone like to ride with me to show Juanita the town? Maybe we'll drive over to Miami." Aileen and Joseph both jumped to their feet, but I shook my head and drifted into the former dining room—where I stayed alone with my thoughts. Jealousy grabbed me by the throat and choked out any compassion or charity I might have felt for a newcomer, under different circumstances. I realized I'd already lost Papa, but now Joseph?

Mama must have stood looking out of her bedroom window while I, from my post in the dining room, joined her vigil. I'm sure we both studied the road with our eyes. No sooner had the car rolled down the road and out of sight, than I heard Mama's door open. Then I heard singing in a loud and pure voice. Peeking through a crack in the curtain, I stood amazed to see my mama's pudgy figure twirling and dancing around the kitchen. She reminded me of a bee dancing to convey a message to other bees. Was there a message in all of this for me? Transfixed, I stood frozen until she stopped.

Tired, perhaps, she entered her bedroom and returned to the kitchen with a darning needle.

"What you doing with the egg, Mama?" I asked, entering the room and peering over her shoulder.

"Oh, there you are Amelia. I thought you'd left with the others. I'm trying to pierce the shell and blow the insides out." Mama put the egg up to her mouth and blew air into one of the holes, forced the liquid contents out the other end, and caught the whites and yolk in a dish. I watched, spellbound.

"Wouldn't it be easier to crack the egg?" I asked.

"Sure, Amelia," Mama said, as she handed me the dish. "Put this in the icebox for me. I need to wash the inside of this shell, and then it'll make a nice hanging decoration for the store. Just you wait and see." Mama looked pleased as she added, "A conversation piece. Brought all the way from Old Mexico."

"What do you think about Juanita, Mama?" I asked. "Tarnations, isn't she rather young for Papa? We don't need her here, do we?"

She didn't speak right away. I thought maybe she hadn't heard me and started to repeat the question, but Mama shook her head and said, "Sometimes, it's better not to think—better to keep busy doing something useful."

"A person has to think," I argued. "I reason all the time, even when I'm doing something with my hands."

"Well, I'll tell you what to think about. Figure out how to triple this recipe for cookies. If we build up the fire, I'm guessing we can bake four-dozen cookies before the others return. What do you think of that?"

"That's a lot of cookies, Mama," I said, as I reached for pencil and paper and started multiplying the recipe by three.

Meanwhile, Mama kept busy poking on the live embers in the wood cooking stove, adjusting the damper and adding short pieces of wood.

"They're not for us to eat," she added. "I've decided to start selling baked goods in the store. "Those that can afford it would rather buy home-baked pastries than stand over a hot stove."

"Extra money will come in useful." She muttered as if to herself.

"You sift six cups of flour and get the rolling pin and cookie cutter out of the drawer. You can be a big help to me, Amelia."

Together we mixed ingredients and had the cookies ready for the oven. "How much will you charge, Mama?"

Mama stood and wiped her forehead with the tail of her apron. "A penny a piece should be a fair price, or ten cents a dozen." She looked over for my approval and added, "We won't get rich, but every little bit helps. Everyone is hard up these days; if you charge too much we'd have to eat them ourselves." Mama laughed at the idea, but the aroma of the cookies started to fill the kitchen and my mouth watered.

"Can't we eat any?" I asked.

"Oh sure, little girl. You and I will eat any broken ones or cookies with burnt edges. There are always a few in a batch that couldn't be sold. Plenty for the two of us."

We'd finished chewing the last of the broken cookies when I heard the truck. Joseph came in the kitchen first. He gallantly held the screen door open for Juanita. "Smells good in here," he said, walking over and taking the lid off the cookie jar. "Hey, it's empty! I'm positive I smell cookies!"

Mama strolled into the kitchen from the store. Without a word she grabbed the large iron frying pan and scooped a dab of butter in the bottom. "Hand me the bowl from the icebox, Amelia. We'll scramble that egg for our supper."

We all ate scrambled eggs from that one large ostrich egg

"I'd like fried chicken tomorrow, Ida," Papa said. "It's been ages since I had a real good home-cooked meal."

Mama didn't answer, but walked over to her chair, sat down and removed her wine colored house slippers, quickly buttoned her high-top shoes and walked out the door.

I followed her.

"You going to decide which chicken to kill, Mama?"

"Land sakes, I'm killing no more chickens. I wish the gate to their pen had a lock, so I could be sure no one else does." As she stood speaking, she moved her hands over the homemade wooden gate covered with chicken wire. "Chickens are mine!"

Mama turned, gazed toward heaven, studied the sky and slowly walked out of the yard and up the road. I stood and watched but didn't say anything. Sometimes I like to be alone, so why shouldn't my mama?

When we three sat alone that evening after supper, I turned to my siblings, "What do you think about Papa getting married again?"

Joseph's face turned red with embarrassment. He didn't comment.

Aileen spoke first. "I don't know what to think. I like her but it may cause friction between Papa and Mama. I tried to talk to Mama but she appears to have withdrawn into a shell and won't discuss it. Maybe it'll wear off as it did with Papa's and Thelma's marriage," she added hopefully.

"In my opinion, Papa should forget about other women," I said. "Mama won't say so but I think he's making her unhappy. It just isn't right!" I stormed out of the room, half mad at everyone.

The next day, Mama ran a string through both holes of the eggshell and hung it on the wall of her store. It looked nice.

So, once again, we were five and gradually a new routine developed. I must say, excepting for Mama and me, all in the family seemed to love Juanita. Wonderfully generous Aileen always made an effort to go out of her way to make others happy. And Joseph, well, I can only say he fell all over himself trying to open doors, push back chairs or whatever he could do for this pretty Spanish girl. After all he wasn't much younger than she, a boy of twelve, mature and tall for his age.

Juanita doted on Papa. She followed him from room to room, touching his closely shaven cheek or sitting on the floor with her head on his lap, cooing, "Daddy Poo." He stroked her, running his fingers through her long silky locks, as she looked up at him adoringly. It made me sick! I could not help but compare her actions to the image of a puppy we had once owned, licking the hands of his master. Disgusting!

Papa stayed with us in Claypool for a few weeks. Then he took his new child bride and moved into the city of Mesa. But he still came to our house on weekends. He did not, however, give us back our bedroom, preferring to use it when in Claypool

One day Mama announced, "A store doesn't need drapes. I don't know why I left them hanging so long." She turned to Joseph. "Go get a ladder and help me unhook them." The two of them removed the heavy drapes that had hung by the windows. Aileen and I stared as she stretched a rope across the ceiling the full width of the room that had once been our dining room, and re-hung the drapes. This created the effect of a wall separating Aileen and my sleeping quarters from the middle of the room.

"This is your new bedroom, girls," Mama said, holding back the drapes for us to see inside. Aileen and I pronounced it "home;" it worked so well that Mama repeated the process, this time using a sheet, creating another sleeping area for Joseph. This left a long corridor in the middle of the room as a passageway to the store without disturbing those sleeping or dressing behind the curtains.

"There are two of you so you should get the windows," Mama said, nodding to Aileen and me. "Anyway," she added, "Joseph, being a boy, can sleep in fewer clothes." Those rooms reminded me of pictures I had seen of railroad sleeping cars, a narrow walkway between two sleeping bunks. With pallets spread on the floor, Aileen and I now slept with our heads in opposite directions, our feet touching.

A few days later, all of us sat under the tree in the yard trying to stay cool. "I hear a car," Joseph said, looking toward the road. "It sounds like a Model T Ford."

How he could tell was a mystery. All engines sounded the same to me. Noisy.

"We once owned a Ford exactly like that!" Aileen announced. We stood in surprise when the car stopped and Papa and Juanita opened the doors.

"Gracious, is that our old car?" Mama asked, walking over to peer in the window.

"Yes," Papa laughed. "While driving through Phoenix I saw the 'for sale' sign. A lady came out when I knocked on the door and she said her husband had died. She didn't drive and only asked $50.00. As luck would have it, I'd finished that carpenter job, repairing a leaky roof, and had been paid today.

Water Under the Bridge

Had the cash in my pocket." He patted his back pocket for emphasis. "Juanita doesn't like to ride in the truck, so I bought the car back." He looked over at Mama and winked. "Isn't that something, Ida, after all these years, the one you and I drove from Missouri to Arizona?"

Mama's face flushed and she looked away. A shocked silence.

"What happened to your truck?" Joseph asked, stepping on the running board and searching the interior of the car with his eyes. "Yes, I see it's the same car. I recognize the tear on the back seat—where I snagged a sharp rock I carried in my pants when too little to know better."

"Oh," Papa said. "I still have the truck. We can't get along without it and keep the store. I may teach Juanita to drive this car. What do you think, baby?" he asked, looking her way.

Juanita smiled her timid seductive smile and I knew she could have anything she wanted from Papa. Once more, I felt jealous, and the joy of having the automobile again was lost to me.

Verna Simms

CHAPTER FORTY-SEVEN—BLANCA

The sun was setting on summer—fall was approaching. It had been a hard day for all of us. Mama's favorite setting hen and the rooster had flown to the top of the chicken coop. Up there, they spread their cropped wings and escaped over the back fence. The fence, built of crisscrossed logs, surrounded our property and had been erected when our lot had only been a parcel of farmland. It was definitely not an adequate barrier to deter chickens from fleeing up the mountainside to freedom. We were frantic to catch them. With the exception of dried beans, chickens and eggs remained our only source of protein.

Twilight fell before we had the birds safely back in their own chicken roost and locked up for the night. Our evening meal had been delayed. Only the four of us, Mama, Aileen, Joseph, and I sat in the kitchen and the room was quiet as we cleared the table. When we heard a soft knock on the screen door, we all jumped and hesitated. We seldom had any evening visitors. No one moved at first. The knock became more insistent. Finally, Joseph arose and strode over to the door. He opened it a crack and Blanca stuck her head in.

"Is Amelia home?" she asked anxiously. "I must see her." Joseph stood back, opening the door wider to let her enter. The cool night air rushed into the hot kitchen with her like a whiff of an ocean breeze. Framed by the doorway, my friend stood nervously.

"Blanca!" I exclaimed, jumping up from my seat and running to meet her. I pulled her farther into the kitchen. "How nice to see you."

Only then did I notice the look of dismay on her face.

"Is anything the matter?" I asked, putting an arm around my friend's shoulders. "Please, Blanca, tell me. What's wrong? Shall we go into the other room where we can be alone?"

"No." Blanca shook her head. "I have no time. Daddy only brought me here because I begged so hard." She took a deep breath and let it out slowly and then told me in short gasps. "We're leaving—tonight." She began to sob on my shoulders.

I could only ask, "Why?"

"Oh, it's the immigration people. They found out about Daddy. How, I don't know, but they know he's in the United States illegally."

I'm sure shock showed on my face. It couldn't be true. How could the government complain about the family? They were such wonderful people and would make excellent citizens. I shook my head in disbelief.

Blanca's eyes searched our homey kitchen as if trying to absorb memories. "Daddy says we must get out of Arizona tonight. Oh, Amelia, I don't want to have to go to Old Mexico. I've never lived there and Mama says the living conditions are awful."

The thought of my life without Blanca was intolerable. We had become inseparable. Next to Aileen, she was my closest confidante.

Then an idea hit me. "You're an American citizen, aren't you?" I asked.

She nodded. "But my parents aren't Americans."

"Stay with us!" I nearly shouted. "May she, Mama?"

"No, I can't," Blanca replied. "I must go. We're trying for New Mexico, Amy. We'll be safe there with our relatives. You remember, they came to visit us for the picnic on the Fourth." She turned and started out the open door. "Here's the address where I'll be." She thrust an envelope into my hand, a large white envelope with upward slanted printing in blue ink. A two-cent stamp was affixed to the right upper corner.

"Promise me you'll write, Amy?" She hesitated and then added to everyone in the room, "And please tell no one. Please—no one at all."

We all nodded in promise and Blanca turned to go.

Just outside the door, while still on the porch, she stopped and beckoned to me. I rushed out to join her. "I never told you this, Amelia," she said, brushing her curls back, stalling for time as if to phrase her words carefully, "but I will tell you now. Our family is psychic. We can feel things. Things that tell us the future or that reveal what is hidden to others."

"What do you mean?" I asked

"I felt a bad aura in this house just now. It worries me, Amy. I feel you will not be here long." She lifted a warning forefinger. "Be careful my dear, dear friend. Be very, very careful!"

She turned and ran to her father's waiting car, and without another word, she was gone.

I stood transfixed where Blanca had left me, clutching the white square envelope in one hand. My other hand waved frantically until I could no longer see the car. I sank to the rough oak floor and began to sob. I already felt as lonely as a missing sock.

It wasn't until two days later that I really thought about the warning Blanca had given me. Whatever could she have meant? It made no sense. I would not be in this house for long? Where would I go? I asked myself dozens of questions, but got no answers. Was Blanca's family really psychic? Could they see into the mysteries of the unknown and predict the future? I'd heard before that Gypsies who traveled through Arizona often claimed such powers. But could Blanca? She was dark and pretty. Was it possible that she was a Gypsy?

No, I argued with myself, and I slowly shook my head. "I will not think dark thoughts about Blanca, but I must write to her at once. Time hung heavy over me. I knew that school would again imprison me. Since that first day three years ago, Blanca and I had always eaten lunch together at school. How would it feel not having her at my side? Each day seemed to drag endlessly.

Papa and Juanita came to our house often and spent every weekend with us, but I never looked forward to their visits. There was a new distance between us. I noticed that every time I entered a room where they were talking, the conversation suddenly stopped or changed to something different. I could not dispel the faint uneasiness and eerie feeling I had developed. I wondered if Papa and Juanita were secretly plotting against me, yet no words passed their lips and not a single facial expression or hints of any kind warranted my uneasiness.

"Am I becoming paranoid?" I asked myself.

In my lonely unhappiness, I turned to the mountain and it called to me. *Come. Come visit with me!* I ran and asked Mama for permission.

"Mama, may I walk on the mountain? I could see if any wild flowers are blooming," I asked eagerly.

Mama didn't answer right away, but fingered the whips of hair that escaped from her bun and readjusted the pins in her hair. She surveyed the mountain with her eyes before studying my face and then said. "Joseph can't go with you today, but I don't see any reason why you can't walk a little way up the slope alone. Just don't stray too far from the path and stay where I can see you. A little fresh air should do you good. You've been looking rather peaked lately."

I didn't wait for her to say more or change her mind, but dashed out on the porch, hopped down to the walkway, and rushed to the back gate. As soon I reached the base of the mountain, I slowed my pace and picked my way through the rocks and cactus, examining each one and savoring every minute of this new adventure. Joseph had accompanied me in the past with one exception, the night a little girl foolishly planned to escape her troubled family. I inhaled deeply of the fresh aroma of the golden-yellow cactus blooms and examined each new shoot of growth finding its way up between the rocks and crevices. It amazed me how much change a fall rain could make. One day the mountain appeared dead, and then, almost as by magic, it was alive and beautiful. I wondered if the resurrection would be like that. Everything and everybody new and perfect. Perfect! Such a nice word; I repeated it over and over in my mind.

I didn't walk down into the knoll where the acacia tree reigned over the land, but turned and waved to Mama before sitting on a flat rock. I picked up a small stick and played in the sandy soil, drawing pictures of stick people, animals and outlines of a house. I erased it all and then wrote in large bold letters. 'I love you, Mama.' I smoothed out the letters 'Mama' and wrote 'Billy.' It felt strange but somehow good to see his name. I frowned. I erased the words and looked toward the house. Mama stood on the porch and motioned for me to come home.

"I didn't find any flowers blooming, Mama," I shrugged, "but it was nice and peaceful where I sat."

I'd never discussed my concerns with anyone, much less Mama. I knew what she'd say—quick to blame any apprehension on "the change"—meaning physical change from childhood to young womanhood. At nine years of age, going on ten—I could be expected to be temperamental, difficult, and rebellious. I only hoped Mama knew best, but the dread stayed with me. Were Papa and Juanita hiding something? Could Blanca foretell the future? Dear, dear Blanca. Oh, how I missed her. She warned me to be careful. I knew that Blanca cared for me deeply. If she felt the need to warn me, I decided, I should take some kind of action. I needed a plan.

The weekend came and Papa drove the truck in and parked in front of the house. I rushed out to meet him. "Where's Juanita?" I asked.

"She's ill. Nothing serious, but she decided not to accompany me this weekend."

Papa started unloading boxes to bring into the house. "Did you need her for something?"

Not waiting for an answer, he handed me a package. "Take this to Ida, Amelia. It's material for new dresses. You and Aileen are outgrowing everything. I'll not have my girls go around with upper body parts pushing out for men to stare at."

I shook my head, and gazed down at my budding breast, embarrassed. With Papa here alone, there'd be nothing for me to overhear, no way to eavesdrop.

Busy at school, time passed quickly. Mama suggested I try and acquire a new friend, but my heart wasn't in it. Even my old friend, Mary, was busy with another girl and I brooded alone most of the week. Each afternoon, I hurried home to see if a letter had arrived from Blanca.

None came.

I'd hidden the envelope containing her address in the secret box. Dejected, I crawled beneath the house after school and sat, hoping that somehow my image would fly over the airwaves to Blanca, but nothing happened. I hunched over, truly alone.

The next Friday evening, I rushed in the house after school to see Mama stooped over the oven, sliding a cookie sheet out and onto the counter.

"I'm home, Mama," I called. "Smells good in here."

I snatched a between, that's what we called the leaving after the cookie cutter separates the cookie dough into darling little shapes, and popped it into my mouth.

"If you'd waited until after school, Mama, I could've helped with the cookies."

"Don't talk with your mouth full, Amelia." Mama separated the cookies on a tray to cool. "You and I'll stir up another batch as soon as Chester brings sugar and flour. We're selling so many I can hardly keep up."

I reached over to snatch another but Mama stopped me. "Don't ruin your supper. Change into play clothes before going outside. And hang up your dress. It's fresh enough to wear again without laundering."

In comfortable clothing, having fastened the two tails of my full skirt together between my legs with a large safety pin, I dashed out to find Joseph sitting on a seat outside the door.

"What're you up to, Amy?"

I tucked as much of the skirt inside my bloomer legs as possible while I bounced down the steps before answering, "Going to practice standing on my head."

I enjoyed this new accomplishment and expected a comment from my brother, but instead he called, "I hear the Model T. Wonder why Papa is bringing it instead of the truck?"

"Maybe Juanita came. I see someone with dark hair huddled close to Papa." He hopped up and rushed to the car and beat Papa opening the door for the young girl. Papa scowled and barked, "Here, Joseph, you unload the back seat. I'll see that Juanita is comfortable in the kitchen. We haven't eaten yet." He turned and spoke to me. "Amelia, for heaven's sakes, get off your head and act like a lady for a change. Now, in the house with you and set places at the table. We're hungry."

Inside, away from Joseph, Papa turned to me. "Young girl, you listen to me. I will not have you romping around like a boy, standing on your head. Of all things! It's an invitation for trouble.

"You're old enough to dress and behave like a lady. Why can't Ida teach you better? Remove that safety pin from between your legs immediately. Also, I forbid you to climb trees." He shook his head in disgust and left the room.

Saturday morning, I awoke early and started what had become my vigil, staring out my sleeping room window, watching for Papa to head for the outhouse. I couldn't see the back door from my window, but I could see the path he must take. As soon as I spotted him, I walked through the empty kitchen and knocked lightly on his bedroom door. I tried the doorknob and found it unlocked. Hurriedly, I slipped into the room asking softly, "May I come in?"

A sleepy Juanita half rose in the bed on one elbow, dressed in a frilly red nightgown. She rubbed her eyes with one hand, squinted in my direction, and pulled the sheet up around her shoulders.

"Oh, yes, Amelia, do come in." She sounded pleased that I'd finally made an effort to be friendly. She patted the bed. "Come sit here beside me."

Now that I was inside the room I didn't know what to say. Embarrassed, I stumbled over my words, "I just came to ask you—I mean—Well, I guess I'm wondering what it's like to be married?"

"Oh, you get used to it," Juanita replied, with a little laugh, tossing up her messed hair. She looked lovely even when half-asleep. "We women must make the sacrifice to please our men." A slight pause before she continued, "But, why do you ask?"

Water Under the Bridge

I didn't answer. What could I say? I hurriedly memorized the placement of the bed, measuring in my mind how many feet Papa's head rested from the window. Relieved that little had changed over the years, I also noted Juanita slept on the far side of the bed, the side closest to the east window.

"I must go," I said, pushing to my feet. "Please, don't tell anyone I came." I prepared to exit the room and dropped my hanky. I stooped to retrieve it.

All is well. Nothing stored under the bed. So far, so good.

Back in my room, I opened my school notebook, tore out a sheet of paper, and, from memory, drew a picture of the room. I marked in inches each piece of furniture, and noted its placement in the room. That finished, I folded my map of the room and tucked it in my pocket.

As Papa and Juanita scooted in the car to return to the city, Juanita leaned over and whispered in my ear, "Maybe you'll find out your answer soon." She smiled and appeared pleased.

Their routine became weekdays in Phoenix and then arriving to our house on Friday night around five, in time for supper. They usually stayed until dusk on Sunday and then returned to the city.

"This way," he explained, sounding pleased, "I can deliver fresh produce every week for Ida to sell in the store. You girls can do our laundry Saturday morning, and we'll attend church together on Sunday."

Mama had stopped attending the Mormon Church, but she allowed Papa to take us. Through the week she would caution us, "Go and learn what you can, so as to make the right choice for yourself when you're grown." She always hesitated and spoke more slowly before she issued this warning. "But be sure you do not marry a Mormon man, at least until you are mature enough to understand and make a sound decision for yourself.

"Remember your school lessons. That is our heritage, why the Pilgrim forefathers came to this country—religious freedom. Each individual has the right to decide for themselves!"

All week I made my plans, but found it necessary to wait until after school to start my project. I rushed home on Thursday, changed into my play clothes, grabbed a ball of string I'd been hoarding, a pencil, the drawing I'd made of the bedroom, and hurried out the door. I snatched the key to Papa's tool shed from its hiding place and tied the key to a short length of string and slipped it around my neck. To lose Papa's key would spell disaster. I glanced around and saw no one. Inside the shed, I selected a hammer, a large nail, a small block of wood, a brace, and the largest wood bit I could find, and then turned to go. I remembered I would also need a rule. I reached up on the shelf above my head for Papa's wooden folding rule. Satisfied with my equipment, I left the tool shed and carefully closed and secured the latch on the wooden door. I held the tools behind my back, my heart pounding, and turned my head first to the right and then to the left to be sure I was alone. The yard remained empty. Stealthy as a thief in the night, I made my way quickly and quietly to my destination—the space under the house, beneath the back bedroom.

It took several minutes for my eyes to adjust to the semi-darkness. I placed all of the tools on the far edge of a box; then I squatted on my haunches and listened. The regular thump-thump of Mama's treadle sewing machine was the only sound I could hear. "Please," I mouthed into the darkness around me, "don't let her stop." I knew the sound of the sewing machine would drown out any noise of a hammer or a hand drill.

Crash! Clang! "Oh, my gosh!"

I dove to the ground in shock; then laughed realizing it was thunder. Mama must have been startled, also. The sewing machine stopped.

I waited.

As soon as the treadle could be heard over the pitter-patter of the rain, I climbed on the box Joseph had fashioned from two orange crates, and resumed my labor. I unfolded Papa's wooden rule but soon realized it was impossible to be completely accurate. Any spot under the bed would have to do. I preferred a hole near Papa's head, but if I missed the bed completely, that would be a catastrophe. I imagined him finding a big gaping listening hole in the middle of the floor and shuddered at the horror of the consequences.

Crossing my heart and biting my lower lip for luck, I held my breath and selected what I hoped to be a safe spot. With the pencil, I marked an x. I scooted the box over until it lay directly beneath the mark. I retrieved the nail from my pocket and, as silently as I could manage, hammered the nail in about one-half an inch. I then turned the hammer around and, using the claw, pulled the nail out.

Now I had a wee hole to start drilling. With utmost caution I stopped to listen. No harm done yet.

Drilling a larger hole was much more difficult than nailing had been. It had looked easy when I watched Papa lean on the round knob with his left hand and turn the handle around and around with his right. I'd watched him many times in fascination and had wished to try for myself. But today, I'd drill a little and then need to lower my aching arms to rest. It took an hour to finish the job and only pure stubbornness helped me succeed.

Water Under the Bridge

The next evening—Friday—Papa and Juanita arrived at Claypool early. Mama's baked chicken tickled my nose but I feared I'd be unable to enjoy it.

"Chicken smells delicious, Ida," Papa said, as he splashed water over his freshly shaved face, rinsed his hands, and sat at the table, waiting to be served. I rolled my eyes to see Juanita waltz over to join him. She looked exceptionally lovely, wearing a new, canary-yellow dress, as she daintily picked at the meat. She saw me admiring it.

"Chester bought this dress for me at a department store in Phoenix. Do you like it? They had another one in green—it would show off your coloring, Amy."

The princess style fit her slim figure perfectly, tucked in tightly at her slim waist and then flared out at the hemline, slightly below her knees. She wore pointed, black patent leather shoes, with dark silk hose covering her shapely legs. Pearly buttons glistened all the way down the front of this creation. I felt a tinge of jealousy. Papa never bought Aileen and me store-bought dresses. Mama made all of our clothing. But I mustn't think of that today.

I nodded to Juanita and tried to smile, but I'm afraid it looked forced.

I retired early, but not for sleep. I arranged my pillow and blankets to appear as if I were lying in bed, completely covered and on my side, with my back turned to face the curtain wall. I knew Aileen would not use a light or disturb me. Fooling her became child's play.

With this camouflage in place, I silently slipped out the window and made my way under the house. At eight o'clock, the solitude and darkness engulfed me. Not the friendly hide-away I enjoyed in daylight. In this spooky spot I waited impatiently, propped up on two wooden orange crates nailed together.

Time passed slowly, having no idea what time Papa and Juanita would retire. I worried I might sit there all night and argued with myself whether to go or stay. After what seemed like hours, I lost hope and stood to go. Just then, I heard the door to our former bedroom creak open, and with a quiet, but distinct click, it closed again.

I clambered up onto the box and tried to press my ear against the low ceiling an inch from the hole I'd drilled. I was prepared to listen—to find out once and for all if my suspicions were real or foolish.

Papa and Juanita were talking. "Baby," Papa said, "don't extinguish the lamp all the way. Just turn the wick down a little. You are so beautiful tonight and I must watch you undress."

Juanita giggled girlishly. Papa continued in a teasing voice, "Pull the shades first. We don't need to give the whole neighborhood a free show. Not with my baby, we don't." he chuckled softly. "You belong to me—only me!"

I could hear Juanita's soft footsteps glide across the floor and then the snap of a shade as it was pulled too far and then snapped back up and rolled around and around—clang—clang—clang.

Papa snorted, "I need to have Ida buy new shades. Now perform for me like you did that first night I saw you in Mexico. We don't have music, but you can sing a song. Sing it in Spanish. Sounds so provocative and suggestive in your native language."

"I don't have my long gloves on." Juanita complained.

"Well, get them," Papa ordered. "I want the whole show, beginning to end—the whole performance. You're mine now, baby doll—all mine!"

I heard drawers open and shut and then Juanita singing seductively in a low, sexy, girlish voice. I knew no Spanish so I couldn't make out any words, but I could imagine her swaying slowly to the tune as she unbuttoned the thirteen buttons and let the dress fall to the floor.

I remember Papa repeating, "Oh, baby, oh baby, what you do to me!" And I wondered how much Mama could hear in her room, with only a closet between them.

"Lordy, come over here now and undress me while I play with your silky hair, so soft. All of you is so soft. I'm a lucky man, I am, that I am—one lucky man."

Then I heard other sounds. The noise came through the hole clearly—much too clearly. With my eyes closed, I could imagine myself in the room with them. Surely what I heard was lovemaking between a man and his wife. Intrigued, fascinated, but most of all embarrassed, I froze as more sounds, now louder, came to my ears through the round hole. I crouched silently in my cramped place on the two uncomfortable orange crates.

"Squeeze it for me, baby—that's it. That's it!" Papa was moaning and gasping for air.

I turned my face from the hole, but could still hear Juanita, "Oh, Daddy Poo! Don't stop, don't stop!" Then low moaning and groaning. The bedsprings creaked and creaked. Will they never stop, I thought, as I tried to force myself to leave but I became glued to the hole with no power of my own.

Water Under the Bridge

The creaking finally ceased and loud snoring could be heard. I started to jump down but hesitated as I heard bare feet pad across the room and the shades roll up.

Blessed silence followed. At last I felt it safe to leave my post.

I vowed to God that I would never return to listen. Next day, I dared not look Papa or Juanita in the eyes. Surely they would see my red face and know something was wrong.

But that very evening I did take up my post under the house again and was pulled over to the drilled hole like a puppet tied to a string. I had barely settled at my 'listening place' when I heard my name. Papa paced around the room and it became difficult to catch every word above the clop, clop of his boots. I pressed my ear closer to the hole. What I overheard sent chills through my bones.

"I've been studying Amelia closely lately," he began. "About time I made a decision concerning my girls, don't you think?"

Juanita's answered so low that I couldn't catch the words. Papa continued, more emphatically, "I hope everything goes well tomorrow for Aileen's wedding," he said. I could hear his footsteps cross the room and then I heard the creak of the bedsprings as he lowered himself.

One boot dropped. Dust flew and I held my nose to keep from sneezing. It didn't work. I only had time to squeeze my nose shut as a weird sneeze almost burst my eardrums.

"Achoo . . ."

"What's that? Did you hear it?"

"Sounds like a sneeze," Juanita answered.

Footsteps shook the floor above me. "I'll not have anyone peeping in our window. "Hand me my gun."

"It sounded like it came from under the house."

I froze, imaging myself drug out by the hair for my misdeeds. I panicked and prepared to make a quick exit; then it came to me. I did excellent imitations of a cat. I made a muffled "Meow."

"It's only that dumb cat of Ida's." Papa sounded relieved. "Let her keep it. That'll be all she has soon." The bedsprings creaked. "You must help me see that everything goes alright tomorrow, Juanita." Papa's voice came through the hole.

A loud thud—the other boot, I thought, dropping inches from my ear. I startled.

"What can I do?" asked Juanita.

"Just stay close to Aileen and encourage her. She'll pretty well do as she's told if we can keep her away from Ida and Amelia. Brother Mathew has only two wives. He'll make her a good husband."

"When will you tell Aileen?"

"Not until after Brother Joshua takes Amelia away. Ten minutes or so before the wedding is time enough. She won't refuse in front of a church full of people."

Take Amelia away? My heart was already pounding, but now the thundering moved into my head. I felt dizzy. I needed to scream. Away! Away—where? One part of me wanted to run—run to Aileen and warn her—run to Mama for help—run far, far away, anywhere—just run—run—run! But I knew that my future life and Aileen's life depended on what I might hear. I stood in the darkness under the house, and there in my lonely vigil I continued to listen.

'Isn't Amelia rather young to marry?" Juanita asked timidly. "Can't you wait a year or two for her?"

Did she say Amelia? She meant Aileen, surely. I held my breath, waiting for Papa to respond.

"Amelia will run for sure as soon she sees I am forcing Aileen to marry. Why do you think I waited this whole last year?"

His voice sounded angry. I heard the bed springs again as if he shifted his weight over to the middle of the springs.

"Don't you give me a bad time, woman. It's enough all the other females in this household do. Brother Matthew is a good man. He's a couple years younger than me, so he and Aileen have plenty of time to raise lots of children—grandchildren for me."

I could feel my face burn hot, then chill, as I shivered uncontrollably. "And Brother Joshua, he'll be good for Amelia. He's good to his four wives. A little strict, perhaps, but that's exactly what Amelia needs—someone to show her how to behave—teach her the needed discipline.

"He'll probably keep her locked up until she's old enough to marry and have a baby. Having an infant born calms a girl down. I'm getting sick and tired of worrying about her—running off and such. That girl is too smart and stubborn for her own good. The sooner she learns that men are the head of the house, the better." He muttered something about an umbrella but his head must have been turned, because I didn't catch the whole sentence.

The bed creaked loudly and I pictured Papa spreading his whole five foot eleven frame across it.

Water Under the Bridge

"I'll keep Joseph with me. We need more young boys to be baptized for the dead. His voice softened and I visualized him turning to Juanita as he spoke.

"Now go to sleep, baby. I want to show off my pretty little wife at the weddings tomorrow and you need your rest. Once I get my family settled, let's you and I take a second honeymoon, pet. Maybe we'll go to Jamaica."

No answer from Juanita. I thought they were sleeping and prepared to move away when a muffled sound slipped through the crack. "Nice town, Snowflake," Papa said dreamily. "My girls will remain good Mormons there."

Terrified of discovery, I stood in the darkness until I heard Papa snore heavily. I felt a chill. My whole body shook. I bent over and with icy fingers I gripped the wooden edges of the box where I'd been crouching. I feared I might stumble and crash to the dirt below.

Unbidden and unwanted thoughts raced through my brain along with the thump, thump of cold blood coursing through my veins and making my temples throb. How much time had passed—whether minutes or hours, I could not say. I only knew that my future life would never be the same. I carefully slumped down from my perch to stand on the dirt floor, but my knees buckled and I fell to the ground on all fours. My palms spread flat; dust billowed up between my outstretched fingers. In this position, I slowly and painstakingly crawled toward the moonlight that peeked in under the house.

Only when I reached the outdoors where the moon and stars lit up the yard did I notice my dusty face was wet with tears running down my cheeks. I had not realized I had been weeping. I continued to crawl through the soft dirt, around the side of the house.

I started gasping for air. I felt as if a mighty rush of wind like a cyclone had swept across me and sucked all the air from my lungs. I sat still again, this time leaning against the concrete pillar that faced east, only inches beneath the open window to Papa's and Juanita's room. Then an idea came to me. I crawled back under the house and inched my way over to my secret hiding place where, in the darkness, I fumbled for the piece of paper I'd hidden weeks before. Finding it, I slipped it in under my bloomers, held there firmly in place by the elastic.

If I could find Blanca, I knew she and her parents would help me. Somehow the plan helped the panic to subside and my courage to return. I left the underside of the house once more and arose from the cramped position to my feet. Cautiously, I made my way around the back of our time-weathered home, hugging the shadows.

A hot flush replaced the earlier chill I'd felt. I was furious. Hatred filled my heart. I hovered under the back porch, the one that led into the kitchen and, with the tail of my skirt, tried to wipe dust from my tired eyes. I must plan. Think, Amelia, think. The knowledge of what Papa was doing made me feel as useless and unwanted as a discarded toy—thrown out with the trash. What to do? I really wanted to crawl under a rock the way I'd seen many lizards hide, up on the mountainside.

I have to run away, I realized. Fast. Right now! But first, I must warn Aileen and Joseph. Maybe they'd come with me. Hope filled my heart. And this time I would take food!

How, oh how, could Papa do that to me—to Aileen, his own daughters—his own flesh and blood? It was more a reaction than a question. I knew the answer. His desire to be a like a god in the hereafter overshadowed the fatherly feelings he'd once had for Aileen and me.

MEN! I screamed silently in my tortured brain. Why do they all believe themselves to be superior? Why do they treat the females of this world as property rather than as human beings? Fortified with anger, I charged out of the safety of darkness under the porch and its morning glory vines. Would I ever smell their sweet aroma again? No matter!

CHAPTER FORTY-EIGHT—BETRAYED

A full moon and numerous stars illuminated the night. I would have enjoyed the beauty of the night if I'd not been so fully engulfed in my problems. I shivered in the cool night air and hurried to the outhouse. I was extra careful not to lose Blanca's address, not to let it fall down into the stinking hole, when I pulled my bloomers down to relieve myself.

Reluctantly, I returned to our darkened house. Entering the same way I'd left—through the window. I did not go to bed, however. I parted the curtain and slipped across our makeshift corridor—my bare feet made no sound. Behind Joseph's curtain, I heard his soft breathing. I knelt on the floor by his head, ducked my upper body under the curtain. I placed my left hand over his mouth and at the same instant cautioned in a barely audible murmur. "Joe, wake up. Make no sound. An emergency! Meet me at the outhouse—now!"

I knew I could count on Joseph. He bolted straight up and gave me a nod I could barely see in the darkness. I soon heard the kitchen screen door close softly and returned to the girl's side of the room. Kneeling, I leaned down and whispered in my sister's ear, "I need to go to the toilet, Aileen. Will you come with me?"

Joseph stood waiting for us near the outhouse on the back of our lot. We three slipped behind it so we could not be seen from the house or road. I could barely hold back the tears.

"I-I sat on a box under the house to listen to Papa and Juanita," I blurted between sobs. "They—they said, oh I can scarcely believe it now!"

"Go on, Amy, tell us." I barely noticed Joseph had his arm around me, I shook so hard.

"Tomorrow when we head for church he's going to keep driving all the way to Mesa and there—once we're inside the church building—he's planning to force Aileen to marry that old man, you know, the one who gave her the locket. You remember, I called him Dandy. He won't tell Mama or Ailie ahead of time, figuring she'll go along with his plan and then it'll be too late for anybody to do anything about it." I caught my breath as if I had run all the way up the mountain.

Aileen looked at me closely and then she turned her gaze on Joseph.

"She's making it up, don't you think, Joe?" she accused, hopefully.

Her words shocked me—the last thing I'd expected. I stomped my feet in frustration and fought to contain my tears and rage.

"No, sis," Joseph shook his head. "It's true all right. I've noticed myself that Papa and Juanita have been acting strangely. Juanita said something I didn't understand and can't remember exactly. She started and then stopped suddenly, clasping her hand over her mouth before—"

"Did Papa mention anything about you and me, Amy?" He stooped down to where our faces were level.

I nodded. "He's going to keep you with him so he can volunteer you to be baptized for dead people and me—me—I'm not sure what he meant. He-he—" I sobbed so hard I couldn't say the words. "Said something about me being too young to marry but having me locked up somewhere until I could have a baby. I'm not sure, but I'm scared!"

The shadow of the outhouse building hid his face, but the next words I heard sounded menacing "Like hell, he will. Dang it all, now, let's plan what we can do about it!"

I could have hugged my brother and swore I'd never be mad at him again. "I have Blanca's address in New Mexico," I offered. "Let's all go there. She'll keep us safe. Want to?"

Neither Joseph nor Aileen liked my idea to try and find the Romac family. We stood in silence, clutching each others' hands in the semi-darkness, as if we broke the chain one of us would vanish into thin air.

Finally Joseph broke the spell. "If we damage the car so it won't start, we'll miss church this weekend and have a week before Papa comes back. In that time, Mama will be able to help us." He turned to Aileen—her being the oldest. "What do you say?" She and I nodded, enthusiastically.

"But how?" Again, Joseph supplied the answer: "Do you remember the day the car wouldn't start and Papa told me to ride to the station to buy new spark plugs?" I was really getting revved up and nodded vigorously. "Well, I have the old plugs in the saddle bag of my bike. I'll jerk out the good plugs and put the bad ones back in."

We all agreed.

The moonlight was not quite bright enough for Joseph to see under the hood of the Ford. Aileen slipped into the house and brought out her hand mirror. By holding it just so, the light from the moon reflected down on the engine. Joseph made fast work of his mission. I stood watch under the shadow of the porch. To be caught around the car at night would be disastrous.

"We need an alternative plan," Aileen coaxed. "Papa knows Amy gets sick going over the mountain and I've heard soap does the same thing if you swallow it. Here's Plan B: She sits in the back seat of the car between us, Joe. Papa takes the turns too fast, especially over the mountains, and sometimes this makes her sick. When that happens, he'll have to stop the car." Aileen looked my way. "You jump out and throw up."

In a way, it seemed a good plan, but I didn't want to wait until we came to the mountains and couldn't see any good it would do anyway to be stuck up on a mountain, sick.

I shook my head. "I don't like it. I hate being sick and stranded on a mountain."

Joseph nodded, "Course not. Don't wait then, Amy. Put some soapy water in that pink purse you carry with you and drink it earlier, while still in town."

I'd never tried drinking soapy water before, but I'd heard that it caused vomiting. I still wasn't convinced.

Aileen said, "Yes, if you're in the middle of the backseat, it would only seem natural for all three of us to jump out. If she vomits all over herself and me, we'll have an excuse not to get back in the car, and can walk back home. Do you like that better, Amy?"

I nodded feebly.

"Amelia can be messy and throw up on all three of us. Just help her by standing close by. Even Papa wouldn't insist we go to church like that, would he?"

I felt very uneasy about Plan A and Plan B. Running away still appealed to me.

The three of us had moved to the semi-darkness under the back porch. Joseph broke the silence.

"Hey, we'd better go back to our beds now." No one answered. Somehow I didn't think any of us could bear to be alone tonight.

"You girls go in first and I'll follow. If we're caught entering the house together, Papa will ask questions."

Without uttering a word, Aileen slipped her hand in mine and we ascended the stairs together. I reached over and slowly opened the screen door, willing it not to squeak. We stepped silently into the kitchen. As I was trying to ease the door shut, my sister bent over and placed Mama's braided rag rug in the door opening.

"One less chance of a bang," she mouthed.

I nodded. We sat huddled together safely on our pallets when we recognized the faint click of the hook that secured the screen for the night. Our conspiracy was finished.

Please God in Heaven, I prayed, *let it work.*

I thought for sure I was much too stimulated to fall asleep, but the next thing I remembered, daylight shone in our window and a loud rap on the wall awakened me. Papa was knocking on the doorframe.

"Wake up, children. Time to get out of bed."

I forced my heavy lids open. The sun shone on the treetops. Night was over and today would decide my fate! I could hear the old familiar sound of our rooster crowing, "Wake up, hens." I always imagined him calling, "Time to go to work laying eggs!"

I rolled over before sitting up, and looked at Aileen. She returned my gaze and without uttering a word, we rose, straightened our covers, fluffed up our thin feather pillows, and started to dress.

We never guessed that September Sunday in 1930 that we would never lie down there again!

Papa's heavy footsteps approached between the two makeshift hallway curtains that separated our sleeping quarters from Joseph's. He stopped. The curtains hanging limp didn't move.

It became difficult for me to breath normally. My chest hurt and I held my hand over it to try and slow the beating—thud—thud—thud!

"Aileen," he said.

"Yes, Papa,"

"Your mama says you have a new white dress she made for you."

"Yes, Papa."

My eyes burned from staring out the closed window into the sky. A black crow flew past the window and landed on a lower branch of the cottonwood tree, close to the tattered old red umbrella.

Papa's voice continued, "I'd like for you to wear it to church today."

"Yes, Papa."

"Do you have any white ribbons?"

"Yes, Papa."

"Put them among your curls. I'd like you to be especially pretty at church today."

Aileen and I exchanged glances. When she did not answer, Papa coughed slightly. "Did you hear me, Aileen?"

"Yes, Papa, I heard you. I'll wear white ribbons."

I could see the distrust and fear in her eyes. Neither had ever been evident in Aileen before. She began to shake violently.

The air hung heavy in our little sleeping compartment. I tried to concentrate on the caw-caw-caw of the crow but stayed acutely aware of Papa standing outside the closed curtain. My chest felt tight. I could hardly breathe. Why didn't he say something or go away? I turned my back to the curtain and stepped closer to the window and raised it a few inches to bring in fresh air. The noise scared the crow away and then the only sound outside was the soft clucking of the hens. Had one just laid an egg? It seemed strange that life around me went on as before.

I could stand the silence no longer. "Papa?" I said in a small voice.

"Yes, Amelia?"

"What shall I wear?" My voice sounded odd and far away. On second thought, I realized I shouldn't have initiated a conversation. What would Papa have me wear for the day he planned to throw me away?

His voice brought me back to the present. "Something appropriate for the Lord's day, Amelia. A nice dress." His voice receded as he turned to leave. "You wear your suit, Joseph." It seemed a rather gruff order.

"My suit is way too small, Papa," Joseph answered quickly. I thought I recognized a challenge in his voice. He continued, "Have you not seen me these last few months? I've grown and in a couple of years, I'll be as tall as you."

Joseph was definitely issuing a challenge, but no answer came from Papa, just footsteps fading into the other room.

As I dressed, scarcely conscious of donning the pink organdy that matched the pink purse, my birthday seemed a lifetime ago. My mind raced. Should I pound on Mama's door and bring her into this calamity? Wake up, Mama! My mind screamed. No use. Mama remained as stubborn as Papa. Ever since Papa brought Juanita into the house, she refused to leave her room on Sundays until she heard the motor of the car start. Today, we children were on our own.

I suddenly felt very small, very fragile and, oh, so scared. "Tarnations, Ailie," I whispered as I watched my sister brush her long curls and try to fasten them with a ribbon at the nape of her neck. "Want me to help? Why bother to try and look nice?"

Aileen didn't answer, just handed me the ribbon and turned her back. I usually loved the feel of her silky blonde hair but today I felt all thumbs and it was with difficulty I tied the crude white bow. What did it matter?

Breakfast offered no improvement. I could scarcely swallow the lumpy oatmeal Juanita had prepared. I worried now that the food would not stay down long enough to execute Plan B, should it become necessary.

"Amelia, eat your breakfast. Stop stirring the oatmeal like it's concrete." Papa looked amused, in unusually high spirits.

Juanita had been scrutinizing me. "Don't you feel well, Amelia? Maybe you should stay home from church today."

I looked across the table, hoping Papa had softened towards me and would listen to Juanita.

His eyes darkened. "No!" said he, emphatically. "We will all attend services today. Now, stop dawdling, hurry up."

I watched Joseph, with fury in his eyes, thankful that he sat on the bench across from me instead of Papa. Juanita sat poised prettily between the two of them. Only Aileen and I could see the turmoil going through our brother's body. Joseph, being naturally left-handed, had been forced by Papa to eat with his right hand. For that reason he usually kept his left hand in his lap at mealtime. I noticed the muscles flexing in his left forearm as he clenched and unclenched his fist under the table. His eyes blazed fire and he furiously worked his jaw.

Aileen nudged me under the table. Always a natural peacemaker, she tried to ease the tension. She'd always been good at placating Papa. She spoke sweetly, "Papa?" How could she look him in the face, I wondered, and with such trust in her eyes. "I think I'll volunteer to lead my class in prayer today. Will you help me prepare the proper words?"

Papa nodded happily. "On the drive to the church services," he said. "We haven't time now."

I tried to do my bit and spoke up rather shakily, dragging out the words, "May I have money to drop in the collection plate? See, I have my new purse Blanca gave me for my birthday."

Water Under the Bridge

Papa pushed his chair back and stood. Reaching in the front pocket of his gray Sunday suit he pulled out a handful of change. He counted out three dimes and laid them on the table. I pushed one over to Joseph. He pocketed the coin and, looking the other way, hastily rose from the table and charged out of the room and into the yard.

I slipped my ten-cent piece into my little pink pocketbook, double-checking to make sure the bottle of soapy water hadn't leaked.

Poking the last two bites of tasteless food into my mouth and pushing our bench back enough so I could slide out without disturbing Aileen, I cleared the table with the exception of her bowl. That finished, I followed my brother outside to find him sitting alone on the large flat boulder under our lone shade tree, fiddling with his pocketknife.

I sidled up beside him and reached back, placed both of my hands palms down on the rock behind me, and made a short jump up to sit beside my brother.

"Try not to let Papa see how angry you are," I said.

"Hell's bells. I can't help it." He fumed. All of his pent up rage of the last three years poured out with his next three words: "I'll kill him—that's what I'll do—I'll kill—I'll kill him before I let him marry my sisters off to those old men!" Then he spat on his small whetstone and savagely sharpened the blade of his pocketknife.

Joseph and I had played many a game of mumble-peg with that very knife. I shuddered to think I might be the cause for it to draw blood now. I jumped down from my perch and hurried over to the rock pile. I chose four round stones, each about the size of a baseball. I returned and lay them on the huge rock in a row. "Can I have your handkerchief?"

Joseph handed it over to me without a word.

"I hurriedly spread the white kerchief on the flat rock. Selecting the largest stone, I placed it in the center of the cloth. Then, I drew the two diagonal corners together and tied them securely. Lastly, I wrapped one of the remaining corners around the knot. It left just enough cloth to make a handle for my small hand. I picked it up and tried swinging it slightly.

"This should make a fair weapon," I announced. "Try and control your temper during Plan A and B though.

I searched Joseph's face to see his reaction. He nodded. "Plan C?"

"Yes, when we get to the stop sign at the far side of town, the one that goes to the mine." I took a deep breath before continuing. "There isn't likely to be anyone there on Sunday. Blanca said the mine only stays open two days a week since the Depression, and by that time we'll know if he is going through with his plan."

Another long pause while Joseph waited, expectantly.

"When he stops at the sign, I'll knock him on the back of the head with this. You grab the wheel. Aileen and I'll hop out, and then you join us as soon as you stop the car."

He didn't object to my wild plan. He just asked, "What are these other stones for?"

"Gee whiz, I don't know." It was true. I didn't have any clear plans for them, but Juanita came to mind. "I'll put them on the floorboard in the back. Just in case!" I said.

Joseph slipped the smallest stone into his left pocket. "Just in case," he echoed. He pulled out the dime Papa had given him and offered it to me. "Here, take this, sis. I'll never attend the Mormon Church again!"

"We'll keep the money for ourselves," I replied. "This dime will buy a quart of milk."

I could see that Joseph hadn't thought of how we would live without Papa, but he rebounded quickly. "I'll quit school and go to work; I'm big for twelve and can easily pass for fourteen." he said. "Yes," he repeated. "I'll go to work and you can help Mama in the store."

I didn't bring up the problem that there would be no supplies for the store without Papa.

Mama would say, "The Lord will provide." I wasn't so sure. I wasn't even one hundred percent sure that the Lord didn't want me to marry a Mormon man and bring a whole brood of little Mormon babies into the world. I only knew I didn't want to do it.

I glanced over and saw Papa leave the kitchen, stepping lively on the back porch and down the four steps. He looked handsome in his dark pinstriped suit, his blue eyes sparkling. He strode over to us and ordered, "In the car."

I slipped into the middle of the back seat according to Plan B. Aileen sat nervously beside me in her white dress clutching her pocketbook, her small white Bible, and a notebook with a pencil attached. Joseph started to walk behind the car but Papa stopped him, mocking: "Here, Joseph," he handed him the crank. You're so big, now? You crank and I'll work the clutch and spark."

Poor Joseph. He cranked and cranked. His face turned the color of a beet, and of course, the car didn't start. Perspiration ran down into his eyes and he needed a rag to wipe it away. I turned to Aileen. "Loan Joseph your hanky, will you?" I said.

"Of course." Aileen slid out of her seat and walked around to the front of the car. I couldn't hear the conversation, but could certainly hear Papa bark, "Get back in the car, both of you! Let a man turn the crank!"

I expected Joseph to be upset but was mistaken. He could barely hide his pleasure. The more Papa cranked the Model T Ford, the more Joseph's eyes twinkled. He couldn't resist a wink in my direction.

With three fingers he fashioned an A and gave me a broad smile, but I wasn't sure what he meant.

Finally Papa gave up and stalked over and raised the hood on the left side of the vehicle; he pulled out a plug and examined it. A dark scowl crept over his face as he dried his brow.

"Joseph, get your bicycle and ride down to Mr. Gilmore's station and buy new plugs. These are bad!" His expression darkened as he handed my brother a $5 dollar bill. "Don't dawdle now and don't lose the change. We've already missed Sunday school, but if we hurry, we can still make it in time for church services."

Juanita and Aileen opened the car doors and we slid out. Joseph was already on his bicycle pedaling down the hill. I watched him turn the corner at the end of our block and out of sight. I knew he would not make it back any time soon.

My starched dress stuck to my body. I pulled it away and shook the skirt to try and remove the wrinkles.

Papa looked my way and slammed the hood down with an angry bang.

"You girls go in the house and wait. Don't change your clothing. If we can't make it to church in town this morning, we'll drive on over the mountain to Mesa for evening services.

"It's time you spent a week with me anyway," he added.

Aileen and I exchanged quick glances with each other. I felt weak. Aileen rallied. "I'll ask Mama."

"No need for that." A pregnant pause followed. "I'm still head of this family and what I say, goes." More silence. "Dang it all, it's high time Ida understands that!"

I don't know about my sister, but my heart sank and for some reason it seemed to land in my bladder.

"I gotta go," I stammered and headed for the outhouse.

It had been years since I'd felt that strong a sense of urgency. I hoped Aileen would follow me, but she didn't. Again, I felt alone in my desperation and deep despair. Papa was determined and I could see that Plan B would be useless. Mama would have to leave her room and help. Our only hope!

With that on my mind, I quickly finished in the outhouse and quietly walked to the house. Instead of entering though, I bent over and crawled under the back porch on my hands and knees to reach the wooden box we kept under the porch.

Who cares how dirty I am? Certainly not I.

If I couldn't save myself, I figured, at least I would not go willingly and all wrapped up in a pretty package.

Upon reaching the box, I sat down in the dirt and scooted, maneuvering it along beside me. When I reached the spot where I judged to be the east window of Mama's bedroom, I emerged from the darkness from under the house into the blinding morning sun.

Squinting, I saw no one. I moved the wooden box directly under Mama's window. Climbing on top of it, I looked in, but the dark-green blinds remained pulled tightly shut.

I pecked lightly on the windowpane. Nothing. Once more time I tried. No response. I tapped louder. Then, as a last resort, decided to break the glass with the stone I still clutched in my brother's hanky, but before I did so, I suddenly remembered Mama telling us about the Morse code used by sailors lost at sea. I was not sure I remembered the code correctly, but at least I could try. SOS, I thought: three dots followed by a dash . . . I waited.

I tried it a second time . . .

This time the curtains parted, and Mama's face appeared at the window. I pressed my fingers to my lips warning silence, overjoyed to see her.

Mama unlocked the window and raised the lower sash. A gust of hot, stale air hit me in the face. Her mouth dropped open and her chubby arms reached out and helped me into the room. I fell on the floor beside her bed like a rag doll. Mama knelt on her knees beside me, cradling me in her arms.

"What on earth is wrong, baby?" she said. She had not called me that in years. "Tell Mama what has happened. What's upset my little girl?"

In a barely audible whisper, I began. "It's Papa. I overheard him planning to take Aileen and me away. He's taking us to Mesa today and he's going to force Ailie to marry an old man!" I buried my face in her lap and sobbed quietly. "He said I should be locked up, and Joe, he'll keep him to be baptized over and over again——for dead people."

Water Under the Bridge

Mama bent over farther with her ear only inches from my mouth. Her arms closed around me tighter, hugging me to her breast. As I continued, "We may never see you or each other again!" I could feel her frame go rigid and although I couldn't see it, I knew her face had paled. I looked up to see that her complexion had turned a sickly gray, but then the color returned and she flushed a shade of crimson. I twisted my head to see unnaturally bright eyes and a wild expression on her face, which startled me even more.

"Hide me, Mama," I begged. "Gosh almighty, I don't want to go away! I don't think Aileen wants to get married either. Papa is not asking her. Please, Mama, oh please, hide us!"

She gently released me. I was wrong when I thought all the fight had gone out of my mama.

"Do exactly as I tell you," she said. "Make absolutely no noise or sound of any kind, no matter what I call or what you hear. I must go rescue Aileen. Let her in the window when you hear the signal. Lock the window when I leave—and don't look out."

With that she rose, squared her shoulders, and marched over to the door. Sliding back the latch with a grating sound, my mama walked out and into battle.

Mama's voice came through the heavy oak bedroom door loud and clear. I could hear every word she said.

"Chester! You still here?"

I could not hear Papa's reply.

"Where are my children?" she asked. Again, no audible answer.

"Amelia," Mama called loudly, "Come out from wherever you are."

Her voice drifted lower now and I didn't catch the gist of the last sentence, but I think I heard something about a chicken. Try as I did to listen, I could understand nothing more. Time stood still for me in that stuffy room. The tick-tock, tick-tock of the windup clock on the marble-top dresser and my own heart beating kept me company.

Worried for my brother and sister and wondering what took so long, I dared not drift off into a deep sleep, even though I was tired, dirty, and very sleepy.

I waited and waited. I knew Aileen had had time to walk around the house and peck on the windowpane. *Should I go look? No, Mama had cautioned me not to chance going near the window. Just a peek, surely a peek couldn't hurt and then Aileen wouldn't have to make a noise.* I argued with myself for what seemed like hours before easing over and fingering the edge of the curtain. Wound up as tight as an eight-day clock, my heart skipped a beat and my hand flew to my mouth when the tap finally came. I rose at once and cautiously peeked out a corner of the bedroom curtain. Aileen's face greeted me from her perch on the box, with Mama standing on the ground beside her.

I unlocked the window and raised the lower sash. Aileen crawled in. She wore Mama's large wrap-around apron. I had to lift it up out of the way to keep her from tripping on it. She stood beside the bed in her stocking feet, her face pale, azure-blue eyes large.

Mama handed her the shoes she'd been wearing and two lunch buckets. Then she blew us a kiss and motioned for us to close and lock the window against any noise that might escape. At the last second, I saw her push the box we'd used to climb in the window out of sight under the house.

"Joe?" I mouthed.

Aileen shook her head. She reached in the generous pocket of Mama's apron and pulled out a small composition notebook. The outside cover said 5 cents. Mama had punched a hole in the corner near the binding and tied a string. A short nub of a round yellow pencil was secured at the end of the string. Someone had notched a groove all around the pencil close to the eraser for the string to stay attached, probably Daniel who had carved the little groove on a hot day last summer, after Mama complained, "Dang it all, I can never find a pencil when I need one."

Aileen opened the booklet, turned to a fresh page, and began to write. I peered over her shoulder and read the following:

Joe is not back yet. Mama plans to stay in the yard and try to intercept him before Papa sees he has returned.

The writing stopped. Aileen dropped the pencil in her lap and cocked her head to one side, as if that would help her to listen. If another person was in the house, he was being very quiet. We two were still seated on the floor directly under the window. I rose up on my knees to see better. My sister again picked up the pencil, touched the lead to the tip of her moist tongue and continued to write. The first four words printed darker as if someone wished to stamp them in her memory:

Mama is as scared as we are. Papa insists we go with him. He has threatened to fetch the sheriff. You remember the sheriff is Papa's good friend, and also a Mormon. They believe girls are merely tools to serve men and a man has last say in everything. We women are used to give them pleasure and babies.

Aileen stopped long enough to look over at me. *You remember the wedding we attended last year. The woman had to promise to serve and obey.*

Water Under the Bridge

The pencil seemed to fly over the words and I could barely keep up with the writing. Again Aileen paused to listen. Hearing no sound, she touched the forefinger of her left hand to her tongue and turned a page.

"*I waited in our room when I heard Mama open her door and go into the kitchen. She said, 'Chester, where are my children?' Papa said to her, 'Our car won't start so I sent Joseph to buy new plugs. I can't understand it. Hasn't been that long since I bought a set. I think I've been cheated, but anyway Joseph should have been back a long time ago.' He paced the floor, stopping to look out the kitchen window.*

"*Mama stepped over to the back door just as I entered the kitchen.*

"*She called, 'Amelia, Amelia—where are you? I need your help catching a chicken.'*

"*I said, 'Amelia isn't feeling well. She went to the toilet.'*

"*Then Mama said, 'You'll have to help me then, Aileen. Go change your dress.'*"

"*Papa interrupted. 'I want Aileen to stay dressed up,' he said 'We may make it in time for the sermon. If we can't, I still plan to go to evening services at Mesa.' Then he told Mama, 'I am going to keep all three of the children for a week, whether you like it or not. I'll get the sheriff if I have to! They are as much my children as yours.' Then he quoted some scripture I forgot.*

"*Mama just said, almost meekly, 'My goodness, Chester, how you do carry on. You're not in the pulpit, you know. Of course the little ones can go to your place for as long as they want, anytime they care to visit.' She turned and looked at him. He now sat on a low stool. 'It's about time you took some responsibility with the raising of them,' she said. Then her gaze shifted to Juanita sitting in Mama's favorite wicker chair close by Papa, as she always does, running her fingers through his hair. Juanita tapping her new pointed black-patent-leather shoes on the linoleum floor made the only sound. I stood close by—too dumbstruck to speak.*

"*Mama glared at Papa and Juanita. 'All the more reason we need to catch a chicken. I'll not have them going off without a good meal in their belly!' She twisted her nose at Juanita as if to say 'your new woman is of no use in the kitchen.'*

"*Mama stretched behind and snatched her big apron—this very one I'm wearing now. She threw it to me and I caught it before it landed on the floor. 'Here, Aileen,' she said to me, 'slip this over your dress while I go into the store and grab some chicken feed.' At the door she turned to me and added, 'Grab a couple of lunch pails. We need water, too.'*

"*I obeyed her. As soon as we were out of earshot she explained everything to me She told me it would be better to play the part and then hide. She said to appease him by promising that our visit to Mesa would just be postponed.*"

I stopped Aileen and made her wait for me to re-read the plan. I wanted to understand it well. I nodded and she started writing again.

"Mama is worried that Joe won't return home before Papa misses you and me. While we waited, we filled the two empty lard buckets with water. You know the ones we usually use for our lunch pails?

"'These are really for you and Amelia,' she said. 'You may get hungry and thirsty while you hide in my room, waiting for Chester to leave. No one knows how long he'll hang around. That man can be awfully stubborn at times, don't I know!' She shook her head as if in disbelief.

"We went into the hen house for a short time and then cornered a pullet. Mama grabbed it by the feet and held it upside down and tied the two legs together over the clothesline. The poor chicken complained something awful! Then Mama pulled that large butcher knife she keeps on the shelf in the chicken coop." Aileen shuddered slightly. "She grabbed the chicken by the head with one hand and with the other she sliced its head completely off in one swift whack. The squawking stopped, but the headless chicken flopped the entire length of the line. It was simply awful, Amy, simple awful!"

I'd seen the drama played many times, but this must have been a first for squeamish Aileen. My guess is Aileen had more to say but she had used up all the paper. She put the booklet and pencil away in the apron pocket that had dropped to the floor.

After a while, she retrieved the apron and extracted three candy bars. She reached over and laid them on the bottom shelf of the washbasin neatly beside the two lard tins of drinking water. I realized she meant to wait for Joseph. I thought it a nice gesture, giving us something to look forward to. The aroma of the chocolate tickled my nose. Breakfast hadn't been filling.

Once more, time dragged. Occasionally we would pat one another and try to smile, but fear and sadness were our constant companions. Uncertainty hung in the air like a limp cloth on a muggy day. I finally gave up and lay my head in Aileen's lap. Before I realized it, I had fallen asleep.

Loud voices awakened me. I sat up with a start and crept over and peeked into the keyhole. Aileen had her hand over her mouth, her eyes wide. I couldn't see Papa but recognized his voice. "Ida, you know I had my heart set on bringing all three of the kids home with me. I had special plans. The bishop will think I am not able to rule my own family. I shall take Joseph at least. You can't stop me!"

"I won't go. You can't force me!" Joseph shouted, jumping to his feet, glaring down at Papa.

"Oh yeah. We'll see about that!" I heard a shuffling of chairs.

Then Mama's voice came through the wall loud and clear, much calmer than the other two, almost beguiling, "Calm down, both of you. I'll have no fighting in my kitchen. Joseph, you apologize to your papa and tell him you'll go next week when Aileen and Amelia visit. And you, Chester, stop and think a minute. How would it look to the neighbors if Joseph and Juanita stayed alone together all day while you are away at work? He does have your hormones and hot blood coursing through his veins and looks much more mature than he is."

A long pause followed, and I heard Mama say, "Juanita, like father, like son."

I could imagine Juanita smiling sweetly, tapping her pretty toes.

Aileen pushed me from the door and put her eye to the keyhole. I tried to pull her away but she shook her head and waved me aside. I could almost visualize Papa's stunned expression and imagine his face turning red, with Juanita tossing her pretty dark curls and smiling seductively.

Joseph's voice was low and husky. I scarcely recognized it and could barely make out the startling words: "You do have a juicy tidbit, Papa." I imagined him turning to the young girl sitting at Papa's feet as he added. "Juanita, you know you are not legally married to Papa, don't you? He already has a wife. If you are tired of sleeping with an old man, I'll go to Mesa with you and you can teach me a few tricks. I feel old enough to learn."

My mouth fell open in shock as I heard the scraping of chairs, the shuffling of feet, a loud crash, and the breaking of glass. It sounded like a crocodile had been turned loose in the kitchen and was using its huge tail to rearrange the furniture. Voices so low and menacing we couldn't distinguish the words were followed by a shrill, hysterical scream.

Aileen backed away from the door, ashen-faced. Her eyes, the size of sand dollars, told me horrible things were happening on the other side of the closed door—as if I couldn't guess from the crashes and exclamations. I dared not breathe for fear the door would crash open and we would both be consumed. Time stood still, then footsteps, a blood curdling scream, and the word '*Harlot!*' in Mama's voice that sounded far away, as if she spoke into a barrel.

Suddenly, a key turned in the lock and the door slowly, slowly swung inward. I shuddered in fear. Mama entered, with Joseph supporting her. Her hair had fallen, covering the left side of her face. Her wild expression reminded me of a cougar I had once seen treed by a wild pack of dogs. In her right hand she held a large butcher knife—covered with blood.

Aileen's scream was the last thing I remember before I fainted dead away, folding up like an accordion in a little heap on the floor. I felt my body lifted, carried by someone or something; a feeling of dread overcame me. I knew I'd be sacrificed on an altar. Fires burned, flames licked the dried tree limbs, ever reaching higher and higher, scorching my tired eyes.

With my eyes closed, I could see the devil with red flaming eyes and greenish-black horns dancing around the fire, his tail swishing this way and that way. As I stared in awe-struck fascination, a glowing ember fell, igniting the tail and as the tail swished back and forth, little fires started all around.

People were screaming everywhere. And then I saw the arm! No body, just a slender, unclothed arm. Long fingers, with little flames of fire, bouncing off each fingertip. The hand held a butcher knife with a sharp, shiny blade and it came down over my body with a loud swish. The breeze felt hot to my parched skin as the heat of the fire burned closer and closer, and always the screaming, screaming, piercing my ears.

"Aileen, stop screaming!" Joseph demanded. His loud, demanding voice penetrating my being. "Amelia, wake up. It's all right. Papa and Juanita are gone. You're safe now." He lifted me from the floor where I lay and gently placed me on Mama's soft feather bed.

"Gone?" I muttered, "as in dead?"

"No—not dead." He turned to Mama. "Please, put the knife down, Mama. You are scaring the girls."

"It's just blood from the chicken," Mama said, shaking her head in disbelief. "It never bothered them before."

I suddenly felt very foolish. Blood from a chicken? Imagination can play strange tricks on a person sometimes, I realized. I sat up on the edge of the bed and looked at the three staring down at me. "After all I've been through last night and this morning, who can blame me?" I said raising and lowering my shoulders in the expression of a sigh, and hoped they understood—the three people I loved most in the world, my family!

CHAPTER FORTY-NINE—RUN, RUN, RUN

"We're wasting time," Joseph warned.

"Time?"

"Time?" echoed Aileen.

"Papa may come back with help at any time. We need to leave before he gets back and snatches us away."

I sat on Mama's bed sweating from the heat and the closed window and had noticed Mama wiping her forehead on her apron tail. I wondered if I should open the window but didn't say anything.

"We'll go to Daniel's." Mama announced, throwing off her apron and trying to twist her disheveled hair into some sort of a presentable knot. "I know he and Thelma will make us welcome." She moved over to her marble-topped dresser and replaced the lost hairpins from a small covered casket. Then she removed her gold-rimmed glasses and wiped the glass on the corner of her apron, before dropping the case into a wicker basket—placed on the dresser.

During the short time this took Mama to do, Joseph had been standing, searching first one face and then another, his legs spread apart in a proud staunch, his brow furrowed. We all three stared at the mirror in front of us, and the reflection that came back. Aileen and I crouched, holding each other, very distraught, Mama, once more trying to keep up appearances; only Joseph standing straight and tall, with his slight shoulders thrown back, trying to appear the man—at twelve—he had not yet become.

"Great guns. No!" Joseph finally spoke, firmly. "Papa'll go there first to look for us. "Amy and I know of a cave where we can safely hide, at least until we decide what's best to do. Papa didn't go with us to the cave that day when I begged him to climb the mountain. I doubt if he knows it's there. The last couple of years, he's never joined us in fun like he used to and we hoped he would." I remembered plans in the past when Papa would accompany us on excursion trips over the mountain.

Three surprised faces turned to gaze at Joseph.

"A cave? But how . . ."

"We'll find a way." There he stood with a manly confidence in his voice that I am sure he didn't feel. He had our attention now and I looked around, hoping to see what the others were thinking.

"How long do we have?" Aileen asked.

I could almost hear the silence during the slight pause it took Joseph to answer, "I'd say one hour if Papa goes for the county sheriff, but thirty minutes if he stops to ask for help from the elders at the Mormon Church in Miami."

"Oh dear, dear!" Mama exclaimed, and stopped adjusting the hairpins in her bun, her face flushed. She dashed from the room, letting her soft brown hair fall, and flew into the kitchen. Stooping, she reached for the handle of the old-fashioned icebox and removed several boiled eggs, dumping them into a bag. Setting the bag on the floor within easy reach, she grabbed a pitcher of milk and carried both the milk and the eggs to the kitchen table.

I followed her into the room. "Get glasses," she ordered, looking at me standing idle. "Add biscuits from the warming oven to the bag of eggs. They can be taken with you to eat later. Drink the milk now. Hard telling how long it'll be before you'll have more." Mama looked around for my siblings. "Aileen, Joseph, where are you? I need you both. Land sakes, hurry up!"

Mama never threw anything away. "Where do you keep Joe and Dan's old clothes?" I asked.

"In boxes under my bed. Why?" She looked at me and waited, open to any suggestions. I didn't answer, just finished dropping the biscuits into the bag and left the kitchen. I found what I was looking for, pulled one pair of overalls on over my dress, secured three extra pairs under my arm and left to find Aileen. I knew she and I could travel faster and safer dressed as boys.

Scared rabbits never scurried around faster than we did in that little house we'd called home for so many years. Mama handed each of us one of her special hand-embroidered pillowcases she'd prized over the years, "Cram personal possessions you wish to take with you in these cases," she said. "Just remember, what you pack, you must carry. Along with bedding for the night."

We held out our hands, took the pillowslips offered, and entered our sleeping area where we kept our clothes. In desperation, I tried to decide what to take and what I must leave.

"What're you packing, Ailie?" She didn't answer. I let it pass.

I tightly rolled a few dresses together and shoved them inside—next the pocketbook Blanca had given me. I can't leave that behind! Lastly, I finished filling the case with stockings and undergarments. I had outgrown the shoes I prized so I left them behind.

"My bag is full, Amy," Aileen said. "You may have anything of mine I haven't packed."

I snatched Thelma's wedding dress, the one she'd given Aileen, and a blue sailor dress I'd always admired. "Aren't you taking your books, Ailie?" I asked.

"No room. Food is more important. Anyway, books are heavy to carry."

Three bundles of bedding were roughly rolled and tied with whatever we could find at hand, our three lunch buckets filled with fresh water, the lids secured, and we three started to leave.

I looked around the four walls to see if I'd missed anything important and a knot filled my stomach. I may never see this room again. Passing through the kitchen, my eyes fell on the woodstove and suddenly I became relieved we no longer had Martha to leave behind. So much time had passed since that day and still the hurt remained. Will it never end?

Finally Joseph paused to catch his breath. "Amy, do you know the way?"

"You're darn tootin' I do," I said.

"Good. You and Ailie take your pack and bedroll and start. I'll catch up."

I would have preferred we stay together, but it was true, I couldn't walk as fast as Joseph, and might hold them back. As I shouldered the heavy bedroll over my left shoulder, it seemed my back sagged a little. Joseph noticed.

He stooped to look at me. "Hey, Amy, do you remember the ledge where we usually stopped to eat?"

I nodded.

"Leave the bedroll there, and I'll return and fetch it before dark."

I signaled in agreement and quickly turned my head. I didn't want anyone to see my startled expression. Dark-dark in a cave. I shuddered, remembering the one time I stood at the entrance and tried to see all the way to the back. I hadn't fully realized the plan involved sleeping in a cave—all night long, no windows to shut—with wild creatures and darkness all around, no way to keep beasts out.

I grabbed my pail and bundles and shot out the door. I knew if I hesitated I might renege, and choose the horror of being locked away and the promise of an old man's arms, to this unknown terror.

"Sis, wait for me," Aileen called, but I could not wait. I mustn't. Her longer strides soon closed the distance between us, and we trudged up the hillside, side by side, in silence. We would see a lizard scamper from a rock occasionally, or a bird fly overhead. Otherwise, we two and the mountain shaped the pattern of our future lives by the action we took that warm September day.

We did not hesitate until we reached the knoll, before the dip down to the old thorn tree. I heard a woodpecker in the far distance. Tap-tap-tap. There we paused and I flexed my aching shoulders before I turned to look back over the rough terrain we'd covered. At the base of the hill I saw movement. Someone swung our back gate open, not taking time to close it, but took long purposeful strides in our direction.

"It's Joseph, don't you think, Amy?" We couldn't make out the face, but who else would carry such a heavy load?

"Where's Mama?" I asked. "I can't see her, can you?"

Aileen shrugged her shoulders, "We'd better head on up. Joe is coming fast. If we can see him, anyone down there can see us."

Aileen turned, and without waiting for me she began the long, slow ascent again. Fear caused a rush of adrenaline and I also turned and rushed ahead and led the way, down into the little dip in the land. I glanced longingly at the shade under the lone acacia tree. A gentle breeze ruffled the leaves and I longed to drop my burden and use it as a pillow to rest in this peaceful spot, but I knew I must not. No longer was I the little girl who had believed problems could be solved by running away. Yet, here I was, running once more, wasn't I? At least this time I had brought food and water. Also company!

On we trudged, up up up the steep, laborious climb. We both became too exhausted to speak until we reached the ledge. I dropped the bedroll and plopped down on it. Even in the autumn, the noon sun beat down unmercifully; sweat poured down into my eyes, and my dry tongue hung slackly. I found myself panting like a stray dog. Squinting into the sun, I noticed a buzzard circling overhead, watching our every move. I shuddered.

To the southwest side of the ledge, a tall rock pinnacle blocked Joseph from our view, but I could hear his footsteps coming ever closer in our direction. Occasionally I heard rocks rolling down the mountain and I held my breath, until I again heard my brother's footsteps. Should one of us fall and break a limb all would be lost. Before, we'd stayed together and he'd slowed his steps to mine. At times he amazed me. Leaning over, I pried the lid from my water pail.

"Don't drink too fast," Aileen warned. "And try not to spill any. This water may have to last you a long time."

"I'm hungry," I complained. "Let's eat." I reached for the bag she'd been carrying.

"Sure. Go ahead. I'll wait for Joe."

I opened the brown-paper sack and saw a fluffy white biscuit. The food was still warm, but I noticed my hands before touching it. They were dirty and we had no spare water to wash them. I sighed and closed the bag. "My hands are not clean, Ailie. How can we eat?" I whined.

I gazed up into the sky. The large hawk soared high in the sky, its beady eyes turned earthward toward us. Searching—for food? It made me shiver to think we might make a meal for some vulture, if somehow we didn't survive. I tried not to look his way and stared at the ground. Dust covered my shoes and I started to brush it away, but stopped.

Just then, Joseph arrived. "Wow, we made it," he said. "No one can see us from down below. You two okay?" We both nodded, glad to have our brother with us.

He placed a bag before us with a clang. "What'd you bring?" Aileen asked.

A wide grin spread on his face. "Look for yourselves." The aroma of the freshly fried chicken wafted up my nostrils and I breathed deep, enjoying the sensation and memory of our homey kitchen.

Dear Mama. She'd thought to drop three wet washcloths into an empty bread wrapper and also sent old thin cloth napkins. Aileen searched through the food and other supplies: fried chicken, pork and beans, deviled ham, tins of evaporated milk, and several candy bars, along with Mama's best silver tableware, a box of matches, a can opener, a pair of scissors, a box of animal crackers, a few raw Irish potatoes, and three oranges.

"I'm glad I waited to eat," I announced.

"What'll we have today? The chicken smells delicious, but I wonder how Mama prepared it so fast."

"Don't you remember—she started frying chicken while we hid in the bedroom, long before Papa and Juanita rushed off in a huff." Joseph looked my way and grinned. Did he have a private joke?

"Fried chicken," Aileen answered quickly. "This other stuff will keep. Chicken won't. Anyway, we mustn't have any fresh food around to attract animals." She gave a little nervous half-laugh.

My mouth watered. I crammed the delicious chicken in my mouth and filled my stomach. Then I stood. The climb became easier without the bedroll, but still too strenuous for conversation.

The terrain changed. I noticed areas covered with knee-high grasses and peppered with small unfamiliar yellow flowers. An old gnarled pinon tree grew between two large flat rocks. Beneath my feet, I heard the crunch of dead leaves and I swore I could smell the acid coppery smell of decomposed leaf litter.

In front of us on this devil's playground, a huge bolder of flat red granite appeared to block our path. "You positive you remember the way?" Aileen asked. "Gracious. We can't climb this!"

"Over here, sis," Joseph called with triumph in his eyes, pulling her to the right. "See, the rock split years ago leaving an opening—as if some higher being knew a path would be needed. Barely room to slide between the boulder, but on the other side we're there. And safe!"

It was true. Joseph led and Aileen followed. She needed to turn sideways to enter an area with rocks so tall they blocked the sun. Halfway through she handed her bundles to him. One by one we labored through the narrow path and entered a low area, where the land dipped down, until we stood before the cave entrance.

At the mouth of the cave, uncertainty of the future loomed large. We hadn't discussed what we'd do beyond escaping Papa's immediate reach.

I brought up the subject. "You have plans for tomorrow, Joe?"

I could almost see wheels turning in my brother's head. He hesitated, chewing on his lower lip, as if trying to decide how much to reveal.

"Sure have. Mama is selling everything she can. When we have money for four tickets, we'll continue over the mountain to the nearest town and catch a train for Missouri. Mama is writing to her brother, our Uncle Willie, to meet us at the train station. He owns a big house and we'll stay with him and his wife, Aunt Cordelia." He looked at Aileen. "Keep the money bag with you, sis. You have all the bills Mama managed to save since Papa married Juanita.

"I think Mama has secretly been planning an escape from Papa for some time. She could have left sooner traveling alone, but couldn't take us with her. Of course, you know Mama would never, ever leave us behind."

Suddenly the letter I'd sneaked from the library table drawer came back to me. *We have room for you at our home. Come.*

"Ailie, Mama said to tell you that if she can't raise enough money to buy train tickets for all of us by Saturday, that you and Amy are to take money from the bag and you two girls go on ahead. Mama and I will follow, when we can." Joseph gazed into our startled faces and then suddenly turned away so we couldn't read his face.

My sister blinked in surprise and turned pale, but she nodded in agreement. Every limb in my body trembled and my knees buckled before I collapsed on a nearby rock. Could we possibly go alone—without either Mama or Joseph? Two girls traveling alone—one thousand miles!

The plan sounded so simple the way Joseph told it. *A piece of cake!* I could almost hear Blanca say. Suddenly her warning came to me with a clear hindsight. Could some people actually foretell the future? I wondered. I closed my eyes and tried to span the distance that separated us. Blanca, oh dear, dear Blanca, I called to her with my mind. As before, no return message came. Joseph's voice broke into my musing.

"Mama made three signals for us. A white sheet hanging on the clothesline means 'all is well and safe' down there. A pair of men's overalls warns it is unsafe—stay away. A large square of white cloth thrown over the back gate summons—'meet me under the thorn tree.'"

"We can't see the yard from here, Joe." I complained.

"After we eat, I'll slip down and bring back the other bedrolls. I'll watch our yard from that vantage point." Joseph nervously paced back and forth. Exhausted, I couldn't see how he could move, much less pace.

"Mama sent a lot of food for us," Aileen said. "I hope she saved enough for herself."

"She has a basket of eggs she can cook," Joseph said, "and chicken—plus canned goods in the store. The store has really come in handy, don't you think?" He tried to sound cheerful as he added. "Guess Papa has done some good over the years."

Aileen nodded and then added, "Do you think Mama will be safe if Papa comes home and finds us gone? Poor Mama."

I wished she'd stop saying that. I was too tired to be sad also. Somehow I blamed myself for all of our current troubles.

Before Joseph left, we gathered dried brush and built three small fires. One in the far end of the cave and one on each side. After the fires burned brightly, he gathered and threw three small clumps of green sagebrush on each fire. "See, that'll make a good smoke to chase any spiders out." He smiled. "Daddy-long-legs won't hurt anyone, but other spiders might."

He gave one last bit of instruction before he left us alone high on the mountaintop. "Papa's shotgun is loaded," He solemnly showed us the way to aim and pull the trigger. "Stay close together and use this if it's needed. I won't be long." And then he left, down the mountain to see what signal Mama had left.

The heeding to stay close together was unnecessary. You couldn't have pried us apart with a crowbar, or bribed us to wander off to explore the area alone.

Tuesday morning, I awakened to darkness in the small wee hours of the morning. In the pitch-black cave with the kerosene lantern turned low to save fuel, I asked softly, "Anyone awake?"

"Yes, I'm awake," Joseph answered.

"I've been lying here wondering what happened, after you told Juanita she wasn't really married to Papa. Aile and I couldn't hear all that went on." I looked over to where Joseph lay on his bedroll, but I couldn't see even the slightest form. At home even on a cloudy night we had some illumination but in this cave, the solid walls blocked off every trace of light. "Tell me."

Joseph gave a half chuckle and a half groan. "I will—best I remember. Mama didn't want me to go with Papa to Mesa. It happened fast and unexpected. Mama mentioned it wouldn't look proper to the neighbors if Juanita and I stayed together alone while Papa worked away from home, our ages being close together. Gosh almighty, I can't think why he wanted me, anyway, unless to make Mama unhappy."

I interrupted his tale. "I know. He wanted you to be baptized for the dead. I can't see what good that does if a person is already dead, but Papa has his reasons and I don't question them. Sorry I didn't tell you. I plain forgot, wrapped in my own misery."

The hoot of an owl broke the silence and in the far distance a coyote howled at the moon. I shivered at the eerie sound and snuggled under the covers closer to my sister.

"That's okay, sis. I hadn't planned on going or volunteering, anyway. But, back to that day. I wasn't really serious and had no idea it would set Papa off." Joe really chuckled this time as he recalled the day. "I took my cue from Mama and it seemed a good idea at the time. Actually, I may have been getting even with Papa for all the mean things he's said and done over the years, especially to Mama—marrying other women, young girls, actually! No woman can be expected to compete with a young girl when that woman has aged and given birth to several children. It just isn't playing fair. Anyway, I really made him mad, that's for sure!"

He stopped talking and I heard him rise up on his elbow. Suddenly, Aileen joined the conversation. "Wonder where Mama is now? Poor Mama." She sighed. "Maybe I should have married whoever Papa wanted me to, and all this wouldn't have happened."

"Tarnations, no!" I retorted irritably. "No way!" I reached over to feel for Ailie. "We'll look for Mama as soon as it's light. Now, let Joe finish his tale."

"Well, Papa jumped up and knocked the table over with a loud crash. I'm surprised you didn't hear it. It took us all by surprise. Someone had left an empty bottle of pop on the cupboard. He snatched it by the neck and hit the glass bottle on the porcelain corner of the cupboard. It broke, leaving a jagged edge. Papa lunged towards me with the broken bottle clutched in his hand. I jumped back to escape him."

I heard Aileen gasp.

Joseph continued, "Dang it all, I hardly know what happened after that. It was so quick. Suddenly Mama stood between us. I saw that long butcher knife in her hand, the one she uses to cut off chickens' heads. Don't know why she brought it in the kitchen with her. She usually leaves it in the chicken house. That's not important. Just enough noonday sunshine crept into the kitchen to reflect off the long, sharp blade. Mama's voice was so menacing it sounded like a growl. It still makes shivers run up and down my spine to recall it." He gave a low throaty laugh. "I'm afraid us men don't fully understand the female, when her young are threatened."

I started to get impatient. "Go on, Joe. What happened?"

"Not much after that. Mama's voice rose, 'Take one step closer to my son with that bottle in your hand and I'll cut you where you'll produce no more sons!'

"Stalemate! They faced each other, glaring like two angry rhinoceros, protecting their territory. Mama broke the deadlock when she screamed. 'Drop that weapon and get out of my house. Get out! And stay out—you and your little *HARLOT, GET!*' Juanita had already been easing toward the door. She gentled it open and escaped, just as Mama flung the word again, '*HARLOT!*' After Juanita had fled, Papa dropped the broken pop bottle, spun on his heels and raced after her. As the screen door banged shut, I heard him call, 'Take my word for it, Ida. You haven't heard the last from me. Not by a long shot.' And then he was gone. You two know the rest as well as I do."

Joseph's voice trailed off as if in the distance, but I knew he had not left the cave.

Verna Simms

CHAPTER FIFTY—THE CAVE

The next day, Joseph sprinted down to be with Mama. Aileen and I sat alone outside the opening to the cave.

"Ailie," I said, "let's cut each other's hair." Her face registered shock. My hair hung straight down to my ear lobes but Aileen had beautiful light-blonde curly hair reaching below her shoulders.

Seeing her distress, I added, "You cut mine first."

I perched on a rock in the sunshine, trying to break the chill of the early morning breeze, as Aileen painstakingly gave me her version of a boy's haircut. We had no mirror but with my hand I could touch it and it felt very short. I liked the feel and decided to wear my hair short from then on.

"Okay, your turn," I insisted. "Gee whiz. You do know we have to make people think we're boys. Come on, Ailie. The hair will grow back," I urged.

With each snip and each curl landing in a pile on a napkin I had placed near her feet, I could hear Aileen gasp. I did my best, but decided that I had better stick to being a lawyer. When I'd finished, Aileen walked over under the tree and started writing in her diary. I wish I knew what she wrote about me that day. I carried an empty bag over and picked up each and every curl and placed them in the sack and took them to where Aileen sat.

A sad day in the desert flashed back into my mind. "Remember the month we lived in the desert, Ailie?" She nodded rather listlessly. "That day Mama cut your hair and the tears streamed down your face.

"I felt sad for you and retrieved all of the curls from the sand. I was only three and carried them in the skirt of my dress. We later pasted them onto cloth dolls. Wasn't that fun? What do you reckon happened to those homemade dolls?"

Aileen reached up and pulled me down beside her, giving me a huge hug. "Oh, Amy, I do recall that day vividly, but can't say where the dolls are. Let's do something fun now."

She hopped up, went into the cave and came back, handing me a package, wrapped in a brown paper bag decorated with different colored stars. It was tied with the white ribbon she had worn in her hair that fateful Sunday.

"This is for you. I had it ready for your tenth birthday, but you can open it now."

As I hesitated she urged. "Go ahead, it'll help pass the time. We might as well celebrate while we have time on our hands."

Eagerly, I untied the ribbon and smoothed it flat, folded it neatly, and slipped it inside my overall pocket. Inside the paper wrapping I found two notebooks, a new pencil, and the cutest little red pencil sharpener—shaped like a Coco Cola bottle. "Oh, thank you, thank you!" I squealed, circling her in my arms.

"Come, let's sit under a tree and record our adventure in our books," Aileen suggested. "I've been keeping a diary for years. I brought it with me. Now is no time to quit. Besides, it will help the day slide by while we're waiting for Joseph."

I sat and started to write:

This book belongs to Amelia Hall—Tuesday, September 23, 1930

Footsteps interrupted me. "I hear someone coming!" I whispered. "Hide in the cave!" Trembling, I gathered my gifts and we hurried inside and shivered on our bedrolls. Aileen cradled Papa's gun in her hand, shaking so hard I became afraid it would fire unintentionally. I scooted over to huddle beside her.

"It's Joe!" Aileen sighed in relief as his form appeared at the entrance to the cave.

"What're you doing back so soon, Joe?" I asked. I knew he was faster than I, but no way could he make a round trip in that short a time.

Joseph gasped his reply, "Overalls are hanging on the clothesline. Danger! I came to warn you. Don't leave the cave and if you hear anyone coming, go to the very back and stay quiet." He gulped a drink of water. "I'm going back to help Mama."

"No, Joe!" Aileen begged. "It may not be safe. I don't think Mama would want you to."

Joseph shook his head. "I must go, but I'll circle around and come in from Dan's direction. In case I'm seen they'll think I was visiting him. Billy will help me see how things are at the house. He's a good friend."

That made me think of something I'd been wondering about. "Does Billy know about this cave?"

"Yes, he came with me the day I discovered it; we were trying to find a way to reach the summit. No one else knows, to my knowledge." He turned to leave but said over his shoulder, "Billy won't tell. I'll whistle a bit of the Lindbergh song when I return. That way you'll know who is coming. Don't leave the cave unless you hear the song."

With that he was gone and we were once more alone—high on top of a lonely mountain. Two very scared young girls!

Time passed slowly for my sister and me. There was barely enough light for us to write, but we whiled away the day scribbling and reading what the other had written. There was little to do but wait.

"I am so glad you brought these books with you, Ailie," I whispered. Aileen nodded. The day crept by, and toward suppertime I heard a noise. "Someone is coming! Do you think it's Joe?" I asked.

"Too noisy for him." Aileen answered. "This person is not being cautious with his footsteps. It may be two people!" I heard horror in her voice. We scooted farther toward the back of the cave, dragging our bedrolls with us. Aileen reached over and squeezed my hand. We were afraid to speak, even in whispers. I jumped when I heard the distant cry of an eagle. And so we waited, trembling and staring into the coming dusk as something or someone lurked outside of our tiny world.

Then, we heard it! The pure strains of whistling—*Lindbergh*—no words but I could follow them in my mind—how he flew over the ocean, all alone. I was overjoyed, but apprehensive for Joseph. The movement still hovered outside the cave out of our sight. What or who was it? Will Joseph see whatever or whomever it is in time to save himself? I worried.

"Scat!" Joseph shouted and I heard loud laughter and Joseph called. "Ailie, Amelia, come on out. It is only a mountain goat. One of you left orange peelings where he could smell them."

The tension had been too great. Aileen and I both laughed hysterically until we cried. And then we thought to inquire about Mama and what had happened at home.

"Is Mama alright?" Aileen asked, wiping the tears from her eyes.

"Give me time to catch my breath and drink a little water and then I'll tell you all about it. Here," he said, handing us each a pillowcase. "Mama put your capes in here, so I wouldn't get them dirty. I told her it was colder up here on the mountain."

"First tell us if Mama is okay," Aileen insisted, but she was just wasting her breath. When Joseph decided to stretch a story, there was no rushing him. It slowed him down to ask questions. I dragged my bedding out into the sunshine to air, plopped down on it and waited, slipped the green cape over my shoulders and hugged it tight. *A little bit of Mama close by.*

"Well," Joseph started to speak as he dropped his burden of food and water. "I swear I've tramped a hundred miles today." He hesitated and took a drink from the pail of fresh water. "First I hurried down to the pinnacle, you know, the one where I can watch for a signal from Mama. The overalls still hung on the clothesline where I noticed them this morning. My heart beat faster thinking of all the reasons Mama had for sending a distress signal." He turned to us, his eyes blazing with excitement. Aileen made a face at him trying to hurry him along, but I'd heard him tell tales long enough to know it was useless.

"Go on, Joe," I said. "We're listening."

"I turned left at that point. I'd never explored that part of the mountain and had to be careful that I didn't get lost. I soon picked up an old cow trail. Maybe it was a mountain goat's path. Anyway, the path showed it had been used a lot in the past and I reasoned if I stuck to it I could always retrace my steps if, by chance, I did lose my way.

"I didn't hear a sound. The woods were eerily quiet, almost spooky. I hadn't gone far and the terrain changed. Instead of boulders and cactus like we found here, trees grew in abundance. Everywhere, I needed to push the limbs aside to make my way. That slowed me down some, but I knew right away I was getting closer to Mr. Wallace's house. I was correct. No one was home, but I stopped to pump myself a drink of water. I remembered the road to take down the hillside from there.

"Refreshed from the drink and knowing I walked the right track, I stepped up my trotting and soon could see Billy's home. I was lucky to find him in the back yard. I ran over and joined him.

"'Billy,' I said. 'I need your help.' I dropped down panting, on the ground by his feet.

"'Joe!' he exclaimed. 'I didn't see you coming and I was staring across the street at your house. I notice you have company?' He made it a question. Surprise showed on his face.

"'That's what I want you to find out.' I said. 'Who is it? I recognize the car but I need to know who is in the store with Mama. Did you see?' I was beginning to be exasperated by the slowness of Billy's response, so I just asked him outright, 'Is it Papa?'

"Billy shook his head. 'Two men, but I've never seen either of them before.'

"I stood up and turned to Billy. 'I'm going over and check if Mama needs my help. Wanna come along?' I grabbed an old rusty hatchet from the woodpile. It was too dull to chop wood but would make a fair weapon. Billy caught on fast this time and pulled his new bean shooter from his pocket and a few round stones. Billy is deadly with a bean shooter.

"We stayed close together, walking across the street and just as I entered the store, I heard Mama say 'The girls are not here and will not be back until sometime next week.' When she took her hand and angrily brushed the hair from her eyes, I could see her blue eyes blazing fire. 'You tell Chester if he wants to see his children, to come for them himself! Even if they were home, I'd not have them riding off with men I don't know. And as for the necklace, I'm sorry Aileen accepted it and she will return it to you at the earliest opportunity.' Mama took a deep breath and looked my way and smiled. 'My son is here now and I'll thank the two of you to leave!'

"That's all that happened." Joseph burst out laughing. "I wouldn't have missed seeing Mama telling those men off for the world!"

I'm afraid that for once I didn't share his humor.

Verna Simms

CHAPTER FIFTY-ONE—TRAVELING

Every morning, Joseph trotted down the mountain and helped Mama sell what could be sold and pack what little we could take to Missouri with us. Each night he returned to the cave in the mountain, bringing food and fresh water.

Wednesday, I awoke before Joseph. I had been sleeping in my clothes while up on the mountains, so I didn't need to bother dressing. "Joe," I said as soon as he rubbed his eyes awake, "how will Mama be able to get through the small opening in the rock? We had to turn sideways."

"She won't be coming this far. We'll meet her half way down and go around the mountain, instead of over it. I must go now. There is still a lot to be done. Mama has sold her bedstead to Mrs. Wallace and I have to deliver it today. Mama will sleep on the floor on the mattress tonight. See you at dusk."

"Wait a minute, Joe. I've decided to walk down to the house with you today. Papa won't come before this weekend and I have to have a bath—or shower if you'll share yours with me. Okay?"

Joseph looked startled, "No way, Amy! You and Aileen must stay here where you're safe. You don't know for sure what Papa is going to do. He sent those men yesterday, didn't he?" He looked at my disappointed face. "Hey, it won't be long. I believe I smell rain in the air, now." He tipped his head toward the sky. "We haven't had any since the last time you used the shower anyway, so the tub's empty.

"Let me show you something before I go. Come with me."

Joseph led the way down the glen and up on the other side. He took my hand to help me over a rocky ledge and around to the backside of the cave opening.

"See those flat rocks over there?" He pointed a short distance beyond a grove of pine trees at a jumble of rocks.

"If it rains, climb over there; you'll find a rock built like a shallow bathtub. It should catch enough water to bathe. But be sure to beat the goat."

He laughed and slapped his legs at my startled face and led the way back to where Aileen stood watching.

I didn't dare go home without permission, so Aileen and I stayed alone on the mountain. We hardly had enough water to wash ourselves, barely more than enough to dampen a cloth and sponge it over our faces and hands. After four days of wearing the same clothes, I began to itch. We had agreed to save the clean pairs of overalls to wear on the train.

"Why are you twitching your nose, Amy?"

"Joe says he can smell rain. I'm trying, but I can't tell any difference in the air, can you?"

"It smells fresh. Tell you what let's do. We'll line up all the empty pails under a drip and if Joe is right, at least we'll have water to wash."

I couldn't help thinking it was useless busy work, but we did it anyway and then I sat, head resting in my cupped hands, half pouting, staring at the sky and trying to will it to open and drop rain. Suddenly, I heard a clump of thunder in the far distance and jumped up. Aileen and I hurriedly consolidated our remaining water supply, placing one more empty lard bucket under an overhang. Next, we shed all of our clothing and draped them over one of the taller rocks. I recalled how fast and of what short duration an Arizona rain can be. When the rain came down suddenly in one large cloudburst, we shared the little soap in my pink purse I'd never used. Standing under the downpour in our birthday suits felt so good. I shall never take an abundance of water for granted again.

"Ailie, let's explore over there." I pointed to where Joseph had led me. "Joe thinks a hollow in a rock will catch enough water for a bath. I'd love a good long soak—while our clothes are drying."

"You go on, if you want; I'd rather stay close by. What if the goat comes back and eats our clothing? I've heard they would eat anything."

I gathered my wet things and took them with me. Joseph was right. A good six inches of water in an area the size of three washtubs waited for me and I spread out and dipped down into the cool water, until—I looked up and there he was—one huge Billy goat with large horns and an ugly face, fur hanging down below his chin. He nuzzled me to one side and began to drink.

"Oh, oh!" I squealed. I rolled out of the water onto my belly, rose to my knees, gathered up my almost dry clothing and headed back to the cave, to Aileen and safety.

Thursday morning, Joseph rose at first light and announced, "Follow me as far as the ledge. If Mama has a white cloth on the gate, we circle around the mountain today." I began to gather the bedding.

"No, sis," Joseph said, "leave everything except your bag of personal treasures, the gun, and the lantern. We'll take what little food and water we have left and eat as we walk. It's imperative that we travel light. Now that Mama has the money for the train tickets, we mustn't hang around here any longer. Papa may come tomorrow and I'm not sure what he'd do. Maybe start a search party."

I'd never seen Joseph so antsy to get moving.

I grabbed Mama's prized silverware, wrapped it in a blue flannel scarf, and placed the package inside my bedroll. I rolled everything together tightly, tied it with a cord and stored the bedroll on a dry ledge as high as I could reach. As I turned to leave, I noticed the long curls I had saved when I cut Aileen's hair. I snatched the packet up and shoved it inside a dry empty lard can and closed the lid securely. Satisfied, I turned my back on the temporary home and walked out into the early morning sunlight.

Would I ever return to see my homeland again? I slung my pillowslip with my possessions over my shoulder. No time for thinking. Joseph and Aileen hurried down the path forty feet ahead and I ran to catch up.

"Hurry up, Amy," Joseph called. "Mama may already be half way up the mountain. With all her worries, we needn't add to it."

I gave one last quick look around; the area seemed to have come alive with the rain. Where before everything was brown, little specks of green began sprouting between rocks and crevices.

Struggling down the mountain was almost as strenuous as climbing up. "Be careful, Amy," Aileen said, "if you step on a stone and it rolls, you could very well break something. And watch out for rattlers!"

I had had a bad scare with a snake years ago.

"There's Mama! Sitting on the rock where we left our bedding. She must have awakened before dark to be there so early!"

Joseph started walking faster as he talked and I couldn't keep up. I turned to Amelia. "Amy, tell Joe that I know the way and I'm going to take a shortcut and we'll meet where the path separates." She gave me a blank expression.

"No, Amy, better not."

But I was determined. "Yes, I am. I'll save fifteen minutes. Joe will know where I mean—one path leads around the mountain and the other heads down to the schoolyard. See you." And I turned right and hurried on my way.

Mama and Joseph were both scowling at me when we met at the designated spot. "Don't you try that again, Amelia Hall! We stay together from now on, do you hear me, young lady?"

"Yes, Mama."

There was no more conversation until Joseph suggested, "Let's stop and eat at the flat rock up ahead. I haven't had breakfast and my stomach is growling."

Once more, Mama surprised me. She unrolled a package and spread it out on the flat stone. The wrapper of the package turned out to be a cut down version of the red-checkered oilcloth, formerly used these many years on our kitchen table. She handed us wet cloths for our hands. "I saved the two best laying hens until last. I fried the chicken this morning. Eat all you want now. We won't have anything but cold food on the train. Let's drink canned milk this morning. Better not carry canned food with us. Too bulky."

"What time does the train leave?" I asked.

Mama's face expressed a worried look. "I don't know, dear. All I remember is what Sarah Jones said that morning when she brought you home. 'Ida,' she'd said, 'if I were you, I'd take my young'uns and hop on the two o'clock Southern Pacific Railroad and ride to that brother of yours, a place where Chester can't get his hands on your girls.' I hope she knew what she was talking about."

Mama wiped her hands and looked behind her, trying to decide what to do with the chicken bones.

We labored the rest of the way over the beautiful mountain in silence. We trudged on in single file, Joseph leading the way, me next, Aileen and Mama guarding our rear. At places the path narrowed and we had to walk bent over to keep from being knocked down by low-hanging branches.

At the next rest stop, Mama pulled out a bundle and handed us each what appeared to be blue overalls.

"What'd you bring, Mama?" Aileen asked.

"I didn't think it would look proper for us to carry pillowcases on the train, so I sewed duffle bags." She unrolled one of them and handed it to Aileen. "See, you fold everything in this. Looks more like a regular suitcase, and the straps can be thrown over your shoulder. It'll be easier to carry."

I admired mine and decided to unpack and rearrange my worldly possessions.

Mama watched me, smiling, "If you leave soft clothing in the pillowcase it will make a fair pillow to rest your head on in the train. I'd place it in your bag last."

I removed everything and started over: dirty overalls and undergarments first, dresses second, and pants and stockings crammed in the slip for a pillow. At the bottom I found the contents of the shoebox I had hurriedly dumped in. I took the time to go through it now.

The little Dutch girl doll I had so admired that first day of school lay on top. Mama snatched it up, "Oh, Amy how nice. Why have you never shown her to me before?"

"You were too busy the first day of school when I tried to show you, Mama."

A sad expression fleeted over Mama's face and I was sorry I'd made her feel bad, even if it were the truth. "It doesn't matter now, Mama. I plan to throw her away."

I put the paper cutout to one side with my old colored broken-glass I used for playing hopscotch, a broken top, the lucky stone Papa had handed me that day as he woke me for school, and dried up gum eraser. "I don't need these items," I muttered as I walked behind a bush trying to find an secluded spot to relieve myself.

When I returned, the Dutch girl was gone. I leaned over, retrieved the lucky stone and put it in my front pocket.

The sun beat down directly over our heads as we sat down to rest at last, fifty yards above the train depot. The loading dock stood bare and empty. My heart sank. What if there isn't a train, today? I bit my nails and looked away.

"Joseph," Mama asked, "will you scoot down and ask what time the train heading east leaves?" Joe got to his feet. "Buy four tickets while you're there. It'll be best if you do all the talking and we stay hidden until right before the train pulls out. Hand him the money belt, Aileen."

Without a word, Aileen reached inside her overalls, unhooked the belt with all the money safely inside and handed it to him, and once more the females of the family played a waiting game.

When I next noticed Joseph's beaming face, I knew everything would be okay. Only a two-hour wait and we would be on our way and free. I fidgeted and found the waiting hard; even nibbling on raw carrots didn't seem to make the time go faster.

"Remember, girls, let Joseph do all the talking and keep your hats low on your forehead. Even that boy's haircut doesn't hide a girl's face."

I glanced around me at the train station. I was hoping it would be busy but only four other passengers planned to board the train. It was my first time to see a train outside of the picture book at school and I held my mouth open in anticipation.

Joseph strolled over to the window and asked, "Will the train be on time?"

The man nodded. "Yep, right on schedule."

Again, Mama reminded us in a low voice, "Do nothing to attract attention to us. It's imperative no one suspects we aren't a man and three boys." Mama had dressed in men's clothing also, even cramming all of her hair in Papa's old felt hat. "Do not speak. Let Joseph do all of the talking."

I missed all of the excitement of the train pulling into the station. Instead of stretching my neck to see, I stood silently, with my bill-cap pulled low over my eyes, focusing my gaze on the wooden planks at my feet.

At last the conductor called "All aboard!"

Mother quietly maneuvered us aboard and breathed a sigh of relief. No one heeded us four bedraggled passengers as we found seats close together in the back of the train.

At last we were on our way and I was free to look out the side-window as the trees and houses seemed to fly by. The smoky ride itself was uneventful. Soot blew into the open windows. Mama sat immobile in her seat like a bronze statue. It was not until we were far past the Arizona border and into New Mexico that she visibly relaxed and changed into a happier person. The closer we came to Missouri, the jollier she became. By the time we were actually in the state of her childhood, she became almost giddy and prattled on about the trees and grass as much as a teen-age girl does on her first date or dance party.

"Amelia," Mama said, "I never did finish telling you how my voting dress got its name. It was like this: married women sometimes wielded their power by influencing their husbands, but single women had no say whatsoever. Women who married bullies had little recourse from their harsh life. Elizabeth Cody Stanton, a woman lawyer, founded the suffragist movement and Susan Anthony campaigned very hard to further our rights. The federal government decided to leave it to the individual states to pass laws governing voting. Arizona gave full suffrage for women in 1912, but it did me no good. We still lived in Missouri."

Water Under the Bridge

Mama paused and looked my way. Her lips twitched and the deep blue eyes appeared clouded. "Any questions?"

I shook my head and Mama glanced out the window. "I'll never forget the morning I ripped open a letter from a relative of mine. My cousin had always been cheerful and optimistic, but today was a sad day. I sat nursing Aileen and wept as I read the small neat handwriting. She told of terrible cruelty that had befallen her and 32 other ladies in Virginia. They'd been jailed and beaten unmercifully. Their crime—picketing Woodrow Wilson's White House with signs pleading for women to have the right to vote. Some received as much as a 60 day sentence."

Mama's face twisted and she closed her eyes, rubbing her forehead as if to erase the memory.

"Finally the 19th amendment was passed in 1919—two short years before you were born. It gave all women the vote.

"I'd been looking forward to voting at the next presidential election in November of 1920." Mama sighed and fingered the sash around her hips. I'd a feeling she'd forgotten I sat next to her on the train. "Fate was against me. As we neared election day, Chester decided October would be a perfect time to start West.

"'We'll be in Arizona where the sun shines every day by Thanksgiving, Ida,' he'd coaxed. 'Won't that be nice?'

"As usual, I let Chester have his way and by the middle of October we'd sold the farm and given away what couldn't be sold. Your papa purchased a new Model T Ford with the proceeds of the farm and we packed everything that rain could ruin on the inside of the touring car, and the running board and fenders held other stuff. An extra gasoline can was tied on the back bumper and canvas water bags hung on the front. At the time I was much too busy to worry about voting.

"We awoke to a steady, slow drizzle the day I am remembering. I never knew in what states we traveled, but I'll never forget the misery of that hellhole of a road, nothing but ruts in mud. Not the rich black dirt on our former farm but hateful red clay that stuck to everything it touched. Every few miles, Chester had to turn off the motor and cut brush to poke under the back wheels to get the car rolling. Of course the vehicle needed cranking again. Twice the road was completely impassable. We could see where others had removed the farmer's fence and cut a detour across the field hitting the road again a hundred yards or so up ahead.

"'You'll have to help move the logs, Ida,' Chester said. I removed my shoes, and together we lifted the heavy logs that made the rail fence, drove the car through and then hefted the logs back in place. Before leaving the farmer's land it became necessary to repeat the procedure at the entrance back to the main road.

"Twice in the same day that happened. Fence moving. Detouring. Logs heaved.

"Around one o'clock it started to rain harder—the rain poured down in a deluge that threatened to last all day and far into the night. The children were restless. I felt bone tired. Chester was glum. At last, about suppertime, he drove the Model T under a large oak tree close to a creek.

"'Great guns, Ida, look at the rushing water. I'll not venture to ford the creek this late in the day. Tomorrow I'll wade across and see how deep it is. Fix sandwiches and we'll eat in the car.'

"After gulping down a peanut butter sandwich and drinking canned milk, the young'uns sprawled out in the back where clothing in pillow slips stuffed on the floor and bedding had made the complete area flat, and in this makeshift bed Daniel, Joseph, and Aileen slept, using each other as pillows.

"I sat staring out the side window at the now steady downpour. My thoughts traveled back to what I had left—my family and dear friends—our farm with fruit trees, a healthy Jersey milk cow, matched horses and wagon, two pigs, and a dozen hens plus a rooster. I longed for the comfortable four-room house. I'd given up my sewing machine, most of my pans and dishes, my braided rugs and the flower garden quilt top I'd started. I did manage to persuade your papa to wrap my prize mirror in a quilt and cover it with canvas and tie the bundle on top of the car but I worried it would ruin. Better I should have given it away, but it was a wedding gift from my dead mother and dear to me."

Mama sighed, and the memory etched sadness on her lovely face. I said nothing.

"Chester broke the silence between us, 'Wonder if Harding is winning the election?' It was too much—the damn of tears I'd been holding back leaked out and ran down in rivulets and I could taste the salty tears mixed with mud. I buried my face in my hands and bawled like a baby.

"Chester must have guessed what I was thinking. He said, 'Oh, come on, Ida. One vote isn't that important.'

"'Land sakes, Chester, how can you say that? It was critical to me,' I blubbered. 'I'd been waiting my lifetime and here I am stuck nowhere between east and west—with nothing. Only three kids and a husband that cares for naught but his foolish dreams. I have nothing. I am less than nothing! Look at me. Just look at me! I married you for better or worse, but how much worse can it get? My toes are encased in mud. My clothing is wet, ragged and muddy. My hair is tangled and hanging down like a wet dog's tail. Not fit to vote if a polling booth was handy. See what you've done. You and your foolishness! See what you've done!'

"I turned to face my husband and noticed he'd removed his wet shirt. He scooted closer to me. 'Wiggle out of that dress, Ida. I have a dry quilt here.' He helped me unbutton the bodice and pulled me to him. Crowded together on the front seat he smoothed my hair and comforted me.

"'You have me as your husband,' he said, 'and I swear to you an oath, darling. At the next presidential election, I will not only see that you vote but I'll buy you the best dress in the store. I'll be proud to accompany my wife to the booth with you dressed like a queen. I promise.'

"'Store-bought?' I whimpered. I'd never owned a store-bought dress.

"He nodded and cradled me in his arms, and the two of us huddled wrapped in a quilt and the long night passed.

"Almost four years later, I'd forgotten the promise, but a week before the election your papa said, 'Don't plan anything for Saturday, Ida. I'm taking you to buy the voting dress I promised that horrible day long ago.'

"So, that's how the dress got its name, Amelia."

She stopped suddenly as if coming out of a trance. I noticed her face was flushed and she averted her eyes. *Mama has told me more than she planned to reveal.*

Verna Simms

CHAPTER FIFTY-TWO—LATE SEPTEMBER 1930

The train lurched to a stop at the Crystal City station. Mama was the first passenger to bounce down the steps.

"My, it feels good to be breathing fresh Missouri air again. I do believe I can smell that old musky river from here. Can't you, Amelia?"

I shook my head but it didn't dampen her enthusiasm "Did I ever tell you about the time we floated down the Mississippi—all the way from Crystal City to Chester, Illinois? Your papa decided to build a boat and two oars. Always was handy that way. He sat behind the kitchen stove all one winter whittling on wooden oars, and then wasted the summer sawing and hammering a flat bottom boat."

Joseph showed interest. "Did it float?"

"Oh dear me yes, it floated. That is, once he rigged a pulley and hoisted the boat onto a trailer. The horses dragged it to the river's bank. Your older brother was four. Wonder we didn't drown—the current was so swift."

Aileen moved closer to Mama. "Was it fun, Mama? Did you enjoy the ride?"

Mama chuckled. "Oh yes, a nice trip—especially thrilling to watch fish jump and your papa trying to grab one. Lost an oar one time and dove in to retrieve it before it floated away. You should've heard your brother squeal in delight."

Mama was silent for a spell. "We'd no way to get back home, so we left the boat in a barn and caught the train. Never saw that boat again. So wasteful. It did make a nice memory, though."

I felt guilty. It was my fault that Mama left Papa and now she was missing him. "You think Papa would take you back? The rest of us could stay with Uncle Willie."

"For crying out loud—I'd never leave you children. I loved your papa very much, but over the years he changed and I changed, in spite of the memory I had of him in earlier years. We had a good marriage at first, but . . ."

She shook her head, as if trying to grab hold of the present.

Personally, I was disappointed the first time I saw Crystal City. The station looked small and dusty. Flies buzzed around a sandwich the stationmaster had left on his desk. The man himself sat chewing and badly needed a shave.

We placed our bundles on the wooden planks that formed a platform, looking to the right and then to the left. I noticed an old frame factory to the south.

Mama followed my gaze. "That's where my brother works," she said excitedly. "He never worked on Saturdays but with these hard times, he only works two days a week. I wonder where he is? I wrote and told him we would arrive at 4 p.m. Saturday. It's not like Willie to be late."

The skies were cloudy. I shivered in the sudden burst of wind that blew the cap from my head. My short-cropped hair whipped in the breeze. Little whirlwinds seemed to be picking up dust and blowing it into my face. I undid my bundle and pulled out my green cape and threw it around my shoulders, pulling it tight around me.

Mama leaned over and picked up a bundle, straightened her back, and searched the area with tired eyes one more time. "We'll have to walk. It's only two miles. Step lively, now!"

We started down a street paved with earth-red bricks. On each side of the road, tall trees grew and met together at the top, forming a thick green canopy. Every yard had green grass and shrubbery. Roses bloomed in some yards. Others had red coxcombs adorning round beds. At last I knew what Mama meant when she said Missouri was God's country.

"Almost there," Mama announced. Four weary travelers finally walked up the gravel path and Joseph knocked lightly on the weather-beaten oak door. It needed paint badly. This had once been a nice home but it needed maintenance.

"We made it!" Mama exclaimed, dropping her burden and collapsing onto the rickety porch swing. She jerked off Papa's old felt hat and her long, unkempt hair tumbled down around her shoulders. That is the way her brother and his wife found her. I stood awkwardly to one side as footsteps could be heard. The door opened and a face appeared.

"Ida," a short muscular man with a friendly, weather-beaten face exclaimed. "Why didn't you let us know you were coming? Come in, come in! Are you and the children alright?"

He held the door open and called. "Cordelia, come see who's here. It's Ida. All the way from Arizona."

Before we could enter the house, a voice from the road called, "Willy, I have a letter for you. It is postmarked Arizona."

We all looked at each other standing there dumbfounded. Mama broke the spell. "Guess the letter came on the same train we did." She shrugged her shoulders and tossed her hair. "I just wasted a two-cent stamp!"

Laughter followed us as we entered this friendly house in God's country.

Verna Simms

CHAPTER FIFTY-THREE—SAFE

Mama, Aileen, and Joseph gathered around Uncle Willie, all talking at the same time. I was too weary to join in conservation, but plopped down on a straight backed chair in the corner and propped my head on the windowsill.

Aunt Cordelia came over and circled me in her arms. "You look exhausted, dear. Let me help you into a warm bath and then you can slip into a soft bed. A good night's sleep will do you worlds of good."

I followed her into the kitchen. I could feel the heat from the cook stove where two teakettles whistled noisily. She pulled back a curtain on the interior wall and revealed a large bronze bathtub standing on four legs. I gasped in amazement. I'd never seen a tub on legs and this one was larger than two of the round laundry tubs we hauled into our kitchen every Saturday for bathing.

"Willie likes a long soak, but he'll be up late tonight, I'm guessing. Plenty of time to heat more water." As she spoke, she filled the tub with buckets of water, adding the steaming water until it tested to suit her.

I slid in and it felt so good.

As I dressed, Aunt Cordelia fastened the handle to a flat iron heating on the stove. She placed the heated iron on a scrap of blanket and removed the handle before she wrapped it securely and took it with her into a bedroom.

"This will be Aileen's and your room." She turned down the covers and tucked the warm iron at the spot she judged my feet would reach. "In you go," she said merrily, and then covered me to my neck and gave me a light kiss on the forehead.

"You never had children?" I asked, thinking what a good mother she would be.

"No dear, I always prayed God would send me a little girl to love." She paused as if in memory of something far in the past, before adding, "Now He has! Sleep tight and as late in the morning as you wish."

She didn't extinguish the oil lamp, but turned it to where it made a soft glow in the unfamiliar room. I remember no more.

Days later, before dawn illuminated the room, voices woke me.

"Amelia may want to come."

I crept to the doorway and stuck my head around the corner.

"Where? " I asked.

"Uncle Willie and I are hiking up the hill to see the sun rise over the Mississippi River. He doesn't think you'd be interested. Are you?" Joseph asked.

"Sure. When?"

"Soon as I lace these old boots," Uncle Willie said.

I loved watching my uncle lace his high-top leather boots, with their eyelets and hooks, but not today.

"Give me two minutes!" I squealed and rushed back into my bedroom. I didn't bother shedding pajamas, but snatched overalls from the hall tree, thrusting my legs into the blue denim overalls and pulled the straps over my shoulders. Rammed my feet into socks and shoes, crammed a sock cap on my head, and slung a coat over my shoulder.

"Ready," I gasped.

Uncle Willie laughed. "We could've waited an extra two minutes."

Although a full moon gave us light, Uncle Willie used a three-cell flashlight. Not talking, we marched in single file, Indian fashion. It seemed long ago and a different world when our small family had climbed the mountain in Arizona—as we fled for safety. I shuddered at the memory. Was it only last week?

I stopped, winded, when we reached the top. Our uncle settled on a large flat rock. I started ahead, but he shoved his arm like a gate in my path. "Not too close, Amelia, until it's lighter. Nature changes."

He spread a blanket and sat. I sprawled face down and slowly elbowed my way forward until I could see over the edge. "Oooh!" I gasped. "It's so dark, deep, and mysterious."

I inched back, afraid. I've never been scared of heights, but this was different. The swirling water lapped at the shoreline, churning up foam and eating away at anything in sight. I had the weird feeling it would snatch and pull me down—down—down.

"Gee whiz, look at that tree, barely hanging on, roots exposed. Think it'll fall?" I asked.

"Someday. The river grabs every handful of dirt it can loosen and carries it down stream. See those fingers of mist rising in the distance—that's the Illinois shoreline. Both states try to keep the water in its boundaries."

Hypnotized by the power of the current below, I lay still, eyes glued to the powerful movement. Branches floated and then became caught in little whirlpools to go around and around—a never-ending battle—fighting to be free but not succeeding—almost like my life.

"Here it comes," Uncle Willie said. "See the pink and red streak across the sky? It won't be long now. The sun shoots up fast."

The river changed as if by magic. A deep red glow bounced from the waves; fish danced in the current and flopped up to catch the sunlight. Eagles flew overhead, calling. The river was no longer dark but sparkled, vibrant and alive. It was beautiful and I loved it.

"I hope it looked as it does now when Mama and Papa floated the river," Joseph said.

"Your papa was handy with tools," Uncle Willie admitted, "And Ida would do anything to please him."

"Almost," Joseph corrected, and winked at me. We both remembered . . .

The aroma of fried chicken caught my attention. I forgot the river and its power and scooted over and gave the man who had offered me safety a big hug. "Thank you for bringing me to see the sunrise over the Mississippi, Uncle Willie. I'll treasure the memory forever."

I snatched a drumstick and a buttered biscuit and began to eat—a contented nine-year-old girl. I turned to my brother. "I'm so happy to be living in Missouri, aren't you, Joe? It's the land Mama calls God's Country—and we live within walking distance of the Mighty Mississippi River!"

Water Under the Bridge

CHAPTER FIFTY-FOUR—SAYING FAREWELL

The next Saturday, Joseph and Uncle Willie took guns and went to the woods searching for meat for the table. I had nothing to do. I decided to explore the area to the west. Mama had told me she had once lived in a small town there and at that time it had been called Tanglefoot, because the streets and paths around town were so winding. I will see this place for myself, I decided.

It was necessary to cross a two-lane blacktop highway, but the traffic was sparse. I felt no qualms about being alone in this strange, but friendly town. Dressed as a boy, no one would notice anything unusual about me. My wanderings brought me to a street that ended at the edge of a small park.

I stood and watched the squirrels scamper across the green grass, gathering walnuts and hickory nuts. The cute gray-brown animals scurried up the nearby large oak tree and back down. Occasionally, one would sit on its haunches, bushy tail waving in the air. Their beady eyes looked at me suspiciously, before they dug a small hole and buried a nut. I laughed at them and then picked my way down the thirteen concrete steps that led to a small arched rock bridge. I sat on the bottom step to rest, and heard something crinkle—a letter from Blanca in my pocket.

Oct. 1930
Dear Amelia,
You'll never know how glad I was to receive your letter. The last letter I mailed to you came back, with no forwarding address and I didn't know how to get your address in Missouri.

We made the trip to New Mexico and my uncle's house without any trouble. Daddy and Mother took turns driving and it was dark when we arrived. I awakened when the car stopped just over the border between Arizona and New Mexico. Daddy said he had to stretch his legs. Then he did a funny thing. He walked back to the sign that welcomed us to New Mexico and continued walking back into Arizona. Then he turned around and came back to the car. He told Mama and me that he wanted to be able to truthfully tell his cousin he had walked from Arizona to New Mexico!

It is beautiful country here. Daddy has not been able to find work yet, but he helps the family in the sawmill to pay for our board. Also, he rises early every morning and walks to the river, never failing to bring back enough fish for the day and sometimes extra to take to the local store and trade for sugar or flour.

We are happy and that's the important thing. We don't know who turned my parents in to the sheriff but they did us a favor in disguise. It is so much better for Daddy to be out of the mines.

I have not enrolled in school here, but Mama and Amos (you remember my cousin that is two years older than I am) are teaching me, so I will not be behind. They think it is best to keep a low profile until such time as Daddy can apply for citizenship. Daddy's cousin is going to sponsor him.

Write soon, dear friend. We must never take for granted the time we have to correspond with each other.

Walk in beauty!

Love, Blanca

I refolded the blue writing paper and returned it to its envelope, smoothing the crumbled paper as best I could. Only then did I reach over and fill my hand with several unshelled hickory nuts scattered on the ground. I got up and continued onto the bridge.

When I got to the middle, I leaned over. The clear, sparking stream trickled over the pebbles, catching the light from the afternoon sun. It seemed to call to me.

The clear, sparking stream held my gaze. It trickled over the pebbles, catching the light from the afternoon sun.

Only one area was deep enough to hide a large fish. This spot beckoned to me and I placed my hands on the wall and raised my body to sit and peer into the blue-green pool of water. All I could see was my reflection, the fuzzy face

Water Under the Bridge

of a nine-year-old girl dressed in boys bib overalls, and a blue, long-sleeve chambray shirt. A straw hat covered my copper colored hair. .

Then, it happened! Another face appeared in the pool of water. Papa's face!

I could feel my heart skip a beat and then pound against my ribs. I looked around, but I was alone. Alone except for the squirrels and the birds. All alone! Again, I gazed at the reflection in the pool of water. The face was smiling now. I leaned farther over for a better look and my straw hat fell into the deep blue water, covering the reflections.

Oh, my! I've lost Aunt Cordelia's straw hat!

Hurriedly, I hopped down and rushed to the other side of the bridge. The hat immersed, swirled, and then picked up speed. It was hopeless to try and catch it.

Then a gust of wind blew, whipping hair around my face. An autumn leaf flying through the air like rain landed on the hat. I laughed aloud and gleefully threw my handful of hickory nuts. Some landed on the brim of the old straw hat.

I could imagine the hat held Papa and his wives as they floated downstream, never to be seen again. As the hat turned the corner and drifted out of my sight, I called loudly, startling the squirrels, "Goodbye, Papa, farewell! Take your wives and sail away. Forever." I fingered the small lucky stone in my overall pocket, pulled it out into the palm of my hand and gazed at it thoughtfully. I recalled that Tuesday so long ago when Papa had given it to me.

A lucky stone for his little girl's first day of school. I touched the rough texture lightly to my lips, and then let it slip through my fingers where it dropped into the water and disappeared from view.

Out of my life. Goo-ood-bye!"

A cloud moved over the sun in the sky and the reflections were no more. I felt a sudden chill, and decided to head home.

I knew in my heart that I had once loved Papa very much, but now it was over. Giving one last quick glance at the empty water below, I whispered under my breath. It is as Mama always said when I was upset over something I couldn't change "Don't worry about it, Amelia. It's water under the bridge!"

Verna Simms

EPILOGUE

As soon as we were settled into two rooms of our uncle's home, Mama wrote to Daniel and informed him of our new address. He answered promptly.

> *Dear Mother, Joseph, Aileen, and Amelia:*
> *I was shocked at your sudden departure. Surely you could have let me know beforehand. Dad came to our house to see me late Friday after finding your house ramshackle and his family missing. He expected to find you here with me. He had both the intended husbands with him. He was furious and the men were disappointed. They all blamed me and threatened to do me bodily harm. Missouri is so far away. Will Thelma and I ever see any of you again?*
> *Daniel*

Mama read the letter through twice, folded it neatly and placed it in her top dresser drawer. Her only comment—"So be it."

I was feeling really sad about Daniel, but a later letter cheered me up.

"Mama," I called. "You have mail. It's from Dan."

Mama jumped up, snatched the letter from my hand, and hastily tore the envelope open. She read the one page aloud.

> *Dear Mama,*
> *We are well. Hope you are, too. Thelma asked me to write and find out about the job market in Missouri. Will you please ask Uncle Willie what he thinks my chances are of finding work there? No one is building houses in this area anymore because the fumes are causing children to contract tuberculosis.*

I miss the family but I understand your concern for Aile and Amy's safety and happiness.

Thelma is homesick for Missouri, and I remember it as a nice state.

Hope to see you soon. Wouldn't it be nice to have our baby born in Missouri?
Love,
Daniel, & Thelma

Mama looked at me and winked, "Wouldn't that be wonderful! I must go and ask Willie at once. With all the repair work needing to be done on this house, why wouldn't he want a good honest carpenter close by?"

Mama got up and left the room with the letter in her hand. I had not seen such a spring to her step for many a year. I walked outdoors and lay in the old wooden hammock made of barrel staves. As I slowly swung back in forth in rhythm to the tune playing in my head, I thought of the possibility of Dan's family moving to Missouri.

Uncle Willie owned ninety acres of farmland, about half in virgin trees. To me he was old, at least fifty, and had no children. Why wouldn't he welcome a nephew? At least not one that looks and acts like the old man himself. In my imagination, I planned. The knoll on the hillside beside the trickling spring that flowed down into a shallow brook would be an ideal place to build a modest home. Not too close to the main house, yet not too far away for frequent visits.

So I planned and so I dreamed—the dreams of a happy child living in a peaceful home in this new land I had found, with relations that loved me. God's Country!

ABOUT THE AUTHOR

Verna Simms was born and lived the first year of her life in an old abandoned garage in Arizona. Her parents, with their five children, moved fourteen times during the first thirteen years of her life, finally settling in Missouri. There Verna finished high school, and met and married Howard Simms and they had two daughters. Verna and Howard lived together happily for sixty-seven years.

At age eighty, Verna joined the Jefferson County Writers' Society and began writing seriously—thus fulfilling a lifelong dream. She has been published in magazines, anthologies, and has a column in the local newspaper—The Leader.

She owes her success to the Jefferson County Writers' Society and says that when she autographs her first few books and hands them to those who have helped her most, she will have accomplished her goal. Her old age would have been dull without this new venture to keep her mind active. Her hobbies are reading, swimming, sewing, gardening, and spending time with her grandchildren.

CPSIA information can be obtained at www.ICGtesting.com
Printed in the USA
LVOW05s1957100214

373118LV00001B/5/P